THE VINTNER'S DAUGHTER

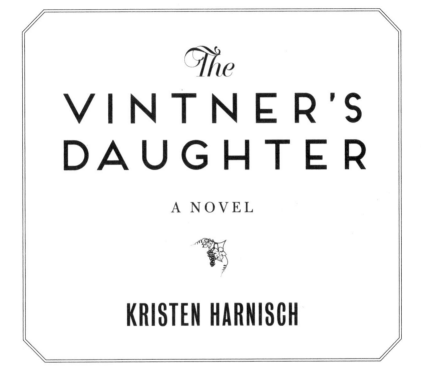

The VINTNER'S DAUGHTER

A NOVEL

KRISTEN HARNISCH

HarperCollins*PublishersLtd*

Published by HarperCollins Publishers Ltd

First edition

HarperCollins books may be purchased for educational, business
or sales promotional use through our Special Markets Department.

HarperCollins Publishers Ltd
2 Bloor Street East, 20th Floor
Toronto, Ontario, Canada
M4W 1A8

www.harpercollins.ca

Library and Archives Canada Cataloguing in Publication
information is available upon request

ISBN 978-1-44342-643-5

Printed and bound in Canada

9 8 7 6 5 4 3 2 1

To my husband, David,
for insisting, "Yes, you can."
And to my loving children, Ellen, Ryan and Julia:
Yes, you can.

THE VINTNER'S DAUGHTER

CHAPTER I

Confession

JUNE 30, 1896, NEW YORK CITY

T he air was thick with the putrid smell of man and horse. Sara Thibault walked swiftly up Mott Street, taking care to lift the hem of her dress and sidestep the heaps of muck without breaking her stride. Like the squabbling of chickens, the street noises swirled all around her. Above her, women beat rugs and draped bedding from the wrought-iron fire escapes, shouting to the children who ran wild in the street below. The clanging bell of an omnibus and the braying of donkeys unnerved her.

This was not the America that Sara had envisioned. Pushcarts lined the muddy road, their proprietors selling everything from potatoes to laudanum and speaking in languages Sara could not understand. Bicycles squeaked by, rag pickers hollered from their doorway perches, and street urchins cried out and tugged at her

1

skirt with their grimy hands as she passed. Sara knew she should not be walking alone, yet to bring a companion would have invited judgment that was reserved for God alone. She wondered if God walked with her now, guiding her down the street toward salvation, away from her sin.

God was a tricky business. Sara believed in the Father, Son and the Holy Ghost, and had even successfully enlisted Saint Anthony on occasion to help her find a misplaced trinket. Yet did she truly believe that God would condemn her to burn in hell for what she had done? If God was everywhere, surely he'd been present that night. He'd seen what had happened.

She could not turn back now. Sara focused her eyes straight ahead. It would be a relief to reach the quiet peace of the church and inhale its fragrant, burning incense.

Sara had arrived in New York four weeks ago, but she had yet to make her confession. She was dressed in her best: a simple dress of pale blue cotton and a claret-colored shawl. A straw bonnet with a wide cream ribbon concealed her reddish-brown hair, which many of the villagers in Vouvray had considered her finest feature. Not anymore, she thought, as her fingertips attempted to smooth the jagged edge of chopped hair at the nape of her slender neck. Sara was unusually tall for a woman and did not possess the plumpness that seemed to be considered so pleasing in females. Her limbs were long, lean and agile. She kept her elbows tucked in at her sides as she approached the corner of Mott and Prince.

The stone facade of the church towered before her, the height of eight men. On its front steps, a squat, balding man in a priest's habit shouted, "Out! Out!" as he wildly waved a broom to chase a group of lively urchins down the steps. On another day, Sara would have laughed, but today her spirits were subdued and her heart heavy.

Inside, the marble altar with its carved reredos, leafed in gold, loomed before her. She pulled three silver dollars from her pocket—which she'd earned for this purpose by selling her hair—and dropped them one by one into the collection box. The sound echoed throughout the massive church. Once the silence returned, Sara could only hear the pounding of her heart.

She made her way to the confessional. Once inside, she sat down, removed her shawl and draped it over her lap. While she waited, she bunched its soft yarn between her fingers anxiously. Sara heard the creaking of wood, and then the carved screen before her was abruptly thrown open. She knelt down, straightened her back and inhaled sharply. She felt her throat tighten. To calm herself, she fixed her eyes on the holes in the screen before her, and then swallowed hard, preparing to speak.

"In nomine Patris, et Filii, et Spiritus Sancti. Amen," she said quietly as she made the sign of the cross. "Forgive me, mon père . . . for I have sinned. It has been six weeks since my last confession."

The shadow on the other side of the partition cleared its throat and stifled what Sara thought sounded like a yawn. "Very well, you may confess your sins."

She was trapped within the walls of the confessional, and she could not leave until she declared her guilt aloud.

"Father, I killed a man."

CHAPTER 2

Clos de Saint Martin

Sara's eyes swept over the land that surrounded her. Clos de Saint Martin was the Thibault family's vineyard and its great pride. Four thousand vines flourished on each of the ten hectares owned by Sara's family. The pineau de la Loire grapes dangled in large clusters on vines that fanned out diagonally on the slopes before her. To the distant south, she could see the Loire River, wide, cool and deep, winding its way through the valley.

Just to Sara's left lay the sunflower field. In July, she loved to watch the blooms sway gently in the breeze, like royal heads adorned with crowns of gold. A cherry orchard, along with fields of oats and corn, stood at the edges of the farm. The main house, off to Sara's right, had been built by her grandparents some sixty years ago. They had named the property after Saint Martin, the fourth-century monk who had first planted grapes on the slopes of Vouvray.

The house itself was made of stucco and clay, and had recently been repaired and scrubbed. Half-moon dormer windows rose up from the slate roof and were flanked by two tall chimneys, one at each end of the house. The austerity of the home's facade was softened by the red-tinged ivy, which twined up the walls and around one of the chimneys.

Behind the house to the northeast ran a ledge of pale yellow tufa rock. This was where, centuries ago, the Vouvray monks had carved a honeycomb of cave dwellings. In one of these caves was the family wine cellar, in which the Thibaults pressed, fermented and stored their barrels of chenin blanc. Each barrel was toasted before it was filled and stored at a constant temperature, a process that had established the Thibault wines as the best whites of Vouvray. Sara's eyes narrowed as they followed the cave line around to the right.

The upper openings of the caves brimmed with activity: the annual harvest had begun. Ribbons of smoke curled upwards from chimneys poking out of the caves' grass-covered roofs. The Roux and Marlette families returned every year to Saint Martin, knowing that the work was plentiful and the master generous, and two new families had joined them this year. The old Gypsy women had once again arranged their food, tools and candles in the small niches of the cave walls and set about their bread-baking and laundry chores in preparation for the long weeks of picking ahead. Earlier this morning, the hardier men and women had headed into the fields to pick grapes until sunset. They would pause only for a luncheon of potato cakes, wine and, thought Sara with a smile, a fair share of coarse jokes.

Sara loved this time of year. Solitude, infinite in wintertime, was scarce now. The night before, when the house was hushed and she knew Lydia was asleep, she had lifted the sash of her window and listened to the sounds of the creaking fiddles and moaning bagpipes drifting in on the cool night air. The caves had been lit up with fires, and from her window Sara could see shadows jumping in a joyful clog dance. How she had wished she could sneak out and join the celebration! But she knew she needed her rest. A fortnight of back-breaking work lay ahead for everyone.

Sara walked along the outer rows of the vineyard, running her fingertips under the broad grape leaves to feel the fruit. She selected a few grapes to taste from the waist-high vines. Their bodies were swollen and their skins thinned from a week of unexpected rains. As she bit into the fruit, she tasted a burst of sweetness. The grapes were ripe. Her father could not have waited any longer to begin the harvest. A week later and the damp weather would have brought the scourge of rot upon the fruit. Sara noted the grapes' sugary flavor and the soil conditions in her field diary.

She resumed her progress toward the end of the rows, where a pair of ox-drawn wagons swarmed with activity. The first day of the harvest was always the most chaotic. Papa had gone with Jacques Chevreau, the estate's longtime foreman, to the cellar to finish preparing the equipment for the first press. This morning it fell to Sara to keep watch over the workers until Jacques returned.

She would encourage them to work hardest now, while they were fresh and cool.

As Sara approached, the pickers' eyes darted in her direction and then back to their work. To Sara's satisfaction, they quickened their pace. They worked in pairs, one on either side of a vine, each employing secateurs. First they thinned the leaves, then their sharp blades severed the golden fruit clusters, dropping the fruit into buckets a foot below. Most of the pickers worked on bended knee in the rocky soil, and everyone would welcome the pots of mustard oil Sara's maman would offer at dinnertime to soothe their aching joints.

A few rows along, Sara eyed a boy with a sunburned neck, no more than twelve years old, struggling in his attempts to cut the vine. She knelt down beside him and corrected him gently: "No, like this." Sara wielded the secateurs expertly. She sliced the vine almost through, then brought the shears in again to catch the tip of the stem in their grasp, free the fruit from the leaves and toss it into the basket, all in one motion.

"Ah, yes, yes, Maitresse Thibault." His voice was deferential.

Sara grinned at his use of the title that her maman so relished. "Call me Sara." She patted him on the shoulder and moved on to the oxen.

Noticing the baskets were nearly full and the wagons empty, Sara clapped her hands and shouted, "Baskets, baskets, if you please!" The workers closest to the wagon scrambled to gather the containers and bring them to the wagon in exchange for empty ones. The pickers at the far end of each row strapped the heavy baskets to their backs, each containing a hundred pounds of grapes, and hauled them toward Sara. As the fruit tumbled from the heaping vessels, Sara used a long pole to guide the grapes from the corners of the wagon's bed to its center.

When Jacques returned, Sara bid him adieu and lifted her skirts to trudge through the mud between the vines toward the other end of the field. There she hunched over to examine one of the vines more closely. She ran her fingers over the leaves' withering edges, fearing the worst. She took her knife from her belt and split the vine's bark. With the tip of her blade, she scraped out hundreds of tiny translucent eggs that lined the interior of the vine. Some had already hatched, producing the dreaded pale yellow insects that were now sucking the vine dry.

Sara looked around cautiously to make sure none of the pickers were watching her. She saw her father approaching, his brow creased. He stood dark and tall behind Sara, studying the evidence.

"Phylloxera." His voice was low. "How far have they spread?"

"I'm not certain, Papa." Maybe this was the first hatching cycle, Sara thought hopefully. Maybe they still had time to correct the problem before it reached the vines' roots. There was only one way to find out.

Papa was a step ahead of her. He signaled to Jacques, who stood by the wagons. In moments, Jacques was bounding up to join their clandestine party.

"Mademoiselle Sara, will you allow me?"

"Yes, Jacques, thank you." She backed away from the vine to stand next to her father.

Jacques wiped his thick neck and brow with his kerchief, stuffed it in his pocket and then lifted his spade. Pressing his considerable weight down on the shovel, he began to dig, creating a circle radius around the base of the vine. When Jacques lifted the plant up, they could all see its shriveled roots. The insects had not only drained the vine of its sap and nutrients, but poisoned it with their venom.

"My God," Papa whispered. Sara's eyes flashed to her father's. They were tired and ringed with disappointment.

After the last plague of phylloxera, fifteen years earlier, Papa and Jacques had replanted half of the vineyard, over five hectares, with resistant rootstock, which had successfully brought the infestation to an end. The infected vines that Sara had discovered today were part of the non-resistant half. Over the last fifteen years, the Thibaults had employed many methods to prevent phylloxera from blighting this half of the vineyard. They had buried a toad at the foot of each vine and injected sulfide into the soil surrounding the most vulnerable plants. They had allowed the chickens to roam freely, in hopes that they would eat the aphids before they reached the vines. These measures had kept the phylloxera at bay, until now.

"The sulfide isn't working," she muttered. How had they not caught this sooner? "We will have to replant this half of the vineyard with resistant rootstock," she continued. Sara knew this would be costly, and they had not yet determined how much wine would be lost as a result of the infestation.

Papa had other ideas. "We can gather the grapes quickly, from both the infested vines and the healthy ones. We'll press them separately, and perhaps we can add some sugar to the drier grapes and still make something out of them." Papa sounded tired. "If our broker discovers the infestation, he may reduce his offering price."

Sara nodded. Right now, they had to make the most of what they had. She turned to Jacques and spoke urgently. "You mustn't say a word, Jacques, not to anyone. We'll examine the other vines for infestation. We'll work double-time to finish the harvest and negotiate the barrel price as soon as possible—without anyone knowing, right, Papa?"

Papa continued to stare at the withered vines. "That is exactly what we'll do."

Luc Thibault took his seat at the dinner table across from his wife. Sara's sister, Lydia, sat to his right, still talking about Wednesday's trip to nearby Amboise. Sara and Papa had decided not to divulge the news of the bug until they knew the extent of the infestation, and its financial implications. Sara doubted that her sister's chattering would have been quelled by knowledge of their precarious situation. Although Lydia was older by two years, Sara was the quieter, more contemplative one.

"Sara, you must come to Amboise with Maman and me next time we go. We dined on truffles and pain au chocolat and bought the most beautiful lace for my wedding gown. It was heavenly, wasn't it, Maman?"

Lydia was engaged to Bastien Lemieux, the elder son of the Thibaults' wine negotiant, Jean Lemieux. Had it not been for a scandalous affair involving Lemieux's younger son and a girl from Tours five years ago, Sara believed Bastien never would have consented to marry a farmer's daughter. Yet somehow her mother had persuaded Jean Lemieux to agree to the engagement last year, and now Bastien and Lydia were preparing to wed.

"Yes, my dear, it was a welcome diversion." Marguerite Thibault reached out to pat Lydia's hand. Her attention then turned to her youngest.

"Sara, you will come with us next time. It is not proper for a girl of seventeen years to be working the land like a common day laborer. Goodness, look at your hands! They are shameful, really. And those dreadful muddied clogs—you look like a peasant."

"Marguerite, that is enough!" Papa's voice boomed across the table. "I have no sons, and Sara is an immense help to me in the vineyard. We're in the middle of the harvest! I need her and that is the end of it."

Sara was quietly pleased. Papa was the one person who always defended her.

"It's not proper, Luc," Maman grumbled.

Silence fell over the table as the family began to eat their meal of chicken and onions. Sara's watered wine tasted bitter. "*Pipi du chat!*" her father might normally have complained. In his frugality, he saved the best wines for sale, rather than for his own enjoyment.

Lydia attempted to change the subject. "I had the good fortune to meet Bastien in town, Papa. He promised to call in a fortnight when he returns to Vouvray."

"Perhaps he would join us for our little fête when we are finished with the harvest, my dear." Papa's spirits seemed to be genuinely buoyed by Lydia's obvious joy.

"See, Luc, you only have to wait a few months and you'll have a son to help you run Saint Martin." Maman would not relent.

"What does Bastien know about growing grapes and making wine?" Sara's voice tightened with frustration. "His family buys wine and sells it for profit. He's an opportunist, not a vigneron."

"Sara is right, Marguerite. Although I'm sure Bastien shows great promise in the wine trade, I think his father's negotiant business and our farm should remain separate for the time being."

Lydia's mouth puckered. "Very well, Papa, but you will see in time that Bastien is more than capable of operating the farm. I've heard that Philippe has established a vineyard in America and fares quite well."

"I'm sure that's the case, my dear." Maman was dismissive. She did not like to hear about Bastien's younger brother, the dark horse of the Lemieux family.

The conversation between Lydia and Sara's parents drifted into more congenial territory. They spoke of the sturdiness of the twice-used barrels Papa was cleaning for this year's vintage, the poor timing of Madame Roux's sixth child, born the day before the harvest, and the pantry items Maman would require for the end-of-harvest celebration.

Sara, however, was lost in her own thoughts, marveling at the audacity of her mother's and sister's presumptions. Didn't they know that *she* was the one who would someday run the vineyard? She would be the vigneron of Saint Martin. She would grow the grapes and make the wine and ship it in shiny corked bottles to America. Papa had said so.

The retreating sun painted the November sky in streaks of orange and gold. The days of picking were nearly over. Every vine had been examined, and Papa estimated that three of the five non-resistant hectares were infected with phylloxera. The seven healthy hectares, God willing, would produce well over two hundred barrels of sellable wine. But only the pressing of the grapes and fermentation in the week that followed would give them a notion of how much wine had been gathered in, and its quality. Sara was keen to help Jacques squeeze the juice from the grapes and was in the cellar, shoveling fruit into the basket press, when Jacques and Papa entered. Sara knew Papa would be required to feign displeasure, for Maman had given him explicit instructions not to allow her to participate in tasks she deemed particularly unrefined, such as grape hauling and pressing.

"Sara." Papa's brown eyes warmed. "I know you are eager to be of use, but your maman swore to me she'd have me drawn and quartered if I so much as suggested you move grapes or turn the press. And I have to wonder, despite your resolve, if you'll break that narrow back of yours."

Sara looked down at the floor to hide her delight, for this was the opportunity she had been waiting for. "As you wish, Papa, but if you are not going to let me work the press, perhaps you would allow me to watch and record my observations in my notebook?" Sara tilted her head to the side and smiled sweetly at Jacques. Jacques just shook his head, and his lip tugged into a half-grin.

"Fine, fine." Papa waved his hand as he turned to walk through the long rows of barrels to the back of the cellar. "Jacques, show

Sara how it's done. I'll be in the back engaged in the sorcery of trying to craft a profit."

Sara pulled over a stool and settled herself down happily. For three harvests now, Sara had tried to wheedle the intricate details of grape pressing out of Jacques, with little success so far. He had always been reluctant to answer her many questions, but this year would be different.

Jacques silently finished filling the press with grapes. He worked the capstan to slowly screw the top plate down onto the fruit. Sara could hear the grapes squish and release their juice. The basket itself was wider than her outstretched arms. Four iron bands held its narrow, vertical wooden staves together. The juice dribbled down between the staves into a trough and flowed to the tub below. The resulting liquid, known as must, would fill a barrel. Once this batch was pressed, the skins would be cleared with shovels and the press would be refilled to begin the process anew. Each harvested grape would be pressed a total of four times. The must from the first three pressings would be fermented in large vats and pasteurized to make a fine wine that would be sold in casks to the Lemieux family for blending and bottling. The fourth pressing would be made into table wine to be sold cheaply to the local villagers. The leftover skins would be given to the pickers or used for fertilizer. It would take ten days to crush the grapes that had been harvested.

"So, I can see I have your undivided attention," Jacques teased Sara.

"You do. Pray, go on. I believe you were just about to reveal your vintner's secrets to me." Sara loved ribbing Jacques, who took great pride in the fact that he was the only man Papa trusted to work the screw press.

"Secrets? I think not. If you want to spend your time recording the ramblings of an old man, suit yourself."

"Did you not teach Papa about wine?"

"About winemaking, yes. But he knows more about growing and pruning." Jacques paused and turned to Sara. "Making good wine is like anything else, my dear. It's only after you've produced vats of vinegar that you are able to master the art of making a fine-tasting wine."

Sara laughed. Jacques cranked the screw down another notch.

"This press is the same design we've been using for almost a thousand years. The pineau grapes require a gentle touch. The mistake many vintners make is failing to add pressure once they hit the cake of grapes at the bottom. With the right pressure and mixing, the wine will sing with the flavors of almonds and quinces—pure, sweet joy. And it will fetch a handsome price. Use too heavy a hand, and you'll end up with cat water."

Sara jotted a few notes down in her journal as she observed Jacques working the press. The process took so much time; Sara wondered why Papa hadn't invested in more efficient equipment, like the new Morineau three-man press she had seen advertised in the wine trade papers. "Wouldn't it be more efficient to purchase a larger press that could work the grapes faster?"

Jacques shook his head. "Faster is never better. Besides, those presses are costly, and when your father had to decide between upgrading the press and purchasing new rootstock, I advised him to spend his money on the fruit first."

Jacques was, above all, a practical man, and Papa had relied on his expertise for over twenty-five years now. Jacques and his wife, Sabine, had moved from Bourgogne to Saint Martin after the Prussian war to help Papa make wine from the ancient vines Maman had inherited. Tragically, Sabine Chevreau died of cholera in 1875, three years before Sara was born. Jacques had often credited Luc and Marguerite for sustaining him through the dark days after Sabine's death. Jacques was part of the Thibault family—a steadfast brother to her father. Sara had never witnessed a stronger bond between two men.

Sara loved to hear how Papa had saved Jacques during the war. It was a gallant tale, one of true friendship.

"Tell me my favorite story again, Jacques," Sara entreated him.

"You never tire of hearing it?" Jacques continued to turn the capstan, speaking between labored breaths. "Your papa was just a babe, ten years younger than I. He barely had a whisker on that cherubic face of his. His heart was aflutter for his new bride, the charming Marguerite, whom I had not yet met. It was near the end of the Prussian war, 1871. Léon Gambetta was entrenched in a muck-and-mire battle with the Germans. He decided he needed reinforcements from his countrymen." Jacques paused for what Sara could only assume was dramatic effect. She obliged him and leaned forward.

"Do you know what that brazen rascal did? He circumvented the German armies by running a hot-air balloon across the border, back into France! He rallied us paysans across the countryside to join him in the effort to defeat the Prussian pigs. Your father and I were assigned to the same regiment, you'll recall.

"During the army's final stand at Le Mans—it was a gruesome and bloody battle, not for the faint of heart." Jacques shook his head at the unpleasant memory. "Anyhow, a steely-eyed Prussian pinned me down, raised his axe and made ready to hack me to pieces. My blood ran cold—I was terrified. All of a sudden, the soldier was struck by a force I could not account for. He was knocked to the ground instantly, and I realized that Luc had shot him clean through the head." Jacques stopped turning the screw and looked at Sara. "We lost the battle, of course, but I won my life that day, thanks to your father. It is a debt I will never be able to repay."

"What in the blazes are you going on about, man? You have more than repaid me—in sweat spent on that blessed press for the past twenty years!" Sara and Jacques laughed, startled to find Papa standing behind them, scratching pen to paper atop one of the empty barrels.

Jacques looked amused. "Well, maybe I'd agree with that today. How are the figures adding up?"

"Why don't you two come take a gander? I want to make sure I haven't missed anything."

Sara and Jacques huddled around Papa to review his calculations. As Papa ran his finger down the column of figures, Sara's anxiety grew. With taxes, vine trimming, fertilizer, plowing, sulfur, harvesting, and new barrels, their costs ran to 7,200 francs this year. The last entry caught Sara by surprise. It listed 600 francs in interest expense, which brought the grand total to 7,800 francs.

"Seventy-eight hundred francs! That's 780 francs in expenses per hectare versus 600 last year. And what is this?" Sara's finger rested on the questionable fee.

"Interest owed on the money we borrowed to replant half the vineyard," her father said evenly.

"That's outrageous! Surely we could find a way to reduce this payment—even just for this year?"

"I doubt it, Sara," Papa rubbed his forehead, sounding defeated. "We were fortunate to get the loan in the first place."

"But that was years ago."

"Yes, but we still owe over four thousand francs in principal this December, and we incur a significant expense each year in interest payments." Papa's face was strained as he reviewed the figures again. Sara knew that expenses were higher this year, but this was not unexpected. What was unexpected was the new aphid infestation that had cost them almost a third of their production.

Jacques seemed to be thinking the same thing. "Luc, what price will we need to secure from Lemieux to meet our expenses?"

Papa scrawled his final estimates on the page:

Expenses *7,800*
Repayment of loan principal *4,100*
Less monies owed to St. Martin. *428*
Total expenses *11,472*

"That's over eleven thousand francs we owe. That means if we produce just over two hundred barrels from the good vines, we'll need a price of"— Papa scribbled some calculations—"over fifty francs per barrel. Considering Lemieux gave us fifty-two last year, I'd say we'll make it, if my estimates are correct."

"And if the buyers are in a generous mood," Jacques added.

Sara knew that Papa was also assuming that he could collect the cash or barrels of wine owed to him by the eight neighboring vignerons, winemakers with small properties who had borrowed bread, milk and tools in return for payment after the harvest. He planned to resell their wine at the market price and make a small profit. In addition, he was assuming that he could persuade Lemieux to pay him promptly, rather than waiting four months after receipt of the casks to make the final payment, as was customary. The odds of all these things happening in perfect sequence seemed slim, even in Sara's limited experience, but she did not want to add to Papa's difficulty by sharing her doubts.

"Jacques, when are they going to set the price?" Papa was clearly concerned.

"The guild is meeting with the curate next Thursday. We'll know then."

"More than last year?"

"Perhaps. It all depends on whether or not the other vineyards are infected and, of course, how many buyers Lemieux has lined up."

"What do you hear from Cazalet and Breuil?" Papa's neighbors produced equally fine wines and might also suffer from an infestation. Their collective misfortune could be their salvation this year, if the low production in Vouvray raised the regional prices.

"Only that there's a lot of demand coming from Paris. That could help us. If the others have been hit hard with the bug, the price will remain high. If not, our price could drop by ten francs or more."

"We'll need at least fifty francs per barrel," Papa repeated.

"Phew!" Jacques leaned in, his elbows resting on the barrel. "I don't know, Luc. Can you call in any of your debts early?" Sara knew they needed the cash now if they were going to make the December loan payment on time.

"No. Everyone, including the growers who owe me, is waiting on that price." Papa shook his head in frustration. "Can we produce the tasting wine before the meeting?"

"Of course. But why?"

"If it is of a high quality, we'll make sure Lemieux tastes it before the meeting. If he likes it, we might persuade him to guarantee us a good price before the meeting, in exchange for our assurance that we will sell him the entire stock. At the very least, perhaps we can persuade him that this year's wine deserves a higher price. I might have more influence with him now that our families will soon be connected. He could be instrumental in convincing the wine merchants' guild to set the buy price high."

Jacques slapped Papa on the back reassuringly. "It'll be our finest quality yet. I'm sure of it, Luc!"

Sara knew Jacques would do his best. She admired his optimism. They would all work their fingers to the bone to produce a premium wine this year. But Sara remained uneasy, and not because of the usual concerns about production or quality of the wine, or even demand for it. Jean Lemieux was the single most influential buyer when it came to setting prices. It was his changeable character that worried her. Evenhandedness had never been his strong suit.

NOVEMBER 18, 1895

All vignerons agree that every grueling harvest, like a guest that has overstayed his welcome, deserves a proper fête to bid it adieu. The Thibault family opened their doors to the whole of Saint Martin, plus twenty-four Gypsy pickers, not to mention ten chickens and three dogs, for a grand celebration featuring a fine meal of roasted goose, pork, cheese, wine and figs.

The doors between the parlor, living room and dining room were opened to connect the three rooms across the front of the house. Marcheline, the maid, had lit the candles on the three iron chandeliers, and Lydia and Sara had decorated the rooms with spicy-smelling, bright yellow witch hazel branches. Once the dinner service was cleared, all the furniture and chairs were moved to the walls, and Maman even asked Jacques to wheel her pianoforte into the dining room, insisting its gentle timbre would be an elegant accompaniment to the scratching of the peasant fiddles.

Lydia pulled Sara upstairs to freshen up. "Aren't we fortunate that Bastien has agreed to come tonight?" Lydia stood at her toilette, peering into the looking glass. She pulled a chestnut strand from her forelock, trained it in a curl around her finger and released it to rest at her temple.

"I suppose it's a comfort to know that your betrothed moves effortlessly between the bourgeois of Tours and us peasants of Saint Martin." Sara stuck her nose up in mock superiority.

"You know that's not what I mean, Sara." Lydia elbowed her, then smoothed her pale peach-colored dress and leaned forward to inspect her décolletage. "I simply feel that his presence is a compliment to our entire family, and we should treat it as such."

"Now you sound like Maman!" Sara rolled her eyes. She moved behind Lydia, studying their reflection. Though Lydia was two years older, Sara was taller. Both girls had long, reddish-brown hair, done up tonight, but Lydia's usually bounced with tight curls, whereas Sara's fell in loose waves past her shoulders. Lydia had wide blue eyes, which were often round with surprise, but Sara's were green and shaded by long, dark lashes. To Sara, Lydia looked like the pictures she had seen in books of Carpeaux's shapely sculpted females, her head tossed back, delighting in life's dance. She sometimes wished she could be as carefree as Lydia, but Sara knew she was more reserved by nature.

Lydia looked Sara over with a critical eye. "You're lovely tonight, Sara. I'm thrilled that I could persuade you to wear your hair up. You're *très élégante*. Trading your field clogs for street shoes certainly made a difference. We may yet find you a husband."

Sara stuck her tongue out, and Lydia ignored her. The idea of marriage to any man was abhorrent to her; she could not imagine being caged in that way. She began to notice the unfamiliar prick of hairpins on her scalp.

Lydia fussed with her earbobs for a few moments longer, then flashed Sara her most radiant smile. Sara's displeasure could only evaporate into a grin of equal proportion.

"Off to the fête!" Lydia clapped her hands with delight.

When Sara and Lydia entered the dining room, the revelers whooped and charged their merriment into full swing. Monsieur and Madame Roux, their children and parents, and Jacques, his sister and her children all paired up for a turn on the floor. The spirits from dinner had already loosened their limbs and tongues, and they spun around the room, elbows linked, striking their clogs on the dull pine to the clipping of the fiddles.

The shiny faces glowing around Sara raised her spirits. As Papa stole her away for a dance, Jacques approached Maman, who accepted his arm, her cheeks flushed from heat and wine. Maman looked bewildered in her effort to mimic Jacques's footwork. Sara could not help but laugh: Jacques looked like a corpulent cricket twitching his legs in mid-leap. Papa chuckled too, then lifted Sara up by the waist and spun her around until she was dizzy. Sara felt her own cheeks warm with pleasure.

Sara's feet landed back on the ground and she steadied herself, clasping Papa's hand. Then the music abruptly stopped; the laughter and ribald shouts were replaced by silence. All eyes turned to the doorway to regard the well-made figure of Bastien Lemieux, who stood a head taller than the average man, with a broad chest and long, fit limbs.

Papa released Sara's hand at once and strode toward the door to greet his future son-in-law. Maman followed in haste. Sara felt Lydia take her hand and squeezed back.

"Thank you, Sara, you are such a dear," Lydia whispered. "I would faint dead away if it were not for you. He is splendid, is he not?" Sara silently opted for "not" but said nothing.

Sara watched Bastien bow slightly to her parents and offer his congratulations on the harvest's end. "You are the envy of every girl in Vouvray, I'm certain of it," Sara assured her sister.

"Save for one," Lydia whispered. "Why do you dislike him so?"

"I have no quarrel with Bastien. He is everything a gentleman should be, outwardly, but how does he regard you as his future wife? That is my concern."

"As any gentleman would, with respect and thoughtfulness."

"Forgive me, Lydia, but do you not find something . . . lacking in his demeanor?"

"You know as well as I, Sara, that Bastien is a man of convention and manners. He does not think it proper to display his most guarded sentiments for all to see."

"Yes, but has there been any 'display' of affection that leads you to believe his love is sincere?"

"Sara! I will not respond to such a vulgar question."

"I'm sorry, Lydia." Sara had not intended to offend Lydia, but her sister always seemed to misinterpret her. They were like two sides of a coin, one minted for pageantry, the other for practicality.

Bastien sauntered across the room toward the sisters, and Lydia lifted her hands in greeting. Crimson crept over her chest and up the length of her fair neck, finally dancing in the apples of her cheeks. Her delight could not be concealed. Sara, on the other hand, felt herself turning scarlet for an entirely different reason. She was embarrassed: Bastien's peacock finery—his waistcoat and top hat—was absurd at this rustic gathering.

Bastien flashed a brilliant smile at Lydia, revealing a row of straight, narrow teeth. His aquiline nose and high cheekbones gave him an aristocratic air. His brown eyes were the color of ripe chestnuts, and his neatly trimmed straight black hair rested just below his tall collar. All in all, observed Sara, it was understandable why so many of her contemporaries found him worthy of pursuit. But his arrogance, which no one else seemed aware of, made her impervious to Bastien's charms. Sara instinctively stepped back as he advanced. She saw Lydia take his hands in hers, and Sara knew proper conduct dictated that she must also greet him politely.

Bastien gave a short bow. "Mesdemoiselles Thibault, it is an honor. I must congratulate your family on what your father informs me has been a plentiful grape harvest this season. My father sends his regards and bids me to say that we look forward to tasting your first press upon its completion."

Bastien paused to look around the room at the Gypsies, who had returned to their gaiety. He continued with a sniff, "I confess, I half expected to find your laborers thick with drink, clinging to the walls with fatigue after their arduous work. But they possess such exuberance. Perhaps because the expense of this grand soirée falls upon your father's shoulders?"

Sara did not know if she should laugh or lash out at his rudeness.

"The harvest has been most adequate, Monsieur Lemieux. We thank you for your good wishes," she choked out.

Lydia clamped her hand on Sara's arm, as if to deter her from any further comment. "Monsieur Lemieux wants only the best for our farm, for we will soon be united as one family."

"Of course. I merely meant to say that your father is very generous."

"My sister is quite protective of our little vineyard, Monsieur Lemieux." Lydia squeezed Sara's hand. "You may find it difficult to believe, but not only has she inspected every stone on our land, she has also recorded every detail of its condition in her treasured diary. She carries that book with her as the curate does his Bible. What secrets of the vintner's trade must rest in her chronicles!"

Sara burned with embarrassment. She was livid that Lydia would trivialize her contributions to the farm's success—and in front of Bastien Lemieux, of all people. As if this weren't upsetting enough, he decided to take a swipe at her as well.

"Mademoiselle Sara is quite modern in her pursuits," Bastien observed. He didn't intend it as a compliment.

"Oh, you've only heard the half of it." Lydia smiled, but her eyes darted uneasily between Bastien and Sara, who didn't understand why Lydia continued to chirp about her work in the vineyard. "She assists Papa with the press and the pasteurization, although I believe it is, in part, to cause our dear maman vexation of the worst kind." Lydia's eyes flitted to Bastien's. "I confess, Monsieur Lemieux, I am caught up in the frivolous preoccupations of young ladies, but not our dear Sara. She would set aside Hugo's novels to read the scientific journals that line her bookshelf. She has a lively mind indeed," she sighed. "If only I could find a comparable passion to which I could devote my time."

"Indeed," Sara said tersely, silencing her sister. She was upset, but could see that Lydia was desperate to please her fiancé. She was about to excuse herself when she realized that Bastien was staring at her. Sara shifted uneasily under his gaze.

Bastien smirked. "I would venture to declare that it is noble to pursue one's passion in life. However, we must admire those who have the necessary grit to sustain such a passion. These enthusiasms are far too easily stolen away with the passing of time and change of circumstance, are they not, Mademoiselle Sara?"

"Indeed they are, monsieur, for those who lack conviction."

27

Without another word, Sara turned on her heel in search of friendlier company.

Weary from a rambunctious evening of drink and dance, the revelers staggered across the back lawn to the caves beyond. Sara imagined them exchanging gossip and telling stories around the fire before surrendering to deep slumber. Maman and Papa had already retired, bleary-eyed and bone-tired. Lydia had slipped away earlier with Bastien; Sara didn't want to think what for. As she climbed the stairs toward her bedchamber, she began to contemplate what she knew of the Lemieux family. They would soon be irretrievably united with her own family, for better or for worse.

Sara had first come to know Bastien when he began working as his father's apprentice and came with him regularly to visit the Thibault vineyard. Farm life was too demanding for much visiting. Sara ventured to town only on market days or Sundays and did not have the time to sustain any lasting acquaintances, aside from her friends at the village school. Moreover, the Lemieux brothers, Bastien and Philippe, were older than Sara by ten and nine years, respectively.

Their mother, Adèle Lemieux, had died eight years ago of a wasting disease. What little Sara had seen of her, she had liked. She remembered one Sunday morning, as a girl of nine, attending Mass with her family and sitting in the pew opposite Monsieur and Madame Lemieux and their two sons. She could not help but stare at the fine figure of Adèle Lemieux, whose shiny yellow hair was pulled back at the nape of her neck in an elaborate twist.

Sara could not imagine how she managed to keep it in its beautiful figure-eight curve. She was taller and straighter than any woman Sara had ever seen; when she stood she reached her husband's full height. Her skin was milk-white and her lips were pressed into a soft pink bow, which held a hint of pleasure, as if she were remembering a happy secret. Sara remembered feeling envious, watching Madame Lemieux take hold of her sons' hands and gaze at them adoringly. Sara had thought that, as kind as she could be, her own maman would never have done such a thing.

Although Sara knew little about Madame Lemieux outside of her incandescent appearance and gentle manner, she was distraught when she heard that Madame had died, leaving her two sons motherless. After Madame Lemieux's death, Sara still saw Bastien and Philippe at Mass on occasion with their father. Bastien seemed little changed, but she noticed that Philippe's hands now hung limply at his sides or remained locked across his chest. His face was expressionless; the light that had animated his young features had vanished.

Sara had spoken with Philippe only once. One morning, six months after Madame Lemieux had passed on to her greater glory, Sara had found herself walking home alone from church. Lydia had skipped on ahead when Sara had gone back to retrieve Maman's Bible, which she had left in the pew. Sara loved walking alone, even though her mother did not often allow it. She kept to the main road, for one never knew what trouble could be stirring in the adjacent wood. Halfway down the road, she heard voices coming from the scrub bushes. Her heart thudded a warning, and Sara answered it by quickening her pace.

But just then, out of the wood, Saul Mittier with pinched face and unkempt dirty blond hair, jumped in front of her, followed by three of his gang. Saul Mittier was a menace in ripped breeches and a stained shirt, wielding a long, pointy tree branch. He had once hidden a foul-smelling grass snake in the teacher's desk, causing her to shriek with fright, and he had a penchant for spying on the girls while they used the school privy. Saul and his gang moved closer, surrounding Sara as a wolf pack would its prey.

"What are you doing there?" He placed his hands on his hips, blocking her path. "You look fetching on this holy Sunday. And looky here, you even have your Bible. Tell me, Sara, does the good Lord, who sees all, know what you're about under there? Let's see that pretty honey pot!" Saul lifted the hem of her skirt with the stick. She batted it away, but not before she felt it scrape her thigh. Even at age nine, Sara did not endure embarrassment for long. Instead, she embraced its more useful companion—anger.

"Saul Mittier, you rat! If your père knew what you said, he'd take the strap to you!" Sara yelled over the taunts and howls of laughter. Their faces blurred, and all Sara could see were their open mouths and crooked yellow teeth.

Saul poked her in the chest. Sara grabbed the stick and tugged, but Saul didn't let go. He landed with a thump—facedown in the dirt. Sara knew if she ran, his jeering friends would chase after her. She held her mother's Bible tightly to her chest. She could not lose it, for it had cost Papa five francs. She looked down the road beyond the boys, lifted her chin and walked straight ahead past them, still clenching the stick in her other hand. She knew she wouldn't get far.

Saul ran up from behind and shoved her to the ground. They tussled, and before long he was on top of her, fists raised. Sara covered her face to protect herself from the blow, but it never came. A large hand grabbed Saul by the collar and yanked him right off her.

It was the hand of Philippe Lemieux.

Philippe had been on the other side of the churchyard when he spied the gang heading down the road after Sara. Sara listened to his version of events as he walked her home. He had run up behind them, pulled Saul off Sara, then threatened that if he ever saw Saul hit a girl again, he'd strip him from head to toe and make him walk through the village naked. Sara had laughed at the thought of that pug-nosed prig running through town in the altogether.

At eighteen, Philippe was nearly twice Sara's height, and seemed to be growing so fast that his skin stretched itself tight in a race to keep up with his bones. He had sandy hair, kind, bright blue eyes and wide cheekbones.

"You're sure you're not hurt?"

Sara shrugged. "No, just a few scrapes." In truth, she felt the sting on her palms and knees, but wanted to appear brave. As they neared the walkway to Sara's house, Sara knew Maman would want to thank Philippe with some freshly made currant buns, which she always baked for dinner on Sundays.

"You must come in. Maman and Papa will want to thank you."

Philippe smiled and waved his hand in polite refusal. "No need to thank me. Something tells me you would have kicked those boys senseless, even if I hadn't shown up." With a quick wink, he handed Sara the dusty Bible, turned and walked toward home. Sara had liked him instantly. As Philippe had figured, Sara was an excellent kicker—and a first-rate pincher, too.

Sara had seen neither hide nor hair of Philippe in almost six years. He had departed for America when he was only twenty-one years old. It was said that he hadn't wanted a place in his father's business, but had ambitions of running a vineyard of his own. More crucially, he had shamed his family when Jacques's niece Marie Chevreau, who lived an hour away in Tours, had become pregnant. When it was discovered, they had left for America together. His father and brother had not seemed disappointed to be rid of him. In fact, they rarely spoke of Philippe.

Sara's apprehension about the impending nuptials of her sister and Bastien Lemieux stemmed from her distrust of wine brokers in general, and an aversion to Bastien in particular. Everyone knew that wine brokers were an avaricious lot, and Lydia Thibault and the expansive Thibault estate were perhaps the most desirable possessions east of Tours. Lydia was known for her beauty, charm and pliable manners, which Sara believed Bastien would take the liberty to shape. Lydia, in turn, would become the wife of a prominent merchant, and eventually a mother, the pinnacle of her aspirations. Everyone thought them an enviable match. Sara disagreed.

Sara's heart was also heavy with the knowledge that when Lydia married Bastien, Sara would no longer have a central place in her sister's life. When they were girls, Lydia had taught her how to roll down hills and to whistle inside the caves where Maman couldn't hear them. She made Sara dandelion crowns and chased her through the sunflower field. She showed Sara how to break open a sunflower and rub out the plump black-and-white seeds. When Sara awoke from a nightmare, it was Lydia who wrapped her arms tightly around her and murmured, "Guardian angels by your side," lulling Sara back to sleep.

Sara sighed and her eyes drifted around the candlelit bedroom they shared. Lydia's wall was adorned with pictures of the latest fashion plates clipped from the pages of *La Nouvelle Mode*, the kinds of costumes she hoped to acquire in her married life, Sara supposed. In contrast, Sara's shelves were stacked top to bottom with books about grape growing and scientific research, many of them translations of American volumes. Glass jars filled with rocks and plant specimens served as bookends to papers written by Louis Pasteur and Madame Aurora Thierry, the French-born Californian whose treatise on grape varieties was one of the best Sara had ever read. Papa was the only one in the family who shared her great passion for learning. She loved to spend the evening hours searching for new ideas that might help their vineyard reach new levels of prosperity.

Sara's thoughts returned to Lydia. She loved her sister, but she struggled to understand her. How could Lydia not see Bastien's flaws? Moreover, why didn't Papa notice them? Perhaps Maman had insisted on the marriage and Papa had acquiesced. Sara's mind often churned over dark thoughts in these small hours. She sighed at the uncertainty of it all and rolled toward the open window to look out upon the stables.

A burst of cool night air alerted her senses to movement below. She shifted her gaze downward and witnessed a peculiar sight: Bastien Lemieux stood at the side of his brougham. Why, on such a fine evening, would he not have ridden the mile between their homes on horseback? The answer came a moment later: Lydia stepped out of the carriage and Bastien handed her down. She smoothed the hem of her dress over what looked to be her bare legs. When she lifted her face, Sara thought she spied tears. Bastien ran his hand along the side of Lydia's disheveled coiffure to replace a comb. How it had become loose, Sara would not allow herself to speculate. Bastien lifted Lydia's hand, kissed it and took his leave.

He did not go far. As Lydia sneaked into the house, Sara watched Bastien round the back of the stables toward the caves. What in the devil was he up to?

CHAPTER 3

Papa

Sara came down the stairs at the unusually late hour of eight the next morning, intending to make her way to the dining room for breakfast. She was surprised to find Lydia standing in the hallway outside Papa's study.

"Lydie, who's there?"

Lydia put her finger to her lips to silence Sara, who leaned in closer to the doorway to listen. She could hear the deep vibration of men's voices behind the door.

Lydia mouthed, "Bastien!" and pointed toward the door.

Sara grabbed her by the arm and dragged her down the corridor. "What are they talking about?"

Just then, the door opened and Bastien was upon them. "Mesdemoiselles Thibault," he said flatly. He made a slight bow and left without another word.

Lydia hastened after Bastien, and Sara poked her head around the entrance to Papa's study.

"That miserable pig!" Papa muttered and crumpled the paper in his hand.

"Papa? What happened?"

Papa was silent. He raked his hand through his hair and stared at the desk before him.

"What has Lemieux done?"

Papa shook his head. "Jean Lemieux is trying to ruin us. He has set a price of forty francs per barrel. He didn't even extend us the courtesy of consulting the curate."

Sara's mind reeled at the implications. "But why? Our wine is excellent this year—the best ever—you said so yourself!"

"Quality is not the issue. Lemieux has brought in low-priced Italian and Spanish wines, which he intends to blend with our Vouvray wines. They will bottle them, label them with the Vouvray name and export them."

"But surely they won't be allowed to do that."

"There is no one to stop them. The winemakers will agree to it because they need the money."

"What will you do?"

"I won't accept it. We will contract with another broker."

Sara was shocked. It was highly unusual to go outside of the village to secure a buyer.

Papa looked up, aware of her silence. "We will go to Tours and sell it barrel by barrel on the rue Nationale, if we must. I'll be damned if I'll be forced into accepting such an insulting offer."

Damned indeed, Sara thought, dispirited. If they couldn't sell their barrels at a minimum of fifty francs each, and in time to make their loan payment, they would be ruined.

Fog thickened the air on the last morning of November. Papa and Jacques hitched the horses and loaded up their wagons with four barrels of wine, a sampling for several negotiants in Tours with whom they were hoping to transact the bulk of their business. Papa had insisted that they bring the barrels themselves rather than hiring a wagon and driver to transport them. One could not take the chance, Papa explained, that a thirsty wine-runner would knock back the contents of his cargo, replace the wine with river water and deliver the breached barrels before the unsuspecting broker was any wiser.

From the scullery, Sara heard the horses start. She ran down the dirt road, a sail of long chestnut hair flying behind her. She waved frantically, but fearing they wouldn't see her in the fog, shouted, "Papa! Papa!" She was clutching a small bag and running in her field clogs, taking care not to stumble.

Papa signaled to Jacques to hold up. As Sara caught up to him, he leaned down to touch the crown of his daughter's head. "What is it, love?"

Sara was breathless, her eyes bright with excitement. "Papa, please let me come with you, I want to learn everything. I promise I'll be as quiet as a church mouse. I have my things right here." She held up her satchel.

"My dear, I would love for you to come, and one day you will make a fine vigneron, but we're expecting heavy rain and I don't think it would be wise. Besides, I need you here, to run the vineyard while I'm gone."

"Yes, Papa." Sara hung her head for just a moment. Then, lifting her bright eyes, she hoisted herself up and kissed her father on both cheeks. "*Au revoir*, Papa!" she said sweetly. She jumped back down and waved once more, watching as the wagons lurched forward. "*Bonne chance!*"

DECEMBER 2, 1895, SAINT MARTIN, VOUVRAY

Sara was the first to see the single wagon winding down the road toward the manor house. Her heart leapt when she thought it might be her father, and she strained to identify the driver at such a distance. It was Jacques alone, and the wagon was empty, save for a long wooden box.

Sara stood in the gated garden. The horses' hooves sucked and plopped down the muddy road toward her. The boards of the wagons rattled. It was a hollow, desperate sound. Drops of perspiration fell down Sara's forehead and over her lips. She did not wipe them away before they fell. She could not move, could not speak.

"Sara! Who—?" Maman's question hung in the air, but then drifted away. Sara recognized the scent of her mother's lavender perfume. Maman stood next to her, gripping her hand. Sara wrapped her arm tightly around her mother's waist.

"Maman," Sara said weakly as she watched her mother's delicate face twist from disbelief to horror and then to blankness.

After Lydia and Jacques carried Maman into the house, Sara watched the field hands lower Papa from the wagon. She followed the cortege in through the scullery door. The men laid the box on the floor and cleared off the long walnut table where Marcheline and Maman would wipe the mud from Papa's eyes and mouth and hair and nails, and gently rub the cleansing spirits all over his body. Then they would dress him in his black wedding coat and breeches from the cupboard upstairs.

Sara stared at the box on the scullery floor and wondered if Papa were hot and scared. She wanted to rest her head on his warm chest, feel his sharp whiskers and brush her lips across his weathered cheek. Marcheline began to boil herbs at the cookstove and the aroma of rosemary and sage broke Sara out of her trance. The herbs would hide the stink of death. Sara could not bear to watch. Papa would not want it.

When Marcheline looked at her, Sara could not stand the maid's pity-filled eyes upon her. She ran outside and down the length of the path, away from the box, away from the stares, away from death.

Sara eased open the oak door to the cellar, just to the point before she knew it would creak, and slipped inside. She squeezed between the jagged tufa wall and the nearest barrel. Alone in the dark, she clutched her knees to her chest. Sara had found this hiding place when she was five. It had always been her refuge from the sun-scorched fields and her carping mother. The damp seeped in from the cave floor through her dress and cooled her skin. Her nose filled with the heavy scent of oak. Sara sat for what must have been an hour or more. Eventually, the door she had left ajar creaked open. She saw Jacques's clogs, caked with dried grass stuck to wet dirt.

"Your mother needs you."

Sara could not see his face. "She has Lydie."

"Ah." Sara saw that Jacques's nails were brown with dirt, or maybe blood. He pushed his hands into his pockets.

Sara knew that if she asked him, it would ruin this special place forever. But she had to know. And Jacques had to be the one to tell her. She sat quietly for a few moments, summoning her courage.

"Tell me," she commanded.

Jacques remained close to the door. Sara heard him breathe in and gulp down a sob. She rested her forehead on her crossed arms, looked into the dark folds of her lap, and listened.

"It was at the Touraine ford. The rain hadn't let up all day, but your papa drove on, not wanting to waste any time. He went down the bank, about two men steep, while I waited above for him to cross the river. The horses, they bucked at it, and they slid a bit on the way down, but they held . . . they held all the way down to the river. But we didn't know how loose the ground was."

Jacques's voice began to shake. "Before he even started to cross, the rain just cleaved off a section of the ledge right in front of me—and it came down on top of your papa. It just swallowed him up. I jumped down into the river and clawed through the mud, but couldn't see him, I couldn't find him . . . then I saw his hand and I reached for him, but my damned feet stuck. The current pounded against us and it pulled your papa right downstream with it. I couldn't get to him, Sara. I couldn't . . . reach him."

Sara looked up and saw Jacques's shoulders quake. She waited for his silent sobs to end before she braved her next question.

"Did he fight?" she whispered.

"What?"

"Did he fight?" she demanded.

Jacques knelt down and looked Sara in the eye. She met his gaze, her eyes shining with tears.

"He fought like the devil, *ma p'tite*. Like the devil."

Sara laid her head back down. So, it was the river, she thought. It wound its way like a snake through every town in the Loire, with its promise of refreshment, of life itself, but this time it had brought only ruination and death.

Later that afternoon, Sara found her sister, who was staring out the hallway window, watching Jacques lead the horses to the stables. She came up behind Lydia, resting her chin upon her shoulder and wrapping her arms around her waist.

"How is Maman?" Sara asked.

"She hasn't spoken yet. She just sobbed until she couldn't any longer and then slept. Now she's locked herself in the parlor with Papa. Marcheline had to send for the neighbors to help her . . . you know . . . prepare him."

"Lydie, dear, this is a terrible blow for Maman."

"But she needs to have her wits about her for the wake and the funeral. She must be able to greet the mourners and do . . . what . . . Papa . . . would want." Lydie broke into a torrent of tears.

Sara held her sister as she shook uncontrollably. When she

could cry no more, Lydia slumped in Sara's arms. "Why don't you sleep a spell before dinner," Sara suggested.

Lydia nodded, wiping her eyes. "You'll look in on Maman?"

"Of course," Sara promised.

Sara pressed her ear against the parlor door, but she could no longer hear her mother's sobbing. It was almost nightfall and Maman needed her rest for tomorrow. Sara's breath caught in her throat as she entered the room.

Papa's casket had been laid across four large picking baskets and it shone like gold in the candlelight. Sara peered in to observe her father more closely. Shadows flickered over his face, bringing a sort of unsettling movement to his ashen features. His pale fingers clutched the crucifix Maman had given him on their wedding day. The broken capillaries on his nose and cheeks had been skillfully concealed by Marcheline's paste of crushed buttercups and powder. What saddened Sara to her heart's core was the fact that she could never beckon Papa to open his soft brown eyes and look upon her again. The life within his battered frame had vanished. The figure before her bore no resemblance to her father.

Sara felt as though she'd been punched in the gut, as if her heart had been ripped from her chest. She swallowed back the bitter-tasting bile in her throat and turned her attention to her mother.

Cloaked in layers of black Saint-Cyr wool, Maman sat on the hard floor next to the casket. Her cheek, framed by the ruffles of her black bonnet, rested against the casket's rough wood.

"Maman?"

"I will rest with him tonight." She was adamant.

"But Maman—"

"I will not leave him alone."

Sara felt the hollow inside her deepen. She had not realized how lost her mother would be without him.

The rooms that had recently hosted raucous revelers were now filled with somber mourners. Sara could not help but think it a disgusting tradition, to invite the neighbors to gawk at a man on his worst day.

Maman stood in the foyer flanked by her daughters. The mourners shuffled by, stopping to offer their condolences. Sara noticed Lydia fussing with the waist of her dress. Then she looked up and saw the reason for Lydia's sudden self-consciousness. Bastien Lemieux and his father approached with their hats in hand. As the two men sauntered toward them, Sara could feel anger pulsing through her veins and her heart pounding in double time. But Lydia seemed pleased to see them. After murmuring a few words in Lydia's ear, Bastien stepped over to Sara.

"Mademoiselle," Bastien said somberly as he leaned in and took Sara's hand in his, "please accept our condolences. I am so terribly sorry." Sara retracted her hand and eyed him cynically.

Jean Lemieux ran a hand over his slick, thinning hair and addressed Maman. "We are at your service, madame, to help in any way we can."

Sara interrupted before her mother could respond. "You'll forgive me, messieurs, if I do not accept your condolences."

"Sara!" Lydia cried.

"Sara is distraught, messieurs. You must forgive her." Maman's tone issued Sara a warning.

"I am in full possession of my faculties, Maman, and I don't need you to make excuses for me."

Jean Lemieux exchanged a knowing look with his son. Bastien addressed Sara. "I am sorry to hear you feel this way, mademoiselle. Madame Thibault, might I have the pleasure of speaking with your younger daughter for a moment—outside?"

"I have nothing to say to you," Sara said pointedly.

"She's a spirited child, isn't she? A bit impetuous, like her father." Jean Lemieux laughed mirthlessly.

"We can spare you, Sara." Her mother's voice was stern. Noticing Lydia's obvious distress, Sara realized it would be best to move away from the crowd. Now she was likely to say something that would render Lydia apoplectic. Bastien took Sara's upper arm and guided her around the corner into the empty back hallway.

"On the contrary, mademoiselle, I think you believe you have something very important to say. I must ask why you treat me and my father with such disdain within view of the entire town." He gestured toward the front door, where a line of people waited to pay their respects.

Sara glared at him. "You killed my father."

Bastien smirked. "You are overwrought."

Sara squared her shoulders and looked directly into his dark eyes. "I am nothing of the kind."

"This is quite a fantastical delusion you have. I'm intrigued. Do go on."

Sara knew she sounded every bit like a seventeen-year-old girl, and she hated herself in that moment for being too young and inexperienced to truly hurt him. The smug look on his face spoke volumes. He thought of her as a silly nuisance, a child, a fly to be flicked from the rim of his glass.

"Do not mock me, monsieur. Everyone knows Jean Lemieux refused to offer my father an honest price. He did so at your bidding. I saw you steal into the caves that night—searching, I presume, for something that would justify lowering the price. Clearly, you found it. Your father cheated us because you told him to!"

"I do not deny it. I found the sulfide you use to treat the vines, and I told my father the truth."

"Not the whole truth. You knew that the majority of our vines bore no signs of infestation. You knew that by offering only forty francs per barrel, you would force us into bankruptcy. My father was forced to seek another buyer in Tours. Had you had the slightest bit of conscience, you would have suggested some sort of gentlemanly compromise, some sort of—" Sara broke off. Tears threatened, and she would not give Bastien that satisfaction. She swallowed hard in an effort to compose herself.

"Sara, you are but a child, and you think like a child. My father may have, as you say, refused your father the price he expected. However, that makes him a shrewd businessman, not a murderer." His voice was gentle, but his eyes menacing.

"I know the truth. I will see to it that everyone else knows, too."

Bastien tightened his grip on Sara's arm. "The truth? Let's examine the truth. Your sister and I will soon be married, Sara." Bastien's eyes drifted from Sara's face and lingered on her bosom.

Lowering his face to hers, he whispered, "You are a fetching young girl, but a girl without protection now that your father has passed. I would hate to see you taken advantage of."

"My mother will never allow you to marry Lydia after she learns what you've done. Your entire family is a disgrace! First the scandal with your brother, and then you and your father, in all your deceit, force us into bankruptcy. And you, sir! You claim a deep affection for my sister, but I have observed you most closely, and it is a lie. All you desire is a pretty girl on your arm and the comfort of a liaison with some land attached to it. You're nothing more than a faithless rogue."

Bastien's eyes hardened. "You and I both know that only my family can offer you continued financial support and a proper dowry for your marriage, once it is arranged. Think carefully before you impugn my character further."

Bastien's grip was so tight, Sara pressed her lips together to keep from wincing. "Take your hand from me." She ripped her arm from his grasp and, steadying her shaking limbs, marched back into the mourning hall with her head held high.

Later that afternoon, Luc Thibault was placed with care in the family's plot at the edge of the oak forest that stood on the western boundary of his much-loved Clos de Saint Martin. The church bells tolled forty-nine times, once for each year of his life.

CHAPTER 4

Despair

The December winds blew in from the west and snatched the last of the leaves from their stems. The nutting season in Vouvray had just come to its end, and Madame Laroche, the miller's wife, had called this morning with bags of chestnuts and walnuts for the Thibaults. She came most mornings to sit with Maman for an hour or so, sometimes in silence, often to pray the rosary, always to offer the news from town. The slight crook of her nose and her dark currant eyes belied her jovial nature. When Sara and Lydia thanked her for her kindness to Maman, she waved them away, saying cheerfully, "Of course, I'm quite a nuisance, but Marguerite must be reminded that there is life all around her, and it needs tending to."

Sara witnessed no improvement in Maman's spirits, but she was relieved to have a respite from worrying about her. She took her winter cloak from the hook near the scullery door, plunged her hands into one of the bags Madame Laroche had brought and pulled up two fistfuls of walnuts. She shoved them in her pockets and started out on her errands without a word to anyone.

She walked half a mile down the road to the cluster of houses near the Église de Tous les Saints. She held a sack to her chest. She would begin by visiting Monsieur Manon to see if he had baked any pain au chocolat, which perhaps would tempt her mother out of her isolation, if only temporarily. Then she would pay Monsieur du Fresne the funds owed to him for the ten new barrels he had delivered to Saint Martin this past summer. She was saving her visit to Monsieur Pepin for last. She didn't know if she had the heart for it.

Papa had been dead for three weeks now, and yet, Sara could see as she walked toward the village, the river still ran and the ships still sailed. Most of the remaining wine had been sold, the empty barrels stacked, the press cleaned and the nuts harvested. The pickers had all left for the north. Christmas was only a few days away.

As Sara waited at the baker's to place her order, Madame Beaulieu, the herring-seller's wife, chattered about village goings-on and made what she clearly thought was a grand pronouncement: *"September de noix, hiver froid!"* The chestnuts had ripened early, which she took as a sign that the winter months would bring only gloom. The baker shook his head. Gloom, indeed, thought Sara. Would the sun ever shine again? She thought not. Papa had vanished from their lives. Sara knew his spirit lived on, but his warmth had abandoned them.

She walked from the baker's to the cooperage, a short journey that nonetheless required numerous responses to sympathetic inquiries about her mother, her sister and the farm. Sara
had perfected her pleasantries and assertions that all would be
well in time, God willing. Small talk required less effort than telling her neighbors that she wandered without aim through the
days, that Maman wasn't eating her meals, and that Lydia spent
all day fussing over silly things like darning their wool stockings
for winter.

After paying the cooper, Sara finally arrived at Monsieur
Pepin's. She clutched her sack tightly to her chest and opened the
door. He sat upon his stool, hunched over a wood stump, resoling
a pair of ladies' shoes. He looked up, a monocle wedged between
his brow line and cheekbone, and squinted at her.

"Mademoiselle Thibault, 'tis good to see you about town
again."

Sara stared at the neat line of polished clogs on the floor next
to the far wall. "I was hoping you could repair these for me." Sara's
grip on the neck of the sack tightened.

The shoemaker stood and gently pulled the sack toward him
until she released it into his possession. He opened the bag. Sara
watched as he examined Papa's buckskin boots, running his hand
over the yellowed leather, and looking closely at the soles.

"I'll fix the toes and shine 'em up right fine for you, my love."

"Thank you." Sara hesitated. "I don't have the money to pay
you, but may I give you these walnuts now and some wine upon
my return? This year's wine is our finest quality yet." She tried to
sound cheerful.

He laid his tools on the stump and took Sara's hands between his own. "*Ma cherie*, do not fret about payment. I am honored to mend them."

Sara felt her eyes well with tears.

Monsieur Pepin looked at her intently. "It is not the boots that hold value, eh? It is rather the path your Papa walked in them, *n'est-ce pas?*"

Christmas was a dismal affair. The downstairs rooms of the house echoed like a cavern; it was not at all the bustling, joyful place Sara remembered from her childhood holidays. Papa was not here to orchestrate the festivities, hide the gifts or hold her tightly by the waist and spin her until she was wobbly and light in the head. How he had made them laugh each year when he chased a rabbit through the house in a mock effort to snare it for their Christmas feast! She never did recall his catching the elusive creature. Alas, thought Sara, without Papa there was simply no laughter, no joy, no expectation.

The smells were different, too. Sara could barely detect her favorite scent of pine kernels and thistles, which Marcheline used every winter to light the oven. Instead, as the three Thibault women sat huddled around the table in the airless parlor, all Sara could smell were the worn furnishings, laden with dust. Sara could not even enliven their day with conversation. She could think of nothing to say. Instead, she watched her mother and sister stare at the steam rising from their cups of wine, their idle fingers wrapped resolutely around the clay vessels. Hardly a useful employment,

Sara thought as she fidgeted in her chair. She longed to be else-where.

At last, the promise of entertainment presented itself. Marcheline entered to announce Jacques's arrival. Maman spoke up first.

"Welcome him in, Marcheline, and bring us some of those honey loaves you've baked." That her mother made the effort to feign pleasure was a comfort to Sara. Maman would at least engage in polite conversation with Jacques.

Jacques entered the room in his usual whirlwind and ran his hand over his head in an attempt to smooth down his few remaining strands of hair. "Bless me! Ladies, there's a wicked tempest kicking up out there, and have you seen that blanket of gray sky? My heavens, if the snow doesn't come by nightfall, I'll eat my own hat."

"A happy Christmas to you, Jacques," Maman responded. Maman always ignored Jacques's colorful turns of phrase, though Sara found his descriptions delightful.

"I've forgotten my manners completely. Happy Christmas, madame, mesdemoiselles! I hope you don't mind my saying so, but I feel Luc's smiling face shining down upon us on this blessed day of our Lord's birth."

"Indeed," Maman answered, "may God keep him." She covered her heart with her hand in a gesture that struck Sara as too solemn given Jacques's attempt at lightheartedness.

Jacques, however, continued with unabated enthusiasm. "I've brought presents, my dears. Luc would have wanted his girls to have some trinkets." Jacques placed three small brown parcels, clumsily wrapped in string, on the table before them. They were all silent. Sara ached for Papa.

Lydia brought Sara back with her quiet words. "How lovely of you, Jacques. You are the truest of friends."

Jacques cleared his throat and shifted in his seat. "It was nothing." He picked up the cup Marcheline had placed in front of him and lifted it ceremoniously. "Go on, don't keep me waiting!"

Lydia and Sara were first to remove the paper wrapping and reveal the necklace inside each package: small wooden crosses secured to gold chains. Sara's was dark stained wood; Lydia's was blond wood. Jacques must have carved them himself. To Maman, he gave the only picture he had of Papa, taken in Reims during the war when a traveling photographer had visited their regiment. Sara took the tintype between her fingers to examine it. Papa's face was so smooth and vibrant.

"That's when your Uncle Jacques still had his hair!" They all laughed.

"You could not have given us anything finer. Thank you, Jacques." Maman held the photograph close to her heart for the remainder of his visit.

Finally, Maman gave the girls their gifts. To Lydia, Maman gave her cherished Bible, for, she said, as a soon-to-be-married woman, Lydia would certainly make use of it. Sara thought this odd, but Lydia seemed to think it the most generous of presents. To Sara, Maman gave a newly knitted wool shawl the color of claret, which Maman said would bring out the green of Sara's eyes. Maman draped it over Sara's shoulders and Sara was comforted by its warmth and softness. Lydia commented that its deep hue added color to Sara's cheeks and fire to her eyes.

Then Maman nodded to Sara in a silent request that Sara retrieve the last gift, wrapped in hessian cloth, from the side table. Sara handed the gift to Jacques. "For all you have done for us." Sara knew Maman had wanted to give Jacques a handsome raise, but with the farm finances in such an uncertain state, this was the next most valuable thing they could give that would be useful to him.

Jacques's eyes opened wide when he saw Papa's favorite boots, cleaned and fitted with new soles and leather laces. Maman had even knitted a beautiful pair of socks to accompany them. Jacques did not speak. Sara knew he had never owned a pair himself, and they would be a comfortable change from wooden clogs, especially in the frigid winter months.

"You needn't say a word, Jacques. Papa would have wanted you to have them," she assured him.

Jacques sniffed loudly and nodded his head. "Thank you." He was in no state to direct the conversation to more buoyant topics, so Sara was relieved when her sister spoke up.

"Tell us the news from town, Jacques." Lydia loved to hear all the city news. Sara noticed today that she seemed to search for topics that did not involve her betrothed, for Bastien had not called at Saint Martin for a fortnight. Nor should he dare show his face here, thought Sara bitterly. Lydia had ceased to mention his name. For once, Sara had to agree with her sister; it would be a welcome diversion to hear the latest gossip from their little corner of the Loire.

"So many things, I hardly know where to begin. Oh yes, well, Mim witnessed a most distressing sight the other day." Jacques's brother and his wife had moved to Tours ten years ago and had opened one of its most popular taverns. "Monsieur Laroche had a few drinks before leaving the tavern. He didn't return home to Vouvray that evening, so Madame Laroche drove into town look-ing for him early the next morning. No one had seen him. She asked Pierre and all the patrons, and it seems he had disappeared somewhere around ten o'clock." Jacques's voice was grave. "Madame Laroche was so anxious to find him, she engaged the local curate to assist in the search."

"Did they find him?" Sara was intrigued.

"Indeed. Mim was tidying up the place before they opened again. Guess whom she found on the cellar floor—au naturel, mind you—reeking of wine and snoring as loud as a woodsman's saw!"

"No!" Lydia cried.

Jacques waved his hands frantically, for he wasn't finished. "But you haven't heard the best of it. Laroche was so crocked, he took one look at Mim, placed his felt cap back on his head and stumbled out of the tavern without a word—*and* without a stitch." Jacques was laughing and snorting so hard, he struggled to catch his breath. "Wait, wait," he gasped, wiping his tearing eyes with his sleeve. "A half hour later Mim found his shirt and breeches inside an open barrel! It seems that Monsieur Laroche had taken himself a bath in the storeroom!"

Sara's shoulders began to shake, and Lydia tried hard to con-tain her amusement by tightening her lips, but to no avail. She erupted in peals of laughter. Even Maman could not resist. She clutched her handkerchief to her lips and giggled until she cried. It was such a relief to laugh again.

JANUARY 15, 1896

Sara passed the afternoon walking on the banks of the Loire and wading into its frigid waters, her skirt knotted up at her knees. She concentrated on the feel of the pebbles beneath her feet—some sharp, some smooth, others slippery with moss. After five minutes, her toes numbed and she could hardly feel the stones at all. Is this what Papa had felt? A tingling sensation, and then nothing? No, she reckoned, the mud that overpowered Papa would have been a thick sludge; he would have felt as if he were drowning in a vat of molasses.

When twilight came, Sara began the climb up the steep bank toward the farm. After fifty paces or so, she heard Lydia calling from the house. She hadn't thought she was late for supper, but perhaps she'd lost track of time. As Sara came closer, she saw the dour expression on Lydia's face. Sara quickened her steps instinctively—maybe something had happened to Maman.

Lydia took her by the hand and led her into the parlor, shutting the door behind them. Before Sara could even ask, Lydia blurted out the unimaginable. She intended to marry Bastien in March.

Sara stared down at her clogs, examining the rough scratches that marred their once smooth wooden surface. She couldn't bear to look Lydia in the eye. When she finally spoke, her tone was scathing. "You would dishonor our father's memory by marrying the man whose family is responsible for his death?"

"Watch your tongue, Sara," Lydia snapped, sounding too much like Maman. "I have no desire to dishonor Papa. I loved him, too."

"I don't understand. You cannot marry into that family. Papa would forbid it. And Maman, surely she has not agreed to this."

"Father is gone and has left us with nothing but debts. The vineyard will need proper tending if we are to survive here, and that will require funds we do not have. If I make this marriage, we will want for nothing."

Sara was shocked by both Lydia's decision and her callousness.

"You cannot be serious, Lydia. You mean to say that you are marrying him in order to *save* Saint Martin? You never cared about the farm. The three of us, with Jacques's expertise, will survive just fine without them. We can ask the bank to extend the loan, Jacques and I can manage the grafting and the harvest and the crush, and I can find a new negotiant, new buyers . . ."

Lydia's voice softened for the first time. "Dearest, I do not doubt your abilities. But Bastien's father holds the loan, not the bank. Bastien has pleaded with his father to ease the terms of the loan on our behalf, but Monsieur Lemieux does not see it as a good investment. He may well be correct. Besides, even if we were all to work our fingers to the bone, the vineyard is simply too much for us to manage without someone to cover our expenses until next year's harvest."

Sara bristled at the mention of those foul people. How could Lydia be so blind?

"I'm afraid it has already been decided, Sara."

"By whom? Why was I not consulted?"

Lydia stared at her hands, fingers intertwined and poised on her lap. She would not look at Sara.

"What is it, Lydie?"

"Maman asked me not to tell. Not just yet. But I fear I must." She took a deep breath and blurted it out. "I walked into the study last week and came upon Monsieur Lemieux and Maman talking. When I asked her later, Maman said that he had offered her a fair price to purchase Saint Martin. It would be enough to repay our debts and give Maman a proper living and you a dowry." Lydia straightened her back. "She had no choice but to accept it. Papa has left us swimming in debt."

Sara attempted to interject but Lydia lifted a hand to silence her.

"Papa mortgaged the farm to purchase those new vines years back. There is little money for repayment, not to mention for our living expenses." Sara wondered where Lydia had obtained so much knowledge about their financial affairs.

"But surely you could have persuaded Maman to wait?" Sara felt her chest tighten.

Lydia shook her head. "Half of the farms in Vouvray are ruined. In Chançay, Noizay, Reugny, it is the same. Look around, Sara," she said quietly, "The phylloxera has hit everyone hard."

"You would marry into their family after they cheated us?"

Lydia's tone was defensive. "They too have a business to run and could only offer a lower barrel price in order to remain profitable. Sara, you should know that I was the one to persuade Maman to accept their offer. She signed the papers this afternoon."

Sara felt heat rush to her face. "But the land is our inheritance! Legally, it passes from Papa to us."

Lydia pressed her palms together and sighed. "As part of their marriage contract, Maman kept ownership of her family's vineyard, and all its dwellings, while Papa managed them. You and I inherit only the furnishings."

Papa had never mentioned such an arrangement. Couldn't her mother have consulted her before she sold Saint Martin out from under them? No, no, she couldn't, because Sara would have fought her tooth and nail. Sara was disgusted.

"Sara, don't you see?" Lydia's eyes brightened with hope. "When I marry Bastien, we keep the vineyard."

"What do you mean? I'm sure Bastien will throw you over and evict us as soon as the ink has dried."

Lydia placed her hands on her midsection. "He would not throw out his own child."

"What?"

Lydia shifted in her chair. "I am carrying Bastien's child. He will inherit Saint Martin and it will stay in the family."

Sara stared blankly at Lydia. "And Maman? Does she know?"

"I have not told her, because I didn't want to compound her grief with scandal. She may suspect it, but I have not uttered a word."

"What if it's a girl?"

"It's a boy. I feel it, Sara."

"But he will be a Lemieux."

"He will have Thibault blood."

Sara was silent. Had Lydia run mad?

"What is the alternative, Sara? Bankruptcy and a bastard? That would help no one." Lydia looked down and smoothed her skirt. "We will be a good match—you'll see."

Sara was appalled by her sister's desperation. Lydia had always been a model of primness and decorum. To think that she had given herself to such a horrible man! Yet Lydia didn't seem the least bit ashamed.

"What about your dowry, Lydia? We have nothing now. Perhaps Bastien would accept Maman's silver or Papa's watch?" Sara said mockingly.

"Bastien has pledged his devotion to me, our child and Saint Martin. He requires no more."

"He requires no more?" Sara's voice was shrill. "What more is there, Lydia? He's taken everything! Are you not angry? Do you not blame him?"

"You are being nonsensical, Sara. It was not Bastien's plan to purchase the vineyard. He asked his father to give us more time to make the payment. Jean Lemieux refused, and that did anger me at first. But Bastien has apologized for his father's actions and is committed to helping us. I trust him, Sara. I need you to trust him, too. As the new owner of Saint Martin, he has told me he will expand the business, and even export our wines to America." Lydia rested her hand on her belly. "Would you rather my child grow up with no land and no fortune?"

Sara couldn't answer. This was ludicrous—every word of it. She felt sickened and helpless. Sara ran from the room without a word and marched toward the stables, filled with rage. What a fool she was to think that her mother and sister would trust her to take over now that Papa was gone! They had thrown themselves at the mercy of Jean Lemieux and his greedy son. They hadn't even stood up to them.

Sara saddled and mounted her bay, grabbing hold of the reins. Her sleeves clung to her perspiration-drenched skin. She clawed at her collar until it broke open, feeling the relief of the cold evening air against her throat. She pressed her heels into her horse's sides and galloped past the back of the house to the western edge of the vineyard, then stopped, breathless, beneath the oaks that stood sentry over her father's gravestone. Sara sat still upon her horse, but inside she felt frantic.

Sara finally dismounted and laid herself down on the cold patch of new earth that covered her father's grave. The ground enveloped her in its smell of clean rain and dead leaves, not like Papa at all. The new shoots of grass tickled the skin of her cheek. They were confused—winter was still hard upon them, but they had emerged to seek the sun during the past few unexpected days of mild weather. She rolled over and looked up at the web of spindly oak branches that hung high above her. They looked to Sara like the bony fingers of a starving hand, straining toward the elusive sky and the coveted place at the crown of the tree. There they would be the first to feel the sun's warmth and the first to catch the spring rain. Only the leanest and wiliest would thrive.

Sara wondered if Papa could hear her thoughts. She imagined hearing his voice echo in the sway of the trees. What would he say? What counsel would he offer? She listened closely, but heard nothing. She did not want to leave her father's grave, but the mantle of darkness had begun its descent over Saint Martin. Sara stood up and smeared cold dirt across her cheek as she wiped away her tears.

The three Thibault women dined in silence that evening. Even Lydia, always the peacemaker of the family, failed to find neutral topics for conversation. Sara had decided she would speak with her mother privately. She concentrated on chewing every bite of food twenty times before swallowing, in an effort to keep from screaming and cursing.

Maman retreated to Papa's study after dinner, as she always did, saying that she was tidying up his possessions or categorizing his books and letters. Sara followed her, stopping in the doorway to scrutinize her mother. Maman sat in the small chair Papa had claimed as his own. Its dark red cushions were threadbare and lumpy, but Papa would not consent to have them restuffed, insisting that should he repair them, their exquisite comfort would be irretrievably lost. Maman was stitching a piece of fabric, and on the floor next to her lay her sewing hamper, draped with chemises, drawers and bed linens, some bearing the initials *LT* in pale blue embroidery. She hunched over her work under the lamplight, threading the needle with expertise. Sara noted that the blue veins that ran like tiny rivers between her mother's delicate hand bones were more pronounced. Sara was saddened to see her mother this way, but she wouldn't pretend Maman hadn't crushed every hope she'd had.

Maman finished a row of stitching and looked up at Sara.

"Lydia has told you." Her eyes flickered over Sara's face and then returned to their work.

"Yes."

"You feel I have betrayed you?"

Sara was quiet.

Maman placed her embroidery aside and said gently, "There are things you don't understand."

"Of course." Sara understood perfectly.

"It was the only way," Maman pleaded.

Sara said nothing.

Maman stood up and peered out the window at the starless sky. "You disagree. You never approved of Lemieux or his sons."

"I know Bastien was snooping around the caves. He found the sulfide and told his father, who used our financial trouble to force you to sell. Now you have given them what they wanted. I only wonder why you waited so long to sell the farm. You never valued the life Papa built for us here."

Maman whirled around to face Sara. "I have just lost my husband of twenty-five years. You cannot fathom how deeply I valued your father." Her chin trembled. "You know nothing of our situation, and yet you question my motives? I have prayed to the Lord for guidance, and it has been given. Now you want me to reject his blessings?"

"If you had just tried to negotiate with Lemieux, or asked our friends and neighbors for assistance, surely we could have—"

"There was no other solution. It was my decision to make, and I took Monsieur Lemieux's offer to secure an income for us and a dowry for you."

"Papa worked for years to make Saint Martin a success, and if it hadn't been for the phylloxera, he would have. How can you turn your back on Saint Martin and sell it out from under us?"

"It was not what I would have wished, but it was the least complicated path."

"For you, and for Lydia. But what about me, Maman?"

"You will marry—to a vigneron, if you like. You would be a wonderful wife to a vigneron."

The idea horrified Sara.

Maman stomped her foot. "Your father would wish you to abide by my wishes, to agree that this is best for our family."

Sara's voice was a cold whisper. "My father is dead."

CHAPTER 5

Sin

The wedding of Sebastien Jean Lemieux to Lydia Marielle Thibault took place on March 14, 1896. The villagers of Vouvray followed the customary rituals without question, though they may have had their suspicions. There would, of course, be time for speculation as the bride's belly blossomed in the months to come.

The bride's door was decorated with pine branches freshly cut from the forest trees. Lydia wore a white woolen dress and, with the exception of a single panel of Amboise lace that adorned her wedding chapeau, her ensemble was noticeably absent of any embellishment, for she was still in mourning for her father. What was noticeable, at least to her sister, was Lydia's expanding waistline. The dress had been altered twice before the wedding. As luck would have it, her bump remained hidden by her long coat for the better part of the day.

Jacques guided Lydia on horseback down the road from Saint Martin to the church, where Bastien awaited her. Sara could tell Bastien gloried in his black top hat and frock coat fastened with copper buttons. The curate performed the wedding Mass, which was followed by a wedding breakfast at the new Lemieux residence—formerly, of course, the Thibault family home. The guests would feast on potato soup, buttered asparagus, tender pork loin, partridge with wild mushrooms, shad, and meaty tripe cooked in chenin blanc. A delectable array of cheeses and prunes stuffed with apricot purée would follow. Sweet fruit tarts, Sara's favorite treat, were among the offerings. It was one of her few consolations on this bleakest of days.

The guests, who had brought gifts of flour and butter to the breakfast, seated themselves around long tables borrowed for the occasion. They chatted amicably and drank wines provided by their host. The accordions and violins played merrily around them. That Jean Lemieux had spared little expense in celebrating the union of his son to Lydia Thibault was obvious. Exactly who would be seated next to Sara was less certain. She dreaded polite conversation.

"Mademoiselle Sara?" A familiar voice inquired behind her.

"Jacques!" Sara beamed at him with relief. "You look smart in your town clothes. Please, sit next to me. I'm in need of a friend."

Jacques took his seat beside Sara. "*Merci.* Lydia and Bastien have fine weather for their wedding, do they not?"

"Indeed."

"Are you not happy for your sister?"

Sara lowered her voice and leaned in. "If she cares for Bastien, I suppose I must be pleased for her. Yet, I cannot bear to see my sister align herself with such an arrogant—" Sara stopped midsentence as her mother walked past. She continued, whispering, "I know this is hardly the occasion to speak of it, but your family, too, has suffered injustice at the hands of the Lemieux family, have you not? How do you bear it?"

"Yes, it is true. You know well that my niece Marie left for America with Philippe Lemieux after he took advantage of her . . . affections." They had never spoken about it before.

"Pierre and Mim must have been enraged! Do they ever hear from her?"

"Pierre is tight-lipped, but I do know that Marie has made a new life in America, and is not unhappy there."

"She has a child, does she not?"

"She does, and although Lemieux does not acknowledge her, he does provide for her amply, from what I am told."

Sara wondered if he meant Philippe Lemieux or his father, but felt it would be intrusive to ask.

"Do you not despise them?"

"I did for a time. One does not easily forgive such offenses. However, I've since come to believe that the vengeful man digs two graves."

Sara chose to ignore Jacques's attempt at advice. "And what will become of you, Jacques? Where will you go now that they have stolen Saint Martin from us?"

Jacques cleared his throat. "Monsieur Lemieux will have his

hands full trying to turn the next harvest into a decent return on his father's investment. Bastien isn't a complete *cochon*. He knows he needs someone to run Saint Martin. He's asked me to stay on."

"That is such welcome news!" Sara grabbed his hand in hers and squeezed it tightly. She would have an ally.

The April rains came early to Saint Martin and the grape shoots burgeoned on the vines. The winter months had been so mournful and staid that Sara delighted in the physical exhilaration of weeding the vines, nipping the buds off the old canes and tying the new canes to their tall stakes. By sundown, her shoulders, neck and knees ached mercilessly, but Sara welcomed any sensation that made her feel alive again. Besides, if she kept herself busy trimming the vines, she could maintain her distance from her brother-in-law, who rarely ventured into the vineyard. There was something peculiar in Bastien's manner that Sara could neither understand nor ignore. He was one of the most ridiculous men she had ever met. On the rare occasions he spoke to Sara, he always stood too close to her. And their most recent encounter had conjured up a whole new set of fears.

She had come upon Bastien standing in her room, rifling through her books. He had told her, in his honey-tongued fashion, that she and Maman would be more comfortable living in the unoccupied watchman's house out by the road. He and Lydia would continue to live in the manor house. Before Sara could object, he rested his hands upon her hips and dug his fingers into her buttocks. When she pushed him away, Bastien did not stop, but instead drew her closer. Sara felt his rank breath, thick with brandy, hot against her ear. "Come, let us be friends," he had whispered. After a long, awkward moment, he finally released her. Sara stumbled back, stunned. After he left the room, she stared at the door.

Bastien had been right. Papa was dead and no longer able to protect her. Jacques could defend her only outside in the vineyard, not in the house, and Maman was useless in her grief. Sara would have to fend for herself.

This incident with Bastien and their exile to the watchman's house had been alarming enough. But Bastien's erratic behavior since the wedding concerned Sara even more. He seemed occupied with little outside his visits to the tavern to discuss "business" with his associates, and was barely involved in the vineyard's day-to-day operations. Jacques asked him questions: Sulfur or flooding to kill the insects? What did Bastien want to pay the vinedresser? Should they purchase a new plow or make do with the old one? But Bastien withdrew and would not respond. He seemed unable to understand that the farm would be ruined if they did not take precautions to safeguard the healthy vines now. When Jacques suggested that they should consult Bastien's father on his wishes for the farm, Bastien flew into a rage and went so far as to pin Jacques against the wall and threaten him. In the end, Jacques was left to make all the decisions, with Sara's help, and the two of them managed the entire business of Saint Martin.

Another might have felt pity for Bastien, with his thinning frame and increasingly colorless complexion, but not Sara. She was too concerned about Lydia. Even in the warmth of May, she rarely encountered her sister outside. Although Lydia was well into her sixth month, Bastien insisted she was ill with morning sickness, and that she couldn't walk well on her swollen feet. But now three days had passed since Sara had last seen her. Dissatisfied with Bastien's explanations, Sara resolved to uncover the truth.

She had waited tonight until she heard his horse's hooves clatter past the watchman's house on his way to the village. Sara then stole away to the manor house. Lydia usually waited for her in the parlor, a single candle in the window, a cup of wine in her hand. Tonight the parlor was empty. Lydia did not respond to her calls. Searching the house, Sara caught a glimpse of Lydia faltering along the upstairs hallway, away from her.

"Lydie?"

Lydia glanced back at Sara for a moment. The pallor of her skin announced her fatigue; her vacant eyes declared her distress. She turned and stumbled on. Sara spied a dark stain spreading across the back of Lydia's dress.

"Lydie!"

Lydia doubled over and clutched the fabric of her dress. She caught hold of the bedchamber door with her hand.

"You are unwell!" Sara rushed to Lydia's side and caught her under the arms as she sank to the floor.

"Sara," Lydia said, then babbled something unintelligible. Her head swayed from side to side. She seemed unable to lift it.

"I shall call the doctor at once."

"No, no, you mustn't," Lydia pleaded.

"But your child . . . we must, for your child's sake."

"The baby is fine." Lydia was breathless and her words slow. "I must rest, that is all." She gripped Sara's arm. "Promise me, Sara, promise me you will not call the doctor. You mustn't tell anyone, especially not Maman."

Sara helped Lydia to the bed. She did not understand Lydia's refusal of help, but wanted her to sleep.

"All right, Lydie," Sara said soothingly, "but you must allow me to tend to your injury."

Lydia did not answer, but simply drifted off.

Sara knew nothing about accouchement or the signs of miscarriage. She examined her sister's dress. The blood had turned from dark red to brown, so the bleeding must have ceased, she thought. She didn't think there was enough blood for a miscarriage. Sara unlaced the stays of Lydia's corset and placed her hands underneath, feeling the hard swell of her sister's stomach. Sara felt the baby roll and kick. Thank goodness, she thought.

Sara set about cleaning and changing her sister. She filled the basin with water and rolled Lydia onto her side. Lydia stirred, but her limbs were heavy with slumber, her breath shallow. Sara pulled her sister's dress and petticoat up to her waist. Lydia's drawers, dirty with blood, had been ripped in the back from the top seam down. Sara ran her hand gently under the torn fibers of delicate cotton that stuck to her sister's skin, matted down with blood. Near Lydia's hip, the garment was not saturated with blood, but bore curious marks. Sara took a closer look.

They were four smears of blood, each in the distinct shape of a fingertip.

Sara's stomach churned to realize that Bastien must have

assaulted her sister. She had known Bastien was sly, even vicious at times, but physically brutal? Certainly, Sara had heard talk in the village of wives being hit or slapped by their husbands. It was not uncommon. Even Madame Laroche had confessed to Maman that Monsieur Laroche had taken the strap to her for lying to him. But this? And with his wife pregnant? Tears threatened Sara's composure. Married or not, this was not to be borne.

Sara wiped her eyes and reminded herself that she must complete the task at hand. She continued the intimate inspection of her sister's wounds. Red scratches—from Bastien's fingernails, Sara guessed—marked Lydia's outer thighs and waist, and the soft flesh on Lydia's inner thigh bled from one deep laceration. Sara exhaled hard. Her sister had tried desperately to fight back. Sara pressed a clean cloth to the cut until she was certain the bleeding had stopped. She rinsed the soiled cloth, wrung it out and then used it to coax the caked blood from her sister's legs and buttocks, steeling herself against the foul odor of salt mixed with excrement. If Lydie could endure such a violent thrashing, Sara could summon the grit needed to tend to her injuries. She blotted the scrapes gently, for purple bruises had already started to form.

Once she dressed Lydia in a fresh gown, Sara fell in a heap on the bed. Lydia did not stir.

What should she do? Whom should she tell? Should she confront Bastien? What if he were to come home and find her here? Sara could not assemble the thoughts coherently in her head. She didn't care if Bastien discovered her. She would decide what to do tomorrow. Tonight, fatigue had outstripped fear.

Early the next morning, the cries of the starlings outside awakened Sara. Bastien had not returned, which was a relief. Lydia's bleeding had ceased and she'd regained her color. Her eyes were no longer hollow; they were fixed upon Sara, like an animal seeking protection.

"Sara."

Sara stroked her sister's cheek. "You gave me quite a fright last night. How are you feeling?" she asked softly.

"Sore, and most vile. I'm so sorry . . ." Lydia sniffed, and shook her head, defeated. "I suppose I can't pretend anymore."

"Why would you pretend? Why did you not tell us? We would have helped you. We *will* help you."

Lydia sat up on her elbow and looked down at her fingers, which smoothed the bed linen. "Bastien said a wife must obey her husband. I have tried, but he is never pleased with me. And then last night . . ."

Sara waited for her sister to collect herself. Lydia shuddered, then forged ahead.

"Bastien demands things of me," she whispered. "Intimate acts. Sinful acts, against the laws of nature." Lydia's face flushed with shame and she squeezed her eyes shut. "I can't even say it."

Sara wondered if Lydia realized that she had seen all her injuries. She rested her hand on Lydia's arm to comfort her. "And you refused?"

"Yes. I told him that as husband and wife our . . . marital congress should be conducted according to Church law. He was so angry." Lydia began to cry. She cradled her belly and turned away from Sara. "He said he had wanted to break off our engagement because I'm dull and dim-witted. But he had already told his father I was pregnant, and his father insisted Bastien marry me, threatening to hold back his allowance if he didn't. Bastien never loved me."

"I'm sorry, Lydie." Sara knew her words were inadequate. At the same time, she wondered how Lydia could not have seen Bastien's true nature during their courtship. She racked her mind for a solution.

"We will tell Maman, and you will divorce him. I will serve as your witness." She hoped Lydia understood that she knew exactly what Bastien had done.

"I cannot afford to be so impulsive, Sara. Bastien will never agree to a divorce. He wants his child. Besides, he would accuse me of adultery if I left him."

Hardly the point, Sara thought. Yet she understood Lydia's dilemma. If Bastien accused Lydia of adultery, she could lose all rights to the baby.

"Then for the sake of your child, you must leave Vouvray and never come back."

Lydia's eyes glistened with hope. "Do you think it possible? Could I hide somewhere? Perhaps across the river in Montlouis?" The desperation in Lydia's voice made Sara realize the severity of the situation. She contemplated Lydia's options.

"You would have to travel farther, but not too far, for I would want to see you and the baby."

"Then I must tell Maman. Perhaps she will know what to do."

"Perhaps." Sara shrugged uncertainly.

"Would you come with me? To see Maman?"

"We shall go see her as soon as you are rested." Sara looked at her sister cautiously. "But what about Bastien? Will he pursue you?"

Lydia shivered. "If he finds me . . . he has such a temper, Sara." Tears streamed down her face and she could not continue. Her eyes said what her lips could not: Lydia feared for her life.

The old watchman's shed, where Sara and Maman now lived, was located on the main road to Vouvray, a stone's throw east of the main house. It was constructed entirely of fieldstone, save for the slate rooftop, oak door and glass windows framed with birch. The two northern windows allowed the shed's occupants to see any visitors arriving on the main road before they made the turn toward the manor house. The interior was divided in two by the hearth and chimney. The front half of the room was used for receiving visitors, cooking and other chores, and in the rear half, behind a wool curtain, was the bedroom. The hearth itself was framed by three oak boards and boasted a base of limestone. Maman's copper pot hung from the center, often bubbling with thick, spicy-smelling broth. Marcheline always delivered the remains of rabbit or duck from the scullery on Sundays, and Maman skillfully transformed this into a stew that would often last the two of them the week. In the early weeks of their marriage, Bastien and Lydia had invited Sara and Maman to dine often, but now it seemed to Sara that Bastien's interest in them had waned as his contempt for his wife grew.

Sara and Lydia entered the shed and moved quietly to the

dimly lit bedchamber, where Sara and Maman shared a featherbed on the floor. There was space for a steamer trunk and the boudoir vanity that Papa had given Maman after his first successful harvest. Sara thought that its elegant carved mahogany legs and ornate mirror were decidedly out of place in their new home, which was otherwise quite basic. Her mother had turned the vanity into a shrine to Papa. Upon it sat his silver pocket watch, the tintype of Papa that Jacques had given her, his dog-eared journal and their wedding photograph. Sara looked at Papa's face—young and happy. Now, when they so desperately needed him, he was only a paper memory.

Maman sat at her vanity now, examining her complexion in the morning light. She had aged since Papa's death, but had persevered in her toilette ritual. First she would chew on a sprig of basil, dried in winter, to freshen her mouth. Then she would wash her face in rosewater and brush her hair, now streaked with white, with long, careful strokes until it was as smooth and shiny as a silk ribbon. Then she would twist it up into a topknot or chignon. She would even heat the iron on the hearth and press the wrinkles out of her dress before rolling her stockings, fresh from the laundry, up each lean leg. Even though she felt certain Maman must feel shamed by their humbled surroundings, Sara admired that she kept her appearance pristine.

Sara felt uneasy about interrupting Maman, but she knew she must protect Lydia.

"Maman? Lydia and I have something we need to discuss with you. A matter of the utmost importance." Maman looked up, a bit startled, and turned toward them.

"What is it, dears?" Maman's eyes widened and her face filled with anticipation, as if she were about to receive a great gift.

Lydia collapsed into tears on the bed. Sara just stared at her. Was she worried about disappointing Maman? Surely the safety of her child and herself were more important!

"What has happened, Lydia?" Maman's eyebrows bunched with concern.

Lydia shook her head, unable to answer. Sara knew she would have to explain things to her mother. She vividly described the harm Lydia had suffered at Bastien's hands. Maman stiffened in her chair as Sara told her story, but she wanted there to be no doubt in Maman's mind as to the nature of his offenses. Lydia nodded in agreement as Sara spoke, and Maman held steepled fingers to her parted lips, her eyes widening at every new horrifying detail.

When Sara was finished, Maman stood up and squeezed Lydia's hands in hers. "How long has this been going on?" she asked, though Sara didn't understand how the timing mattered.

"Over a month, Maman," Lydia choked out.

Maman nodded. "Sara," she said gently, "It was kind of you to help your sister, but . . ." Maman turned to Lydia, resting her hands on her shoulders. "I wish you'd come to me sooner." She sighed heavily. Maman's eyes were filled with sweet concern, but lacked the fiery indignation Sara had expected to see. Had the trauma of Papa's death robbed her of all passion, even for protecting her daughters?

"If she had come to you, Maman, what would you have done? What will you do *now* to help her?" Sara cried.

Maman walked over to the hearth and leaned on the mantel. She rubbed her forehead, staring down at the cinders from last night's cooking fire. Sara watched her mother struggle and prayed she would have the courage to help them. Lydia remained seated on the bed, staring at the floor. When Maman faced the girls again, she laid a hand against her chest. Her mouth turned downward as she walked over to sit down beside Lydia. "Oh, don't look so forlorn, my dear Lydie," Maman said, patting Lydia's knee. "The first years of marriage are often the most difficult. Bastien's . . . appetites will subside once the baby is born, and all will be well."

Sara's stomach dropped. She would never understand why their mother always placed her own comfort ahead of theirs. First by selling Saint Martin, and now this. "Maman, you cannot be serious!" Sara railed. "Papa never treated you with such contempt!"

Maman did not respond, but her eyes floated to their wedding photo: Maman in a wide-brimmed flowered hat linking arms with a beaming Papa in his suit and tie. A tear ran down her cheek. When she finally spoke again, her face was determinedly composed, but her voice trembled. "Indeed, he did not, but we had our scuffles. Marriage is not for the faint of heart. The woman most often bears the brunt of its difficulty and, at the same time, enjoys the privileges that arise from her husband's success. Bastien provides well for you, for us and for your child. Be grateful, and you will receive your recompense in heaven."

Sara was astounded. Maman had swept their concerns into the closet, locked the door and tucked away the key, just as she did with every unpleasantness she faced. Lydia wiped fresh tears from her eyes. Sara's heart broke for her sister. "But what is Lydia to do, Maman, when Bastien beats her, endangering her unborn child?"

Maman looked up at Sara, and then at Lydia. "If it happens again, I will speak with Bastien. I will move back into the house."

"Bastien will never allow it, Maman," Lydia declared, shaking her head, "and if you speak to him, it will only anger him. Lord knows what he's capable of doing." Sara nodded, proud of her sister for speaking up.

Maman placed an arm around Lydia. "My love, you are exhausted. Get some sleep, and I assure you, time will take care of things. You'll ease into your marriage, and Bastien will discover what a treasure you are, once you present him with a child." Sara wondered if her mother actually believed what she was saying.

Lydia's shoulders slumped, and she turned away from Maman. Sara was so exasperated, she couldn't even summon the words to lash out. Instead, she stormed out of the cottage. She would seek Jacques's help. She found him inspecting and pruning plants in the center of the vineyard. She knelt down beside him and began to do the same. They continued in silence for some time.

"What is it?" Jacques seemed to know something was amiss.

Sara did not meet his eye. "It's Lydie. Bastien has violated and beaten her."

"He's a son of a bitch. Where is he *right now*?"

Sara caught Jacques's arm to keep him from marching off to thrash Bastien. "We can't confront him. He'll just hurt her again." Sara's eyes pleaded with him. "We must help Lydie leave him in secret."

"What about your mother?"

Sara shook her head. "We told her everything—all of it—and she has advised Lydia to stay with him. She is steadfast."

"I'm afraid your mother has not recovered from losing your father."

"Don't defend her! What mother would not shield her daughter from violence?"

Jacques sighed, squinted up at the sky, then turned back to her. "Your mother is frightened, Sara."

"Well, if she won't do something to help Lydia, we must."

"Lydia is set on leaving? She understands that she will not be able to return?"

"Yes," Sara replied firmly.

"She may be a stranger to her mother." Jacques's voice filled with regret.

"Yes." Sara knew that could not be helped.

Jacques stood up and Sara followed. "All right. I'll set to work on it. In the meantime, you and I will find a reason each night to visit the house, to make our presence felt. Perhaps Bastien will not injure your sister if we are near."

"Thank you, Jacques."

"You were right to tell me. What I'd like to do is skin the bastard alive, but that would end badly for all of us. We'll find a way to protect her. Now get on back to the house and tell your sister."

The grandfather clock in the hallway chimed ten o'clock. The sound reverberated in Sara's head. Her heart raced and her steps quickened as she walked down the corridor toward the kitchen.

Bastien had assaulted her sister again tonight, striking Lydia square across the cheekbone. Marcheline had rushed to the shed to tell Sara as soon as Bastien left the house. Sara had found Lydia whimpering on the floor of her bedroom, her face purple, her hairline matted with blood.

Sara had been correct: Bastien would never stop mistreating Lydia. Lydia would have to leave Vouvray, with her unborn child, and Sara might have to accompany her. But to where? The question weighed heavily on her mind. It had been over a week since she had confided in Jacques, and he had agreed to form a plan. However, Jacques had yet to communicate exactly what the plan was.

Sara had sent Marcheline home, for she preferred to nurse her sister's injuries unobserved. When they were children, the warm milk Maman fixed them would always, as if by magic, ease their minds and relax their muscles. Perhaps it would soothe Lydia's spirit tonight. In the kitchen, Sara placed her lamp on the butcher-block table by the basin. She poured goat's milk into the copper pot and placed it on the cookstove. On a small tray, she arranged dried elderberries, crusty bread and soft cheese she hoped would replenish Lydia's strength. In an effort to calm her own nerves, Sara steadied her hand and concentrated on laying the cheese knife and metal fork precisely atop a freshly pressed white linen napkin.

The house was quiet, save for the rush of heat to the warming pot, until Sara heard the scrape of footsteps on the walkway outside leading to the kitchen. She swallowed hard. The last thing she wanted was to exchange words with Bastien this evening. She didn't have her wits about her.

Bastien threw open the door to the small, dimly lit room. The lamp cast the flickering shadow of his figure on the stone wall.

"Mademoiselle Sara, it is a pleasure," he said, the corners of his mouth curling. "You are like a guardian angel to my ailing wife."

Sara did not wish to spark his anger, so she simply nodded a greeting and began to stir the milk.

"Why do you dislike me so? Am I not amiable? Am I not pleasing to your eyes?" he demanded. Sara felt him come up behind her. He rested his large hands on her hips. "Let us be friends, sister."

She willed herself not to shrink from his touch, or betray her anger. His hands felt heavy on her slender frame. "Brother, you mistake me. Of course we are friends."

Bastien shifted her around to face him. His hand cradled her jawbone and lifted her eyes to his. Sara shuddered.

He clearly mistook her trembling for excitement. "I desire to have a deeper friendship with you. You see, I have grown to admire your tireless devotion to your sister and your clever plans for the vineyard. You are most valuable to me."

"Monsieur, you flatter me. May we discuss this later? Lydia is tired and needs her meal." Bastien was obviously not going to acknowledge the beating he had just given Lydia. Sara heard the crackle and spit of the boiling milk flooding over the rim of the pot onto the scalding cookstove. She tried to turn away from Bastien to tend to it, but he halted her with the firm grip of his hand under her chin, jerking her back around to face him.

"As my friend, you must give me your complete attention, if not devotion. Have I not protected you and cared for you as I promised? Even now, I have the intention of offering you a more . . . suitable situation . . . than the one you have at present in that little shack beside the road. We could make an arrangement that would benefit us both." Bastien began to stroke her jaw with his thumb. "You are not the prettiest of girls, but you have a certain appeal—a fiery spirit that I admire. And those eyes, those bewitching emerald eyes of yours. I feel them on me, watching me, whenever we're in the room together. That's why I am determined to convince you of my sincere affection."

His voice was smooth and deliberate. Bastien moved his thumb to rest on Sara's lower lip. His caress was intolerable, yet unexpectedly tender. A man had never touched her so intimately. Every sense, every fiber in Sara's being was awakened to his energy, however repulsed she was by him. She was at once drawn to him and fearful of him. His scent of sweet liquor mixed with bitter tobacco overwhelmed her. She stood motionless. Bastien rested the tips of his fingers on Sara's throat and with his other hand smoothed her hair, then her cheek. His hand wandered down the length of her neck and grazed her bodice.

"I chose wrongly, Sara. All this time, I was convinced that Saint Martin was the prize I sought. Not so," his whisper was hoarse. "Not so." Before Sara could utter a word, Bastien's lips crushed down upon hers, his sour tongue twisting into her mouth.

Sara could not breathe. Panic rose up within her. Her immediate reaction was that she would rather die than endure this violation any further. Then, fighting against her every instinct, she decided to return his kiss, slowly and deliberately, until she at last felt his body relax into hers.

When she was certain he was convinced of her willingness, she brought her hands up, grabbed his ears and bit down with all her strength, slicing her two front teeth deep into his lower lip. Bastien roared in pain and stumbled back into the wall. Sara continued her assault, kicking him squarely between the legs.

She knew Bastien would not be deterred for long. She reached for the tray on the counter, meaning to use it as a weapon, but in her haste sent it crashing to the floor. Bastien lunged toward Sara, grabbed hold of her hair and snaked it around his arm. He dragged her down to the floor.

"You little bitch!" Bastien moved astride Sara and pinned her skirts to the floor with his knees. Sara tried to scream, but only a guttural moan escaped her lips. Her arms flailed, but she was unable to strike him. She spotted something shiny on the floor, just inches away. She strained to reach it and caught it up just as Bastien slammed one hand down on her chest, and, with the other, split the front seam of her dress wide open.

Sara saw a kind of wild excitement flash in his eyes as he looked over her body. Terror seized her. Bastien held her arms down. He leaned over her with his bloodied lips and sucked her left nipple. Then, with blinding force, he bit into her tender flesh. Sara heard herself scream, but this seemed to incite Bastien further. In one swift motion, he pulled down Sara's underdrawers and thrust his fingers inside her. Instantly her fear turned to fury.

Using every last bit of strength she had, Sara propelled her free arm up and toward the side of Bastien's neck. She hit her mark. Sara pushed and twisted her weapon deeper into Bastien's flesh. His face contorted in a grisly pantomime of pain. Only when she had carved a large and grotesque gash did she finally pull her hand up and out. Sara sprang up to a crouching position, ready to strike again if he lurched toward her, but Bastien seemed wholly unaware of her. He cupped his hand to his neck in a futile attempt to stem the flow of his blood. He was choking on it, trying to spit it up and clear his throat. His eyes widened and he began to sway. He tumbled back down onto the hot wood floor, grabbing Sara's arm and pulling her with him.

Sara studied his face carefully, for she could not look away. Bastien's eyes stared blankly at the ceiling. His grip weakened and the hand that clutched her sleeve fell to the floor. Sara heard a sickening gurgling sound erupt from deep inside his throat. Within a few moments, it ceased. Only then did she loosen her grip and release the dull, blood-stained fork to the floor.

She collapsed, exhausted and numb. The walls of the room began to spin. The acrid smell of burnt milk and blood overwhelmed her senses. Sara's world went black.

She awoke to Jacques shaking her shoulder and calling her name. Her head throbbed, but her vision cleared enough to see him kneeling beside her.

"Jacques? Oh, Jacques!" The memory of what she had done flooded back to her. Sara gripped his arm to steady herself.

"He hurt you." Jacques's face crumpled.

"Only a little, but I . . . stopped him."

Jacques turned to Bastien's body, lying face up in a river of blood. Jacques's expression was blank.

Sara looked down at her torn, blood-soaked corset and felt a thick, salty substance on her lips. She realized it was Bastien's blood mixed with her own. She began to retch.

"All right, there, all right. You'll be okay, my love," Jacques consoled her. He offered her a cloth.

"Where is Lydia? What time is it?" Sara could not bear to ask the most obvious question. When she observed the vast amount of blood that had pooled around them, she knew she had killed Bastien.

"Upstairs. It's nearly midnight. Where is your mother?"

"Asleep. In the shed." Sara's mind was a haze.

"Is there anyone else in the house? Marcheline?"

"No, just Lydia. Where is she? When I left her she was asleep." Sara clutched Jacques's shirt with both hands. "What should I do, Jacques?"

He pulled Sara up by her forearm. "First thing you do is wash yourself, your hair. Put on a fresh dress—borrow one of Lydia's. Then pack a small bag of things. You'll need a change of clothes and money, however much you can put your hands on. Bring Lydia to meet me at the caves in a half hour. Hide there, no matter what happens."

"Where are we going?"

"I'll explain it all later. Just stay out of sight and don't wake your mother."

"But—"

"Do as I say! Now go!" Jacques commanded.

Sara did exactly as Jacques had ordered. While Lydia slept soundly, Sara disrobed and threw her soiled dress into the bedroom fire. The flames surged up, curled around it and consumed it. Sara examined herself by the light of the fire. She had scrapes on her arms and legs and blood everywhere: on her skirt, in her hair, smeared over her thighs. The pale, once unblemished skin of her breast was now torn and bleeding, and hurt almost more than she could stand. She winced as she pressed one of Lydia's folded handkerchiefs over the wound. Once Sara had washed herself and put on one of Lydia's ruffled cotton day dresses, she gathered items into a small bag—a dress and shawl for Lydia, a spare pair of clogs and undergarments, a brush, some matches and candles, and Maman's Bible. Then she began to search for money.

She spent a few minutes rummaging through Bastien's room for coins he might have stashed away. It unnerved Sara to be in his chamber: the bed was made, each pillow in its place, and Bastien's red velvet morning coat hung on the valet by his dresser. She was now no better than a common criminal, she observed silently, as she searched the coat's pockets and found a money clip containing twenty francs. There must be more. Sara hurried to the study downstairs.

Sara ransacked Bastien's desk and found nothing useful. Her eyes searched the room and came to rest on a wooden box with an intricate pattern of roses and lilies inlaid on its polished cherry finish. Sara lifted the top and sifted through the papers inside. There was a latch on the lower edge of the lid. Sara pulled it up to reveal a false bottom and the drawer it concealed. She removed the contents and found a bundle of over a thousand francs and two sheets of paper. On the smaller piece, someone had scrawled, *Notre Dame, 197 Mott, New York.* On the other document, she recognized her mother's signature below the words that had officially signed their land over to Jean Lemieux. It was the deed to Saint Martin.

Sara could not think of Maman right now. She shoved the money and documents into her petticoat pockets. She had broken at least two commandments in the space of one hour, God forgive her.

Sara raced up the stairs and shook Lydia gently, whispering, "Hurry, Lydia! We must make haste!"

"Why? Where are we going?" Lydia murmured sleepily. At Sara's prodding, Lydia dressed and followed her out the back of the house to the vacant caves. Although the caves were not far away, Sara could barely make out their shape, for a thick fog had crept in during the evening hours.

"Watch yourself on the way down, Lydie, the steps are mossy," Sara warned. They descended to the lower caves that, in her grandparents' day, had stored most of the family's wine. Lydia obeyed and kept one hand wrapped tightly around Sara's. With her other hand, she cradled her stomach.

The dank chamber stank of rotting wood. Sara struck a match and lit one of the two precious candles she had in her satchel. Only a few ramshackle oak casks remained within this cave. The walls were decorated with chalk drawings of the girls' childhood imaginings. Lydia's fingers grazed the outline of four stick figures holding hands—two tall and two small. Sara remembered sketching them when she was ten. That moment now seemed a lifetime away.

Lydia finally choked out a few words: "Why have you brought me here?"

"Jacques is coming. He will tell us what to do."

"Am I to leave Bastien tonight?" Lydia's voice quivered.

"Yes, if you still want to. And I will come with you," Sara said with conviction.

"I cannot ask you to leave Maman," Lydia's eyes filled with tears.

Sara did not know how much she should tell Lydia. How much could she bear to know in her condition?

She caught Lydia looking at the scratches on her neck. "I have no choice. I must go with you," Sara said sharply.

Just then, Jacques appeared. He handed Sara a sack containing a jug of wine, some cheese and bread. "For the journey. Did you find any money?"

"Yes. Thirteen hundred francs."

"Good, you'll need it, and the extra two hundred I've put in there. The horses are hitched. We'll leave at once."

"Where are we going?" Lydia asked.

Jacques's eyes darted to Sara. "Under the circumstances, I think you should both go abroad."

"To America?" Sara was shocked.

"So far from France? We don't know the language. We don't know a soul there. Could we not live in Paris, or perhaps Spain?" Lydia sounded confused.

Jacques looked at Sara. Sara knew it could not be helped— they must tell her. "Lydie, I need you to listen and not ask questions." She took Lydia by the shoulders and looked her directly in the eye. "Bastien attacked me tonight. Bastien is . . . he is . . . dead," she stammered.

"Oh. Oh—but how?" Lydia asked, shaking, her eyes wide with shock.

Sara pleaded with Jacques. "Must we truly leave for America? Could we not stay on the continent, at least until the baby is born?"

"Bastien is dead. His father will assume one or both of you had something to do with it. You must go where he wouldn't suspect—where he won't find you."

Sara hesitated. "You cannot suppose that I would be brought to trial."

"If you are, the judges are known to be unsympathetic to women. You could be imprisoned, or worse." Jacques's voice trailed off.

"The guillotine?" Sara whispered in horror.

Jacques lowered his head.

"But I struck him in my own defense! He was going to—I did not intend to—" a sob escaped her. Sara felt Lydia's arm drape protectively around her shoulders.

"Of course not, love, but Lemieux's oldest and favorite son, a bourgeois, is dead. Lemieux will want someone's head for it," Jacques reminded her.

Sara brought her eyes to meet Lydia's, fearful of what she would see there.

Lydia put her hand over her belly and straightened her shoulders. "You were Papa's best friend, and you have never failed us, Jacques. We will trust you and do what you believe is best."

Jacques nodded and instructed them gently: "Go to the

wagon. I'll be back in a few minutes and we'll leave for the train station." He handed Lydia some apples. "Feed these to the horses. That will keep them quiet while you wait."

When Jacques met them at the wagon, he was breathless from exertion. He loaded up a bag, three lanterns and his shotgun. The three headed north on the dirt road away from Saint Martin. Sara was too exhausted to argue with Jacques. For now, she would have to rely on him and Lydia to tell her what was best. The wagon rattled down the road at a snail's pace. Sara could barely see the road through the shroud of fog before them. She instinctively looked back, searching for the outline of the house and the watchman's shed where Maman slept soundly, unaware that her daughters were running for their lives.

A flash of orange broke through Sara's hazy thoughts. It flared up, illuminating the line of rectangular windows in the front of the house. In less than a minute, tongues of flame darted up the timbered stucco walls of her family's ancestral home.

Saint Martin was ablaze.

CHAPTER 6

Philippe

Philippe Lemieux hated to lose. It did not irritate him that another man might best him; his pride was not that brittle. But he was precise and self-demanding, and hated to put forward anything less than his best effort. Despite this, Philippe did not allow a trace of frustration to register upon his face. As he sat at the card table, leaning his chair back against the saloon wall, he reminded himself that, in this particular game, a calculated loss would benefit him the most.

Philippe examined the faces of his opponents after the first betting round. Lamont, the most senior of the four Frenchmen, was a seasoned vigneron, but a novice at the game of poker. Still, he had proven himself much more sportsmanlike than the other two at the table. Courtois and Gautier were new to both wine-making and the game. Courtois drew two new cards and shifted

93

in his seat; Gautier drew one and let out a telling sigh. Lamont stayed pat, as did Philippe. He guessed from Lamont's blank face that they held the two lowest hands. Lamont's was a consequence of bad luck, Philippe's of deliberate design.

It was a small stakes game: no bet exceeded five dollars, a laborer's weekly wages. When the cards were revealed, Gautier had bested the other men with a straight flush. Philippe was surprised. Courtois had the next best hand, a full house. Philippe and Lamont showed down with three-of-a-kind and two pair, respectively. Philippe was pleased with the outcome, although he feigned mild disappointment. He was just about to launch into a friendly commiseration with Lamont when he was cut off by Gautier.

"At least the old lady will let me in for supper tonight," Gautier announced with satisfaction.

"With those winnings, you'd best bring supper home with you, Gautier." Philippe motioned toward the butcher shop across the street. "I bet the missus would enjoy that nice haunch of pork hanging in the window." Philippe figured the best way to get rid of him was to locate the nearest foodstuff and point him in that direction. If Gautier's ever-growing paunch was any indication of his habits, Philippe could be assured that he would act on the suggestion with gusto.

"Indeed she might. A fine idea, Lemieux, and a pleasure taking your money, messieurs." Gautier corralled his winnings off the table and into his saddlebag. He then pushed his hat firmly upon his head and sauntered out the tavern door.

Lamont shook his head and mumbled, "You'd think he'd struck gold."

Courtois forced a laugh. He was the quintessential bootlicker, thought Philippe. Lamont glared at Courtois with unveiled disdain.

Philippe knew Lamont well enough to understand his dislike for Courtois and his kind. Courtois had the air of an aristocrat but the nerves of a tree squirrel. He had made his money in trade on the San Francisco docks. At his doctor's bidding, he had moved his family to the country last year for the air. Better for his chest, he said. Courtois had purchased a small vineyard, just a mile north of Philippe's, and half-heartedly made an effort at grape farming. From Lamont's prickly demeanor, Philippe judged that he viewed Courtois as a pretender. Lamont's heroes were the forty-niners and the silverados and the year-round farmers—those who had earned their livelihood and his respect from working the land. Lamont's kind had built California from the ground up.

"Another drink, gentlemen?" Philippe wanted to keep Lamont there a bit longer.

Courtois shook his head and stood up to leave. "If I keep showing up stewed for dinner, the missus is going to cart me off to the Castle for certain." Philippe cringed a bit at Courtois's humor. The Castle, as it had been nicknamed, was the enormous asylum just south of Napa City for the area's drunkards and those in need of "moral treatment." The immense building near the Napa River boasted seven towers, six hundred patients, a lumberyard, an amusement hall and its own mortuary. It looked like a palace, but if you walked by its looming exterior, you could hear the shrieks of its inmates.

Lamont changed the subject as soon as Courtois quit the tavern. "So, Lemieux, your first harvest is coming up, right? How are the vines looking?"

"Actually I had a small harvest last year, mostly zinfandel and cabernet, but I expect well over a hundred tons this October, and five hundred by the '97 harvest. I'm actually about to drive to the depot to pick up some equipment I ordered. It came in on the nooner—a bottling machine." Philippe waited to see if Lamont would take the bait.

"You know, I've always admired you for your forward thinking, Lemieux." Philippe could guess what was coming next. "As a friend, though, I have to warn you off of bottling. I tried it three years back—I told you this—it was a bust. Not only is it expensive to bottle the wine, the railway charges three times what they would to transport barrels. Besides, it'll be another year before you're ready to sell this year's vintage." Lamont shook his head and scratched his graying beard. "It's just not worth it, son."

"I thought I'd start off small. Bottle half of last year's vintage and sell the rest by the gallon." Philippe would tread lightly at first, because he knew that before he could make his pitch to Lamont, the man's ego would have to be sated.

"I was in your shoes a few years back." Lamont smirked. "Don't make the mistakes I made. Hell, I've got a third of a cellar filled with top-notch bottled chardonnay, and I can't move it. It's just too expensive. You should ship your barrels east, maybe as far as Chicago. That's what I do, and I make a decent living off it."

"Yes, but you know as well as I do, half our wine doesn't even make it to the Second City—the rail men drink it and then swap it with water, or even worse, vinegar. The other half of our wine is poured into bottles, slapped with a French label and sold for double the price. Shouldn't we be taking that profit? Shouldn't the people in Chicago and New York be able to enjoy your chardonnay and zinfandel, both of which are superior to their French counterparts?"

"Ah"—Lamont shook his head and waved his hand dismissively—"but French wine is French wine. It has a unique appeal, an air of sophistication, if you will. Who will ever choose bottled Californian wine over French?"

"Let's not try to sell it to the high falutin' class, then. Let's sell it to the everyman. Let's sell it to the city clerk who wants to surprise his wife for their anniversary." Philippe stopped there. He didn't want to belabor his point.

"Go on."

"Why do we work so hard? So we can bust our bollocks selling barrels of wine to drinkers who don't even know where it comes from? Do we really want to eke out a living that way? I don't. I came to Napa to produce the best wine I can off the best land there is and sell it across the country—in Chicago, New York, New Orleans." Philippe paused to gauge Lamont's reaction, but his expression was unreadable. Philippe decided to appeal to the man's sense of nationalism. "France's wine production is on the rebound, and they'll be active in seeking out new American markets. Don't you think we should at least throw our hat in the ring to show them we're a contender?"

Lamont looked appraisingly at Philippe, all the while smoothing his mustache from its bushy midsection out to its twisted tips. He shrugged, unconvinced. "Maybe."

Now it was time to lay it out for him in black and white. "Hear me out on this, Lamont. We know that McKinley will likely get himself elected in November, and if he does, one of the first things he's going to do is pass the tariff on foreign dry wines. The import duty will go from thirty to fifty cents. Now you may think this will work to our advantage, but let's think it through. Our wines are already protected by a thirty-cent tariff. A fifty-cent tariff is going to artificially inflate domestic wine prices, and that will spur a vineyard land grab like we haven't seen in a decade. Every last Gautier and Courtois will be running into these hills to plant grapes, and they will overplant, ruining the soil and the reputation for quality our wines have earned. Over time, that will crater wine prices. Napa vintners have just started turning a profit these last two years, now that wine is selling at over twenty cents a gallon in most cities. Do we really want to jeopardize that?"

Lamont shrugged. "I do see your point, Lemieux."

"But there's even more to consider. I just read that the meat packers and shippers in Chicago want to propose a reciprocity agreement with France and Germany. They're going to increase their exports overseas. Guess who they're going to throw to the wolves to get their way?"

Another shrug.

"Us."

"What! How?" Now Lamont was incensed.

"In return for permission to export their meat to those countries, they're proposing a bill that would allow France and Germany to ship their wines to America with little or no duty— not even the thirty cents that exists now."

"They're proposing to eliminate the duty altogether?"

"Yup. At least for France and Germany. Our markets— Chicago, New York, New Orleans—will be flooded with foreign wines, and prices will nosedive. We may even be forced to sell our wines overseas, at the blending centers in France, alongside the Spanish and the Algerians." Philippe hated this idea, and it was evident in his voice. "Let's make that quick calculation. Those wines sold last month for an average of fourteen cents per gallon. If you deduct seven or more cents for cooperage, shipping and insurance, you're looking at, if you're lucky, seven cents of profit. Versus the sixteen or so we could be earning now. All to fill the coffers of some rich, power-hungry butchers and pork packers!"

Philippe had been persuasive enough to render Lamont speechless. Looking closely, Philippe realized Lamont's face, under his well-groomed beard, had lost its color entirely. He felt a twinge of regret for scaring him, but sometimes it was the only way to get people moving—to shove them out of their complacency.

"I have a plan."

"What do you propose we do?" Lamont was eager to listen now.

Philippe sat back in his chair at last and laced his fingers together behind his head. He had to say this just right. "California does a fair business in the East—260,000 gallons to New York last month and more than 55,000 to Chicago. Between us growers here in Carneros, we also have plenty of contacts in the East, wouldn't you agree?"

Lamont nodded, waiting.

"We need to set our Carneros wines apart from the other California wines, even the other Napa wines, in both price and quality. We need to ship bottles, not barrels, to guarantee high quality and name recognition. We need to offer samples to the merchants in Chicago and New York in order to distinguish the Carneros wines from all other California wines." Philippe thought of Agoston Haraszthy, the pioneering Sonoma vintner he greatly admired, who decades ago had garnered worldwide recognition for his sparkling wines. "We need to make our inroads now."

"Of course, but price is the major consideration. Without the right price, we won't be able to finance the shipments."

"Up until now, only a few Napans, like you, have been progressive enough to bottle some of their wine. Even then, most of those bottles make it only as far as the Embarcadero, not even out of California. You and I both know that the California Wine Association has five million gallons sitting in the warehouse, waiting for the shippers to agree to the twenty-cent price they're demanding. Why shouldn't we arrange our own shipments and secure a higher price right now directly from the buyers, instead of waiting for the CWA to negotiate on our behalf? The key to securing business will be to offer the buyers an assortment of our wines. Their clients can choose the wines they prefer and reorder accordingly. We just have to make it more appealing for them to work with us and buy the bottles." In Philippe's mind, the possibilities were limitless.

"So what you're saying is that we need to form some sort of cooperative to get the Carneros name out there, into the restaurants and stores, and then the orders will follow?"

"Exactly. I have associates in Chicago and New York who have already agreed to sample our wines and store what they don't purchase until we find buyers. Up to 100,000 bottles to start with."

"What would our cost be?" Lamont still sounded skeptical.

"To store them? One cent per gallon annually."

"Not bad. But isn't that why we formed the Napa Corporation in the first place? To arrange these types of things?"

"Perhaps, but then why do you have so much wine sitting in your cellars? They're too big to make efficient decisions. Let's form our own smaller group of Carneros vintners."

"Hmm." Lamont took one last swig from his drink and stood up. Philippe was worried he was going to reject the idea before he'd even heard him out. Lamont settled the tab, throwing two silver coins on the table.

"I'm damn tired of sitting in this hole and wasting the afternoon away. Let's ride over to the depot and take a look at this newfangled machine of yours. I want to make sure you didn't get swindled."

Philippe took his words as a good sign—he was willing to listen to more. Philippe found it amusing how Lamont, a squat, balding man of forty, seemed to fancy himself Philippe's mentor. Truth be told, Philippe was grateful to him for it. Having lived here just over five years, and now on the cusp of running a full-scale winery, Philippe appreciated the ease with which the Napans took an interest in him and his business, although, at times, the scrutiny could be overbearing. Philippe chuckled to himself, for he knew that was just their American nature. He grabbed his hat, and followed Lamont outside to the horses.

Philippe hitched his team to the wagon and Lamont joined

him up in the seat, instead of riding his own bay. Once they started down Main Street, Lamont resumed his analysis of Philippe's plan.

"It sounds smart, Lemieux, but let me get something straight. You're proposing that the ten or so vintners here in Carneros, including myself, who have bottles in supply, sell these bottles just to make inroads for you, so that when you're ready to sell yours, you have the connections. We will stake our reputations and the money we spend to ship the wine—what do you stand to lose? You have no reputation, no real business to lose."

Philippe cracked his riding whip and the team lurched forward. "I stand to lose my future bottle sales. But here's my real offer: I will pay a third of your shipping costs. I'll reimburse myself from the profits. This fall, I'll travel to Chicago with the wine to make sure it reaches the merchants. You can provide me with letters of introduction to the merchants who have placed orders with you in the past. If there's any excess, I'll go door to door to sell the remaining bottles and make new contacts. All I ask in return is for you and the other wine men to front two-thirds of the shipping costs and deliver your labeled bottles on time to the depot the day I depart."

Lamont's eyes narrowed. Philippe could not tell if it was skepticism, or a response to the brilliant sunlight.

"Why should we go to all this trouble just to sell our inventory, possibly at a loss?" Ah, definite skepticism.

Philippe thought that, for such an accomplished vintner, Lamont was not much of a salesman. "Because we're not selling wine. We're selling Carneros."

Philippe's conversation with Lamont had ended successfully. Lamont had agreed to arrange a meeting of the most prominent winegrowers in Carneros within a fortnight, so Philippe would have a captive audience to whom he could deliver his pitch. Lamont claimed he could bring the others around to seeing things their way. All in all, it had been an afternoon well spent.

Philippe turned his thoughts to a hot bath and a warm meal. After sitting in the darkness of a tavern losing at five-card draw, he enjoyed the warmth of the evening sun on his skin. He guided his wagon down Main Street, watching the people bustle by. Ladies strolled down the sidewalk, clutching baskets filled with vegetables, bread, meat and poultry, and men steered horses and buggies down the dirt street, all beneath American flags flapping in the breeze high above the buildings. Philippe noted with great satisfaction that the butcher, wearing his stained apron and locking up his store for the night, was missing a sizable haunch of pork from his window.

The white hand-painted direction signs nailed to poles on each side of the street pointed to the right for plows, freezers, camp stoves and tinware, and to the left for the hotel and bar. Philippe always turned left. The three-story Palace Hotel, the largest in Napa City, was where he always rented a room. He lingered in the stables, which held forty-five horses, to ensure that Red and Lady were properly groomed and fed. He left his wagon, with the new machinery, in the capable hands of the hotel stableman.

Philippe made his way through the lobby to the stairs, taking them two at a time to the third floor. He rapped twice on the door at the end of the hallway. She opened the door quickly. He rested his shoulder against the doorjamb, taking a moment to appreciate her delicate features. She was wearing a pale yellow dress of airy fabric with sleeves that ruffled demurely over the curve of her fair shoulders. Her hair cascaded down to her mid-back like a golden cape. The warmth of intimacy flickered in her eyes, and he thought she might be planning to seduce him right there in the hallway. A mischievous smile on her lips beckoned him closer.

"Linnette."

At the sound of her name, she moved her face close to his. Philippe could feel her petite hands glide down his back. Her kiss reminded him of biting into a ripe strawberry. He stepped in and she closed the door behind him without a word.

She helped him remove his riding boots, breeches and shirt, and eased him into the steaming tub of water she had prepared for him. Within minutes, Philippe felt his thigh and calf muscles begin to relax. Linnette sat on the edge of the tub and dangled her fingers in his bath. She soaped up a cloth and rubbed it down his chest and back. He was not modest, but even if he had been self-conscious, she had a way of looking at a man that made him feel like he was the most desirable in the room.

Their conversation was comfortable. Linnette never pried into Philippe's business.

"So, what's the talk in town?" Philippe rested his head against the tub.

"Molly Reynolds is happy the Italians are here," Linnette chirped, and described how the arrival of several new families in town, settling in before the harvest began, had spurred a run on supplies at Molly's grocery store. "She's going to start selling their homemade gravy and pasta in the store."

Philippe doused his face with water. "She's happy for the Italians because she hates the Chinese."

Linnette put her hands on her hips and cocked her head to the side to mimic Molly. "Them Chinese want darn near five dollars a week for working the fields, and they don't even have the decency to spend any of it in here. They take their slanty eyes and cone hats on over to Sam Kee's, fer sure, but the day they condescend to spend any of their cash in my store, I'll swallow my own tongue. What are they doing with all those greenbacks anyhow? Hoardin' 'em, I say. I tell you one thing," Linnette wagged her finger, and Philippe laughed at the accuracy of her impression, "they ain't spendin' it on food, 'cause all they eat is rice and sticks and that stinky water soup. Maybe if they bought some meat at the butcher's once in a while, they'd grow a foot or two."

Philippe chuckled. Linnette's mockery of Molly's prejudices was spot-on. It probably never occurred to the shopkeeper that her bigotry was the reason the Chinese didn't frequent her store in the first place.

Linnette recounted the past month's big news: the local suffrage conference held at the Napa Opera House in May, and the upcoming California ballot measure to give women the vote. "Philippe, it was inspiring. Right on the heels of Susan Anthony's visit, the most influential women favoring political equality rallied support for the ballot measure." Linnette held up a finger. "I remember one in particular: Mrs. Taylor, I believe, said, 'We cannot claim that our Constitution is of the people, for the people and by the people when one half of them are disenfranchised.'" Linnette wrung out the soapy sponge, leaned over and began to wash Philippe's arms. "How's that for common sense?"

As she scrubbed, his eyes wandered down to the beribboned edge of her thin chemise, which strained under the weight of her ample breasts. She was a beauty who could have had her pick of men, but she had made it clear from the moment Philippe had met her, while strolling past the infamous Clinton Street House, that she had chosen him, not the other way around. Philippe was comparatively well-off, it was true, but Linnette had also revealed to him that he was the only man she knew under forty and over seventeen who understood the finer workings of a woman's body.

After they retired to the bed for an unsurprisingly satisfying liaison, Linnette drifted into a deep, untroubled sleep. Philippe looked out the window to watch the last rays of sun disappear behind the distant mountains. He was happily preoccupied by the feel of Linnette's flesh upon his and the tangy taste she left on his tongue. She gave him what he craved: an evening's escape from the weight of his responsibilities. Theirs had always been an affair of convenience. He provided Linnette an allowance for food and clothing, and a room at the hotel. She, in turn, provided only for him. He was glad he'd been able to help her out of the Clinton Street House and give her more independence, though it still upset him that for years she'd had to entertain other men to survive. She didn't deserve that kind of life.

Their arrangement had been in place for well over a year now and had proven satisfactory for both of them. Before he arrived in town, Philippe would send a note to Linnette, and she would book a room for him in the hotel. He was very cautious about their liaisons, for he was well respected in Napa and wanted to make sure that the appearance of propriety was maintained. Linnette understood this, and he appreciated her practicality. She was youthful and lovely, but she did not subscribe to the theatrics enjoyed by so many of the younger girls in town. She did not cling when he left her; she did not discuss their relationship with anyone. If he passed her in the street, he did not tip his hat to her, as he would to other female acquaintances. He held eye contact and smiled, their silent acknowledgement. Philippe did not care if his fellow Napans suspected the truth of his relationship with Linnette. He only sought to avoid its confirmation. As far as he knew, most people accepted Linnette's story that a wealthy uncle from San Francisco had discovered her working in the parlor house and come to her rescue, setting her up in grand style.

Although Philippe considered the restraint of one's physical desires to be a virtue, he had no wife and, at twenty-seven, no aspirations to enter into a lasting union. His ambition was to create the largest-producing and most profitable vineyard in the valley by 1900. The arrangement with Linnette kept his libido from becoming a distraction.

Linnette stirred beside him. Philippe felt her fingers twine through his chest hair and her leg stroke his beneath the bedcovers. Clearly, she was ready for another round. He had no choice but to comply.

When in town, Philippe always made a stop at the post office to retrieve his mail, the bulk of which came from his solicitor in New York or his merchant contacts in the East. Content after a night of physical exertion, Philippe walked out onto the wide veranda of the post office and sifted through several weeks of letters.

He was surprised to find that a large envelope from his solicitor, William F. Briggs, contained another letter within. He recognized the large scrawl at once—his father's handwriting. Correspondence from his father in France had been scarce, limited to occasional notes such as the one announcing the marriage of his brother, or apprising him of new business contacts his father had established in America. The communication was always perfunctory and displayed little sentiment. Jean Lemieux had never been an affectionate man. This note was brief and typical of his father:

May 25, 1896

Philippe:
I regret to share with you this news. Bastien is dead. Come to New York at once. Briggs has the details and papers for you to sign.

Your father,
Jean Paul Lemieux

Philippe reread the note, struggling to comprehend its meaning. The words scattered on the page. How had Bastien died? Why? Philippe tried to see Bastien's face before him, but the picture was hazy. Slowly, the memories of his family edged forward, loosed from their carefully constructed hiding place in the back of his mind. Grief for Bastien gripped his heart. He mourned not only for Bastien's lost chance at a good life, but for their shared childhood.

It had not been an easy one. Philippe remembered how the winter of 1880 had raged hard upon their family, with the root cellar depleted by year's end. Eleven year-old Bastien had been the hero that night in early January when, after a day's work on the half-frozen lake, he had proudly offered five pike to Mère for the evening meal. They ate like kings that night, thanks to him, and Philippe could still remember his father's booming laugh, fueled with food and brandy, and his mother's face glowing like an angel's in the firelight while they feasted on the fish. But Bastien made a mistake that night. Père had caught him feeding Chance, his hound, the leftover table scraps. Bastien should have known better. Mère pleaded with their father, but he shook her off, commanded her to stay put and marched outside holding Bastien with one hand and his rusty Enfield in the other.

Philippe could still hear the shot as it pierced the frigid night air. He could smell the curl of acrid smoke rising from his father's rifle, and feel Bastien's weight as he caught him up in his arms. Philippe remembered gently lowering Bastien to the ground and coaxing the rifle from his shaking hands. He looked to his father for help, but Père only grumbled, "A worthless mutt—that'll teach you to steal from my table!" and walked away from his sons. Philippe was the only one to see Bastien crawl across the dirt yard to cradle Chance's head in his lap. Looking back, Philippe realized that was the only time in his life he'd seen Bastien cry—for the dog, his best friend, whom his father had forced him to kill.

Mère cared deeply for them and did her best to counter their father's brutality with a lullaby, a slice of warm bread or a bedtime embrace. Philippe could now appreciate his mother's emotional strength, tireless work and the keen interest she took in other people and their concerns, and understood how much she had endured for the love of her two boys. Although Philippe was formed, in part, by her kindness, it had never seemed to take hold in Bastien. Even before Mère's death, their father had forbidden them to see their mother's parents—good, honest people who might have protected them, or lent a compassionate hand to their upbringing. Years later, Philippe had discovered that they had tried to communicate with their grandsons, but with little success.

Meanwhile, Philippe stayed out of his father's way. He learned about grape farming and the wine trade from books and his apprenticeship with a wine broker in Tours. Bastien, as the oldest and favorite son, worked with their father. Under his tutelage, Bastien had become wily and self-consumed. Philippe had been surprised to learn that he had married one of Luc Thibault's daughters. Thibault's reputation was impeccable. The daughters he knew less of; he recalled little more than seeing them occasionally at Sunday services. He was shocked that Bastien had managed to charm his way into such a fine family and secure such expansive property for himself.

Philippe crumpled his father's note in his fist and tossed it in the rubbish bin. He was not prepared to sort through the details right now. He would write to his father and explain that he couldn't possibly leave the farm until after the harvest; he would make the trip to New York after the fall crush was complete. He tucked the rest of his letters in his bag and climbed up into the seat of his wagon.

After the previous afternoon's tête-à-tête with Lamont and the night with Linnette, Philippe welcomed the solitary five-mile journey back to the vineyard. He had named it Eagle's Run because on the very day he'd taken ownership of the property, he'd spied two eagles soaring back and forth over the length of the vineyard. They looked like they were racing, and their cries of exhilaration had echoed through the vale. Philippe had wanted an American name for his vineyard because he viewed this new endeavor as the beginning of his transformation into a true citizen of this country. He had found freedom here, not only from his father and brother, but from his former self. He had been able to give Marie and her daughter a fresh start in New York, and now he was reinventing himself out here in California. Here he'd finally found the space to breathe deeply, as though every breath he'd taken before had been shallow and stunted.

Philippe had chosen this part of the country carefully. He could have sought property in upstate New York, where he'd heard the grape farming was superb, but he had a wanderlust that a day's train ride would not quell. Once he laid eyes on Napa's rolling hills, lively city streets and friendly faces, he simply couldn't bring himself to leave. The valley itself had everything a farmer could want. It ran the full length of the county and was thirty-five miles long by five miles wide, bounded by mountain ranges on its eastern and western sides and irrigated year-round by the Napa River, which wound along the valley's eastern foothills. Five years ago, upon his arrival in Napa, Philippe had taken a train ride up the western side of the valley and a wagon ride back down the eastern side to survey the vineyards.

He was captivated by the majestic grandeur of Mount St. Helena, which rose high above the neighboring peaks, its summit poking through the lower-lying clouds. An even more stunning sight, however, was the number of phylloxera-stricken farms that had been abandoned. The parasite had afflicted half of the six hundred vineyards in the county. Philippe had heard that many were owned by San Francisco's social elite, European-born aristocrats who had purchased the vineyards with dreams of a bucolic escape from the demands of city life, and the bragging rights that come with the creation of one's own wines. Their abandoned properties presented an opportunity that Philippe decided he could not pass up.

Eagle's Run was the most idyllic land Philippe had ever laid eyes on. He immediately saw the advantage of settling in Carneros, in the southern Napa Valley. Its morning fog and the cool afternoon breeze from the San Pablo Bay made its climate perfect for growing zinfandel, cabernet and chardonnay grapes. After discovering that the property had been abandoned, Philippe headed immediately to city hall and paid the monocled clerk twenty-seven dollars in back taxes owed on the land to the town. By the end of the day, on Tuesday, January 27, 1891, the city had signed the land over to him, the deed was recorded, and he had acquired the property.

He could not believe his good fortune. Eagle's Run was located five miles south of downtown Napa, between the Napa

River and Carneros Creek. Of its 350 acres, nearly two-thirds was dedicated to the vineyard and the other third consisted of pastureland, meadowland and a small orchard. The northern section included a white-painted oak house, set on a verdant knoll conveniently close to the public road. The house could have easily accommodated a family of six, though Philippe spent little time indoors. It featured two floors, a stone basement and five gables, two of which crowned the long front porch. The tidy white-fenced yard, adorned with columbine, mountain lilac and herbs, pleased him greatly.

But like any bargain, Eagle's Run had a sizable hitch. Almost all the vines were dead—gnarled from the ravages of the phylloxera. Philippe knew that it would be five years before he could produce a reasonable harvest. He planned to sell the yield of unscathed mission grapes for table wine until his replanted vineyard was thriving. With some of the money Philippe's father had given him when he left home, and against the advice of several well-established Napa vintners, Philippe purchased specimens of the rarely used St. George rootstock from a friend in France. He hired ten skilled Italians to bench graft the resistant rootstock to new vines. Today the vineyard was flourishing, with 120 acres of zinfandel and cabernet and 80 of chardonnay, and he expected a yield of over one hundred tons this year—a good start.

The bottling machine tied securely atop his wagon would complete the winery's modernization. Philippe had poured his soul into making his vineyard a success, but if he left for New York this fall, who would be capable of running it in his absence? As he rounded the final bend toward the vineyard, he saw a woman waving wildly to him from his front porch. Of course, he thought.

Madame Aurora Thierry was a lively and unconventional woman. Her white farmhouse, whose upper balcony overlooked her ten-acre farm and orchard, was located north of Eagle's Run, in the heart of the land known as Rancho Rincon de los Carneros. Aurora, as she insisted Philippe call her, had given him invaluable advice when he was scouting out land to purchase. She had schooled him in the terroir of the Napa Valley and, specifically, its three distinct climates.

The northern portion from St. Helena on up was best suited to grow grapes for making fine white wines. The middle valley's warmer temperatures and flatter land was best suited to grow cabernet sauvignon and sauvignon blanc grapes. Her favorite region, and the one she called home, was Carneros, in the lower valley. Its moist conditions were best suited to zinfandel, cabernet, malvoisie and berger, she had told him. Under Aurora's astute guidance, Philippe had replanted with disease-resistant zinfandel, cabernet and chardonnay grapevines. She had many connections in Napa, and had helped him find experienced bench grafters and reliable laborers. She advised him as much as he asked, but never intruded on his management of the farm. Philippe could not think more highly of any other Napan.

Aurora was waving her hat in the air with such vigor, he was certain she would bounce right off his front porch. He returned her wave. She was indeed like the dawn of a new day, and her enthusiasm for life was contagious. Philippe guessed her age as somewhere in the range of forty-five to fifty, old enough to be his mother. Her face was like a lady apple just past its ripened peak. Soft lines appeared around her eyes and creased her brow when her face lit up with excitement at sharing one of her rebellious schemes with him. Her coiled, fiery red hair had only recently begun to show a few stray strands of white. Her eyes were bright blue and her skin clear, with the exception of a smattering of freckles on her nose and cheeks, which lent her a childlike charm. She was always fashionably dressed and sported a wide-brimmed straw hat to shield her fair skin during long days out of doors conducting her research. No matter what she was wearing, her ensemble always included a gold suffragette button fastened to her lapel.

According to Linnette, Aurora had met with her share of misfortune. Her husband, with whom she had shared a tempestuous but ardent relationship, had died ten years earlier, leaving her with no children and a farm to manage on her own. She had since thrown herself into an abundance of pursuits. She taught botany and husbandry at the Ladies' Seminary in town and campaigned tirelessly with the likes of Susan Anthony to secure the vote for women in California. In addition, she was the area's foremost expert on olive farming and had even completed her studies in the subject at Berkeley two years ago, much to the displeasure of the male authorities who dominated the field. Linnette had observed that Aurora was such a fixture in town and so well credentialed that it was difficult for even her most outspoken critics not to secretly admire her, or at least tolerate her passion and unorthodox ways.

Aurora marched off the porch and right up to Philippe as he drove up. He was surprised to see that her face was flushed and pinched with anger. The Winchester she brandished in her right hand reinforced the impression.

"Where in the blazes have you been?"

"In town. Why? What's happened?"

"You mean you haven't heard? Your foreman beat a Chinese worker senseless last night and nearly killed him. Down by the river."

Philippe had known that Jip Montagne, who'd worked for him over the past year, was a bit unpredictable and harbored a strong dislike for the Chinese, but he'd never seen him driven to violence before. Philippe wondered if the victim had been one of the twenty-five traveling Chinese pickers Eagle's Run usually employed. Most of them lived south of Napa City, in dilapidated houses on the riverbank.

"How did it happen?"

"He'd been drinking and went down looking for a Chinese man he said had ripped him off. A bad deal of some sort. Tan told me—the man was his cousin." Tan had been Aurora's loyal man-servant since her husband had died.

"Where's Jip now?"

"He ran off like a streak of greased lightning, I'm told." Aurora drew her rifle up, cocked it and took aim at some fictional figure in the distance. "When I find him, I'm going to give him a piece of my mind."

Philippe raised his eyebrows at Aurora's overreaction. Nevertheless, he understood her indignation, and he knew her aim to be sharp. "Holster the gun, Aurora. I'll handle this. Stay here and watch the wagon for me, would you? I'm going to look around."

Philippe set the brake, hopped down from his rig and set off toward the winery. After searching its length, he checked the larger of the two barns out back, which housed his plows and fertilizer. He found Jip slumped over a bag of seed, snoring. Without a word, Philippe dumped the water-filled bucket sitting by the door over Jip's head. Jip sputtered and shook his head like an angered grizzly. Philippe would have laughed if he hadn't been so infuriated. Instead, he picked Jip up by his shirt collar and pinned him by the neck against the wall. Jip coughed and his eyes bulged with shock.

"I'm giving your week's wages to the man you thrashed. If it happens again, I'll be giving him your job, understand?"

Jip nodded and gasped for air. Philippe dropped him to the floor and walked out.

He had considered sacking Jip outright, but by taking his wages and keeping him employed, he could hit him where it hurt and at the same time keep a watchful eye on him. Besides, with the fall crush around the corner and his plans to go east, Philippe didn't need a disgruntled foreman wreaking havoc in his absence.

Jip Montagne hated the Chinese because, for the past twenty years, they'd been hired for field jobs that he felt should have gone to white men—namely, the Italians, Germans, and French. Philippe knew the truth: the Chinese worked harder and complained less than the Europeans, and their typically small stature was an advantage when it came to picking off the smaller vines. Townspeople like Molly Reynolds resented them because they earned Napa dollars but spent the money sparingly, and only in Chinese-owned shops. Most had left for San Francisco's Chinatown by now, fed up with the discrimination and violence. Only a handful of families remained;

some were house servants to the larger landowners, while others ran businesses in town, like Sam Kee's laundry.

Jip didn't understand that there were twenty equally qualified men in the area who would line up for the chance to manage a major vineyard. Hopefully, Philippe had made his displeasure clear to Jip this afternoon. Arrogance, Philippe reckoned, was a useless quality in a man.

Philippe returned to a newly composed Aurora, who sat fanning herself on his porch.

"So you found him?"

"I did indeed. We shouldn't have any more trouble. Now, if you're free this afternoon, I'd like you and Tan to accompany me down to the riverbank."

"Why?"

"Because I want to give Tan's cousin an apology and compensation for his injuries."

"That's very generous of you, but it's not necessary. An apology should suffice."

"Oh, it's not me. Jip has graciously offered to pay Tan's cousin a week's wages to make amends for his behavior." Philippe smiled broadly.

Aurora smirked with satisfaction. "How very unexpected of him."

Convincing Aurora Thierry to oversee Eagle's Run while he journeyed back East was not as easy as Philippe expected. In fact, she was downright obstinate in her refusal. She argued that she had far too much research to conduct over the winter months to prepare for the spring planting. Philippe waged a campaign to win her over on their ride to the river. He offered to pay her handsomely for her time and explained she would only have to oversee Jip's efforts to prune the vines, turn the soil and build the straw fires to keep the frost at bay. She would also mind the payroll and pick up his letters in town.

"What if Jip acts up? He's certainly not going to take orders from a woman."

Aurora made a good point. Jip didn't value chivalry, but he certainly valued money. "I'll promise Jip a bonus upon my return if you report to me that his work and behavior have been beyond reproach. And, of course, you always have your Winchester."

Aurora ignored his last comment. "I suppose that would be satisfactory. But I'm still not certain I can afford the time away from my research."

Philippe could tell that Aurora was warming to his proposal.

"Wouldn't it absolutely *enrage* the big toads in town to discover that Aurora Thierry is running one of the largest wineries in Napa this winter?"

Aurora gave Philippe a sideways glance. A smile began to play upon her lips. Philippe had his answer. In early December, after the last of the wine was barreled, he would set out for New York.

CHAPTER 7

America

Sara waited in the quiet of the confessional. It was more than a minute before the priest's voice broke the silence.

"Who was this man?" He could not hide his surprise.

Sara thought it best to keep her answers succinct. "My sister's husband."

"Why did you kill him?"

"He attacked me." Sara pressed her hand over the scar Bastien had left on her chest. In recent days, she had felt a prickling sensation there.

"So he harmed you?" Sara detected a hint of sympathy from the priest.

"Yes, and he nearly raped me. That is when I stopped him."

"You were defending your virtue and your life?"

"Yes."

"Did the courts rule as such?"

Sara hesitated. "No, the case was never tried in a court."

"Why not?"

"Because I left France before anyone would discover my . . . offense." Sara's voice quivered at the memory.

The priest was silent again for a few moments, and then cleared his throat to speak. "Exodus 21 tells us: 'An eye for an eye, a tooth for a tooth.' The Beatitudes, as described by Matthew, remind us that the meek will inherit the earth and the peacemakers will be called children of God." The priest sighed and his voice deepened. "If your words are truthful, then you have killed a man in defense of your virtue. This is not a sin in the Lord's eyes. However . . ."

Sara anxiously awaited the priest's next words.

"You must tell me truthfully, daughter. Do you regret it? Ending your brother's life?"

Sara gripped her hands together. "I regret that my brother-in-law was so hateful as to inflict pain and suffering upon my sister, and my family, over and over again. I regret that his actions forced me to defend myself by breaking one of God's most holy commandments. But Father, I will never regret killing that man to protect my family."

"This is unfortunate, for in your refusal to surrender any uncharitable feelings you harbor toward your brother-in-law, you continue to ignore the second greatest commandment: Love thy neighbor as thyself. I cannot absolve you of your sin in the Lord's eyes until you have made amends."

"Make amends? How do I do that, Father?"

"Do you wish to be forgiven and have this dark stain removed from your soul so that you are rendered clean in the Lord's eyes on Judgment Day?"

"I do."

"Then you must seek out your brother-in-law's kin and confess your sin. And you must abide whatever punishment the law assigns you."

"I see." Sara sighed in defeat.

"Do not lose heart, child. All things are possible with God's love."

Sara did not know if that were true. She was about to say as much when the priest ended the sacrament.

"Let us say the Lord's Prayer together before you go."

For the first time, Sara felt the full weight of her sin. She uttered the words to the prayer she had said her entire life, hoping they would serve as a magic elixir, to summon the guilt she could not bring herself to truly feel. *As we forgive those who trespass against us.* As she spoke the words, Sara's cheeks burned and her tears began to fall. Forgive him? She could not bear to do it. She knew she was a wretched creature. But then, if that were true, Bastien had made her this way.

Sara stood outside the building she now called home. The convent's stone structure was vastly different from the neighboring wood-framed tenement houses. From the street, its facade looked to Sara like a rock wedged between two planks, but its narrow appearance belied the virtual village that lay behind its imposing carved oak doors. The Thibault sisters had been residents here for nearly four weeks. The convent, managed by Les Religieuses de Notre Dame, had been built in 1848 on the Lower East Side. Its address was of course the notation Sara had found written on the scrap of paper in Bastien's cash box that fateful evening. She had brought it to America with her, along with the deed to Saint Martin. To her surprise, the address turned out to be a place of refuge for them in this strange new country.

Sara had booked them into steerage on the great steamship *La Champagne*, out of Le Havre, at Jacques's insistence. As he had advised, she had given her mother's maiden name, de Coursey, for their surname. Sara could see he was fearful for their safety. Their goodbyes had been tearful, but brief. Sara's stomach knotted when she thought of how they had left their mother without saying goodbye, but to have alerted Maman to their departure would have implicated her in Sara's crime. Sara had begged Jacques to take care of Maman, and promised to send word when they were safely settled in America.

The journey to New York had lasted twelve days, and although the winds were light and the seas calm, Lydia had suffered bouts of nausea throughout the crossing. Fortunately, she had found the fat, juicy pickles served on board to be a satisfactory remedy and had eaten through nearly a barrel of them. They shared the basket of saucissons and hard cheese Sara had purchased before their departure. After eleven nights on a swaying hammock in a room shared with thirty other men, women and crying children, Sara was more than eager to disembark. Upon docking at Ellis Island, she and Lydia had signed their names in the register as planned: *Sara de Coursey* and *Lydia de Coursey*. The pock-faced man who tended the register stabbed a dirty finger at the line they had left blank: *Address*. Sara was perplexed. Should she invent an address? She barely knew any English. Panicked, she recalled the crumpled piece of paper in her pocket. She lifted the pen and scrawled their destination in the narrow space: *197 Mott Street, Manhattan.*

Before they were allowed to board the ferry to the island of Manhattan, Sara and Lydia endured a degrading examination. They may have traveled in steerage for economy's sake, Sara thought, but this did not mean they should be inspected like a farmer would his cattle. The men, women and children who disembarked from the ship were separated in a vast waiting area filled with long wooden benches carved with initials and words in what looked like scores of languages. When it was Sara's turn, a brusque woman stuck a tongue depressor in her mouth and peered inside her ears. She motioned for Sara to lean forward, then pulled the pins from Sara's hair and roughly examined her scalp. Lastly, the gruff woman flipped up Sara's eyelids with what Sara believed was, of all things, a buttonhook. She had not expected a warm welcome, but to be poked and prodded like this was humiliating.

Sara felt even worse when Lydia told her what she'd endured. Lydia's right shoulder had been marked with the letters "Pg" in chalk. Lydia guessed that was the reason she had been required to see the doctor. He laid her on a waist-high board inside a small room, lifted her skirts, and gracelessly examined her belly and between her thighs. When Sara found Lydia afterwards, she was squatting outside the booth, red-faced and agitated. Sara put her arm around her sister and guided her into the ferry line. They had been lucky. They had heard shrieks of sorrow from families whose loved ones had been pulled away from them and herded back onto the ship, sent back to Europe because they did not pass the medical exam.

Sara and Lydia squeezed their way through the crowd to find a spot at the ferry railing. The blast of the ship's horn shook the deck beneath them. Soon they were on their way to Manhattan, which they could see clearly, for it was a fogless, sunny day. Fishing boats and barges cluttered the harbor. The jagged Manhattan sky-line fascinated Sara, with its sleek skyscrapers and multi-story buildings, all packed tightly together like wine bottles in a case. The sharp, cool wind on her face instantly refreshed her and lifted her spirits. Perhaps the fear that had settled in the pit of her stom-ach would soon begin to subside.

Lydia jabbed Sara with her elbow. Her face registered a look of amazement. Sara followed her gaze out into the harbor until her eyes found the Statue of Liberty. The statue's head was adorned with a spired crown and her fingers were wrapped around a torch, which she held high above everything else in sight. Her left hand supported a tablet, and Sara wondered what was inscribed upon it. She knew the statue had been made in France, and filled with pride at the thought of her countrymen having fashioned this beautiful creature as a gift to the Americans. Perhaps she and Lydia might actually belong here. The statue's smooth face and clear eyes seemed to beckon to her: "Come." Sara felt an instant kinship with this towering protectress. Like Sara, she possessed a woman's heart: strong and steadfast.

Lost in her memories of their arrival, Sara lingered on the wide flagstone steps that led up to the entrance of the convent. The door slammed shut at the top of the stairs, jarring her back to the present. "Ma'am," a delivery boy greeted her as he bounded past her down the steps, disappearing into the Mott Street morning rush. Sara nodded and blushed with embarrassment. She must have looked silly, standing here idle.

Sara pounded the immense iron door knocker. The porter, a snowy-haired scruffy old soul who seemed to manage a kind word for every stranger he encountered, soon answered. He gave Sara a nod of recognition, and she passed through the vaulted passageway and the two side parlors into the heart of the convent. Sara walked down the long cool hallway. Its grey stone walls lacked decoration, save for three Bible verses that had been chiseled by hand into their surfaces. Whenever Sara passed Psalm 5:8, etched in French, she made the sign of the cross and touched the wooden cross she wore around her neck to her lips. *Lead me, O LORD, in your righteousness because of my enemies—make straight your way before me.* Today, Sara walked down the corridor without seeing another soul and climbed the rickety stairs to her room on the second floor. Sara found Lydia there, still sleeping. She was relieved. She did not have the strength to speak to anyone just yet.

Sara had expected the priest to instruct her to recite a few prayers, perform some charitable works or perhaps say the rosary every day for a month to secure her forgiveness from the Lord. The weeks of travel and seclusion in the convent had given her time to reflect, and some of the rawness from her frightening ordeal had begun to dissipate. She had made an honest confession this morning, and

127

had not expected her confessor's rebuke. How would she ever obtain forgiveness now?

Lydia began to snore softly next to Sara on the straw mattress they shared. Sara watched her face as she slept, her knees tucked under her growing belly. Perhaps the priest was correct, and Sara would have to make amends to Bastien's family. But the priest wasn't here to see Lydia's contentment, or witness the deep slumber Lydia had experienced ever since they'd left France. He did not understand that by taking Bastien's life, Sara had saved Lydia's. She had no regrets about that.

Sara awoke the next morning to the smell of rain and a light rapping on the door. Oh, she'd nearly missed matins again! How could she have slept through the clang of the bell? She jumped out of bed, donned her dress from the day before, and ran a handkerchief across her teeth. At least she no longer had to pin up her hair, Sara thought wryly, running a hand over her newly shorn head.

She peered out into the hallway and saw the flash of a white robe before it disappeared down the stairwell. Thank goodness for the postulants. She guessed it was her friend Anne, a new applicant to the religious life, who'd administered the reminder knock on her door. At least Sara had a few allies in this austere corner of the world. Like her, they were still trying to adjust to this rigidly scheduled way of life, with its morning and evening prayers, daily rosary, communal meals and never-ending chores. Sara closed the door gently and walked quickly toward the chapel, leaving Lydia behind to sleep.

The room was dark, lit only by candles set in the alcoves along the wall. Sara took her place next to the postulants in the last pew. The advantage to sitting with the lowly in the back was that Reverend Mother, now perched upon her kneeler at the front of the altar, might overlook Sara's tardiness.

Reverend Mother was as formidable as her title suggested, a barrel-chested, high-bosomed woman who was easy to disappoint and hard to please. She ran the convent with the precision of Napoleon during his first Italian campaign. She managed the spiritual life and daily activities of sixty nuns, five postulants and ten boarders, typically widows who had donated their wealth to the convent in exchange for an escape from the secular world. At any given time of day, Reverend Mother knew the whereabouts of all who resided within her convent's walls. Almost every nun in the convent was French, or at least spoke it fluently.

Sara had been a bit surprised by Reverend Mother's abrupt manner. When she and Lydia had arrived, Sara had stood in the convent doorway, her travel bag on one arm, the other wrapped around Lydia's waist, pleading with Reverend Mother to admit them. The imposing nun, who spoke with a Parisian accent, asked several questions: Were they Catholic? Were they healthy? When was Lydia due? After what seemed like an endless deliberation, she waved them inside, on the condition that they pay rent and complete daily chores. She also added an additional caveat: they could stay only for the duration of Lydia's confinement. After Lydia gave birth and the child was sturdy enough to travel, Sara and her sister would no longer be allowed to trespass on the goodwill of the convent.

They were in no position to argue with Reverend Mother's terms, and Sara knew that the ten dollars she would charge them for each month's stay was more economical than the rent in one of the surrounding tenements. They gratefully agreed. Soon Sara not only thanked the Lord for their good fortune, but also, a bit begrudgingly, came to admire Reverend Mother for her practicality, thrift and skill at matching individuals to suitable tasks.

The rituals of the convent could be timed down to the second. Sara was expected to be at matins at sunrise and Mass at noon every day, plus vespers on Sunday and holy day afternoons. Lydia was excused from matins because of her condition, but was expected to attend all the other prayer services. Breakfast was served at six o'clock sharp following matins. After a meal of porridge and strong coffee, Lydia headed to the laundry to fold countless bed linens and towels; Sara took up her chores in the garden. The courtyard garden, enclosed by the three-story stone walls of the convent, was divided into quadrants: two for the vegetable garden, filled with leeks, potatoes, carrots and cabbage; one for the fruit garden, complete with grape vines, an apple tree and raspberries; and one for the poultry yard, which emitted the foulest of odors. Even the fragrant jessamine that bloomed in the courtyard could not mask the stench of those dreadful birds. If Lydia so much as passed the window that overlooked the yard, Sara would inevitably find her retching, arms wrapped tightly around the chamber pot, within two minutes' time.

On this fine summer day, the skies promised an abundance of sun and only a sliver of cloud. Sara greeted Sister Paulette, one of the nuns with whom she worked in the garden. Sister Paulette's figure was hidden by her black veil and robe, but her white wimple framed a regal neck and lively pink face. Sister Paulette was the gentlest of souls, and Sara believed her to be twenty years of age, at the most.

"I have something for you," Sister Paulette said, reaching into her gardening bag and pulling out a broad-brimmed hat. She handed it to Sara. "I know it's a little too fancy for gardening, but it's the only one I kept. Now that you haven't any hair to speak of, it's the best protection from blistering in the summer heat. Reverend Mother would surely disapprove to see you under the veil."

Sara fingered the yellow straw, which was adorned with a thick cerulean blue ribbon tied in a bow. Even Maman had never worn such a fine hat. "It's beautiful, Sister. Where on earth did you get it?"

"Oh, well." Sister Paulette shifted and blushed, as if she were embarrassed to be caught with such finery. "My life before the convent was a charmed one, Sara. My father was a gentleman, and my mother a lady of society. I had the most gorgeous dresses and pinafores and ribbons and hats that a girl could ask for. We lived in a grand house with a cook, a housekeeper and a copper tabby named Lily."

Sara could see Sister Paulette's thoughts turn, and the brightness of her eyes faded to a mere shadow. "Then one day Mother opened the front door and there were some men who had come to take the furniture. You see, Father had lost everything at the gambling tables. Mother said we were ruined. I was sixteen, almost of marriageable age, though I had no beaux to speak of. Mother said I would have to take the veil, for they could no longer supply me with the dowry to make a suitable match."

"And so you came *here*?" Sara tried without success to hide her dismay.

Sister Paulette laughed. "It wasn't all that bad, Sara. Besides, it was my duty to obey my parents—to lighten their burden—and I did. In time, I found peace here, a real purpose, which I doubt I would have found on the outside. I took my vows last year and have been quite content ever since."

Sara thought perhaps Sister Paulette was trying to convince herself of just that. She could not imagine forsaking her desire to have her own vineyard, but she did not question the young nun further. She had to respect the sacrifice she had made.

"I thank you for the hat, Sister, and I'll wear it gratefully."

Sister Paulette nodded and knelt down to pull a few weeds that had sprung up overnight. Suddenly she stopped, looked up at Sara, and beamed. "Lord forgive me for my vanity, Sara, but I'll tell you one thing I do miss." She let out a sigh. "My gold taffeta gown. Do you know it actually rustled when I walked down our winding staircase into the parlor? Heavenly."

As Sara and Lydia crawled into bed that evening, Sara regarded her sister's protruding belly, which looked enormous. Surely, Lydia's time must be near.

Lydia put her hand to her head and grimaced. "It's dreadfully uncomfortable at times, you know."

"Yes, I suppose it is. But at least you'll have a beautiful baby in another month or two." Sara tried to sound cheerful.

"I do wish . . ." Lydia's voice trailed off.

"What?"

"I do wish sometimes that Maman were here, you know, to tell me more about the whole ordeal. I'm a bit frightened of it."

Sara felt a sudden shame that she had been the one to commit the act that had separated Lydia from her mother. "I'm sorry I'm useless that way. The midwife will visit tomorrow, and she'll instruct you, I'm sure."

"Yes, of course." Lydia was satisfied. "When can we send word? After the baby's born?"

"Yes, I told Jacques we'd send word when it was safe. After the baby's born, I'll write to Jacques, with a letter for Maman. Then we'll leave here, so that there's no risk of Lemieux finding out where we are."

"Do you think Jacques told Maman we're alive? He wouldn't let her believe we died in the fire, would he?" They had discussed this before, but Lydia needed reassurance, Sara could tell.

"I'm sure he wouldn't want Maman to suffer so. He will tell her, if he has not already."

The sisters were silent for a few minutes. Sara absentmindedly rubbed the dark wooden cross that Jacques had carved for her, which hung around her neck as a remembrance of home. Her thoughts were lost in her own regret for having abandoned their mother.

Lydia lifted her hand to Sara's head and smoothed her spiky hair. Her voice was gentle. "We have all suffered, Sara."

Sara could only look at Lydia for a moment, then had to turn away.

"Sara, what did he do to you?" Lydia whispered.

Sara did not know how to answer. The recently healed scar on her chest began to itch, and she remembered the searing pain she'd felt that night and how she'd sworn, in that moment, to never allow herself to become powerless in the shadow of a man. Sara had always hidden this evidence of Bastien's attack. When disrobing in their room, she carefully turned her back to her sister, for she knew that if Lydia caught a glimpse of it, she would feel nothing but enormous guilt. But now, should she tell Lydia that Bastien had tried to rape her? How much could she bear to hear? Sara realized she owed Lydia an answer that was as candid as her question.

"He tried to force himself on me. When I resisted, he pushed me to the ground and . . ."

"Did he . . . ?" Lydia was near tears.

"No. I stopped him before that happened."

Lydia closed her eyes and sighed. "Thanks be to God." She was quiet for a few moments. When she spoke again, her voice trembled with emotion. "I am so sorry, Sara. It's my fault."

"No, that's not true, Lydie. Bastien and his father duped us all."

"They didn't fool you. You saw them for what they truly were. How could I not see?" Lydia's hands covered her face.

"You loved him." Sara's tone mellowed.

"But he never loved me. I was foolish and selfish. I should have never married him. Or at the very least, I should have left him as soon as he started treating us with such contempt."

"Yes, and Papa shouldn't have tried to travel to Tours during a torrential rainstorm, Maman shouldn't have sold the farm, and I shouldn't have—" Sara shook her head. "It's no matter, Lydie.

What's done is done, and we must look forward to caring for this new little Thibault who will soon arrive. Although . . ."

"What?" Lydia's face was still etched with distress.

"I still think you may be surprised with a daughter."

Lydia looked pleased and squeezed Sara's hand. "If so, I shall name her Sarette, after my dear sister."

CHAPTER 8

Cloistered

The following day, Sara and Sister Paulette had finished weeding and collecting raspberries and were washing up for the afternoon when Anne appeared.

"Mademoiselle de Coursey, your sister is with the midwife in her room and wishes you to come at once to meet her."

Sara hurriedly dried her hands and followed Anne up the stairs. As they reached the top stair, a little girl, whom Sara had seen before with some of the sisters, greeted them with a large smile.

"Hello, sister." The girl spoke flawless French.

"Hello, Adeline. This is Mademoiselle de Coursey."

Adeline responded, "I am happy to make your acquaintance."

"Likewise," said Sara.

"This is the midwife's daughter, Adeline," Anne continued. "She is quite precocious for a five-year-old, but a pure delight,

I assure you. She has been very patient waiting out here in the hallway, and I think such patience should be rewarded with a little treat, don't you, mademoiselle?" Anne moved aside the heavy wooden rosary beads that hung from her waist and slid her hand into her pocket. She pulled out a paper-wrapped confection and handed it to the child.

Adeline deftly unwrapped it and popped it into her mouth. Sara crouched down to speak her. "Indeed, I can't think of anything more delightful than a sugary sweet, can you, Adeline?"

Adeline strained to speak, for her tongue was employed in the arduous task of removing the glob of candy now stuck to her top teeth. Once she freed it, she heartily agreed. "Oh, no, mademoiselle!" The girl had an air of sprightly intelligence.

Sara excused herself and made her way to her room. She knocked before entering, for she did not know if an examination was underway and she certainly did not want to intrude upon her sister's privacy more than was needed. Her sister's voice bid her to enter.

"Sara. Thank you for coming." Lydia smiled, but her eyes darted over to the midwife, whose back was turned as she pulled something from her medicine bag. The woman turned and greeted Sara with a warm smile. To Sara's surprise, she was young and petite, with dark brown hair and deeply set brown eyes.

"Pleasure to meet you, Mademoiselle de Coursey. Your sister fares quite well. My guess is that her confinement will end in two months' time. Perhaps a little sooner." She handed Lydia a vial, then fastened the latch on her leather bag. "Ginger root to calm your stomach, Lydia." She then turned back to Sara. "Oh, I am sorry." The woman extended her hand. "I am Marie Chevreau."

Sara was stunned. She could not utter a word. Lydia, who must have sensed her bewilderment, spoke up. "Mademoiselle, my sister is most pleased to meet you. Do tell us, how should we compensate you for your care?"

Sara turned her attention immediately to the concrete question of Mademoiselle Chevreau's payment, searching for familiar ground.

"Don't you worry your head about that, Lydia," Sara said calmly, trying to mask her confusion. "Mademoiselle Chevreau and I shall speak of these matters on her way downstairs. Might I accompany you?"

"Indeed, but I insist that you call me Marie." She turned back to Lydia. "Make sure to rest and take two drops of the ginger root serum—one in the morning and one before you retire. I shall examine you in a month's time, unless you call for me sooner."

"Thank you for your kindness, Marie."

"Not at all." Sara followed Marie out of the room, and they walked in silence while Sara's mind swirled with confusion. Marie Chevreau? A five-year-old daughter named Adeline? Was this the same Marie Chevreau whose child was fathered by Bastien's brother? Jacques's niece? Lydia obviously thought so. Sara could not bring herself to believe it fully, until her thoughts came to rest on the undeniable evidence. She recalled Bastien's handwriting as if she were reading the note for the first time: *197 Mott Street*. When they had arrived, she couldn't fathom why Bastien would have been connected to a convent, but he had recorded Marie's address in America. Had he been in contact with her all this time? And why?

Sara should have been more careful; they should never have

stayed here. It appeared as though the three of them were now linked through their shared history with the Lemieux family, but Marie had given no indication that she knew anything of their background. When Marie spoke, she confirmed this.

"Sara, if I may call you so, Lydia tells me you two came over from the Loire—from Angers, is that right?"

Thank God Lydia had kept her head about her and lied. "Yes. What town are you from?"

"You'll hardly believe it—I come from Tours, just up the river. Indeed, it's true! I believe our towns were once rivals in the race for the best whites, were they not?"

"Yes, I believe so."

"Oh, I miss my family desperately sometimes," Marie said wistfully. "You know what else I miss? Wading in the river up to my knees and waving to the barges coming down from Amboise, loaded with their treasures of lace and chocolates and wine. Are there as many ships now?"

"No, actually, the river is not as busy as it used to be. Most of the merchants use the wagon or railcar these days. They tend to be more reliable." Sara remembered herself and changed the subject rather abruptly. "Tell me, Marie, what is your fee? I want to make sure I have it by the time the child is born."

Marie seemed taken aback. "Yes, of course. Because of Reverend Mother's great kindness to me when I first arrived here, I've always halved my fee for her boarders. I shall do the same for you. Six dollars."

"So you also boarded here when you first arrived?"

"Yes, and I now have an apartment in the back, though I'm

usually out tending to expectant mothers or delivering babies. You may have heard that I was also with child when I arrived, like your sister. Only, unlike your sister, I was not widowed, but rather . . . shamed." Marie's cheeks reddened a bit, and Sara felt sympathy for her. "I would understand if you didn't wish for such a woman to deliver your sister's child. But I am a Christian woman, and from the time of my daughter's birth, I have lived in a Christian manner, I assure you."

Marie turned to Sara expectantly. Sara admired her direct-ness. "The sisters speak very highly of you, Marie. I have nothing but confidence in your abilities."

"Thank you." Marie hesitated uncomfortably. "Reverend Mother asked me to speak to you of another matter."

"Of course." Sara wondered what the shrewd abbess had up her sleeve.

"When I told her that I had my hands full with expectant mothers, she said she has more than enough help here at the con-vent and that she could spare you until Lydia has her child."

"What could I do?"

"I was hoping you'd agree to come with me to visit new moth-ers and even assist in some of the deliveries." Marie looked askance at Sara. "Do you faint at the sight of blood?"

"How much blood?"

Marie put her arm on Sara's. "Never you mind, my dear. I'm sure you'll manage just fine. We're of strong stock, we women from the Loire."

Sara had to agree with that and, although she had no medical training, she felt excited to have a reason to explore the world outside the stone walls of the convent. Besides, Marie did not seem to know their identity. Sara would just have to be cautious not to reveal anything while they were working together.

"I would be happy to help."

"Then it's settled. Shall we shake hands on it?"

Sara took Marie's hand in hers. She did not know what this new association would bring, but her instincts told her that Marie Chevreau had a good heart and that she was not someone to be feared. She hoped those instincts were correct.

Sara had no idea what to expect when she set out with Marie the following morning to visit her patients over on Mulberry Street, in the heart of this mostly Italian quarter. Marie gave her a large basket lined with cloth to carry, but Sara could not muster the courage to ask its purpose. Marie carried only her small leather bag. She had left Adeline in the care of the sisters.

The morning sun blazed so fiercely that one could have cooked an egg on the cobblestones. Newly laundered clothing, hung on twine strung high above the street, billowed like a parade of flags when the occasional breeze blew. Sara began to perspire heavily in her shirtwaist as she walked toward the Bend, the elbow's crook in Mulberry Street, and the most infamous slum in New York. Striped and solid-colored awnings shaded shopkeepers haggling with their customers, and a row of wagons waited in the street to make deliveries or haul purchases home. Sara and Marie crossed to the opposite side of the street, dodging men wheeling handbarrows filled with peaches and plums for sale.

The smells of the street—garlic and stale Roquefort—over-powered her. Every time a passing horse or cart kicked up dust, Sara could taste it on her tongue. She tried to ignore the assault on her senses and instead listen to Marie. It was a great comfort to converse in French and not have to strain to think of the correct phrase in English. Sara was still learning the new language, but Marie, on the other hand, seemed comfortable speaking English and Italian. She was well known in this part of town. Several shop owners came out to greet her as they passed. Each of them gestured vigorously and invited Marie in; each time she would make a polite refusal in Italian. Inevitably, her admirers would duck back into their stores and reappear with a hot loaf of bread, a savory sausage or even some fresh eggs. Marie would thank each one by name and place the gift in the basket Sara held.

"I may not be paid too well, but Lord knows Adeline and I are well fed!" Marie patted her stomach and puffed her cheeks up. Sara could not help but laugh.

"They are friendly, aren't they?"

"They are indeed. Good folks, and grateful. They would be mortally offended if I refused their gifts, so alas, we must feast on all this tonight."

"Sounds delicious."

As they neared the Mulberry Street tenement Marie had just pointed out, Sara became uneasy. She began to notice people loitering in dark corners and cellar stairwells. Sara took pity on a painted woman in a cellar-way whom she saw calling to the young men who passed, her cheeks brightly rouged and breasts nearly popping out of her tight bodice. It was clear that she was trying to entice men into her apartment below. While Marie was engaged in conversation with another shopkeeper, Sara broke off a piece of bread and knelt down, handing it to the woman. She hoped Marie wouldn't mind. The woman grabbed the bread with a dirty hand and shoved it in her apron. Then Sara felt the woman's hand under her skirt, stroking her calf. The woman uttered something in Italian, licked her lips and rubbed her other grubby hand between her own fat legs.

Sara blushed with embarrassment—such wickedness! She stumbled back into the street at the shock. Marie caught Sara up by the armpits, steadied her and then linked her arm in hers. She guided her away from the licentious woman and they made haste down the street.

"I can't leave you alone for a minute," Marie said, chuckling.

"Apparently not. Thank you for your help," Sara replied, flustered.

Marie was obviously amused that Sara had fallen into the woman's trap. Sara was just glad Marie had extricated her from it.

Now Sara noticed more suspicious creatures lurking about, always on the periphery of the sun's light. Their skin was pale and their eyes hollow. Most of them just blended into their surroundings—passersby would give them no more thought than a plank of wood. Yet when Sara looked closer, she found their blank faces unsettling; each had the vacant visage of a mannequin.

She was relieved when they finally reached the building. Marie instructed her, "Just stand aside while I examine the mother. I will let you know what I need from my bag." She hesitated, looking as though she wanted to say something else, but then turned and led Sara up the three flights of stairs to the top floor.

No warning would have prepared her anyway. A sad-eyed girl, whose belly jutted out from under her threadbare yellow dress, greeted them at the door. When they entered the room, Sara noticed that the girl had tied cardboard to her shoes to bolster their worn-out soles. Sara counted five adults and seven children in the apartment. Three women sat at a table, darning socks and mending shirts. The floorboards in the corner behind them were rotted and damp from the rainwater that dripped from the ceiling. Two large husk mattresses were pushed against the far wall. Three children were huddled together upon one mattress. An infant boy had sores on his lips and an open blister on his right cheek. The older children, who were perhaps ten and twelve, carried the same sores on their hands and cheeks. Their red, sickly eyes followed their visitors carefully as they walked into the room, and each little cough and sniffle they released tugged at Sara's heart. The other four were squatting around a pile of a something black that she did not recognize.

Marie whispered, "Tobacco. The children roll cigarettes during the day to earn money for the family." Of course, Sara thought. The bittersweet smell had reminded her of Papa's evening pipe.

Sara marveled at Marie's ability to ignore her surroundings and speak in authoritative Italian. She shooed the other tenants outside the room so she could conduct her examination in private, pulled the empty mattress to the brighter side of the room and instructed the girl to lie down. She moved her hands around the perimeter of the girl's belly, pressing down as she did so. The girl winced in discomfort. Marie spoke in Italian to the girl and patted her arm reassuringly. Then she helped her up and asked Sara to take vanilla balm and ginger root from her bag.

"The baby is coming soon, but she's not in labor yet. We will come back every day this week until it is her time."

In the hallway outside, Marie knelt down and picked up the baby to inspect his sores. The boy squirmed and tried to free his chin from Marie's grasp, but she spoke calmly, and he soon stopped his wriggling. He never took his eyes from Marie's face. Marie asked Sara for some salve from the bag.

"Aloe. It will help the wounds heal. Give them the extra vial."

Sara handed it to the woman standing nearest, whom Sara suspected was the baby's mother. The woman grasped the bottle with both hands. For the first time since she left France, Sara felt as though she were being useful.

Once they were back on the street, Sara delicately inquired how Marie had become used to confronting such indigence with steady hands and a degree of detachment.

Marie replied in her matter-of-fact manner, "If I get carried away with the why and the how of a girl's circumstances, then I cannot properly concentrate on giving her the care she needs to deliver a healthy child. I cannot mend what God or man has rendered. I can only ease her suffering for a time, and in some small way, affirm her and her child's importance in the world."

Sara was silent after that. At just twenty-three, Marie was a wise woman indeed. Sara felt as if she'd learned quite a lot from a few hours in Marie's company. She was about to say as much when she spied two young boys down a side alley beating another boy with broken sticks.

All three of the boys were barefoot and dressed in rags. A closer inspection of their dirty faces and hands confirmed a life of wanting. The taller of the two assailants kicked the littlest boy down and pounced upon him, barreling his large fists into the boy's averted face. The little boy fought back. Marie rushed over at once, shouting in Italian, and one of the boys dropped his stick and ran away. It took more effort to stop the larger boy, but Sara rushed to Marie's side and the two of them pulled the attacker off. Marie chastised the boy, who stood before her defiantly and wiped his bloody nose on his arm. He spat a tooth on the ground and then bolted into the street. A few coins fell to the ground in his wake.

The small boy, whom Sara had just helped up, scurried to claim the coins. She followed him with the intention of soothing him or perhaps giving him some of the food in their basket, but the child recoiled from her touch. He turned and staggered away, stumbling a bit until he regained his balance and broke into a full run.

Sara felt sorry for the boy, for he reminded her of a stray dog left to fend for itself. Marie must have read her thoughts, because she said, "Do not pity him, Sara. You don't know what happened here. He could have stolen money from the other boys. We don't know."

Sara thought it unlikely that such a small boy would provoke such harsh retribution. "Do they not have any family?"

"Orphaned, most likely," Marie shrugged. "Guttersnipes do what they must to survive."

"Are there no orphanages?"

"An abundance, but they run away from them. I've visited a few. The food is dreadful, and it's about the same as living on the street to them, but with less freedom."

Sara wondered if her compassionate nature would serve her well in this new city. America was not at all what she'd imagined.

Soon the sweltering heat of July was upon them, and Lydia suffered from it. The air was so oppressive that she would retire to the privacy of their cell just so she could remove her stockings and unbutton her collar for some relief.

One day, when Sara came upstairs to make certain that Lydia hadn't fainted in the heat, she found her seated in the corner, fanning her face with a piece of cardboard. Her other hand was pressed to her midsection.

"Feel this, Sara. I believe he's practicing to be a circus performer with his constant somersaulting. I barely slept a wink last night. I thought he would kick my insides out!" Lydia's face was sweaty, but aglow with pride.

Sara placed her hand on Lydia's belly. It was firm and smooth, like a river stone. Just then, the child kicked.

"Oh my, he's a strong little one, isn't he?" Sara was a bit worried for her sister.

"Eager to meet his mother and have a good stretch, I would imagine."

Sara looked at her sister admiringly. She had endured their ordeal without complaint. Sara had been surprised by Lydia's forbearance in these past two months. "I like to see you content, Lydia. It suits you."

"Yes, I suppose it does." Lydia held her stomach with both hands and smiled. "Do you think he has all his fingers and toes and such from the beginning, or does God shape him in my womb right before he's born, like a piece of clay?"

"I think the baby must grow as the fruit on the vine grows. A grape starts as a smaller version of its ripened self. So did your baby, I would guess."

They were interrupted by a knock on the door. It was Anne, who would soon be taking her vows. "I come bearing presents, ladies."

Lydia clapped her hands together with delight. "I haven't had a gift in so long. They are most welcome here. Do come in!"

"Now, it's nothing grand. First, something for the baby." Anne handed Lydia a package wrapped in newspaper. Lydia opened it and carefully fingered the brown cap and blanket Anne had knitted from soft, warm wool. Lydia's eyes welled with emotion.

"Thank you, Anne. They're beautiful, and perfect for the cold winters here."

Anne looked pleased. She turned her attention to Sara. "And for you, Mademoiselle de Coursey." She handed Sara a stack of colorful magazines. Sara tried to pronounce the magazine's name, but she simply couldn't cajole her front teeth into pronouncing the American "r." She always reverted back to the throaty French consonant. Anne corrected her gently. "It's pronounced *Harper's*."

"Ah, yes." Sara was not sure of the purpose of Anne's gift.

"Mrs. Bourse, my patron, sneaks these to me through the turning box when she comes to visit each month. Look at the beautiful pictures! The articles are very modern. I thought these could help you learn to read English. We can read together in the evenings, if you'd like."

What a clever idea, Sara thought. These looked a vast deal more interesting than the English Bible the Reverend Mother had given her to read. Sara began to thumb through the tattered pages.

"That sounds wonderful, Anne. Would you mind helping me? Won't it take you from your other duties?"

"No, Reverend Mother gave me permission to tutor you. Although"—Anne grinned conspiratorially—"I believe I failed to mention exactly what we'd be reading."

"Our secret, then?"

"Yes, our secret." She giggled.

What a shame, Sara thought, that such a spirited girl would spend the rest of her days in a nunnery.

As the weeks passed Sara learned many things from Anne, who turned out to be quite an accomplished young lady. Anne not only spent time reading with Sara, but told her much about America's history and peculiarities. The magazines themselves, some of which dated back to the 1880s, were filled with articles on subjects Sara had never thought about. She found herself particularly drawn to a section entitled "The Editor's Easy Chair." One story, titled "Women's Rights," took Sara, under Anne's tutelage, a whole week to interpret, but the endeavor was certainly worthwhile. Mr. Curtis, apparently a writer of some distinction, argued that because no one would deny a woman's right to earn her own living by her own industry and talent, then no one should deny that same woman the privilege of voting alongside the men. Sara thought this argument made perfect sense. Anne did not agree. One afternoon, their debate on the topic lasted well into the evening. Anne, taking her cue from the Bible, believed that women were made by God to be inferior to men and, therefore, voting could not be seen as a suitable womanly activity. Sara did have to admit that since this article had been written, ten years prior, little progress had been made toward securing the vote for women. She was about to concede this point to Anne, when Lydia, who had been listening, snatched the pages from Sara's hands.

"God save us all from your tiresome nonsense. I know my sister well, Anne, and I'll tell you that if I don't interrupt this conversation, she will ride her side of the argument to hell and back again just to prove her point." Lydia gave them a sly smile and flipped through the magazine until her eyes rested on the colorful fashion plates of society ladies, dressed from head to toe in lace, frills and flowers. Lydia ran her fingers over the sketches and let out a wistful sigh.

Sara shook her head and rolled her eyes toward the heavens. Lydia was just so *Lydia*.

One evening, after Sara had intelligibly pronounced nearly every word in a long article written by Mark Twain, she came across something remarkable. It was a story dated March 9, 1889, seven years earlier. The article spanned three pages, and Sara could only navigate a small portion of the type that evening. She read the words slowly, not understanding them all. She knew the article described grape growers in California, but she could not decipher many details. Growing frustrated, she begged Anne to translate for her.

Anne graciously obliged in French: "The two best known valleys—those having soil and climate adapted for the production of the choicest grapes from the Médoc, Bordeaux, and Rhine Valley districts—are Sonoma and Napa. I cannot imagine a more sheltered, pretty nook than the Napa Valley . . . it is a little world in itself. Several of the Napa growers own estates that have no counterpart in America."

"Napa," Sara whispered with reverence. She pulled her eyes away from the page just long enough to address Anne. "Have you ever been to California?"

"Heavens, no, it's clear on the other side of the country, nearly three thousand miles away."

"How does one travel there?"

"The fastest route would be by rail. I believe it goes from Chicago to San Francisco. I'm not sure whether this Napa Valley is north or south of San Francisco, though."

"I see." Sara's mind raced with the possibilities of moving west to a new land, where she could once again grow grapes and make wine. She would work hard and save the money to purchase a small vineyard of her own. She would eventually make enough of a profit to return to France. Yes, she would return, and she would reclaim Saint Martin. It seemed so far away, but Sara could still smell the sweetness of Saint Martin's fruit and taste its earth on her tongue.

"What are you thinking, Sara?"

"Oh, nothing. Shall we continue?" Sara could not have put her longing into words, and it would have been dangerous for her to do so. She doubted that Anne could have ever understood the strength of her desire, in any case. Sara was born to make wine. Nothing else made sense.

Sara soon realized that catching babies was not her calling in life. She had, of course, witnessed the birthing of mules and the occasional pig at Saint Martin. Still, she had not been prepared to observe the birth of a child. After assisting Marie in the delivery of five healthy, two breech and two stillborn babies, Sara was still shocked at the sheer violence of the undertaking: the sweat, the screams and the blood seemed to be never-ending. The vast quantity of bodily secretions alone was enough to make anyone turn green, she thought. She knew her mother would be horrified if she knew what Sara was doing. How life had changed in the past three months.

Sara was amazed at the courage of the women she encountered. In the face of their great labors, she could not possibly succumb to her own squeamish desire to faint. For this reason alone, Sara forced herself to concentrate on handing Marie the necessary instruments as they worked, although Sara was not above sneaking a whiff of Marie's smelling salts to revive herself. Marie, for her part, reassured and instructed the expectant mothers: how to breathe, when to relax, when to push. She seemed sure of what to do in every situation. Sara was certain of only one thing: she had no desire to endure such an ordeal, even if God had designated it a woman's most important function.

It was a late August afternoon, and Sara and Marie had delivered a lusty baby boy to Hettie Smyth, who lived in a tenement located just south of the Bend. Both mother and child had survived—a good day. Marie was eager to get back to the convent to check on Lydia, because she believed Lydia could begin her labor at any time. After spending all day in a smelly tenement, Sara wanted some fresh air, so she told Marie to go on without her and to inform Lydia that she'd return by dusk.

She did not tell Marie that she had a secret errand. Sara had decided that since Lydia was about to endure the rigors of childbirth, she should have the treat of a new travel dress. Sara quickly reviewed their finances in her head. Of the 1,520 francs she had taken from Bastien and Jacques, which had converted to a little over $300, she had spent $90 on the tickets for their trip here, $30 on rent at the convent and another $20 for cotton flannels and clothes for the baby. The remainder of the money, plus the $7 that remained from selling her hair to a wigmaker on Mulberry Street, she kept hidden under the husk mattress in their room. If Sara bought a dress and hat for Lydia for $20 or less, she would have enough left to purchase two one-way tickets to California with a small cushion left for rent and food once they arrived. She would simply have to find work as soon as they reached California. Having made up her mind, Sara walked into the modest dress shop on Mulberry.

She had her eye on a dark blue wool dress, fairly plain, but with a black ruffled collar and matching trim on the cuffs. It cost

$22, including the matching hat. She held the dress up to her face, inhaling the fragrance of fresh, unsoiled wool. It smelled like Saint Martin when Papa was alive. It smelled like the place Sara desperately wanted to find again.

Sara's reverie ceased when she realized that the well-dressed woman behind the counter was glaring at her. For the first time in her life, Sara felt self-conscious in a place of business. She looked down at her own dress and realized that, although its linen fabric was not torn, it was stained and rather dingy compared to the fine wool dresses and silk skirts that lined the shop's walls. Sara flushed with embarrassment. She carried the dress and hat to the counter and counted out the bills and change she had saved. Without a word, the shop clerk picked up the money using the tips of her fingers. She wrapped the dress and hat in brown paper, tied the package with string, and gave it to Sara.

Sara took a deep breath upon exiting the store, in an effort to keep her stinging tears from running down her cheeks. You will not, she chastised herself, allow that nasty woman to make you feel worthless. She straightened her back, lifted her chin and walked on, holding her purchase tightly to her chest, for the streets were lined with people.

The crowd was mostly women, Sara noticed, and they seemed to be looking eagerly down the street. She heard a drum beat in the near distance, and then she saw why the faces around her were etched with expectancy. A throng of well-dressed women carrying a wide banner marched down the street toward her. They were singing in unison and although Sara did not understand the words well, the song sounded like a church hymn.

The women leading the group wore smart hats, striped sashes and gold buttons fastened to their lapels. They clutched a banner, which they used as a sort of fortification to push pedestrians off the street and out of their way. Sara was amazed at their boldness. Then she read the one word on the banner she understood, for it was the same in French: *prohibition.*

At age eight, she had assumed prohibition was a deadly disease of some kind. The word had been strictly taboo in Vouvray. One did not speak of it nor think upon it, for fear it might eventually come to pass. When Sara eventually did discover what the dreaded word meant, she realized that if the French government were to successfully prohibit the sale of absinthe, it could one day strike at her own family's livelihood, too. Yet to Papa, prohibition was more than a potential threat to their winemaking business. He had considered it to be a threat to man's liberty, and vehemently opposed the right of religious conservatives to rule on such personal matters. Sara laughed to herself as she remembered what Papa used to say: "There's no cuckoo like a religious cuckoo."

Sara stood aside while the block-long parade of marchers passed and wondered how in the world they expected to convince an entire nation to give up its diversion of choice. While Sara was ruminating upon this fanciful idea, her eyes landed on another odd sight. Pushing through the crowd was a woman who looked like a seraph, draped and veiled in spotless white on the filthy street, waving her arms and shouting to be heard above the commotion. Sara's heart leapt into her throat when she recognized Anne. She pushed her way toward her.

"What is it? What has happened?"

Anne took a moment to catch her breath. "Oh, thank goodness I've found you. It's Lydia. The baby is coming. She's with Marie right now. Come, we must make haste."

Sara fell in step behind Anne and elbowed her way through the crowd. She did not know if it was apprehension or the afternoon heat that caused her cheeks to prickle and her heart to beat frantically. Only the wall of humanity blocking her path kept her from casting decorum to the wind and bursting into an all-out sprint to reach her sister's side.

CHAPTER 9

Make Straight Your Way Before Me

lthough she ran to their room, Sara still hesitated outside the door and knocked before entering. She did not know how far Lydia's labor had progressed. Marie answered with an uncharacteristically forceful "Come in." Sara opened the door and was shocked by what she saw. She smiled as though everything were fine, but was filled with fear for her sister.

"Sara." Lydia's face was pale, and her hair was matted to her forehead in a sweaty tangle. She gripped the bedsheet and, arching her back, let out a howl unlike anything Sara had ever heard.

"Don't be alarmed," Marie interjected. "It's the normal course of things, but the pains are coming more quickly than expected. I wouldn't be surprised if she birthed this baby before vespers."

"Before vespers?" That was less than two hours' time. "Good Lord." Sara was incredulous. "What can I do? Lydia, can I get you some water, or a cool cloth for your head?"

Marie did not wait for Lydia to respond. "Yes, do that, and Sara, I want you to ask Sister Paulette to prepare some boiled towels, soap and vinegar, and a clean basket for the baby. Tell her to ask one of the novices to wait outside the door. She'll need to fetch hot water when I call for it."

"Do you have your knife and twine?"

"I see you've been paying attention." Marie sounded pleased. "Yes, I have both." She turned back to Lydia, who by this time was experiencing another pain. "Now set yourself to work. Your sister's about to have a baby."

The hours passed more slowly than Sara had expected. She sat beside Lydia, stroking her head and reading to her from the Bible, as Lydia requested. Marie read her dog-eared midwifery handbook. Over the course of the evening, Lydia's groaning became louder, and with each contraction, Sara feared Lydia would break her hand from gripping it so hard. At last, Marie placed the book aside and opened Lydia's knees to examine her. Lydia looked exhausted and Marie cautioned her to rest. She would need all her strength to push when the time came.

The time had come.

"Lydia, listen to me. I can feel the baby's head with my two fingers. It will only be a little time now before you'll need to summon all your might to push, all right?"

Lydia nodded. Marie busied herself readying the basket with clean linens and lining up her instruments. After she was done with her preparations, she seated herself on the stool at the foot of the bed.

"Sara, I'll need you to encourage Lydia to push when I tell you. Say whatever you need to. The firstborn babes are often the most stubborn."

Lydia turned to Sara and whispered, "I hope you don't find this difficult, Sara. It is all so awkward." Lydia glanced at her legs, now sprawled out for Marie's inspection. She wrapped her hand around Sara's and looked at her pleadingly. "I need you to stay right here, dearest, to give me courage, or I don't think I can bear it."

Sara pressed Lydia's fingers to her to her cheek. "Nonsense. You have traveled across the ocean and freed yourself from miserable circumstances, and that took great courage," she whispered. "You can do this, Lydia. Only a little longer, and you'll meet your new son."

Lydia smiled and closed her eyes. "Yes."

Sara fanned Lydia's face with one of the old magazines that had been stacked neatly in the corner of their room. Marie poked her head into the hallway and instructed the novice to fetch a pail of hot water. "Her time is near," Sara heard Marie whisper.

Marie washed her hands and arms up to her elbows with the brick of soap in the basin of water that rested on the small table. She then covered her hands in antiseptic and handed the bottle to Sara.

"Be certain to scrub between your fingers," she instructed her.

Lydia moaned and then cried out, wincing, "I need to push, I need to push!"

"Wait for it. Let me make sure." Marie lifted her head and nodded. "You go right ahead, Lydia. Push with all your might—bear down as hard as you can!" She looked at Sara. "Sara, lift her up a bit. Place that other pillow behind her."

Lydia's face scrunched with effort, and she let out a deep guttural moan.

"That's it, Lydia, don't be afraid. Push him out, push him out, that's it!" Sara prayed silently between each of Lydia's pushes. *Please, God, please.*

Marie's face was knotted in concentration. She looked up at Sara and Lydia. "The baby's head is right here, Lydia. Give me one more big push."

"I can't. It's too much," Lydia responded breathlessly.

Sara took Lydia's face in her hands. "Listen to me, Lydia. You can, and you will birth this baby right now. Push!" She helped Lydia up onto her elbows. "Push!"

Lydia began to bear down and Sara persisted, "There's the head! Keep going! Shout as loud as you want, no one can hear. That's it!"

Lydia released the most terrifying shriek Sara had ever heard. Her eyes reddened with the strain. She fell back on the pillows and heaved a sigh of exhaustion.

Marie cradled a slippery boy child in her arms. To Sara, he looked healthy, pink and vigorous. But her concern grew when he did not make a sound. Marie squeezed his nose and used her index finger to clear his mouth. Then she pinched his foot. His lip quivered and he wailed in protest. Sara thought it was the most beautiful cry she had ever heard. Marie expertly clipped the spiraling cord, tied the stump, wiped the baby clean and wrapped him in a swaddling blanket. She handed Sara her nephew. Sara turned her attention to Lydia, who had not said a word.

Lydia's eyes were half shut. Sara brought the child's face close to her sister's. "It's a boy, Lydia, just as you said it would be. Your little boy."

Lydia touched the child's fine, matted black hair with her fingertips and pulled his tiny face near to her cheek. Sara kept a firm grasp on him, as Lydia did not appear to have the strength to hold him. Lydia kissed his pink cheek and his cries continued. Then her hand dropped to her side, and she drifted off, exhausted.

Sara had been so enraptured to see Lydia's new son that she only now realized Marie was standing next to her, kneading Lydia's abdomen like a ball of raw dough.

"Place the baby in the basket—let him cry. I need you to move the bucket underneath her. The placenta will emerge soon."

Sara placed the bucket at the end of the bed and gathered the sterile towels beside it.

"It's coming, Marie." Sara stepped aside so Marie could position herself on the little stool. She proceeded to pull a twisted blue and red mass out from between Lydia's legs until blood began to flow. Although Sara had witnessed this stage of the birthing process many times now, it was another thing entirely to witness this bulbous mass being expelled from her sister's body. She would have fainted had Marie not shocked her into clearheadedness with her next words.

"She is torn, Sara, and the bleeding has not yet ceased. Listen closely. Take these towels and hold them here firmly to staunch the flow of blood. Don't stop until I tell you. Use both hands—yes, like that. Press harder!"

Marie shouted to the novice waiting outside to bring more warm water. She then filled a syringe with vinegar and water. By this time, the towels Sara was holding were soaked through and her fingers were bloodied. This, combined with her nephew's crying, felt like too much to bear. Her sister's blood was pooling around her shoes. The smell pulled Sara back to the night she stabbed Bastien, and she began to panic.

"What is happening, Marie? Is she, is she . . ." Sara could not bring herself to say the words.

"Lift her legs, ankles together, now."

Sara did as she was told and watched as Marie emptied the contents of the syringe into her sister's birth canal. Lydia did not react. Her legs were limp in Sara's arms and her skin was colorless. Sara's chest heaved as she tried to catch her breath. For minutes that felt like hours, Marie worked to revive Lydia, but nothing appeared to be happening.

Marie put a small mirror to Lydia's mouth and observed it intently. All Sara's hopes and fears hung in the balance.

"Sara, Lydia is not breathing." Her words were unthinkable to Sara. She ignored Marie and squeezed Lydia's slack hand with her own. She rocked back and forth at the bedside, whispering, "Stay with us, Lydie. Stay with us." Sara placed her head on Lydia's chest to feel for her breath. She could not hear anything over the cries of her nephew, but she could not feel the natural rise and fall of Lydia's breast.

This could not be. Sara rose to her feet and shook Lydia's shoulders. "Lydie . . . Lydie! You must awaken for your son. Your son!" Lydia's face was unresponsive, her neck and limbs slack. Her bright eyes would never look upon her son again. Sara's hands fell to her sides and she began to sob.

Marie gently pulled down Lydia's nightgown and placed the baby to her breast. After some coaxing from Marie, the baby latched on to Lydia's nipple and began to suck with vigor.

"What are you doing?"

Marie's voice was soft. "He is hungry, Sara. He must suckle."

"But she has no milk and she . . ." Sara could not choke the words out. She shuddered.

"He's drinking the foremilk, and it has soothed him—see?"

After a few minutes, the boy was full and drifted off to sleep in Marie's arms. She offered Sara his tiny body to hold, but she protested. "No, he must remain with his mother."

Marie placed the baby in Sara's arms nonetheless, and wrapped her arms around the two of them. Sara shook her head in disbelief. Marie held her cheek to Sara's. Her voice was quiet but firm. "You are his mother now."

CHAPTER 10

Rebirth

ydia was buried in a small patch of earth near the end of Mott Street. Before the nuns came to place her body in its pine casket, Sara had cleaned Lydia's delicate skin with rosewater and vinegar and brushed her curls out until they shone in the candlelight. She turned her sister gently on her side and fastened the line of delicate black buttons down the back of her new blue dress. Sara knelt beside Lydia's body and took her cold hand in her own. Her stomach lurched with grief. Holding Lydia's hand to her lips, Sara prayed that God would deliver her sister's soul into his eternal light. Then she opened the door to the sisters and postulants who were waiting silently in the corridor. Anne held the newly christened Luc de Coursey, who had fallen fast asleep.

Sara asked them all to wait and took the boy in to his mother. She nestled him into the crook of Lydia's arm so he could feel her embrace for the last time. As it should have been, Sara thought. As it will never be.

For the next two days, all Sara felt was exhaustion. She could not eat or care for Luc. She could not bear the whispers and sympathetic conjecture of the sisters when she went to the refectory for meals, and instead hid herself away in the silence of her room. In the small hours of the morning, she lay awake, shining a light on her darkest thoughts. Was this God's punishment? Had her family not endured enough suffering? What hope was there now of a new life in America when she had no family to share it with? What on earth was she to do with a baby? She knew nothing of his needs. She had no answers, and sleep was her only escape.

But it was short-lived. On the third morning there was an abrupt banging on her door. Sara's heart jumped with fear. Then she heard Marie's familiar voice.

"Sara, Sara! Wake up, my dear. If you don't open this door, I shall be forced to break it down, and Reverend Mother will be cross indeed! Open up!"

Marie's voice was annoyingly cheerful, and Sara would have ignored her entirely had she not realized that it was very early— half the convent was still asleep.

Sara opened the door. "Marie," she sighed.

Marie entered the room without invitation. "I have something for you, or rather, for your little Luc, but you must dress and come downstairs to the courtyard."

"I'm truly not ready, Marie." Sara leaned against the door for support.

"That's nonsense," Marie said maternally. "You've been holed up in here for two days, and that's quite enough. You have a little boy who needs you, and you'd best get dressed and start tending to him."

Sara, taken aback by Marie's stern tone, realized she had no choice but to obey. At that moment, Adeline poked her head in the door. "Maman?"

"Oh, yes, yes, bring in the water, my love." Adeline brought in a large pitcher of warm water that looked heavy for her to manage. She set it down and retrieved a red apple from her apron. She offered it to Sara.

"For you, mademoiselle."

Sara managed a slight smile and thanked the girl. Her stomach rumbled at the sight of the fresh fruit, which made her conscious of how hungry she was. She bit into it with relief.

"Come down when you're ready—no longer than ten minutes. I don't want Adeline to have to come fetch you." Marie smiled and closed the door.

Sara washed her face and hands, tidied herself and made her way down to the courtyard. There her eyes met with an odd sight. Sister Paulette held baby Luc in her arms as he sucked from a bottle.

"He's a lusty little drinker, isn't he?" Marie's enthusiasm was met with a quizzical look from Sara, whose attention had turned to a four-legged, shaggy creature with drooping ears. Marie explained, "I have supplied you with a goat."

"A goat?" Sara was mystified.

"Yes. I could not find a cow, which would be far too large for the courtyard anyhow. So here you have our little goat friend. Adeline has named her Josephine."

"A goat named Josephine," Sara repeated.

"She wanted Napoleon, but I suggested that perhaps Josephine would be more suitable for a milk-giving goat." Marie took Sara's arm. "Baby Luc can't live on sugar water, so he will have nourishing goat's milk, the next best thing to mother's milk. Look, see how he's lapping it up?"

Luc made an unabashedly loud sucking sound that almost made Sara laugh.

"Sister Paulette," Marie cautioned, "that little man is going to need a sizeable belch after such a feast. Please see to it." Sister Paulette nodded and turned her attention to her charge.

"Such a creature is surely costly. I must repay you, Marie," Sara said gently as she stared at the animal.

Marie faced her with a determined look on her face. "I failed you, and for that I will be eternally sorry. Please allow me the small comfort of providing food for Luc and helping you care for him. In your generosity, grant me this kindness."

Sara looked at her nephew. "Don't reproach yourself, Marie. I will gladly accept your gift and your assistance with the baby." In all honesty, she didn't know whether or not Lydia's death was Marie's fault, but she didn't believe any doctor could have performed better. Lydia's life had been in God's hands, and he had stolen her away from them.

Sara felt Marie's hand squeeze her own. When she looked

over at her friend again, she saw her silent anguish. Marie's eyes were filled with tears.

Sister Paulette, who had remained silent, handed Luc to Marie, took Sara by the arm and guided her over to the bench beneath the chestnut tree.

"One of the things you may not have guessed about me is that I have experienced the kind of grief you suffer," said the young nun. "I did not tell you, that day in the garden, that my father not only left us destitute, but the day after he told my mother the news, he shot himself in the head with a pistol. Convenient for him—not so for my mother and me."

Sara's shock must have shown on her face, for Sister Paulette spoke again quickly.

"Don't pity me. I tell you this because I don't want you to despair. It's only natural for us to lose hope when suffering is heaped upon us time and time again."

"Indeed it is," Sara replied, growing weary of their conversation. "Forgive me, Sister, but I daresay it is not a benevolent God that permits the kind of violence and death that I have witnessed."

"This God you speak of—is he the same that led you to the safety of this convent and delivered a healthy nephew into your arms?"

Sara did not answer.

"All I am saying, Sara, is that your suffering is not in vain."

"Really? Then pray tell me, Sister, in your wisdom, what grand purpose does all this suffering serve?" Sara asked bitterly.

Paulette looked away, and Sara worried that she might have hurt her friend. The nun, however, was not so easily discouraged. Her eyes filled with kindness as she placed her palm gently against

Sara's cheek. "If we do not struggle and suffer in this life, then what need would we have for God?"

Yes, perhaps, thought Sara. However, with her own survival and Luc's at stake, she would not accept this suffering in any measure. She would fight it every step of the way.

Josephine the goat turned out to be a blessing. Over the next two months, Luc grew to be a happy and hearty baby. By October, Sara was thoroughly immersed in the routine of caring for him. Marie had shown her how to diaper, clothe, swaddle, feed, burp and bathe him. Sara thought the feeding and sleeping regimen strict, but Marie insisted that babies needed a predictable schedule and that deviation from it could result in disaster—or sleepless nights. Luc was a source of amazement to Sara. How could a creature so tiny relieve himself over ten times a day? He produced more soiled clothing in one day than any other human would in a week. Marie assured Sara that in the first few months of life this was, in fact, perfectly normal.

Despite Luc's robustness, Sara still feared pneumonia or typhoid—many children died before their first birthday—so she paid close attention to Marie's instructions and, just as she had for her grapes, kept a detailed journal for Luc's care. Marie advised that he should be allowed to cry himself to sleep and should not be held or kissed except during feeding time. Sara disregarded this advice entirely. When she swaddled him and rocked Luc in her arms, his sweet face, his warmth, comforted her. She knew that she needed to hold him for her own sake, if not for his.

Sara was relieved to have a purpose. Caring for Luc took up most of her time, energy and anxiety. She had no time to despair or think upon the past, for she fell into bed exhausted each evening, to be awakened by Luc at least a few times during the course of the night. She would have had no idea of the month, or even the season, if it had not been for Sister Paulette's mention of the convent preparations for All Hallows'.

When she realized it was almost November, Sara knew she could not stay with Reverend Mother and the sisters for much longer. No matter how much sympathy they felt for her and Luc, they would soon ask her to leave. Sara couldn't bear to think of life on her own with Luc. What if something happened to her? What would become of him? Where before she'd found the convent confining, now she didn't know how she could leave its safety. Sara dragged her heels on the question for several weeks until an unlikely turn of events made her departure not only imaginable but necessary. In late November, while Sara was helping Marie with her laundry, Marie announced that she had received a letter from Adeline's Uncle Philippe.

Sara did not understand. Was this Philippe Lemieux? Wasn't he Adeline's father?

Adeline clapped her hands and spun around. She peppered Marie with questions. "When? Do you think he'll bring presents, Maman?"

"He's coming in three weeks." Marie chided her daughter for her impertinence. "Perhaps he will bring a present, but we shan't ask him. It would be impolite."

"Yes, Maman." Adeline snatched the letter from Marie's hands and pretended to read it. Marie returned to the laundry, which she'd hung on a line above the wood-burning stove. She slipped two clothespins onto her belt, removed the hanging sheet, shook it out and folded it into a neat square, with Sara's help. The cotton warmed Sara's hands.

Marie explained, "Monsieur Lemieux has been our most generous benefactor. He takes good care of Adeline."

Sara was curious, but spoke carefully. "Yes, of course. Um, forgive me, but I wasn't aware that you had any family in America."

"He's not my family, but he is the brother of Adeline's father. When her father abandoned me, Philippe took me under his protection and brought me to New York."

Sara could not help herself—this was all too strange. She waited until Adeline had disappeared into the bedroom before asking, "Where is Adeline's father?"

Marie hesitated before answering. "In France. He married into a family with land." She lowered her voice to prevent Adeline from hearing. "It was apparently not enough for him to be in line to inherit his father's wine brokerage. He wanted land as well. That's why he betrayed me. He had promised to marry me, but it was a lie," Marie said, her voice tightening.

Sara could not believe it. She had thought Philippe was Marie's seducer when, all along, it had been Bastien. To conceal her surprise, Sara knelt down to cover Luc, who was dozing in his Moses basket. "Where is Monsieur Lemieux visiting from?" Sara asked.

"He has a farm in California, and he is coming to New York via Chicago on business. He says he has some news to share with us. I don't believe all of it is good, though. The tone of his letter was rather serious."

Serious indeed. He had probably received word of his brother's death. "Did you ever consider going with him to California?" Sara asked.

"No. I was still with child when we arrived here at the convent. From what I gather, he gave Reverend Mother a substantial sum to look after me. He stayed in New York for the rest of my pregnancy, but I insisted after Adeline was born that he make his way out West, which had always been his dream. He had sacrificed a great deal for us, and I was quite content not to travel any more. The thought of long wagon and train rides at that point was less than appealing."

"I see." Sara's mind swirled.

Marie finished folding the last garment. "Monsieur Lemieux is a good man. I am grateful that Adeline has such a gentleman to admire."

Sara was relieved when Adeline, twirling around the room, broke into the conversation. "May I sing Uncle Philippe a new song?"

"We'll see, my dear. Now, I'm sure mademoiselle has better things to do than help us with our chores." Marie rose from the settee. "Thank you for your help." She squeezed Sara's hand slightly. "And for listening."

"Of course." Sara was happy to help her friend. She wrapped a shawl around her shoulders, picked up Luc, still sleeping in his basket, and stepped out into the brisk winter air.

There was no entrance to the main convent from Marie's

apartment in the back, so Sara walked down the narrow alley leading to the front of the building. These new revelations confounded her. About several things, however, Sara was very clear. She could not return to France, for she might be caught and executed. She could not stay in New York and wait for Lemieux to discover her. Lastly, no matter what the old priest had said, there would never be an apology from her lips. The price had already been paid: her innocent sister for that ruthless son of a bitch.

As she thought of Bastien, bile began to rise in her throat, and her fists clenched in anger. No, even if her actions landed her squarely in hell, she would make sure she and Luc were taken care of here on earth.

Sara resolved to depart at once.

Sara's anxiety grew every day she remained at the convent. If Philippe met her and discovered who she was, who knew what would happen to her—or, worse, to Luc? Though running might be a coward's way, she could not risk his future.

Sara knew she must go where she could find work. She could not cook or even sew adequately. She was a vintner's daughter, and the only work she knew well was grape farming. Winter was almost upon the wine country in upstate New York. The journey to California would be much more difficult, but she had read that the milder climate and terroir were exceptional and that the fruit farming was very successful. California was a large state. They should be able to avoid Philippe Lemieux. She counted the money she had remaining: $135. Who knew when she would next have the means to travel? She would seize the opportunity now and head west to Napa.

Sara purchased a train ticket to Chicago on the New York Central Railroad. Once in Chicago, she could buy a ticket to San Francisco on the Southern Pacific Line. From what Sara could ascertain from her map, San Francisco was the closest major city to the Napa Valley, and the southern route was her best option during the winter months. The entire rail journey would last about ten days, with stopovers in Chicago and Santa Fe, during which time Sara would purchase milk and supplies for the next leg of the trip.

Before Sara left, she wrote a long letter to Maman explaining what had transpired in New York. She apologized for leaving France, and expressed her deep pain over the loss of Lydia, her mother's favorite. Sara had gained a new compassion for her mother now that she had experienced firsthand the demands of motherhood. She promised to write again when she was settled, and expressed hope that once she had established herself she could send for Maman and they would be together again. In her last line, she begged her mother not to tell a soul of her whereabouts or her grandson's, for fear that Bastien's father would try to find them. Jacques could know they were safe, but no one else. She instructed her mother to burn the letter once she read it. She almost wished her mother a happy Christmas, but stopped short. Sara remembered the horror she had felt when Lydia died, and imagined what her mother would feel when she read that Lydia was gone: disbelief, anguish, frustration, guilt. Holiday wishes would not lessen her pain. Sara signed the letter with love, and dropped her pen. She would mail it from Chicago.

Sara made her final preparations for the journey. She packed Lydia's well-worn shoes, a size too small for Sara, and her Bible, which Luc would want one day. For Luc, she packed cotton flannels, safety pins, a knitted wool soaker to contain his waste, soap and a small bag of burnt flour for his rashes. She wrapped it all up in a wool blanket and placed the bundle in the satchel along with twenty cans of condensed milk. These supplies left little room for her own belongings, so she decided she would wear, under her traveling dress, her work dress, apron, three pairs of undergarments and wool stockings. She had no coat, but hoped that the layers would keep her warm during the winter weeks of travel. She could use her shawl as a sling to bind Luc to her chest.

Saying farewell to the nuns, and to Marie and Adeline, proved heart-wrenching. They had been loyal and amiable companions over the past six months, and Sara felt as if her departure were a betrayal in some way. They promised their prayers, and Sara promised to write when she reached her destination. Out of an abundance of caution, Sara said she was headed to upstate New York.

As Reverend Mother handed little Luc up into the carriage, Sara was surprised to see that her eyes were puffy and red. Right before the door closed, Marie hoisted herself up on the carriage step and kissed both Sara's cheeks, tears shining in her eyes. She squeezed a small velvet purse into her hand and whispered, "The one who gave me this loves me—loves both of us—very much. *Bonne chance, mon amie.*"

The carriage lurched forward, bound for the station. Someone who "loves both of us"— what in the world had Marie meant?

Sara clasped the purse Marie had given her and felt something small and hard inside it. She opened it and shook it gently. A hand-carved cross of dark-stained wood fell into her palm. Her hand flew to the identical cross that hung around her neck, given to her by Jacques last Christmas. Had Marie seen it? Did she know Sara's true identity? She must—what else could she have meant? Sara panicked, her guilt washing over her anew.

Bonne chance, Marie had wished her, the same words Sara had spoken to her father the last time she saw him. Marie had implied she would protect Sara's secret. Sara could only hope this was true.

Mercifully, the rocking of the carriage on the way to Grand Central lulled Luc to sleep. They passed Lydia's unmarked gravesite, but did not stop. Lydia's heart would always be with her son, and Sara's duty now was to take infinite and fastidious care of him. She was tired of saying goodbye to family and friends. She resolved that when they reached California, she and Luc would stay put. Then she would form a plan to take back Saint Martin. Although there was sorrow in her heart, Sara was excited for the new life that lay ahead of them in Napa.

CHAPTER 11

Ambition

William Briggs, Esquire, sat behind his oversized, leather-inlaid mahogany desk and fussed with the stack of documents in front of him. The attorney's face was gaunt, and under his pale eyes was a sliver of shadow, which hinted at a less than perfect night's sleep. His nails were trimmed, Philippe observed, and immaculate—absent of any sign of manual labor, unlike his own. Before heading east, he had scrubbed his hands with a horsehair brush to remove the wine stains from his palms and fingernails. Philippe imagined the greatest injury this man had ever confronted within the confines of his office was a vicious paper cut.

That thought made Philippe smile. Thank God he didn't spend his days behind a desk dealing in legal jargon. He would go mad. Even now, as he waited, he shifted in his chair with a restless energy he couldn't quite account for. Philippe eyed Briggs and thought, For God's sake, man, let's get on with it.

As if he sensed Philippe's impatience, Briggs sat up in his chair, dropped his monocle and began.

"Your father suspects murder."

Philippe had not expected this. "Why?"

"I don't know how to say this delicately. Your brother's body was found burned in the fire. However, there was a wound to the left side of his neck that is thought to be the true cause of his death. The fire, we believe, was deliberately set to hide murder."

Philippe felt a charge of adrenaline throughout his body. He stared at Briggs. Bastien was not well liked by many. But would his brother's behavior really have incited someone to murder him? Philippe's voice faltered. "And the weapon? What about his wife? Was she found with him?"

"There was no weapon found, not a knife, not anything. Mrs. Lemieux was originally thought to have perished in the fire, but her body was not recovered. Upon further investigation, it was discovered that she and her sister were missing. They haven't been seen since that night."

"They could have run away on foot. Made it to the river and stowed away on a barge or something," Philippe theorized, his thoughts spiraling.

"But she was heavy with child."

Philippe hadn't known this, but felt a mixture of suspicion and sympathy toward Bastien's wife. "You'd be surprised what a woman can do if she sets her mind to it."

"Jealousy?" Briggs sounded unconvinced.

"I don't know." Philippe drummed his fingertips against the arm of his chair. "My brother was certainly known to enjoy his diversions."

"There's no evidence that she did anything."

"Of course not. No one can find her. Did you talk to the gendarmes? What about this sister? What about the foreman, Jacques Chevreau? Where is the girls' mother?" To Philippe, it sounded like a sloppy investigation.

"They have been questioned and have denied any knowledge of the ladies' whereabouts. The mother was quite distraught, understandably, and appears to believe that the wife and sister may have also died in the fire."

Yes, understandably. But for once he agreed with his father. Something was amiss. The girls had always seemed congenial enough. He remembered the younger one better—what was her name?—with skinned knees and a defiant tilt to her chin. But girls grow into calculating women, and who knows what could have happened?

"Are there any other suspects? Bastien was not a popular figure. Any business associates who would have had a motive?"

"He had gambling debts, but that alone is not a motive. In fact, his debtors would have wanted to keep him alive to—" Briggs lowered his voice. "Forgive me, but . . ."

"But what?"

Briggs exhaled. "You should know that there has also been talk of suicide."

Philippe shook his head. Clearly, Briggs had never met

Bastien. "Mr. Briggs, that is not possible. First of all, if my brother planned to end his life, he would have done it with a shotgun, not by stabbing himself in the neck. Second, he thought too highly of himself to end his own life, no matter how great his debts were." Philippe leaned toward the solicitor. "You see, Mr. Briggs, I regret to say that my brother was indeed a scoundrel."

Briggs shifted back in his seat and interlaced his fingers tightly. "Be that as it may, Mr. Lemieux, your father has decided to offer a bounty of five hundred dollars for the capture of either Mrs. Lemieux or Miss Thibault. You see, they've exhausted all leads in France and he suspects they've come here. He wants retribution, and he also wants his grandchild, who, by our estimates, would have been born sometime in September."

Philippe was surprised his father would go to such expense to track down his son's killers, if that's what they were. Then it dawned on him. His father wanted custody of the child, presuming it was a boy. Bastien's legitimate son would inherit half of the Lemieux business and land holdings.

"What makes him believe they've come to America?"

"It's in the latest gendarme report." Briggs pointed at the papers on his desk. "When they searched the stables the next morning, two horses and a wagon were missing. They showed up later that afternoon, with Chevreau driving them."

"Where did he say he'd been?"

"In Tours, but the horses were too winded and tired for that to be the case, or so the officer thought. When they searched the wagon they found a soiled lace handkerchief—it looked to be blood. Chevreau claimed he had a bloody nose on the way home.

They think he's hiding something. Maybe he took the girls to Orléans, and from there they caught a train to Paris and on to Le Havre. The timing works. He could reach Orléans and be back by the following afternoon. In addition, your father sent an emissary to check the passenger lists of the ships leaving from Le Havre and Nantes on the days following your brother's death."

"But they wouldn't be foolish enough to use their real names. It's like looking for a needle in a haystack, is it not?"

"Perhaps, but apparently they found something." Briggs grabbed the papers, licked his finger and peeled them back one by one until he found what he was looking for. "Two women, Lydia and Sara de Coursey, sailed from Le Havre on May eighteenth. It looks like they did use their Christian names."

"And they traveled to America?" A long journey for an expectant mother, Philippe thought. They must be guilty of killing Bastien if they fled here.

"To this very city, aboard *La Champagne*."

"I'll be damned." Philippe was incredulous. He'd missed them by a few months. Or maybe they were still here. "Did you check the Ellis Island records? Did they list a specific destination?"

"We just learned about all this two days ago. I've instructed the men I've hired to search for the girls' names in the ship's manifest."

"Who does this type of thing?" It sounded shady to Philippe.

"Bounty hunters—ruffians. But they always get the job done."

"They will bring them back alive, will they not, so we can question them?"

"Of course." Briggs waved his hand nonchalantly. "But more than likely a bit . . . bruised."

Philippe nodded. "Sounds reasonable."

Briggs shifted the conversation to the Saint Martin property. He gave Philippe a full accounting of what remained and asked him to sign the documents that would transfer Saint Martin and all the estate's debts from his father to him. Philippe asked for the evening to review the paperwork. His father might just be pulling him back in to clean up Bastien's mess, or the acquisition of Saint Martin could be a real opportunity. Briggs gave him a stack of documents: a copy of the deed, inventory lists, written interviews and the official gendarme report. With the expectation of meeting the next day, Briggs bade Philippe *bonne chance.*

With his mind reeling, Philippe decided to focus on the afternoon he had planned with Marie and Adeline. He walked slowly through the city streets toward the convent, paying little mind to the shouts of the scuttling street vendors. He was consumed by the knowledge that he'd have to impart the news of his brother's death to Marie. What would she think?

Bastien had kept quiet about his relationship with Marie Chevreau and had certainly never acknowledged Adeline. Philippe assumed that everyone back home in Vouvray believed the child to be his own and that he had taken Marie to America to live a life of sin. He didn't care; he knew the truth. Philippe remembered how Bastien had pursued Marie relentlessly and even promised her marriage. Her parents were outraged when Bastien did not make good on his offer once she was pregnant. When the Lemieux family discovered the truth from Marie's parents, Philippe, disgusted by his brother's boorish behavior, took pity on the girl and decided that he must help her. Her prospects for marriage had been ruined. What would become of her?

Philippe realized that Marie could be his ticket to a new life, away from his father. He had stood in her parents' humble parlor and offered Marie the chance to come to America. He'd been surprised when Marie jumped at the opportunity to leave France. Even though Pierre and Mim Chevreau had objected to their daughter leaving them before she gave birth, Marie had insisted. She did not want to shame her family any further, she had said. With promises to return one day, Marie set off with Philippe.

Finding a suitable situation for Marie in a convent in New York City had delayed his journey west by six months. His only communication to his family that year was a note letting his father know the two had arrived safely and giving him the address on Mott Street where they could be contacted temporarily. Philippe stayed in New York until the baby was born. When he had first seen the pink-faced girl, he knew he'd done the right thing. His mother certainly would have approved, even if his father had no sense of responsibility toward his only grandchild.

Philippe had wondered if Marie would want the Lemieux name for his niece, but Marie refused. Adeline, the child's Christian name, would go well with her own surname of Chevreau. It was a proud French name, she had told him. Marie explained that because she did not have a hold on Bastien's affections and he did not acknowledge their child, she could not in good conscience lay any claim to the Lemieux name or fortune. Marie's character had grown in motherhood: she was now a strong, independent and, despite her youthful indiscretion with Bastien, morally scrupulous woman. Philippe admired her courage.

Over Marie's protestations, Philippe had given her a portion

187

of his funds to cover her starting expenses and promised to send more. With the support of the convent nuns, Marie apprenticed to train as a midwife. Satisfied that Marie and Adeline would be safe and well cared for in New York, Philippe set out for California's wine country to make a name for himself in America.

It felt strange to be walking alongside the convent, down the long alleyway to Marie's apartment. With its impenetrable stone walls, this place had always looked to him more like a medieval fortress than a nunnery. Philippe checked his pocket for the tickets he had tucked away there and quickly smoothed his hair before knocking.

Adeline bobbed in her seat, clapping her hands with glee. In her excitement, she dropped the freshly shelled peanuts she had clenched in her fist. Philippe didn't mind. He was happy to continue in the post of nut sheller, and had spent the better part of an hour cracking and serving peanuts to the little one. Philippe took more pleasure in watching Adeline squeal and giggle at the Irish tenor, the juggling monkeys and the clumsy muscleman than in watching the acts himself. He could not remember when he had last laughed so hard.

The Union Square Theatre was a marvel. Its stained-glass lobby was teeming with costumed players, all eager to take your fifty cents in return for what they promised would be a great spectacle. A statuesque moor, dressed in the Turkish style, complete with curled-toe slippers and silken turban, had ushered them inside the building and directed them to the gallery. Adeline could not take her eyes off the purple ostrich plume that was fastened to his turban with a huge brooch made of faux rubies and diamonds. "Look how it sparkles, Maman," she had exclaimed, her eyes as wide as saucers. The threesome took their seats in the lowest level, just to the right of the rounded stage. Gas lamps burned brightly all around, illuminating the stage and the tall walls of the theatre. Two levels of ornate box seating framed the sides of the stage. The vaulted gold-leaf ceiling reminded Philippe of the dome that topped his favorite cathedral, in Reims.

The vaudeville was quite a change from the bawdy acts he'd witnessed the last time he was here, over three years ago, with a group of city wine merchants who insisted on bringing him to a burlesque show. The garlic-smelling, smoke-filled, foot-stamping gallery Philippe remembered was populated today with midday shoppers, mostly women from all classes who were happy to remove their hats so as to not obstruct the view of their fellow patrons. Now it smelled of roasted nuts and cherry soda, a welcome change from tobacco and sweat. Nonetheless, at either side of the gallery three hulking bouncers stood ready to whisk any unruly patron away at a moment's notice. With this crowd, they'd be more likely to bounce a cuckolded husband than a drunk.

He looked over at Marie, who was also caught up in the whirlwind of pageantry on stage. He had forgotten how strik-ing she was. How foolish Bastien had been to toss her aside. She was smart, hardworking and attractive. He wondered if she still cared at all for Bastien and how she would react when she learned of his death. He would have to tell her soon enough. He

189

shook the thought off, determined to enjoy his few hours with Marie and Adeline.

They followed their afternoon of vaudeville with sodas and candy at the fountain on Fourteenth Street. Later that evening, in their apartment, Adeline squeezed the fair-haired doll that Philippe had given her and asked politely, with her childish lisp, "May I give you a good-night kiss, Uncle?"

"Right here, if you would." Philippe tapped his finger to his cheek. Adeline raised herself on tiptoes.

"Off to bed, my love," Marie nodded to Adeline.

"And thank you, Uncle, for all the fun!"

"You are most welcome. I hope you will convince your mother to bring you to visit me on my farm in California sometime."

"Oh, yes! Maman, can we go?"

"I promise to think about it, Adeline." With that, Adeline scooted off to bed.

Marie sat down on the ottoman across from Philippe and sighed. "This has been such a wonderful day. I so needed to laugh. The winter days have been long . . . though I've managed to keep busy with my work."

"I'm glad I could offer a little diversion for you and Adeline. I have so enjoyed seeing you both again. It's been far too long. And Adeline—she seems to be thriving."

"Yes, thank you. But then, children are always more resilient than we adults, are they not?"

"I suppose so." Philippe did not know how to broach the subject of Bastien, and racked his brain for another topic.

"Come to California with me. It's so bleak and depressing and crowded here, and Adeline would love the farm—the wide open space to roam. We could eventually send her to the city for schooling. I'm sure the town's in need of a midwife."

Marie shook her head. "You've been generous enough. Besides, you have your own life to lead. Eventually, I'm sure you'll want to marry and have a family, and we wouldn't want to stand in the way of that." Marie's hint was sisterly.

"You would never stand in the way," Philippe replied earnestly. "You know how important Adeline's well-being is to me—and yours, too. I would feel better having you closer to me, so I could keep an eye on you," Philippe teased. Marie was more than a friend to him; she was family.

"We're grateful for your kindness, but you are not responsible for us. I am." She hesitated just a moment before straightening her back and continuing, "I was hoping to ask you for something, a loan, which I'd repay over time."

"Of course. What is it?"

"I want to study midwifery at the Women's Medical College at the New York Infirmary. It's an elite program, and I need to improve my knowledge." Marie's voice trailed off, and her eyes wandered to a dark painting of the Madonna that hung somewhat menacingly on the parlor wall. When she turned back to face him, Philippe was startled to see her eyes reddened and shiny. "You see, I lost a woman, a friend, this past summer in childbirth." She was distraught. "I've gone over and over it in my mind, trying to figure out what went wrong . . . what I could have done to save her. She was young—it was her first child. It devastated all of us."

"But these things happen. They are not always in your control."

"Yes, but I need to study and keep learning. You may laugh at me, and I daresay I've been afraid to even say the words aloud until now, but I want to become a doctor someday. I really think I have the strength of mind for it. Would you loan me the money for tuition?"

"Absolutely not." Philippe gave her a generous smile. "I insist it will be a gift."

"No, it will be a *loan*. I have some money saved, but the balance I'd need is five hundred dollars over two years. That includes textbooks."

Philippe took some cash from his wallet. "This is half, and I'll send the remainder in a few months' time. I'm glad you asked."

"Thank you, Philippe. I'm truly grateful."

Philippe looked down at the cracks in the wood floor. Now he could no longer delay the inevitable. He knew it was tactless to move from such a hopeful topic to one so upsetting, but he didn't know how else to proceed. When he spoke next, his voice was low and thoughtful.

"Marie?"

She must have seen the distress on his face, for she leaned in closer. He took her hands in his.

"It's Bastien. I'm afraid . . . he is dead." Philippe took a deep breath and continued, "It happened in May."

Marie placed her hand over her mouth and, rising, moved wordlessly across the room to peer out the half-shuttered window. Her back was rigid and she stood motionless for several minutes. Philippe did not dare interrupt. When she finally spoke, her voice cracked.

"How?"

"We don't know. Murder, perhaps. There was a fire, but he was found with a wound to his neck. We've initiated an investigation." Philippe's voice was flat. It was still unreal to him.

Marie swept across the room to sit down across from him. Her delicate features were creased with pain. She placed her hand on his arm sympathetically. "I'm so sorry, Philippe. How are you managing?"

Philippe looked down and ran his thumb along his wallet's worn brown leather strap. He was not prepared to share his emotions—they were too complex, too raw. Marie must have sensed this, for she withdrew her hand and did not press him further.

"What about his family—his wife?"

Philippe looked up. "You knew he had married?"

"Yes, my uncle wrote me in April," she said slowly. "Uncle Jacques said that he was kept on to help your brother after the marriage."

"Bastien's wife and her sister are missing. Madame Thibault is still in Vouvray, living in the gatehouse of Saint Martin. Neither she nor Jacques knows their whereabouts, apparently. They may have perished—or they may have murdered him."

"Is that what you think?" Marie exclaimed. "Why?"

"I don't know. To escape something, perhaps," Philippe ventured tentatively.

"His viciousness, no doubt." Marie's sharp tone startled

Philippe. She exhaled. "I'm sorry, Philippe. I'm sorry for you and your father, and I'm sorry that Bastien abandoned Adeline. Or rather, that her father was not the man you are. But, Philippe," she spoke intently, "that is where my regret ends."

"I know. However, my father, in his grief, has seen fit to offer a bounty for the capture of the Thibault sisters. You see, we think they've come to America."

"How do you know their actions were not justified?" Marie's tone was mildly combative. Philippe realized that he'd just reopened a wound that had barely had time to heal. Nonetheless, Bastien was his brother, and it was his duty to set things right.

"Does anyone deserve to be killed in cold blood?" he asked mildly.

Marie was silent.

"I have to find them, for my own peace of mind."

"How will you find them? Do you have any leads?"

"Yes, one. Apparently, Lydia and Sara *de Coursey* sailed from Le Havre to New York in May. Bastien's wife is Lydia, as you may know, and her sister's name is Sara."

Marie moved toward the window. When she turned back she had transformed her face into a serene mask. Philippe studied her with concern. Perhaps the news was just too much. Or perhaps she knew something she didn't want to tell him.

"Our attorney is checking the ship records at Ellis Island to see if we can find an address," he said.

"And how long will that take?"

"A few weeks, no more."

"But you leave in a few days for Boston, no?"

"Yes, and then back home via Chicago. My attorney will forward the information to the bounty hunters and they'll take it from there."

"Bounty hunters? Isn't that a little much?" Philippe saw fear flicker in her eyes.

"We need to find them, Marie. Even if we don't press charges, we need to discover if the child was born alive. My father intended Saint Martin for Bastien's family. The baby would have been born in early September, by Madame Thibault's estimation."

Marie crossed her arms and her shoulders hunched in concentration. "And what have you learned from my uncle?"

"He has been questioned. When Jacques awoke, the house was on fire. He saw the flames and rang the bell for help. He searched the upstairs bedrooms before the heat forced him out, but he didn't find anyone." Philippe hesitated for a moment. "Tell me something, Marie. Is your uncle a trustworthy man?"

Marie's features softened as she faced Philippe. "He is the best of men." Her eyes, a deep mahogany, widened with feeling. "As are you." She moved to kiss him on the cheek. "Thank you again for the outing. Adeline and I enjoyed spending time with you."

"You are most welcome." He wanted to offer more, but couldn't find the words. Instead, he stood and took her small hands in his. "It is good to see you again."

He collected his belongings and moved toward the door.

"And Marie?"

"Hmm?"

"You would tell me if you knew anything about the Thibault girls, wouldn't you?" He was now certain she was hiding something.

"Of course I would. I'll ask around and see what I can find out."

"That would be most helpful, thank you."

"Philippe?"

He eyed her speculatively.

"Prepare yourself. Some stones are better left unturned."

He nodded, but in his mind, Philippe dismissed her warning. He would find them, with or without her help. "Just remember, Marie, they're involved in this somehow, and I doubt they are innocents." He inhaled deeply, trying to shake off his frustration and remember instead their pleasant day together.

He donned his hat and spoke kindly. "*Adieu*, Marie. Tell Adeline that I'll write as soon as I can."

"God bless, Philippe. Safe journey home."

Philippe was exhausted. He shut the door to his small hotel room on the Lower East Side, and dropped down onto the narrow bed. He squeezed the bridge of his nose between his finger and thumb and then rubbed the inner corners of his eyes. His head throbbed with a dull pain. It was a lot to absorb in one day.

Listening to what Briggs had said about Bastien had made it all real. Philippe realized that when he'd read his father's letter in June, he'd not actually thought of his brother as being *dead*. He had not allowed himself to feel it. Here, alone in his rented room, the weight crashed down upon him. The truth was that he grieved for his brother. For all Bastien's wretched behavior, now there would never be a chance for Bastien to change, to become a better brother, a better man. Above all, Philippe was angry that someone had killed his brother in cold blood and just run off, taking with her all the chances that would never be. The injustice gnawed at his gut.

Philippe let out a sigh. As if that all weren't enough, now he had to figure out what to do with the land. Christ, Bastien had made a mess of things. From what Philippe remembered, Saint Martin had been fairly prosperous and had produced a decent white under Thibault's stewardship. Now it was plagued with debt and the main dwelling had been destroyed in the fire. It appeared to Philippe that Bastien had given up long before his death. With a pang of sorrow, he wondered why.

Philippe sprang from the bed and made his way across the cramped quarters to the desk. He began his examination of the papers Briggs had given him: the newly drafted deed naming Philippe as the owner of Saint Martin, signed by his father, and the list of what had survived the fire. The watch house was intact, but only a stone skeleton of the main house remained. All the valuable furnishings and draperies had been destroyed. Copper pots, a curio cabinet and three glass panes had been salvaged. Two horses, one wagon, a mule, two pigs and five chickens. That was all.

What was impressive was that only the hectare of land surrounding the house had been damaged by the fire, and over sixty percent of the vines were unscathed and thriving. According to Briggs's scrawl at the bottom of the inventory list, thirteen barrels of wine sat in the cave, unsold at the time of the fire. They would fetch about 700 francs. Philippe read on. The estate's debts, most of them a result of his brother's gambling, totaled 3,800 francs, according to Chevreau's tally. Bastien's cash holdings added up to a paltry 990 francs, so the burden was considerable. He doubted his father would finance the deficit. Philippe sensed that his father had transferred the land, or, in reality, Bastien's debts, to him so that he could use his own resources to fund the search for his son's killer. Retribution was already exacting a heavy price.

Slowly, his mind began to form the framework of a plan. He now had to manage the production, marketing and distribution of wines in both France and America—and at the same time. Still, the pieces began to fall together, and within a half hour, he had organized his ideas on the back of the official gendarme report.

The business side of Philippe's trip east had been a moderate success so far. With Lamont's endorsement, he had convinced three other Carneros wine men to join him in his endeavor. Philippe had left Napa with two hundred thousand bottles of their best chardonnay, zinfandel and sparkling wines. In Los Angeles and St. Louis, he had sold nearly half of the bottles, at an average price of twenty-three cents per gallon. It was satisfying knowing that he was generating a larger profit for his fellow California vintners back home than the Wine Association had in years. And this was only the beginning. He had also secured orders for another twenty-five thousand gallons to be delivered after the next bottling. He planned to spend the next few days calling on New York merchants to forge relationships with them. On his way home, he would stop in Boston, Chicago and other cities to sell more bottles and secure more future orders. Next year, he would try his luck in New Orleans.

His mind began to break free from its earlier malaise. Ambition edged forward to inspire the hint of a smile on his face. Saint Martin, a sizable vineyard by Loire standards, had just fallen into his lap. Combined with Eagle's Run, his was now one of the largest holdings of vineyards that he knew of: 233 acres of fruitful vines. It was only a matter of time and persistence before the Lemieux wines would dominate on both continents.

He would sign the papers tomorrow.

CHAPTER 12

Napa

The exhilaration Sara felt as she disembarked from the steam train at the Napa depot was only mildly tempered by fear: here she was, arriving in a new city, not knowing a soul and with only fifty-four dollars to her name. Her limited means were the most obvious concern, but there was an even more pressing matter at hand: what would her new name be?

She had thought about this endlessly during this final leg of their journey. She could continue to use the name de Coursey, but Philippe Lemieux had just been to New York and visited Marie Chevreau. What if Marie had unwittingly, or, heaven forbid, intentionally, mentioned her? If Lemieux cared enough to check the ship's manifest, he would find their names there; even more incriminating, Lydia's pregnancy would be recorded. Sara needed to manufacture a new surname—again. This was the last time, though, she promised herself.

Sara decided to take her middle name, Landry. Sara Landry. Perhaps it was paranoid, but Jacques had put the fear of God in her with his talk of the guillotine. She'd never truly thought it would come to that, but so many terrible things had transpired over the last year, how could she not anticipate the worst? Sara Landry and Luc Landry. So it would have to be, for their shared protection. At least it was a pleasant name to say, and easy for the Americans to pronounce. No one would suspect that Sara Landry was a Thibault, of the Vouvray Thibaults. No one would suspect that the boy she cared for and now considered to be her own son, was not. Even Sara had to admit how strange it all sounded. In her wildest imaginings, she could never have envisioned her life taking these turns.

Sara stepped off the wooden platform of the train station and down into the dusty road. The afternoon winds kicked up, and silt swirled around her and the baby. Luc squeezed his eyelids shut, balling up his pudgy fists against his face while he squealed with displeasure. Once Sara had wiped his eyes clean with the sleeve of her shirtwaist, she propped him on her hip with one arm and picked up her satchel with the other. It was sunny out, but colder than Sara had expected. On a bench behind the station, Sara set her satchel down and unlatched it with one hand. She reached in for Luc's worn gray blanket while balancing him precariously on her thigh. Luc wriggled violently until his legs were free of Sara's hold. He would have slipped to the ground had Sara not scooped his legs back up and held him tightly against her chest.

Motherhood was more challenging than she had ever imagined. Now she could add the dubious distinction of contortionist to her list of newly discovered talents.

The steam train roared to life again, startling both of them. Luc erupted into hysterical crying. To make matters worse, the iron horse left a billowing cloud of black smoke in its wake, causing both of them to cough. Trying to soothe Luc, Sara headed away from the commotion, to a quiet patch of grass nearby. Sara sat on her bag on the parched grass, and rocked Luc to quiet him. She watched the train until its caboose disappeared from sight, then looked down at her little cherub. He was calm now and his eyes were closed, but he still inhaled sharply and sniffled. His tiny lips quivered slightly, forming a perfect pink bow. Sara couldn't think of anything more beautiful. She kissed his forehead and murmured into his smooth hair, "Welcome to California."

It was half past three in the afternoon, and the streets were fairly empty. She walked up Soscol Avenue and then headed west toward Main Street. She would need to find some inexpensive lodging. The fifty-four dollars she had left would last them about a month, if she was frugal. Because it was late in the day, she would find a hotel room for the night. Tomorrow, she would look for suitable lodgings to rent and begin her search for work.

The town's buildings were modern compared to what Sara was used to. Most were made of freshly painted wood, not stone or brick. The sunlit streets were wide enough for a wagon to turn around, not dark and narrow like the streets of the Lower East Side. As she made her way down Main Street, she heard the pleasant chatter of pedestrians in English, French, Italian and German, and the whistle of a steamboat docking at the nearby riverfront. Sara made a mental note of the places she'd need to return to: the Semorile Sons' grocery store, the gothic-style Catholic Church, the hardware store. When she reached the three-story Napa Hotel, she was relieved to find they had rooms to let, and at a rate she could afford. Once settled in her room, she changed Luc's diaper and fashioned a makeshift bed for him from a spare quilt she found in the closet. Then she strapped him tightly to her chest and made her way to the grocery store.

She had hoped to slip in unnoticed, but the store was small and surprisingly busy. To make matters worse, the proprietress was a stout, loud-mouthed busybody who had decided that Sara would serve as her entertainment for the afternoon. After introducing herself, the shopkeeper barraged Sara with rapid-fire questions.

"The name's Molly. Where'd you come from? How long you staying? Married? Widowed? I don't see a ring, but that doesn't mean anything these days. Need milk for the baby? Place to stay? Job? Family in these parts?" She finally came up for air and glared at Sara expectantly.

Sara felt as though she'd been riddled with bullets. While she understood almost every question, she didn't possess the English vocabulary to formulate coherent responses. Her eventual reply was heavily accented and brief.

"Sara and Luc Landry from France." She ignored the question about her marital status. "Milk?"

The woman smiled and came out from behind the counter

to show Sara where the milk, diapers and baby supplies were located.

"Thank you." Fresh milk would be a treat for Luc tonight. She placed a bottle into her basket and continued. "Apartments?"

"Well, there's best and then there's the cheapest. Which do you want?"

Sara was confused. She pulled out a dollar bill with one hand, and held up five fingers, indicating she could afford five dollars per week. The woman shook her head and made a clucking sound inside her cheek. "Here's what you'll be wantin', honey—at least until you find a job." She hauled down from the top shelf a thick, folded piece of cloth and placed it at Sara's feet. "Tent. Pitch it down by the river."

Sara just stared.

"Now, let's set about finding you some work. Seamstress, are you?"

Sara's brow furrowed with frustration. Molly pantomimed sewing with a needle and thread.

"Ah—*non.*"

"Waitress?" Sara didn't have a clue what that meant.

"*Non.*"

Molly threw her palms out. "What kind of work do you do?"

Sara thought carefully. "I. Grow. Grapes. *Vin?*"

"Oh." The woman seemed genuinely disappointed by Sara's response, but she was trying to be kind. It occurred to Sara to have a little fun to keep Molly's interest.

"And I dance burlesque." Sara had lost nearly everything, but not her sense of humor.

Molly let out a gasp, her lips pursed, her eyes bulging. Her face turned crimson. Sara thought the woman might faint dead away from the shock.

Sara's carefully arranged face crumpled with laughter. "*Non, non!*" She waved her hands. Sara could have sworn she heard a giggle erupt from the other side of the store, somewhere behind a shelf of canned goods.

Molly's face returned to its usual color, but her breathing was still heavy. She eyed Sara cautiously and grinned nervously, not yet convinced that Sara had been joking. After she regained her composure, Molly shook her head and looked down at the tent on the floor between them. "The Chinese and Italians do the pickin' and prunin' around here."

As Molly began to turn away, she offered one last piece of advice. "What you need is to pitch your tent down by the river. The Chinese will show you where the work is." With a quick bob of the head, Molly turned to search the store for her next victim.

After a restless night and an unsatisfying breakfast of stale bread and canned peaches she'd purchased at the grocery store, Sara packed up her satchel, figured out how to carry the heavy cloth tent she'd purchased, and set out with Luc to find work. She followed the west bank of the Napa River south. After a mile or so, she detected the faint odor of smoke. She walked a few more yards and caught sight of a clearing with a fire at its centre. Narrow ribbons of smoke circled upwards through the dense shadow of oaks before evaporating into the veil of morning fog draped over the trees.

Sara walked toward the fire quietly. She heard laughter and the low talk of women and children in an unfamiliar tongue, which she guessed must be a Chinese dialect. When she entered the small clearing, the women halted their conversation and stared at her, their faces cool and suspicious. Their attire was like nothing Sara had ever seen: ankle-length, wide-sleeved robes, almost like dressing gowns, tied at the waist. Their hair was slicked back into a tight knot at the crown of their heads. The children hovered near their mothers, dressed in similar garments with brightly colored wool caps. There were no men or teenage children in sight. Sara presumed they had already started their work for the day in the vineyards.

The women looked Sara up and down, nodding, then returned to their cooking and weaving, unconcerned. Sara would have lost her nerve then and there if a slight woman had not gestured toward her with delicate fingers and then pointed to the fire. She said something Sara could not understand, but her tone was friendly, and Sara nodded and smiled. She cleared a space for Sara and Luc next to her and offered them a wooden bowl of what looked to Sara like hot water with roots floating in it. Sara didn't know what it was, but, not wanting to be rude, she ventured a spoonful. It really didn't taste much like anything. Regardless, the simple broth warmed her to the core and she was grateful for it. She even managed to spoon some into Luc's mouth.

The same woman offered Luc something runny and brown from her own bowl. She must have sensed Sara's hesitancy, because she answered her unspoken question.

"Wice."

Sara repeated the strange word. "Oh, rice!"

The woman nodded. She had warm eyes, the color of coal.

Luc lapped it up eagerly, the overflow from the spoon dribbling down his chin. When he had finished and belched contentedly, Sara's new friend picked up Sara's tent and suitcase and motioned for her to follow.

They walked to the end of a long line of small houses, which looked as though they'd been built with mismatched planks of wood and rusted nails, perhaps salvaged from building sites in town. Beyond the simple buildings was a smattering of canvas tents of varying sizes, staked to the ground with twine, each entrance held open by a tall tree branch or pole.

It was here that Sara pitched her tent and established a new life. Three days after her arrival in Napa, on Christmas Eve morning, she gathered the courage to leave the circle of women around the fire and ask about working with the men in the vineyards. She strapped Luc to her back and approached the tall Chinese man who organized the vineyard workers. Like all the men, he wore his hair cropped short, with a long braid hanging down his back. Sara pointed to herself, then to the wagon. He was surprised, and glanced at his wife, who was heating broth over the fire, watching them intently. His wife nodded. Without a word, he signaled to Sara to climb aboard. She couldn't have imagined a better Christmas gift.

Sara and Luc established a routine. Luc would wake at five o'clock and drink his milk contentedly, and Sara would dress and gather a satchel of foodstuffs for the day. Luckily, she needed only canned milk and rice for Luc, for all the workers were fed a midday meal with wine. In the evenings, she ate heartily by the fire and heated bricks, which she'd wrap in flannel and place against their feet to keep them warm in the biting night air.

As the vines slept for the winter, Sara and the Chinese workers clipped the old growth back to the spurs that would grow into next year's crop. After pruning, they chopped up the piles of canes lying between the rows and disked them into the ground. Every week or two, they would move to another vineyard to work for a different white foreman. Worried she would draw attention as a pale-skinned female traveling with a band of Chinese men, Sara kept her head down, worked as quickly as the men and hummed to keep Luc calm. The Chinese paid her no mind, which suited Sara fine. The one time a vineyard foreman did question her about her experience, her fellow workers huddled around her. Sara was startled, but grateful for their protection.

During her stay in New York, Sara had grown accustomed to the cadence of the harsh-sounding American English, but Chinese was altogether different: shrill and choppy to Sara's ears. She yearned to hear the beautiful lilt of her beloved French. The only time she spoke it anymore was when she sang Luc to sleep at night, her voice competing with the incomprehensible chatter around the evening fires.

One early March evening, right after the vine buds broke, Sara went for the first time to tend the frost fires in one of the largest vineyards she'd ever seen. Although her neighbors by the river had offered to care for Luc, she didn't want to let him out of her sight. She hadn't been able to keep her sister alive, but she would do everything in her power to protect Luc.

She trudged into the vineyard at twilight with ten other workers. The foreman, an unfriendly hulk, pointed Sara in the direction of the closest fire, near the vineyard house, and directed the others to the central and outlying fires. They would all keep vigil over the vines to make sure the frost, or heaven forbid, the fire, did not overtake them during the winter night. The fire looked as though it had just been ignited, and its flames climbed waist-high. The vineyard at night was a beautiful sight—otherworldly, Sara thought. The diagonal vines formed a labyrinth up the hills, stretching toward the outermost edges of the farm. The smaller pyres, spaced twenty or so rows apart, glowed like brilliant candles on a holiday tree.

Sara laid her blanket down on the cold earth and covered Luc with two wool blankets and his brown wool cap, and then tucked him face out into the front of her jacket, taking care that if she did fall asleep unexpectedly, she would not smother him. The heat two yards from the fire warmed Sara's cheeks. She relished being alone outside with just the baby, instead of huddled inside their too-small tent surrounded by a noisy throng of people.

Now six months old, Luc was robust and fattening up, his arms and legs like chubby tree trunks. Sara gave him his bottle and rocked him, as usual, while singing "Au claire de la lune," her father's favorite lullaby. When his long lashes fluttered closed, she stroked his head until it fell gently to one side in slumber. Sara herself could hardly stay awake after a day of pruning and cutting weeds. It was Sunday, and after attending early Mass, she had joined the workers in the vineyard. Now, spasms of pain rippled through her back. She removed her gloves to examine the small red cuts that stung her fingertips, the inevitable result of pruning in near-freezing temperatures.

Sara's fatigue finally prevailed, and she curled up on her side with Luc nestled contentedly against her belly. Though she tried to fight sleep, she drifted off before long. She might have been asleep for five hours or five minutes. Sara bolted upright at the crack of a gunshot not ten feet away from her. A small creature howled in pain. Luc followed suit, erupting into high-pitched sobs. Sara staggered to her feet, clutching Luc to her chest. Her heart was in her throat as she turned around, frantically searching in the dark for the cause of the ruckus.

She saw the dead animal first, a dog, or maybe—yes, a fox, she guessed by the red-brown coat and long bushy tail. It had fallen on its side. Its tongue lolled listlessly and blood trickled from the hole in the side of its skull to the dirt below.

"Come on then." Sara jumped. The voice was directly behind her and speaking fluent French. Sara whirled around to see a short, busty woman, rifle in hand, gas lamp at her feet, wearing a plain white cotton nightdress. Her fiery red hair was braided, and cloth ties wrapped around disheveled curls in the front.

"What—how?" Sara stammered. She blinked several times to make sure she wasn't dreaming. She could smell the smoke from the waning fire; she could hear the embers popping. Her hands were trembling. It wasn't a dream.

The woman, who Sara guessed was about forty years of age, shook her head disapprovingly. "This is no place for a baby. Either he'd die of frostbite when the fires fade, or that fox would have made a meal out of him. You'd best come inside, the two of you." She turned and started walking toward the large white house. Sara, assuming she was to follow, scrambled to gather her satchel and blankets and called after the woman.

"That won't be necessary. I'm sorry, I must have fallen asleep. Thank you for—well, for shooting the fox. We'll go home now." Sara faltered with embarrassment.

The woman didn't break her stride and didn't bother to turn around as she answered. "Home? Isn't 'home' a tent down in Chinatown? No place for a baby, either." She shook her head again and glanced over her shoulder at Sara. "Yes, I know all about you. Saw you in the store—heard about you from Molly Reynolds. Not much gets by us locals, especially if you're new to town," she chortled.

"No, I suppose it doesn't," Sara muttered to herself.

Luc had finally drifted back off to sleep once they reached the house, which was about a hundred paces from where Sara had been stationed. The front door creaked softly, and the woman held it wide open for Sara as she stepped into the kitchen.

"I'm Aurora Thierry. And you are . . . ?" She smiled warmly, her eyes dancing with secret amusement. Sara took in the woman's pleasant features: face like an apple, kind expression, straight white teeth.

"Sara . . . Landry. And this is my son, Luc," Sara said softly.

"How old?"

"Six months."

Madame Thierry showed Sara to a bedroom. "You'll sleep here tonight." She held out the lamp, and Sara took it, overcome with gratitude. Madame Thierry looked Sara over and then nodded in approval. "We'll get acquainted in the morning."

Sara awoke to the sun streaming through the unshuttered windows. Her body was still racked with fatigue, and her head was heavy. The room was still and quiet: something wasn't right. She jumped up and searched the room for the baby. She had laid him last night on the floor, tucked into her new overcoat. He had purred and drifted off to sleep contentedly sucking his fingers. But now Luc was gone. She disentangled herself from the blankets and listened. She heard a gentle cooing coming from outside the bedroom door and the low humming of a vaguely familiar melody.

Her heart rate began to slow when she heard Luc giggling in the background. Madame Thierry had taken him to the kitchen. Under normal circumstances, Sara would not want Luc to be held by a stranger. But these were not normal circumstances, and Sara was so grateful to have been able to sleep deeply and awaken to find him safe and sound. She was truly a mother to Luc now, she realized. Sara rubbed her eyes, which were still lazy with sleep. She was trying to piece together the events of the previous evening when she was hit with the smell of fried eggs and ham, maybe even buttered potatoes. Her stomach gurgled violently.

Sara quickly combed her fingers through her hair, removing pins and rearranging runaway tendrils. She wanted to appear presentable. She inspected herself in a small looking glass that hung on the wall over a low four-drawer pine dresser. On top were a basin and pitcher of fresh, albeit nearly frozen, water. Sara poured a bit of the water into the bowl and doused her face. She cupped some water in her hand and swished it around the inside of her mouth before spitting it out. Freezing, but refreshing. She might have looked worse after the night she'd had.

She opened the door gently, unnoticed by Madame Thierry or Luc. Madame Thierry was working at the stove, spatula in one hand, Luc comfortably hitched on her hip. She had tilted her head sideways toward him and was singing in a low voice and swaying her wide hips back and forth to the rhythm. Ham sizzled on the iron griddle.

Sara was struck by how Luc's eyes were riveted to Madame Thierry's animated face. For the first time in many months, Sara ached for her own mother. She imagined Jacques was caring for Maman while she grieved for Lydia. Sara felt a twinge of guilt, for she had not written a second letter to her mother, nor had she given Jacques an address. She was terrified of being discovered. Even here, in this warm and safe Napa kitchen, she had to proceed carefully.

She softly cleared her throat. "Good morning, you two." She loved hearing her own language rolling off her tongue.

"Ah, my dear, come—sit." Madame Thierry waved at the table with her spatula. "Your beautiful baby boy is making his maman a full breakfast, California style: eggs, ham, hash browns." She bounced Luc up and down on her hip and Luc cooed in return. "We need to fatten Maman up!" she said playfully.

Sara's cheeks reddened. Her growing hunger was not just the result of a long night. For weeks, she had eaten only watered-down rice soup. All the milk she could get her hands on, fresh and canned, went to Luc. She had noticed that her stomach, which usually stretched flat between her hipbones, actually curved inward now.

She must look worse than she thought if a perfect stranger had noticed she was thinning. She would gratefully accept a hearty breakfast this morning.

Madame Thierry served her and sat across from Sara with Luc contentedly on her lap, sucking on her apron string. She watched Sara's face intently as she nibbled at her own food. Sara could not meet her eyes, for her need to eat overpowered all else. Only when she had scraped the last bit of egg from her plate with her fork did she finally look up. She let out a sigh and glanced happily at her new friend.

"Madame, I cannot thank you enough for your hospitality. The meal was delicious."

"Aurora—call me Aurora. And you were ravenous. Help yourself to more." She nodded toward the stove, where an ample helping of potatoes remained. "Your son already feasted on fresh goat's milk this morning." She shook her head in disbelief, scowling. "When's the last time you had a proper meal?"

Sara chuckled and stood to spoon more food onto her plate. "I honestly can't remember. Maybe two months ago? On the train, before I arrived here. I've been living on the soup the Chinese women share with me."

"Good Lord in heaven! There's a reason the Chinese are so small, even the men. You need meat to fill out those bones, not rice meal. Well, that settles it. You're staying here."

"I'm sorry . . ." Sara was flustered. "I couldn't—we couldn't trespass on your kindness any longer."

"Where else will you go? Back to your tent by the river? This is the coldest March we've had in years. I won't have the death of your baby on my conscience, no ma'am. You will stay and help me out here for the next few weeks, in return for room and board, until you can find a suitable situation in town. You *are* on your own, correct? Not married?"

"Widowed." Sara looked down at the potatoes she'd just heaped on her plate. She was acutely aware of the fact that any details she gave Aurora about herself and Luc had to be carefully chosen to conceal the truth. And Aurora appeared to be all about the details.

"*And?*"

Sara hesitated. "And we were left with nothing, so we came to America to start a new life." But this did not satisfy Aurora's curiosity.

"Mm-hmm. Why did you leave France? You must have had some family there who could help you?"

"No, madame." Sara speared the last potato.

"No one?" Aurora sounded skeptical.

Sara began her well-rehearsed lie. "Henri, my husband, was orphaned as a boy. He died of pneumonia, last winter." She paused, lowering her head. "My parents, too, have passed, and neither of us have siblings." Sara's eyes welled with tears for her real, fragmented family.

"You poor thing. So your husband never lived to meet his son?"

Sara wiped her cheeks with her napkin. "No, madame."

Aurora exhaled deeply. "You seem a clever girl. Surely you could get work as a seamstress, or perhaps a housekeeper?" she ventured gently.

Sara shook her head. "My father was a vigneron from Angers, my husband, too, and so am I. It's all I know, really. Besides, I would hate to be cooped up inside all day—I like to be outdoors, even in these cold temperatures."

Sara cleared the table and began washing the dishes. A good time to change the subject, she thought.

"And have you lived here long?"

Aurora chuckled. "I was born in Bordeaux, and came to America when I was twelve. I married when I was twenty." She continued wistfully, "My husband died of consumption ten years ago. Left me childless, but with a substantial pension that allows me to pursue some of my interests, like teaching."

As the truth dawned on her, Sara could not believe her good fortune. This was *the* Madame Aurora Thierry whose papers Sara had read and whom she'd admired for years. How could she run a vineyard this immense and find the time to teach and write? Sara's confusion must have registered on her furrowed brow.

"Oh no, this isn't my vineyard. I live west of here. I'm watching the place for the owner, a friend, who has traveled east on business. He should return in a little under a fortnight, I'd wager. I usually spend my days teaching agriculture at the seminary in town or experimenting with new farming methods. Sounds a bit mundane when you say it like that, I suppose."

"You must be an accomplished farmer if he left his property and livelihood in your hands." Sara was impressed, but not yet ready to confide that she knew exactly who Aurora was.

"Oh, I've been around a long time—I'm old enough to be your mother, I'd wager. And I've farmed grapes, currants, olives. You name it, I've grown it." She shrugged. "I was flattered that he trusted me enough to leave me in charge." Aurora had a self-effacing yet sturdy demeanor that Sara instantly admired, but her words left Sara chagrined.

"In charge of protecting a witless mother and her poor baby from a menacing fox?" Sara's shoulders slumped.

Aurora laughed. "Not at all. Having reason to fire my shotgun is just one of the perks." She smiled unapologetically.

"We both thank you." Sara gestured to Luc, who squirmed a bit in Aurora's lap until she began to bounce him on her knee.

"You can thank me by staying here to help me out. When my friend returns, we'll move back to my farm. There's a spare bedroom, and I would welcome the company, if I can persuade you, that is." Aurora's eyes danced with hopeful sincerity.

Decorum dictated that Sara should decline Aurora's offer. She barely knew her. Yet, as she stacked the clean plates in that warm kitchen filled with all the aromas of home, Sara believed Aurora to be a kindred spirit of sorts. This was a new country and a new year, and Sara did not suffer from an abundance of friends in this part of the world. Besides, it would be safer for Luc to sleep indoors. She made up her mind.

"You are very generous, and I will accept, but you must allow me to continue to work in the fields or do something useful to earn my keep. I'm afraid I'm not a very good cook."

"Don't worry, I have other plans for you." Before Sara could respond, Aurora stood and propped Luc on her hip. "Let's bundle up, and I'll take you two on a tour, so you can see what you're getting yourselves into."

CHAPTER 13

Fight or Flight?

The morning fog swathed the vines in its gentle embrace, making it nearly impossible for Sara to see more than a dozen feet ahead. She walked closely behind Aurora, for she wasn't sure she could find her way around in the mist.

"So, this is Eagle's Run, the largest vineyard in Carneros, on the Napa side." Aurora swept her hand across the vista. "Over two hundred acres, replanted with resistant rootstock five years ago. Chardonnay, cabernet, zinfandel. The first significant harvest, this past October, yielded one hundred twenty-five tons—fairly impressive, I'd say. All told, there's over seventeen thousand gallons—290 barrels—aging in the cellar. He hopes the harvest will yield five tons per acre next year."

Sara followed Aurora as they walked past two small barns and modest stables that probably kept three or four horses and a rig. They were headed east toward the rising sun, and the river. Sara's eyes became fixed on a wide gable that poked out of the fog and pierced the light from the awakening sun. Gravel crunched beneath their feet, and soon Sara could make out the outline of a huge building that looked brand new.

Aurora nodded her head. "The new winery." Sara recognized its purpose right away. The first floor was constructed entirely of stone, and the second and third floors of wood and large-paned glass windows. Most wineries in these parts were built into hillsides, so the horses could unload the grapes on the highest floor, but this winery utilized a large mechanical conveyance that ran from the ground up to a third-floor door. Ropes and pulleys hauled the grapes up to the top level for crushing. Perfect, Sara thought.

Her eyes widened. "It's so . . . modern." She stood still, wondering who had the resources and foresight to build such an amazing structure. "It's beautiful," she whispered in awe.

Aurora beamed. "Spoken like a true vintner."

Once inside, Sara enjoyed the smell of freshly milled pine, oak and damp stone.

Aurora proceeded with her tour. "It *is* impressive, actually. And well planned. Plenty of oak and redwood cooperage and all the most modern crushing and bottling equipment."

As they walked from the first floor to the third, Sara marveled at the bottling machinery, the huge fermenting tanks and the three-man press. "May I?"

"Of course," Aurora encouraged.

Sara moved in to take a closer look. She ran her hand over the smooth, cold metal of the press handle, and her eyes wandered to the rows of sparkling empty wine bottles stacked perfectly against the stone wall on a wooden platform, ready to be filled. A surprising burst of emotion pressed heavily against her chest. Sara took a deep breath and held her tears back behind her closed eyes, overwhelmed by admiration and intense, palpable envy. She was standing in the midst of her heart's desire. This winery, this vineyard, right here, was exactly what she'd envisioned for Saint Martin. And it belonged to someone else.

The pain of that realization must have flashed across Sara's face, for Aurora was immediately concerned. "Are you well? What is it, Sara?"

Sara waved her hand to brush off Aurora's concern and forced a smile. "Nothing at all. I'm fine. Would you kindly show me the cellar, too?"

Aurora took a long look at Sara before continuing. "There's a large one underneath us, and the original adobe cellars are located just a few feet south of this building. The reds and whites are aging here, and I think Philippe's planning to use the adobe cellars to store the bottles."

Adrenaline coursed through Sara's veins. Her tightly wound nerves threatened to unravel. She attempted to say the name without faltering.

"Philippe?" Relax, she chided herself. It couldn't possibly be the same Philippe.

"Oh yes, the owner. I suppose I should call him Monsieur Lemieux, but we're a little less formal here and tend to call our friends by their Christian names."

Sara felt the urge to run as far and as fast as she could.

Aurora's hand pressed gently on her arm. "Is everything all right, my dear? You look—well, positively distressed. Really, maybe you should take a glass of wine, to calm your nerves."

She mustn't raise Aurora's suspicions. She must play this calmly. Sara shook her head, hoping to shake off her agitation as well. "Not at all. I'm just . . . tired." She glanced at Aurora, trying to invent a reason to leave. "It just occurred to me that I should—I need to gather my things by the river. There's not much, just a few items. Where should I bring them?"

Aurora answered as Sara expected she would, unfortunately. "I'm installed in the main house until Philippe returns, you know, to keep an eye on everything, especially his foreman, Jip Montagne. So you should stay here with me for the next week or two in the bedroom where you slept last night, if that would be agreeable."

Sara tried to ignore her numbing fear and to speak naturally, "Of course, yes, that makes perfect sense. I'll go now and—well, I'll see you later this afternoon, if that's all right?"

Aurora looked puzzled by Sara's sudden change of mood. "Yes . . . that sounds fine," she said slowly.

Sara attempted to sound sane again. "Thank you so much for the breakfast and for helping me with Luc here. Oh, and for the wonderful tour." Sara looked around again at the inside of the winery, at all the bottles and equipment. "Truly, I have never seen its equal."

"When you return, I'll show you the cellars. In the meantime, I'm going to head downstairs to examine the casks." Aurora smiled pleasantly. "And don't you walk that distance. Tan should be here by eight o'clock." She lifted the pocket watch that was chained to her belt. "Less than a quarter hour. He'll take you in my rig and bring you back."

"I'm much obliged. Thank you, Mad—Aurora."

"My pleasure. I'm so pleased to have some company here. It was getting a bit lonely."

Sara's mind reeled as she walked back to the house to wait for Tan. This must be God's doing. She had traveled over sea and land to escape punishment for her crime. She had run from her responsibility, from her penance. And now the Lord was going to force justice upon her, and at the hand of Bastien's own brother. Philippe Lemieux wasn't her enemy, but she was his. Would he even recognize her from nine years ago? That she doubted. Would Marie have told him about her, about Lydia and Luc? Had Marie even known about her crime? How would he react if he found out that she was living next door to him, and had worked on his farm? He would probably drag her back to France to be imprisoned and prosecuted.

She expected to feel panic rise up within her. She should run—again. But she was tired of lying and running. She didn't feel panic, but resentment and anger. Would she really allow Philippe Lemieux to drive her from the place she so desperately wanted to be? In that moment the die was cast. She'd had enough. She wasn't going to leave, and she wasn't going to apologize for ending the life of a man who had brutalized her and her sister. She had defended herself against Bastien. If Lemieux discovered who she was, then so be it; she would take what she had coming. Until then, she would build a life for herself and Luc here in California, and plan to take back Saint Martin.

It occurred to Sara that she was just like—what was that expression?—a moth to a flame. Naive and fluttering, captivated by the beauty of this place and by the allure of a chance to realize her life's ambition. Perhaps she was a stupid, reckless girl, but she was resolute. She would stand and fight for what was rightfully hers. For what Lemieux *owed* her: Saint Martin. She wondered anxiously, would she survive the flame, or would she burn?

For the next fortnight, Sara stayed on at Eagle's Run, helping Aurora inspect the new buds and trim the new shoots from the base of the vines to keep rabbits from eating the wood. Aurora had graciously given Luc a basket for sleeping, tightly woven from willow shoots and lined with a small blanket. One morning, Sara placed his basket on her bedroom floor for his morning nap and quietly closed the door behind her. She waited until he stopped fussing, opened the door slightly to observe him hugging his Pup, the stuffed toy Aurora had given him, and then headed out to work.

As she left the house, she was surprised to see Aurora out among the rows standing on her tiptoes, shaking her fist and yelling up at Jip Montagne, the surly foreman Sara had disliked since the moment she'd laid eyes on him. Even stranger, a slight Chinese girl, not more than fifteen years of age, stood behind Aurora, her head hung and shoulders shaking. Sara hurried over and placed her arm comfortingly around the crying girl. Aurora paid no attention to Sara, but continued her tirade in clipped French while Jip stood unapologetic, hands on his hips and legs spread obstinately. His face reddened with anger as he practically spewed his words at Aurora.

"You can't fire me! You're nothing! I won't leave," his deep voice boomed.

Aurora was so incensed that she was screaming. "You will leave, or I'll get the sheriff to escort you off the property! Or maybe I'll just shoot you myself." She lowered her voice slightly and nodded to Sara. "Take the girl in the house and bring me back my rifle."

Sara whirled around and guided the girl back toward the house. Her steps quickened when she heard Jip growl menacingly at Aurora.

"You wouldn't *dare*!"

Within moments, Sara had seated the girl at the table, retrieved Aurora's rifle from the back hall cupboard, and checked to make sure it was loaded. Thank God Papa had taught her a thing or two about shooting. She cocked the rifle and started back out toward the vineyard. By now, Jip had Aurora by the arm and was shaking her violently. The wild look on his face, eyes bulging from their sockets, warned Sara that he'd lost control.

She had to stop him before he broke Aurora's arm or worse, but he stood a brawny six and a half feet, and Sara didn't believe she was strong enough to do it on her own. She would have to use the gun. It took just one shot, and a bullet breaking the dirt near his feet, for him to release Aurora's arm and stumble back, flabbergasted.

In no time, Aurora was at Sara's side, gingerly removing the rifle from her hands. Sara's fingers trembled slightly, more from anger than from having fired the gun. Well, Aurora had the rifle now and Jip would have to stand down. Sara had no doubt that Aurora would shoot him clean through if he so much as batted an eyelash.

"Nice shot," Aurora muttered. "Follow me. I may need you."

Aurora approached Jip and pushed the tip of the gun barrel into his chest, forcing him to step back. "Turn around, go pack up your stuff and leave." Left with no choice, Jip started toward the barn, but he wouldn't let it go.

"When Lemieux returns, he's—"

Aurora had no patience left. "When he returns, you'll be lucky if he doesn't kill you himself. I suggest you run and hide . . . *now*." Her voice was strong and intimidating.

After they had watched Jip Montagne ride around the last visible turn in the road, Aurora turned to Sara, unruffled, and rolled her eyes.

"Now we've gone and done it. This is going to leave us with heaps more work to do." Aurora shook her head and wiped the sweat from her forehead with her handkerchief. "Thank the Lord you were here. I don't know if I could have fought him on my own."

"I was glad to help. What did he do, anyhow?"

"Disgusting pig tried to have his way with that young girl in there. He's the foreman, you see, and if she refuses, well . . ." She shrugged and nodded toward five Chinese workers in conical hats weeding between the vines about twenty yards away. "Then they all lose their jobs."

"Just tell me what to do."

"Come with me."

Sara spent the afternoon at the western end of the vineyard pulling up weeds alongside the Chinese family and their daughter, and worked at twice their clip. She was in her element and could do this work in her sleep. Luc lay quietly strapped to her back while Sara hummed his favorite lullaby, "*Dodo, l'enfant do, dodo l'enfant do, L'enfant dormira bien vite.*" Her hat shielded both of their faces from the sun, although it was still cool enough that Luc needed his wool cap and Sara wore gloves.

Partway through the afternoon, Sara spied a tall figure approaching from the stables. Her heart skipped a beat when she thought it might be Jip coming back to take his revenge. But although this man stood nearly as tall as Jip, he was more graceful, and his hair a bit fairer in the afternoon sun. She dropped her head abruptly and looked down at her hands, seeing nothing. Could it be *him*? She was almost certain it was. Sara glanced up to surreptitiously study him as he walked toward their group. The thin, gangly boy she remembered from Vouvray was almost, but not completely, unrecognizable. His shoulders had broadened, his jaw had sharpened and squared, and he moved with a confidence she didn't recall. But then, he'd only been eighteen, and she nine.

She would have sworn it was a different man, if she hadn't, in that last stolen glance, caught sight of his eyes. They were exactly the same. Cool and brilliantly intense, like blue topaz. And they were fixed on her.

Sara ducked her head back down again and tried to remember how to breathe. Thank God Luc was quiet—she didn't need any more attention drawn to her. She could hear Lemieux's footsteps scrape the clay and small stones as he neared. In response, the Chinese family increased their working speed to match Sara's lithe movements. They spoke quietly among themselves, but soon the chatter ceased. He was close now.

A deep, melodic voice rang out. "Good morning. *Zao an.*"

The workers next to her said nothing but simply bowed their heads. Sara didn't want to draw attention to her and Luc by seeming rude.

"Good morning." She knew her voice was too heavily accented to pass for American.

"*Ah, bonjour, mademoiselle—ou madame? Vous êtes française?*" He seemed surprised.

"*Oui*—yes, I am." She looked up briefly, then forced herself to break away from the magnetic hold of his eyes. She trained hers downward, willing herself to move on to the next vine, though her limbs had gone rigid with fear. Her face was hot. It took a considerable effort not to stare up at his exquisite face.

"*Bienvenue.*" He sounded amused. Sara couldn't fathom why. She looked up again, just in time to see him walk away.

She was a ridiculous, fanciful girl who'd let her imagination run wild. Why had she thought that he would remember her? Of course he'd all but ignored her. She was a stranger, a vinedresser, a hired laborer on his land. She was of little consequence to him, thank God. That she had thought otherwise, even for a moment, was merely evidence of her paranoia.

Lemieux did not return to the field that afternoon. At the end of the day, Sara knew she would have to return to the house, his house, to change and feed Luc, and to collect her things. She assumed that she and Aurora would move back to Aurora's house immediately. She had always known that she was an interloper here. Though she could leave to start a life elsewhere, she had decided to stay, to hold her ground. And now she would have to stand by her decision, whatever the consequences.

Sara walked with trepidation toward the house. In the time it took to cross the acres from where she'd met him in the vineyard to his front porch, Sara had come up with at least ten ways she could skulk off to Aurora's house without having to be formally introduced to him. But all her contrivances were for naught: Aurora appeared on the steps before she could make her escape, beckoning Sara to come in.

Philippe was lighting a fire in the hearth and leapt up to greet the women as they entered. His movements were lithesome, his limbs long and graceful, not like any farmer she'd ever known.

Sara's heart thudded with dread as Aurora made the introductions. "Madame Sara Landry, may I present Monsieur Philippe Lemieux."

Philippe extended his hand. She returned his handshake and smiled as warmly as her fear would allow.

"Sara?" he asked with curiosity.

Her heart raced, threatening to explode. "Yes," she replied, as lightly as possible.

When she realized Philippe was studying her face, she wanted to hide, but instead forced a pleasant expression. He chuckled to himself, and shook his head.

"We've already met, Aurora—out in the vineyard this afternoon,"

Philippe said cheerfully. Relief washed over Sara; he didn't suspect her.

"Sara is the daughter of a vintner from the western Loire, near Angers," Aurora declared.

"Indeed, down the river from where I grew up." He glanced appraisingly at Sara. "Hmm . . . a vintner's daughter. We can always use more of our countrymen in these parts. After all, no one truly knows wine like the French, wouldn't you agree, madame?" He gave them a radiant smile that nearly melted Sara's bones.

Before Sara could voice her agreement, Luc began to cry.

"And who is this little fellow?" said Philippe with sudden interest.

"My son, Luc Landry. He's six months old."

Philippe rubbed Luc's fine brown curls with his palm. Luc calmed immediately under his touch and grasped Philippe's extended finger.

"Is he cooperative when you work? It seems so." He looked at Sara again and smiled crookedly. "It must be a bit of a strain to carry him on your back while you're working. He's quite big for six months, isn't he?"

Sara felt oddly irritated by his remark. What did he know about babies? She supposed every mother was overly sensitive to what was said about her child.

"Not at all," she replied. "He's no trouble and average weight for his age. If you'll excuse us, Luc needs a change. I should also feed and bathe him."

"Why don't you tend to him here and stay for dinner? It's the least I can offer to thank you ladies for your help with the vineyard." He looked at Aurora with kind eyes. "I really am most grateful."

Aurora smiled in return, but shot a sideways glance at Sara. "It wasn't without its . . . difficulties. But we'll talk more of that over dinner. All in all, we had fun, didn't we, Sara?"

Sara wasn't sure she could share a meal with Bastien Lemieux's brother, no matter how charming he appeared. Her wits had left her. She needed more time—for what, she hardly knew. To decide how to make small talk with the brother of the man she had killed. Her mind reeled at the absurdity—no, the tragedy of it all. She realized that Philippe and Aurora were staring at her. She had to invent something to say.

"I'm so sorry, I have to leave you two to discuss these matters without me. Like I said, I need to tend to Luc and . . . he's teething and a bit irritable right now, so I don't think it would be a good idea for us to stay."

"Oh." Aurora seemed disappointed, but recovered her good humor quickly. "Oh, of course. Take the wagon home. I'm sure Philippe can drive me back after dinner, if it's not too much trouble."

"None at all. Perhaps next time, Madame Landry." Philippe bowed slightly.

Sara knew she should suggest the idea was appealing. "That would be delightful, thank you."

APRIL 2, 1897, MADAME THIERRY'S FARM, NAPA, CALIFORNIA

"What is this?" Sara held out a jar filled with dark, glossy chips of glass.

"Obsidian. It's volcanic glass, from the northern valley. The Mey'ankmah—some of the first inhabitants of Napa—traded

231

obsidian and used it to make spears and arrowheads. I collect it." Aurora moved around her workroom, organizing books by subject and stacking them on the new bookshelves she and Sara had constructed from pine boards.

Sara placed the jar back on the long table and picked up the next one. "And these dried flowers?"

"Oh, that's my latest experiment, blue elderberry. I'm told the Mey'ankmah used it for children's fevers, so I thought, with your permission, I'd make the tea and we'd give it to Luc the next time he's feverish. Don't worry, it won't hurt him."

"I'm not worried. I'm just in awe of your knowledge. And . . . I do have to make a confession."

Aurora's head turned in interest. "Which is . . . ?"

"When I was a girl, I read all your treatises on grape and olive farming and now, to be working with you—well, it is unfathomable to me and quite an honor."

"Well, I'll be!" Aurora's hands moved to her hips. "I didn't know those writings had even reached Europe." She smiled, satisfied. "I'm feeling rather proud of myself right now."

"As well you should be. All the best farmers back home read your work."

"You don't say? Actually, I've been fortunate. Living here has given me the opportunity to research and publish, whereas I probably wouldn't have had as much success in France. There's not as much . . . openness to female writers there. The old ways, you know," she said wryly.

"How long have you lived in California?"

"Since 1861, when my father brought us to Pope Valley, in

northern Napa County—first for the silver mining, then, when that didn't work out, red cinnabar provided a nice living for us. My husband bought this place in 1875. As stubborn as he was, he was also very patient and taught me most of what I know about farming. Renaud was amazing: he could grow anything." Her voice was matter-of-fact, with no trace of sadness.

"And how did you meet Monsieur Lemieux?" Sara grabbed the broom and dustpan from the closet and began to sweep up the dried plant cuttings and dirt from the floor.

"When he was looking for property in these parts, he dropped in to ask me some questions about the land he was interested in. I've never been one to keep my opinions to myself, so I told him exactly what I thought."

"Which was?" Sara tried to sound nonchalant, but was eager to learn more.

"That he'd be *mad* not to take it, and replant the vines and orchards. Plant an olive grove. Would have done it myself if I'd had the money. The place could be a goldmine," Aurora said enthusiastically.

"It *is* enormous."

"Yes, but Philippe's just the man to put it right." Aurora sounded impressed.

"How so?"

"He's savvy—not just about grape growing, but about selling what he produces. And I've never seen a man want something more."

Sara could relate to that. She was surprised that he hadn't married yet. "Does he not want a wife and family as well?"

"Why? Are you volunteering?" Aurora teased.

Sara blushed a thousand shades of red. "Of course not. I barely know him. I'm just saying, he's not young."

"Twenty-eight hardly qualifies him as ancient. Besides, he has his . . . diversions, from what I understand. He's had a relationship with a woman in town for the past year or so."

"Oh, is he engaged?" Sara tried to sound offhand.

"I don't think she's the marrying kind." Aurora gave her a knowing glance, but Sara wasn't sure what her friend meant to imply. After all, Sara herself was the only girl she knew of who wasn't the marrying kind, who would rather spend her days and nights growing wine than taking care of a man.

"Do you miss your husband?" Sara asked cautiously. She had loved her father, but from what she had seen, husbands could be tricky.

"Every day," Aurora sighed. "And you?"

Sara felt a pang of shame for deceiving Aurora into thinking she was also a widow. "Sometimes. I regret that Luc doesn't have a father, you know, to teach him things."

Aurora nodded. She took a few moments to line up the jarred specimens on the edge of the workroom table before she spoke.

"I had a son. Not many people know—it was before Renaud and I moved here. René was four when he died. Pneumonia, they said. He always had weak lungs. Anyhow, it was a long time ago."

"I'm so sorry, Aurora. That must have been, must still be, unbearable."

"And yet, here I stand," she said bravely, and looked away. "I miss his smell—not at all flowery, mind you. Pure boy. All musk and sweet-scented perspiration. And I miss running my fingers through his hair. Paintbrush hair, Renaud used to call it. It was so thick it never needed brushing, always fell right back into place, like the bristles on a painter's brush." Her laugh was wistful, sad. "So you see, when I met Philippe, although he looks nothing like my son, I couldn't help but think: what would René be doing now if he'd lived? He would have been the same age as Philippe. I wonder if he would've been a farmer, like his father. Sometimes, when I'm alone, I think about things like that."

She glanced back at Sara and smiled warmly. "Which is why it's good to have you and Luc here—to keep my mind on the present. But you understand, you've lost your husband."

"Luc and I are so grateful to be here and to have you as our friend." Sara said, trying to dodge Aurora's unspoken question.

"Thank you. Speaking of which"—Aurora clasped her hands together in excitement—"I'm having a dinner party next Saturday. You, because you are new to town, and Philippe, because he's just returned from the East, will be the guests of honor."

Sara tried to hide her horror. "I don't think—"

"Oh, no, I insist, Sara. You absolutely cannot say no. You have no idea how I love my dinner parties. I'm inviting all the best wine men and some of the worst, so you'll get a real understanding of what's going on around here. And their wives are quite tolerable in small doses."

Sara laughed at Aurora's enthusiasm. She would not dream of disappointing her one true friend in this part of the world.

"It sounds wonderful. You must allow me to help."

"Not one bit. You worry about you and Luc. I'll take care of the invitations, the food, the drink. We'll ask everyone to bring a bottle of his best wine. It will be positively lavish!'"

Sara felt apprehensive and hopeful in equal measure. So much time had passed since she'd dined in proper company that she decided to take extra time with her toilette before going downstairs. She tried to remember Lydia's painstaking beauty routine as she stared at herself hopelessly in the looking glass. She did not have her sister's peaches-and-cream complexion or silky hair. Nor had she much of Lydia's charm. Sara sighed wistfully, and her chest tightened with longing. She missed her sister's infectious smile, her easy laugh and, most of all, her unfailing ability to diffuse Sara's darkest moods.

Sara concentrated on her appearance to calm her nerves. She didn't have any rosewater, so she used the water from the pump to wash her face. She chewed on a mint leaf and then inspected her teeth meticulously. She had splurged on a few special items at the general store for the occasion. On her farm-worn hands—Lydia would have been appalled!—she slathered a thick honey cream, rubbing it into her shredded cuticles until they looked smoother. She brushed her chestnut hair fifty times for shine and pinched her cheeks for a healthy radiance, as Lydia used to say. Dusting powder under her arms was essential in this surprising spring heat. A simple twist at the nape of her neck was the best she could muster with her hair, which had not yet fully grown back.

She could almost see her sister standing in front of her, smell Lydia's lavender filling their bedroom back at Saint Martin. Lydia would have tugged a few tendrils from Sara's slicked-back coiffure to frame and soften her face. Lydia always knew how to make the most of their features, while Sara had never paid much attention to fashion or beauty. Now she wished she had. Sara's eyes, a fleckless, verdant green, were her most attractive feature, she believed. Would Lydia agree?

Attire was another conundrum. She really only had one choice: Lydia's old white summer dress, cinched at the waist with a black ribbon, with elbow-length puffed sleeves and a high ruffled collar. She had swallowed her pride and asked Aurora to advance her money to buy some new soles for her only pair of shoes. Fortunately, as Aurora kept reminding her, the people here did not stand on ceremony. They were more likely to judge someone's intellect than their attire, her friend insisted. Let's hope so, Sara thought anxiously. Although she had to admit it was a bit senseless to worry about hair and clothing when a much more substantial challenge lay ahead of her this evening.

Sara hated being the center of attention. The only good thing about being one of the two guests of honor was that Aurora would seat her and Philippe at opposite ends of the table, so Sara would not have to make polite conversation with him. She was determined to conceal her identity. Sara had lain awake for hours the night before, racked with anxiety, refining her story until she had the details memorized. She tried to anticipate the group's questions and manufacture believable but concise answers. The string of lies had to be consistent with what she had already told Aurora. Despite the fact that she would have to act all night, she found herself looking forward to an interesting evening, even though it meant putting all thoughts of her real family and her former life out of her head. That would not be easy with Bastien's brother sitting a table's length away from her.

Sara descended the stairs, prepared to meet Aurora's friends. Candle sconces lit the parlor, which was decorated with a plush velvet settee, carved wooden chairs and faded gold scrolled wallpaper that reminded Sara of a tapestry she'd seen inside the Château d'Amboise. As Aurora welcomed the guests, she introduced them to Sara. Instead of staying for refreshments in the parlor, however, Sara ducked into the kitchen to see if Tan, Aurora's manservant, needed any help feeding Luc. Tan was preparing dinner and entertaining the boy, who sat strapped into his chair, happily drinking from his bottle.

Before long, Aurora popped her head into the kitchen. "Tan, dinner smells wonderful. Is it ready to serve?" He nodded, and opened the cookstove door, releasing a burst of heat. The aroma of roasted poultry made Sara's mouth water. Aurora took Sara's hand, sensing her hesitation. "Come along, dear. They won't bite," she teased.

Sara studied the guests as they took their seats. Philippe, of course, was seated at the head of the table, directly across from Sara. Aurora had seated the couples, Monsieur and Madame Lamont, Monsieur and Madame Courtois, and Monsieur and Madame Gautier across from one another. Aurora was seated to Sara's right, and Father L'Enfant, the village curate, to her left, to even out the numbers. The evening's early pleasantries showed the guests to be amiable enough. Sara was so delighted to be in the company of her own countrymen again, it did not matter how

American she found their manners and tastes. The elegant lilt of her native tongue, spoken around the table, enveloped her in its soft timbre and warmed her lonely heart. The fire was warm and the wine abundant, and Sara began to relax.

She realized, sitting at the table as Sara Landry, that she was completely in charge of her own life. As long as she kept her identity concealed, she was free to do as she pleased in this small corner of the world. She felt suddenly protective of this newfound autonomy.

"These sun-kissed hillocks are the very essence of God's country, do you not agree, Madame Landry? I daresay our California scenery rivals the very best offered by the French countryside." One could always rely on Aurora to voice strong opinions.

Sara had to agree. "I could not think of anything more satisfying than to cultivate one's own patch of vines here. The land is constant and loyal, something a person can cling to." Perhaps she had overstated her sentiment, but it was genuine.

"Well said, my dear." Aurora raised her glass.

"And why is that, madame?" Philippe interrupted from across the table.

"Monsieur?" Sara did not understand the question.

"Why would you 'cling' to the land?" His eyes searched hers with unexpected intensity, as if he were trying to solve a riddle.

She would have held his gaze, but the incandescence of his eyes, as brilliant as sapphires, unnerved her. She looked down at the napkin in her lap and smoothed its edges with her fingers. In a moment, she had formulated her answer and could look at him again.

"Perhaps because it does not disappoint."

He was clearly amused. "No, no, I suppose it doesn't. While wind, hail, disease and quake may wilt the vines and wither the fruit, the soil persists. Even scorched by flames, it comes back to life with a vengeance."

Sara shifted uncomfortably in her seat at this. She forced herself to hold her voice steady. "Yes, I suppose."

"And one day, it will gather us up and restore us to itself—dust to dust, as they say." Philippe finally broke the intense eye contact and speared another morsel from his plate. Was his last remark made in jest? Sara wondered. She decided the best response would be none at all.

"Now you've become positively morose, Philippe. Let the poor girl eat her dinner in peace, would you?" Aurora's eyes sparkled. She clearly enjoyed a bit of sparring at the dinner table.

"Lemieux, how do the vines fare this year? Do you anticipate any difficulties?" Gautier queried. He was a jovial, stout man with a ruddy complexion, who ate voraciously.

Philippe took a sip of wine, and it seemed to Sara that he was buying time. Serves him right, Sara thought. Let's see how he fares under scrutiny.

"I examined the entire crop yesterday, and I can say, from my own observation, that the vines are robust and in good health this year. The St. George took to the vines flawlessly," he announced. "No sign of infestation or decay at this point. It looks like it will be a plentiful harvest."

"Excellent! Glad to hear it! And your trip back East? I heard it was most profitable."

"Profitable to a degree, yes. More importantly, it was product-ive," Philippe gave a satisfied grin. "We made significant inroads with the largest eastern wine merchants and secured our orders for the fall."

Lamont, an experienced Napa vintner, chimed in. "Philippe's being modest. He sold every last gallon and made a stunning profit. We can't wait to send him out to New Orleans next win-ter to see what riches he can unearth for us there!" He slapped Philippe on the back.

"That is wonderful news! You didn't tell me all that." Aurora was delighted.

"I'm cautiously optimistic, I guess you could say." Philippe smiled genuinely at her.

Aurora laid down her fork. "The vines have rebounded, busi-ness is plentiful, and for these blessings we are grateful, but there are still dangers. Indeed, there is a storm blowing in from the East, maybe not this year or next, but within five years, I'd wager. It will be an unyielding blight, more obstinate than the phylloxera or the rot, and longer lasting." Aurora sipped her wine before adding, "Madame Landry has advised me so."

Sara's head shot up at the mention of her name, and Aurora nodded at her with a knowing twinkle in her eye. Sara's cheeks flushed.

"What is it, madame? What is this grave prediction of yours?" Courtois's face was ashen.

Sara tried to diffuse the tension at the table. She did not like being the focus of controversy.

"Madame exaggerates the importance of my remarks, of course.

I mentioned to her my concerns regarding the possible . . . impediments to the California wine trade in the coming years."

"We're intrigued," Lamont said, sounding amused. "Please, do educate us."

Sara had the sudden feeling that this was some sort of test. She knew her views were well-founded, whether or not they all agreed with her. She may not have been blessed with her sister's charms, but she knew she had a sharp mind and could spar with the might of Hercules himself. She took a deep breath and started slowly.

"Monsieur, the temperance movement is gaining popularity, especially in the eastern cities—New York, Boston, Chicago. The Women's Christian Temperance Union in particular has many supporters. They even tried to stop McKinley from serving spirits at his own inaugural last month."

"And Hayes's White House was free of spirits, thanks to his wife, ol' Lemonade Lucy," Lamont laughed, and the others joined in. "Her temperance leanings may have influenced her husband, but not the entire country."

"Yes, I've heard the stories, monsieur," Sara continued, "but to witness their demonstrations with my own eyes was something different entirely."

"Where did you see all this? In Chicago? New York?" Lamont was skeptical. "It's a fleeting fashion, I'm sure. If it becomes anything at all, we will just reroute our trade to other parts of the country until the hysteria passes."

Sara noticed that Philippe was listening attentively but had not yet spoken up. Courtois looked as though he might suffer a stroke of paralysis right there at the table.

"Forgive me, madame, but you've only recently arrived in this country. What qualifies you to make such judgments?" Gautier challenged.

Aurora interjected before Sara could speak. "She came from Chicago, and before that, Angers. She is a vintner's daughter. She's very knowledgeable about many subjects, not just picking and pruning as you may have been led to believe, Gautier."

"It's not my intention to prophesize about what will or will not happen. I simply mean to inform you of my . . . concern," Sara offered gently.

"What do you say, Lemieux? Is this not overblown rubbish?" Courtois, it seemed to Sara, wanted reassurance that the world would never change. He was not a modern thinker, she guessed.

Philippe dabbed his napkin to his lips, placed it back in his lap and answered with a confidence that, to Sara, bordered on arrogance. "Absolutely. It's like all other movements. Housewives, in need of a reason for their husbands' infidelities, and preachers, forgive me, Father, in need of something to rail against in their pulpits, try to strike terror in people's hearts and convince them that intoxicants are the devil's elixir."

At this, Sara could not hold her tongue, even though she knew she should. "Yes, and in a few years' time, those housewives and women, right here in Napa, will secure the vote, and do you know what they will do with it?" Sara looked at Philippe. "They will use it to pass the prohibition laws, a move that could decimate your trade, monsieur."

Philippe chuckled. "I doubt they would."

"How can you be so sure?" Sara inquired, tilting her head.

"For one, such a vote would also destroy their husbands' livelihoods."

Sara faked a smile. "I am not speaking of the vintners' wives. I'm speaking of the prune, apple and raisin farmers' wives. They could account for over sixty percent of the vote, could they not?"

"Woo hoo!" Aurora's whole body shuddered with laughter. "Clearly, Madame Landry has done her arithmetic. She may have you there, Philippe."

Philippe shrugged his shoulders mildly and seemed unruffled. "Forgive me, Aurora, for saying so, but that is precisely the reason why the association spent a fortune lobbying for the defeat of your beloved suffrage referendum last year. Some of our colleagues agree with Madame Landry. They fear prohibition will follow the women's vote."

"And what do you think, Philippe?" Aurora countered brashly.

"What I think hardly matters. However, I am of the opinion that although they may try to prohibit the drink, in the end, man will find a way—legal or otherwise—to procure it, and will pay handsomely for it."

Courtois raised his glass in agreement. "Hear, hear! Lemieux, you're a keen rascal. God bless you, sir!" he blustered.

Sara found Courtois's heartiness a bit forced, yet she could not help but feel agitated. Her first introduction to the locals and she had already managed to kick a hornet's nest. She did believe, however, that she was right, and that the gentlemen were short-sighted. No matter how stinging their rebuke, Sara was proud of herself for holding her ground. She was relieved when Aurora steered the discussion in a more light-hearted direction.

"I, for one, cast my vote in favor of chocolate cake." Aurora pushed her chair away from the table and the men rose. "Do I have any takers?"

Everyone nodded enthusiastically and complimented the meal. Sara leapt up to help with dessert. When she walked into the kitchen, she found Tan putting the kettle on, his back to Luc, who was still seated in his chair, wide eyes transfixed by the enormous cake before him. Before Sara could reach him, Luc launched himself headlong into the chocolate-frosted confection. The fluffy frosting covered his entire face, but Luc didn't seem to mind a bit. He licked the cake and clawed at it, wedging the frosting under his greedy Lilliputian fingernails.

"Luc!" Sara was horrified. She heard the door swing open behind her. It was Aurora, and on her heels, Philippe.

The cake was utterly ruined, crumbling around a huge hole the size of Luc's face. The little criminal rubbed enough frosting from his eyes to open them and flashed Sara an unapologetic grin. Sara and the others could not help but burst into peals of laughter.

The following day, after Mass, Sara slung her shawl around Luc and hitched him to her hip for a walk down by the pond. Now that the warmer weather was upon them, the wildflowers were blooming and the cattail plants swayed in the offshore breeze.

Luc tugged on Sara's hair, which she had loosened from its usual pinned-up style. He was dexterous for his age, and was busy twisting a thick lock of hair around his wrist. She was concentrating on untangling herself when she was startled by the thud of approaching hoofbeats. She looked up, blinded by the midday sun, to see the shadow of a horse and rider slow to a walk, then stop only a few yards away. The tall rider dismounted and tethered the horse to a nearby maple tree.

Sara froze when she recognized him. Philippe Lemieux's chiseled face and coolly appraising eyes came into view as soon as he removed his hat. He offered her a broad, relaxed smile, and he was suddenly so attractive, she nearly lost her footing. Sara wrapped her arms protectively around Luc, trying to calm her own fluttering nerves. Her momentary bedazzlement was soon offset by the memory of his less than civil behavior the prior evening. What could he possibly want? Hadn't it been enough to undermine her at dinner? After challenging her with such determination last evening, he had the audacity to give her this breathtakingly beautiful smile today? It was unfair, not to mention disarming.

"May I walk with you?" His voice was like silk, but his eyes were cautious.

"As you like, monsieur." She tried to sound indifferent. She glanced up at him. He was half a head taller than Sara, over six feet, she'd guess. He was dressed as though he'd just come from church, although she hadn't noticed him there. With a twinge of irritation, she realized she had been looking for him. If he had been there, she wondered, did he notice that she hadn't received the Sacrament? Would he have wondered why?

Philippe tucked his hat under his left arm, and his blond bangs, disheveled by the breeze, swept over his forehead carelessly. He wore a gray coat and contrasting navy waistcoat, dark trousers, a short turnover shirt collar and black riding boots. He didn't wear the mustache and pointed beard considered fashionable these days, and she had noticed at dinner that this accented his square jaw. She liked his clean-shaven looks—when he wasn't undercutting her in public, of course.

They started walking together along the dirt path that encircled the pond. Philippe didn't speak right away, but Sara could feel his eyes upon her, and she instinctively straightened her back in an effort to quiet the conflicting emotions his presence had triggered.

"Did you enjoy supper last night?" Another exquisite smile.

"Indeed. It was quite a lively exchange, wouldn't you agree?" Sara tried to sound light, as though their disagreement hadn't affected her.

"And a most interesting party. Aurora is a unique character, is she not?"

"Yes." Sara's voice softened at the mention of her name. "Her kindness toward Luc and me—well, her generosity is overwhelming."

"It must have been difficult arriving as you did, baby in tow, not knowing a soul here."

"Yes."

"And it must have been difficult to cope after your husband passed." He shook his head and then looked up to the sky, squinting at the sun. "My brother died last year. Nothing compared to a spouse, I'm sure, but it leaves its mark." His voice, tinged with melancholy, sent Sara's dormant guilt spiraling.

"I'm sorry." She could say no more, for she was in danger of losing her composure.

"Thank you." Philippe pressed on. "Forgive me, madame, but I am . . . curious."

"About?" She kept her tone cool and businesslike.

"I was wondering something at dinner last night."

"And what was that?" She supposed she would have to continue answering his questions. Otherwise, he might grow suspicious.

"Why have you traveled so far from France? Did you not have any family you could rely upon back in Angers? The Landry clan is spread widely throughout the Loire, is it not?" His tone was pleasant, even if the questions were somewhat prying. He seemed to be honestly interested in her situation. She didn't know whether to be flattered or wary.

Sara recited her well-rehearsed story. "My husband Henri died—he had no family to speak of. My parents are dead. I have no siblings. I am a vintner's daughter, and grape farming is all I know. It's what I'm skilled at. It seemed time for a change, a new life for Luc and me, free from the established ways and old prejudices." She managed a wistful smile. "Perhaps you came here for similar reasons?"

"Yes, I daresay I did." He sighed and looked east toward the rolling hills. "Perhaps you think me impertinent. I apologize. I'm intrigued, that's all. I can tell you're well educated, although I would speculate that your knowledge is mostly self-taught."

"Primarily," she allowed. "I attended school until the age of thirteen. The rest I learned on the farm or from books."

"How large was your farm?" Philippe asked politely.

"Fifty hectares." A lie.

"So it was sizable for Angers?" He sounded impressed.

"Yes," Sara said happily, remembering Saint Martin.

"What did you grow?"

"Chenin blanc."

"And who inherited the farm?"

Sara glanced at him, surprised again by his directness. She squinted at the water, now shimmering in the midday sun. "It came to my son and me. However, after my husband's death, I had to sell it to repay his debtors and secure a small living for us." A partial truth.

"That must have been a disappointment."

Yes, especially the part where your father cheated us, caused my father's death, then coerced my mother into selling Saint Martin— my rightful inheritance. And now, to protect herself and Luc, Sara had to pretend that Papa, Maman and Lydia had never existed. Sara was in no mood for his questioning, even if his assumptions were accurate.

"If you'll excuse me, monsieur, we should head back."

"Ah—I have offended you." He touched her elbow lightly. "Forgive me."

She recoiled reflexively from his touch. "There's nothing to forgive." She hurried ahead of him, but she could hear him walking in step behind her. Why couldn't he just leave her alone? Unable to take it any longer, she whirled around to confront him.

"Monsieur, why did you seek me out today when you did not take any pains to hide your disdain last night?"

Philippe raised his eyebrows in surprise, but quickly recovered with a laugh. "You are spirited! And I admire your directness."

His face smoothed into a serious expression. "You misunderstand me—it was not disdain. I admired your conviction. You don't seem like the type of woman to trifle with people's confidence in their livelihoods. If you were willing to voice your opinions last night, then you must have also determined a path around the dilemma."

"Monsieur?" Sara was befuddled.

"Let me speak plainly. You are concerned enough about the gains the prohibitionists are making that you didn't hesitate to announce that a prohibition is inevitable. Therefore, I presume you have an idea about what we vintners should do to safeguard ourselves against such a catastrophe." He stopped walking and turned to face her. "It's just that I would very much like to hear your ideas," he said encouragingly.

Sara was still skeptical, even if Philippe's manner was persuasive. "You didn't give me that impression last night."

"And why would I have? I was seated at a table of friends, and although we may be comrades-in-arms, we are still rivals. Monsieur Courtois is a man who needs reassurance. He's not comfortable with anything that might disrupt his life as a gentleman farmer. And the others are not the most forward thinkers." He looked down, seeking her eyes and surveying her expression. "Besides, I knew nothing about your experience. I wanted to talk to you about your theories privately—not with an audience."

Apparently the two of them had acted their parts convincingly. Despite herself, Sara admired his competitive instincts. "You flatter me, monsieur. I only have one idea, still in its infancy, untested."

"I'm all ears." He gazed at her intently.

250

Sara began to walk again. She could not think clearly while he was staring at her. Philippe mirrored her stride effortlessly, waiting quietly.

"We have to act preemptively. Fight the temperance movement in its own backyard, if you will. What groups do you think will most likely propagate the move toward prohibition here in the West?"

"Social groups and churches, I would imagine."

"Exactly. Ironic, isn't it?"

She could almost hear the click in his head as he grasped her meaning. His eyes widened with understanding. "Ah, yes. The Catholic Church. The archdiocese needs wine for the Sacrament."

"Yes. You should arrange things directly with Archbishop Riordan."

"How do you suggest I secure a long-term arrangement? Surely there will be others vying for the business?"

"From what I understand in speaking with the curate at dinner, sacramental wine is currently purchased from a variety of suppliers—all small, all from the local parishes. If it were me—" she shook her head, realizing her error. "Let me rephrase. If it were me, and I were a man, I'd go directly to the archbishop with a case or two of my best red, and offer a long-term contract at three cents per gallon lower than his best supplier."

She looked over to assess his reaction. His expression was contemplative, expectant. She took that as a good sign and continued, excited now.

"You could specify in the contract that you're willing to match any lower bids in the future, and that you'll meet their quality requirements." Sara glanced at Philippe, who nodded in reply. "In return, you should ask for the archbishop's guarantee that the church will purchase a certain number of bottles each year," she suggested.

Sara stopped abruptly and faced Philippe, feeling even more enthusiastic about her ideas. "There's no question that you'll be taking a cut in your profits the first few years, but think of it as insurance. Within five to ten years, a prohibition could completely dry up your other markets—and you will have created an alternative, legal market for your wines. Let's not forget that the archdiocese includes all the churches north to the Oregon border, east to the Colorado River and south to the Diocese of Monterrey. The opportunity is vast."

Philippe looked impressed. "It is indeed. But what if the Catholic Church goes dry during the prohibition?"

"I doubt that will happen. The use of alcohol will have to be permitted for medicinal purposes—so why not the Blessed Sacrament as well? Besides, what will you care? You'll have a contract, and we all know that any prohibition could only be temporary, and the archdiocese will need to have a supply of wine on hand." She did not give Philippe time to respond. "And to your point, just in case, you really do need to make Eagle's Run . . . prohibition-proof. In other words, take Aurora up on her offer to help you cultivate those extra acres of land into a viable fruit orchard. Apples, raisins, prunes, olives—whatever you like, just so long as it's not grapes." Sara could have gone on, but decided she had been bold enough already.

Philippe stepped back, and Sara could sense his surprise. "I can see you've had some time to think this through."

She shifted Luc to her other hip. "I'm not naive enough to think that you haven't considered it as well."

"Yes, but I confess I never thought of securing the business so far in advance. Or starting the orchard right on the heels of my first decent harvest."

"But who's to say it *is* that far in advance? Prohibition might not be as far off as we think. Can you really afford to put off planning for it?"

"Perhaps you're right. Hedging my interests certainly would have its benefits—peace of mind being one of them. But why would you share your ideas with me?"

"Well, obviously, I have yet to acquire my own vineyard. Besides, it takes something to admit you don't know everything," Sara teased. "Perhaps it's because you were interested enough to ask."

Philippe contemplated that for a moment and then turned the full force of his azure eyes upon her. "You are a feisty one, aren't you?"

Sara was pleased at the compliment. *May you never know the full extent of it,* she thought with a twinge of remorse.

Philippe bid them goodbye with a bow and ruffled Luc's hair before riding off. It was well past one in the afternoon. By the time they arrived back at Aurora's, Luc was sleeping contentedly in Sara's arms. She laid him in his crib and glanced in the mirror. She was surprised at her reflection. Her hair was disarranged, but not unattractive, and flowed loosely down to her shoulders. Her eyes had a new brightness about them, and her cheeks were flushed a becoming shade of pink. She looked alive and young, and for the first time in over a year, she felt that way, too.

What was she *doing?* She should run from Philippe and never look back. But she was tired of running, of just surviving. She wanted a life. And despite who he was and what she had done, she was drawn to this magical place, and moreover, drawn to him. She felt as though she belonged here. For the first time since Lydia had died, Sara felt an inspiring surge of hope. She would eventually have to own up to what she'd done. She would have to tell Philippe, make him understand, hope against hope that he'd believe her and see her side of the story. But she knew that even if he did, even if he understood that she had killed Bastien in self-defense, there was one fact that Sara couldn't escape. After he had attacked her, she had *wanted* Bastien to suffer. Maybe she had even wanted him to die. Sara closed her eyes, trying to remove the memory from her consciousness. She couldn't think about it now.

Sara had endured the loss of her family and traveled so far. To succumb to her buried guilt and confess would be to surrender her future—and Luc's. But to leave now would cast even more suspicion on them. That she could not do. She would stay and create a new life for them among their new friends and hope for the best.

It was six weeks before Sara was once again thrown into the path of Philippe Lemieux. She had kept busy planting beets, corn, tomatoes and herbs in Aurora's garden, and helping write lesson plans for Aurora's classes at the Ladies' Seminary. Today she was pushing Luc down Main Street in a pram, a generous gift from Aurora. The balmy June weather was exhilarating to the senses.

She had journeyed to town to purchase cloth and pins for Luc's diapers, and notebooks for Aurora. Downtown Napa bustled with an energy Sara had not witnessed when she arrived here in the bleakness of December. The streets were flooded with people and wagons laden with French and American wine barrels, bottles and farming implements. Winemaking in the valley was in full swing; the vintners were racking, blending and re-barreling their wines in anticipation of the bottling that would take place in midsummer. Sara was so absorbed in observing all the people passing by that she was startled when Tan pulled up beside her in Aurora's rig. It was amazing he had found her in the crowd, but Sara had always admired his quiet efficiency.

In moments, Tan had loaded Sara, Luc, the pram and all her parcels into the wagon. Since they each spoke limited English, Sara understood only that she was to meet Aurora at Eagle's Run.

"Madame Landry!" Philippe exclaimed upon their arrival, emerging from the winery to greet them, his spirits high. Tan halted the rig, and Sara looked around, perplexed to see no sign of Aurora.

"Monsieur Lemieux, my apologies. I thought I was supposed to meet Aurora here."

"You are indeed, but I believe she's coming a little later. Come, let me help you two down."

Sara was rattled. Philippe's charm was disarming. She had to look away to assemble her thoughts, and she despised herself a bit for it. Despite her resolve to form an intelligent phrase, she stumbled over her words. "I'm sorry but—well, I don't really know why I'm here."

Philippe chuckled. "You and Aurora were invited because I require your counsel." He took Luc from Sara, securing him in one arm, and then helped her down from the wagon. When he wrapped his rough fingers gently around hers, their touch was electric, the air around them instantly charged. Sara tried not to flinch from the heat of his skin on hers. She thanked Tan for driving her, trying to compose herself, then willed herself to turn her attention back to Philippe. She released her hand from his.

"And what kind of advice do you seek?" Her voice was calm, businesslike.

"I need you to taste the chardonnay and tell me what you think."

Sara shrugged. "I am hardly qualified, monsieur."

"Have you not grown grapes your entire life?"

"Yes, but—"

"And are you not a vintner's daughter, trained in the art of pressing and blending white grapes from the Loire?"

"Yes, but those were chenin blanc."

"And wouldn't it be fair to say that because you've been drinking wine from—I'm guessing—the age of eight, you are able to distinguish between fine wine and swill?"

Sara smiled a bit at that. "Yes," she agreed reluctantly.

Philippe grinned. "Then you are completely qualified, I'd wager."

He held Luc while he led Sara into the dim cellar, which was lit only by a table lantern and slivers of daylight peeking through the window wells. After seating Luc carefully on the floor, Philippe used a pipette to transfer chardonnay from a barrel to three glasses. He handed one to Sara.

256

Sara held it up in the natural light. The wine was a brilliant pale honey color. She placed her nose over the edge of the glass and inhaled deeply. Oak and vanilla. She took a sip, rolling the cool liquid over her tongue. It was creamy—she tasted butter, oak and perhaps, yes, pear. Philippe was watching her intently. Sara would reserve her opinion until he answered all her questions.

"When was the final racking?"

Philippe looked surprised. "We just completed it. All the wine has been siphoned off the lees," he added.

Sara took another sip and this time detected a refreshing hint of lime. "And you sweetened with . . . ?"

"A little beet sugar."

It had a nice bite, perhaps a bit heavier on the tannins than she'd expected for a white, but not unpleasant. She liked it. Philippe leaned against a nearby table, absentmindedly drumming his fingers on its surface.

"American oak?"

He looked up. "Of course."

"And who will be buying this chardonnay?" She met his eyes, and he cocked his head, brow furrowed in confusion.

"How is that relevant? Either it's good or it's not." There was an edge of irritation in his voice. This was turning out to be much more fun than Sara had imagined.

She laughed. "Bear with me, monsieur. I promise you I shall come to a conclusion soon. Now, are you marketing it to the local merchants or back East?"

"If you must know, we'll be shipping the bottles to New York, Boston and Chicago."

"Hmm. The wine you've produced is dry, but with a bit of a bite, which I enjoy immensely." Philippe seemed pleased, but Sara wasn't finished. "Unfortunately, I am not the person, or rather, the kind of woman, to whom the merchants back East will want to sell your chardonnay. The middle-class and well-off females there prefer a much sweeter drink. My recommendation would be to blend it with a lighter, French-oaked chardonnay, or perhaps a fruity pinot gris, before you bottle it."

Philippe's eyes widened. Clearly, he had expected only praise, not advice. "And what if I leave it as it is and take my chances in the marketplace?"

"You can ask Aurora for her opinion," Sara said matter-of-factly, scooping Luc up in her arms, "but I'd say you risk that the eastern merchants will not renew their orders for next year. Why don't you blend half, offer both chardonnays to them and see which their customers prefer? It would be an interesting experiment, would it not?"

"Perhaps, but I'd rather not 'experiment' with my livelihood." His voice was tight.

Before Sara could speak again, they heard a wagon lurch to a stop outside. "That must be Aurora. Will you excuse me for a minute, madame?" His voice was softer, more civil now. Philippe bounded up the stairs, two at a time, making Sara wonder at a physically robust farmer taking such pains to craft so delicate a wine. She admired him for it.

"Yoo-hoo!" Sara heard a winded Aurora call to her as she descended the creaky stairs to the cellar. "Sorry I'm late, my dears. I was cornered by Dean Montrose at the seminary. Oh, and my apologies—I simply can't stay, for I'm already late to Madame Maude's for my suffrage meeting." She rubbed her palms together. "What do we have, Philippe?"

He handed her a glass of chardonnay. Aurora took a sip, swishing it about in her mouth. She peered up at Philippe over the rim of her glass.

"And what did Sara make of it?"

Philippe touched Sara's elbow lightly and whispered, "Don't you dare utter a word." He flashed Aurora a smile. "I want another unbiased opinion before I make my decision as to what should, or shouldn't, be done."

Sara bit her lip to keep from laughing as Aurora made a display of savoring the wine. She swallowed loudly and emitted a satisfied "Aaah!"

She handed the glass back to Philippe and turned toward the stairs, calling over her shoulder to the pair of them. "Excellent. Particularly bold on the finish. But I enjoy a sweeter white myself. Sara, dear, are you coming to the meeting with me, or walking home?"

Sara smiled triumphantly, and Philippe rolled his eyes. "Coming, Aurora," she replied.

Sara chuckled and, taking her leave, turned back to address Philippe. "In all seriousness, Monsieur Lemieux, please save a few of the pure, unblended bottles for me. I sincerely enjoyed it."

It was a half-mile ride to Madame Maude's estate. This would be Sara's first introduction to Aurora's friends, the women who campaigned for the Napa branch of the National American Woman Suffrage Association. Sara had agreed to attend their monthly meeting with Aurora, but, although she was curious, she didn't intend to do any campaigning anytime soon. She planned to sit quietly and observe the meeting.

When they arrived at the large, turreted stone house, there was scarcely any space by the roadside for Aurora to park her runabout. Wagons, carriages and surreys were scattered all over the yard. Some were modest, others lavishly decorated. Aurora picked up a book that had been wedged in the seat they shared and showed it to Sara. "This will entirely change your thinking— you must read it." Then she shook her head. "Unfortunately, its radical views are alienating some of our most fervent supporters across the nation. Today we have to figure out how we're going to respond to the criticism . . . and how we're going to regroup after the defeat of the equal suffrage referendum in November." Aurora smiled with nervous enthusiasm. "Should be an entertaining meeting!"

The book's title was *The Woman's Bible*, and it had been translated into French. The title alone seemed blasphemous to Sara, but she supposed it would help her learn more about the plight of women in California. Gathering Luc in her arms, she followed Aurora into the home's immense front parlor and took a seat in the back row. Aurora perched herself right up front.

A tall, well-dressed woman stood up before a crowd of fifty, and addressed their host, Madame Maude, while stabbing a finger toward her copy of the offending text. "Mrs. Stanton says right here that the Holy Trinity is composed of 'a Heavenly Mother, Father, and Son,' and she goes on to say that prayers should be addressed to an 'ideal Heavenly Mother'! This is surely blasphemy, and that's how the majority of our sisters in suffrage will view it!'"

The group began to nod and grumble, some in agreement, some opposed. The angry voices in the room became shrill, and Luc began to cry. Sara nestled him to her chest to soothe him. Madame Maude tried to quiet the crowd, but to no avail. Finally, Aurora popped up out of her seat, clearly upset, and began to bang the book on the desk next to her.

"Ladies, ladies, ladies!" she shouted. Finally, the voices dimmed to a murmur so Aurora could address them. "There are many assertions in this book. We will agree with some, and we will disagree with others. We are a branch of the NAWSA—our mandate is to campaign for the women's vote." Aurora waved *The Woman's Bible* in the air, holding the crowd's attention. "Ladies, this is an important work because it states that women are just as important and productive as men, and it demands that we receive equal rights. There will be plenty of time in the future to campaign for the rights to which we're entitled, but if we do not first secure the vote for ourselves, then we will have no power to do anything!'"

Cheers and applause erupted. Sara was bewildered by the passion and solidarity. Never in a million years would she have seen a similar display among the women of Vouvray. Sara began to feel that, despite her longing for Saint Martin, perhaps she was better suited to a new-fashioned town like Napa than the staid, traditional French hamlet of her birth.

Once Madame Maude had wrestled back control of the meeting, the gathering lasted another hour or so. New committees were formed, and there was excited talk about pamphlets, banners, pins, Susan Anthony and speaking engagements. Each committee had a list of items they were responsible for accomplishing by the next meeting. Sara was impressed with their organization.

"So, what did you think?" Aurora asked on the ride home.

"I thought you made a good argument. The group seems very committed to the cause."

"And might you consider joining us?" Aurora raised an eyebrow.

"Would they want me to? I make wine—I can't support their prohibitionist views."

"Only a handful of the women in that room are active prohibitionists. Most of us are just working for the vote."

"I would like to attend another meeting," Sara said cautiously. "I think that for now, though, I need to spend my time learning more English and working to pay my way."

"Fair enough," Aurora said cheerfully. "But it's young women like you who will benefit from having the power to vote. It's for women like you—our sisters, daughters, granddaughters—that we continue to campaign so tirelessly for this."

And Sara was grateful to them. "I understand, but perhaps I should read your book and become a little more informed on the subject first."

"Sounds reasonable—I won't pester you anymore! Let's change the subject. What did you think of Philippe's chardonnay?" Aurora gave her a sideways glance.

"I told him that although I enjoyed it, he should blend it with a lighter chardonnay or a fruity pinot gris before he bottles it."

Aurora chuckled. "And how did that go over?"

Sara smiled. "I think he was a little taken aback by my suggestion. It made me laugh when you told him that you preferred a sweeter wine—then he couldn't ignore my idea."

Aurora laughed. "Oh my dear, even if he put considerable effort into it, Philippe Lemieux could never ignore *you.*"

CHAPTER 14

Proposition

S ara had no idea how long Philippe had been standing in the doorway of Aurora's workroom. Her stomach somersaulted when she looked up to find him there, keenly observing her as she catalogued her friend's medicinal herbs.

"Aurora told me I'd find you here."

"And what else did she tell you?" Sara was surprised by her sudden irritation, and to judge from the look on Philippe's face, so was he. It had been weeks since she'd seen him, but he always caught her unawares.

"She told me that you're bored," Philippe said, gesturing to the bottles and plant cuttings and papers on the workshop bench, "with all this."

"That's ridiculous. It's fascinating, you know, the research." Sara tried to sound enthusiastic, turning back to her journal and doodling aimlessly on the page to make it look as though she were in the middle of something desperately important.

"Well, if you feel this is your . . . raison d'être, then you probably wouldn't be interested in what I came here to ask you." He leaned casually against the wall, arms crossed, a grin tugging at his lips.

Sara knew she shouldn't ask, but her curiosity got the better of her. "And what is that?"

A triumphant smile now. "I came to offer you a job."

Sara hesitated. "Doing what?"

"As you're well aware, Jip Montagne is gone, and you may have heard that I've sacked my housekeeper too."

"What does that have to do with me? You know, I don't cook or wash clothes very well."

Philippe laughed. "No, I didn't think you did."

"Why is that funny?"

"Because I find you . . . charming."

"You're laughing at me?"

"Not at all! You have mistaken me entirely." Philippe glided toward her. He stopped a foot away, his eyes penetrating, serious. "I want you to be my foreman, or forewoman, or maybe we'll have to come up with another name for it."

Sara was flabbergasted. Surely he was teasing her now, though his eyes were bright with sincerity. She felt a wave of elation rush over her, but would not give in to it without considering the prospect before her. She wanted her own land, not to work someone else's. Yet maybe this was a way to get what she wanted, eventually.

"I have fewer qualifications than an experienced foreman."

"Whatever qualifications you lack, you more than make up for with your hard work and quick mind. Aurora has observed your work and finds you highly knowledgeable and capable."

"She does?"

"Yes, and let's not forget, you also speak my language. You are exactly what I—what Eagle's Run needs to grow."

Sara had never heard him speak so flatteringly to anyone. *Don't get ahead of yourself*, she thought. There were still many obstacles to working with Philippe.

He seemed to sense her reluctance. "And I'm going to need someone reliable to blend, bottle and arrange the transport of my wines to over half the parishes in the archdiocese . . ." Philippe's voice trailed off, but his face was positively beaming.

"What? You made the deal!" Sara was amazed.

"I sure did. You are a genius." Philippe gathered her hands in his, exclaiming, "They jumped at the offer!" Sara had never seen him so euphoric.

"Congratulations," she said, gently pulling her hands away, unsettled by the warmth of his touch.

"Congratulations to us. I wouldn't have done it without your encouragement. I owe you a great deal."

Sara shook her head, but Philippe was not easily thwarted. "I'm prepared to offer you sixty dollars a month in wages, plus food and lodging." Sara studied Philippe closely. Even standing still, he exuded a restlessness and vitality. He was a force of nature.

"What do you say?" His words snapped Sara out of her momentary bewilderment.

"Um . . . who will care for Luc? I can't do both."

"No, of course not. I've hired a new housekeeper. She has excellent references, and she's worked as a nanny before. Luc can stay with her when he can't be with you, until he's old enough to work, you know, with us . . . on the farm," Philippe offered, slipping his hands into his pockets.

Sara was more excited than she would have imagined at the thought of working with him for the long term. Her heart began to fly.

"Where would we live?"

"In the barn. There's a small apartment where Montagne lived. I'll clean it and add some furniture and a crib for Luc. It's modest, but it should do . . . temporarily." His eyes shifted to the floor, as if he wanted to say more.

"And what about Aurora? You've spoken with her?"

"Yes, and she has agreed to it, provided I give her full access to the farm, and of course, to you and Luc whenever she has need of you."

Sara gave a half-smile. She and Aurora had become close, and she suspected Aurora thought of her as the daughter she'd never had.

Philippe appeared to understand. "I knew she would ask for something in return for sacrificing her only apprentice."

"She drives a hard bargain."

"Indeed." He smiled broadly.

"I guess you've thought of everything." Sara paused and thought of the absurdity of his offer, and the abundance of his trust in her. She pushed aside the guilt that lurked under the surface with regards to the Lemieux family, and instead focused on the opportunity: they would do great things together. They could make the Eagle's Run wines world-renowned. One day she would have to tell him the truth, but in the meantime, she would impress him with her work. At the same time, she could save for the one thing that mattered more than anything—the ability to buy back Saint Martin.

"Your deliberation is torture. Tell me your thoughts at once," he said playfully.

"I'm not in a position to refuse your offer, for I know I could do the work credibly. But you know one of my biggest faults is my boldness . . ." Sara hesitated only briefly. "I must try your patience and ask you for one more thing."

"Name it."

"Ten acres."

"What?"

"Ten acres, which I will purchase from you over time. Give me forty dollars a month and apply the other twenty toward the purchase of a share of your land."

Philippe stared thoughtfully at Sara, who became uneasy. Would he turn her down?

"I want to provide for my son. With my own land, I can do that."

Philippe continued to scrutinize her for what seemed an eternity. She felt like a toddler having a tantrum because she wanted chocolate instead of vanilla ice cream. But perhaps he was actually considering her request. Then a conspiratorial grin spread across his face, as if he knew something she didn't.

"I won't provide any laborers. And you'll have to rent any equipment you need—plows, the press . . ." His tone was matter-of-fact.

"Yes."

"You can have ten acres that have yet to be planted, near the creek—for five hundred dollars."

"Five hundred!" Sara couldn't believe his audacity. "That's uncleared land, not even worth three hundred!"

"But it's the only land available to you," Philippe replied calmly.

True, Sara thought grimly. "Three hundred and fifty dollars."

"Plus half of your first harvest's profits."

He would not give her preferential treatment because she was a woman, or a widowed mother, that much was obvious. But then, she wouldn't want him to. "Agreed."

"Excellent. You start work on Monday. We'll move you in on Sunday. Shall we shake hands on it?" Philippe extended his arm.

As his sinewy fingers gripped hers, she felt a rush of joy sweep over her. She would have jumped with excitement had not another thought suddenly intruded.

He noticed her change of mood immediately. "What is it?"

"There will be talk, you know."

"What kind of talk?" Philippe had yet to release her hand from his.

"You are an unmarried man, hiring a young widow to do a man's work while living fifty yards from you. It's highly improper."

"Perhaps." Philippe pulled her gently toward him and bent down to whisper in her ear, "But I wouldn't have it any other way."

Philippe had offered to drive Sara and Luc over to Eagle's Run right after Mass that Sunday, but Sara insisted that he meet them at Aurora's house to minimize the gossip and judgments that she knew would come. The speculation would begin soon enough, but Sara was willing to take the risk. As long as she and Philippe didn't cross any of the lines of propriety she had established in her mind, she could hold her head high, knowing that her conduct was irreproachable in God's eyes. She didn't really care about what anyone else thought—anyone except Philippe, of course.

Sara had practically nothing to bring to her new accommodations at Eagle's Run. The carriage carried only a trunk containing clothes, diapers, toiletries, and her mother's Bible. In a separate basket, she had packed Luc's food and bottles, and his favorite toy. Poor Pup had seen better days. Over the last three months, his fur had become threadbare from Luc's constant biting and sucking. She would have to patch him up a bit when she had a chance, so that his stuffing wouldn't fall out.

Philippe was in high spirits during the five-minute journey from Aurora's to Eagle's Run. He spoke of the new cooper he'd hired and the Italians he'd lined up to help during the summer and fall months. When they arrived at the barn, Sara was surprised to see that its small windows glistened pristinely in the afternoon sun.

They entered the upstairs apartment, which was divided into two rooms by a dark green cotton curtain. The pleasant fragrance of freshly milled Ponderosa pine filled the barn, and Sara looked down at the wide floorboards, which were peppered with dark knots and had been shined to a beautiful shade of golden-brown. There was a small bed covered with a pale green and yellow quilt, and a bedside table just large enough to hold an oil lamp. On the other side of the curtain, Sara found a crib, a long table with a porcelain washbasin, and the most beautiful rocking chair she had ever laid eyes on. It was amply wide, painted black and decorated with golden scroll accents and colorful Botticelli-type angels. A soft blue blanket was carefully folded over one arm. She realized she had never rocked Luc in a chair. The care and time Philippe had taken to prepare the rooms left her speechless.

Philippe stood in the doorway, having graciously given Sara and Luc a chance to look around. He must have mistaken her silence for disappointment. When he spoke, his voice was tight, almost anxious. "Is it all right?"

Sara finally exhaled. "It's perfect."

Philippe relaxed. "I can't take all the credit. I laid the floors and bought some of the furniture, but Aurora bought the linens and made it look—well, made it suitable for the two of you."

"This chair, Philippe—what beautiful workmanship." She sat in it, with Luc on her lap, and ran her hand along its polished, curved arm. She knew he must have chosen it—a woman would never have picked a black chair for a baby's room. Yet it suited the apartment.

"I thought so, too. I'm glad you like it," he said.

"Thank you . . . for all this." She shook her head; his generosity amazed her. "But this must have taken—" Sara suddenly grasped that, for Philippe, his hiring her had been a foregone conclusion. "How did you know? You only asked me last Wednesday."

He beamed confidently. "I was certain that I could persuade you if it came down to it."

"I'd better get to work then, and uphold my end of the bargain."

272

Philippe laughed and scooped Luc up in one arm. Sara was surprised at his easy way with the boy. "It's Sunday. Come meet Rose. She's prepared a meal for us and she'll entertain Luc, or put him down for his nap, while you and I talk grapes."

Sara hardly heard a word. For the first time, she could see an undeniable resemblance between Luc and Philippe: a similar curve to their cheeks, the same wave in their hair, the same round shape to their eyes, the same dimple when they smiled. The only difference was that Luc was dark-haired and brown-eyed, as Bastien had been, and Philippe was fair-haired and blue-eyed. A shiver ran down Sara's spine, and she could feel guilt tightening in her chest. Let's hope, she thought, that the difference is enough to keep everyone—most importantly Philippe—from wondering for some time.

Philippe looked at her with concern. "Are you okay? You look . . . startled."

Sara shook her head and waved him off. "Dinner, you said, right?" she asked cheerfully. "That sounds great. I'm starving."

At the house, Philippe and Sara sat down to a meal of roasted chicken, potatoes and carrots, served with white table wine, followed by plum pudding. Sara hadn't enjoyed such an exquisite meal since Lydia's wedding. "You certainly know who to hire," she said between bites. "This meal is delicious."

"Indeed, Rose cooks almost too well." Philippe patted his stomach. "Her meals are very rich. They're starting to compromise my waistline."

Sara shook her head. Philippe, she had reluctantly observed, had the muscular torso of Adonis. The thought made her flush, and she couldn't muster a word, even to change the subject. Fortunately, Philippe filled the silence.

"There's something I've been meaning to ask you."

"What is it?"

He hesitated before speaking. "Does it really bother you—the idea of people criticizing us behind our backs?" He took a sip of wine, but his eyes held hers.

"Not as far as my reputation is concerned. This is a business transaction, and Luc and I live separately from you. But," she admitted, "I am new in town, and it bothers me that buyers might be reluctant to transact business with you because of me. That, perhaps, is something to consider." Sara scooped pudding onto her spoon and ate slowly. She was self-conscious to be alone with Philippe, and at the very least wanted to make sure she didn't have a sliver of plum stuck between her teeth.

"You have a point. And I *have* thought about that. I think it's important that we both understand that that kind of . . . retaliation is a possibility. But in my opinion, the positive effect on my wine sales far exceeds the probable risks. Never forget that, in France, winemaking may be an art, but here, it's an industry."

"And a very competitive one, from what I've observed. That being said, people here in California tend to hold a more modern view of the world than, say, those in France, don't you think?" Sara tried to sound hopeful.

"I do. So we'll hope for the best and get down to business, agreed?" Philippe raised his glass, and Sara clinked hers to his.

CHAPTER 15

Moth to a Flame

S ara thrived in her new role. During late June, she led a crew of
eight men, turning the soil to uproot the weeds between the
vines. To turn the soil on the slopes, they used a stationary
winch to hoist a plow up the hill on a long cable. Sara left the heavier
tasks to the men, though she was proud that she could manage the
horse and plow by herself on more level ground, even if Philippe
did object. After all, if she'd been a man, he would have expected
her to do it. She was young and capable and wanted nothing more
than to be useful. Working with plows was much more cost-effective
and faster than working by hand, but still physically taxing, Sara
noted. She felt the pain in her neck, shoulders and legs.

By mid-July, they'd racked, blended and re-barreled the wines
inside the winery, including the remaining forty-five barrels of the

1895 vintage, making sure the red met the high standards set by the archdiocese for sacramental wine. By the end of July, they had finished bottling twenty thousand reds and nineteen thousand of the Eagle's Run white blend.

On the first evening in August, after a long day of transporting wine for the archdiocese to Napa Junction, Philippe and Sara sat down to a simple dinner of beef pie and a bottle of the 1895 zinfandel. They reviewed their plans for the upcoming harvest, deciding how many pickers they needed and the wages they'd offer.

Sara was impressed by Philippe's organized approach and the short time in which he had managed to test the red wine for purity, bottle it and label it. It had been less than three months since he'd put her idea into action. He handed Sara a list of contacts in the archdiocese, along with a list of parishes and the approximate number of parishioners registered in each. He instructed her that she would be responsible for anticipating demand and supplying the Church's warehouse at the Embarcadero. The priests who worked for Archbishop Riordan would be responsible for periodically testing the purity of the wine and distributing it to the parishes. It was a daunting project, but Sara was excited by the challenge. Philippe seemed to think she could handle all of it.

"I should stop talking and let you get Luc settled down for the night. Make sure to give Rose whatever instructions she needs for tomorrow." Rose was a soft-spoken, gentle woman who seemed delighted to be caring for Luc in addition to keeping the house and making the meals. She was a widow with three grown children. For Sara, Rose was a godsend.

"Tomorrow?"

"We have to be on the road early."

"Where to?" Sara hadn't realized they were going anywhere.

"The Embarcadero."

"We're going to San Francisco *tomorrow*?"

"Absolutely. The wine will arrive there by tomorrow morning, and I don't want it left unattended." He hesitated. "But there's something I need to tell you. It may . . . upset you." A smile began to appear at the corners of his mouth.

"And what is that?" Sara asked warily.

"Monsignor Finnegan, the archbishop's right-hand man, gave me a list of rules that we must adhere to."

"Certainly. Sacramental wine requires—"

"Yes, some are about the quality of the wine, but there are other restrictions regarding who can enter the residence of the archbishop and who is allowed to deal with the archdiocesan staff, even in the warehouse."

Sara raised her eyebrows.

Philippe cleared his throat in an effort to hide his amusement, Sara guessed. "You see, they only allow men."

"That's ridiculous! Why? They allow women in church. Did they say why?"

"I would presume it's to protect the priests and laymen working there from . . . temptation."

Sara exhaled with a huff. "I suppose that's their prerogative, although it's unnecessary. I mean, really, I work at a vineyard. It's my employment. What, do they imagine that all women are depraved?"

Philippe just laughed. "No, but I'm not concerned with *all* women. And besides"—he paused for a second—"I don't think you realize how very tempting you are." He was teasing her now.

"You're exaggerating again." Sara returned to their dilemma. "So, what does that mean? How am I supposed to accompany you and, more importantly, serve as the liaison between Eagle's Run and the archdiocese?"

"I thought about going alone, but then I realized you would want to see your idea through."

"And, so?" Sara asked expectantly.

He pushed his chair back from the table, stood and waited for Sara to do the same. "Come with me. You have some new clothes to try on."

The next day, they rose with the cock's crow and left Eagle's Run at dawn. Sara relished the opportunity to ride her horse astride, just as Philippe did. It was invigorating to be on horseback again. She felt like she was flying.

What a strange turn her life had taken. Here she was, living in America, dressed like a teenage boy. Philippe had stifled a laugh when he first laid eyes on her in one of his shirts with a buckskin vest, and breeches cinched with one of his black leather belts. She had had to tuck the legs deep into her boots to make sure they wouldn't slip off while she was walking. Her hair was shoved up under a hat. Philippe shook his head with a grin and insisted that if she lowered her voice and adopted a slow swagger, she could perhaps pass for a fifteen-year old. The breeches afforded her certain advantages. She no longer had to worry about crossing her legs or covering her ankles—it was divine! Maman, were she here, would have been horrified.

It took just over three hours to ride to Vallejo and ferry across the bay to San Francisco. Once they reached the Embarcadero, Sara followed Philippe to the train station to retrieve the bottles. With the flat wagons and drivers Philippe hired, it took them four trips to bring the bottles to the warehouse, just a short distance away. There was little time for sightseeing, or even conversation. In spite of Philippe's objections, Sara insisted on helping the men unload and stack the cases of wine. She reminded Philippe that today she was his teenage employee and would be expected to lend a hand. It was a small victory. She might not have a man's strength, but she could still carry her fair share. She knew she was equal to the task, although she did not relish the toll a day's riding and heavy lifting took on her body. She ached from her head to her toes by the afternoon's end.

By the time they had stacked a thousand cases and received their payment, it was four o'clock. She and Philippe had just enough time to catch the five o'clock ferry and make it home before nightfall, at around eight. When they arrived at the wharf, however, they were dismayed to find out that the five o'clock crossing had been canceled. Mechanical problems forced the steamship authority to turn away a crowd of rowdy passengers. Sara was silently relieved—she was too sore to ride tonight, though she'd never admit it aloud.

Philippe shrugged and looked up and down the dockside streets. "There are a few hotels I know of nearby. We could see if they have two rooms available . . ." His voice trailed off.

"What?" Sara asked, suspicious. "Did you have another idea? I'm in favor of anything that won't eat too far into that check you have burning a hole in your pocket. Any money we save goes back into the vineyard."

Philippe nodded in approval. "I knew I made the right choice hiring you. Yes, I do have another idea . . . but . . . well," he stammered, "I don't know if you'd—"

Sara cut him off midsentence. "Would you even hesitate to suggest it if I were a man working for you?"

"Ah, no. No, I wouldn't."

"Then?"

He shook his head and gave her a crooked smile. "I usually camp out at the beach. We can get supplies nearby." He looked up at the sky. "It looks like it'll be a clear night. I just find the beach more convenient and less stuffy than a hotel."

"Great—let's go."

Philippe looked surprised. "Really? You don't mind?"

"Of course not. I know how to pitch a tent and besides, I'd rather sleep outside. San Francisco is beautiful."

After stopping for supplies—blankets, a tent and feed for the horses—Sara and Philippe galloped down California Street, past the Presidio to a small crescent beach. It took some effort to coax the horses down the steep, rocky incline. At the bottom, they tied their mounts to a hitching post. Sara's wide eyes scanned the tall dark cliffs and jutting rock formations that sloped upwards from the shoreline, sheltering them on this small sliver of beach. Across the stretch of ocean before her, the lush green Marin headlands rose up from the bay in unbroken splendor. Everything in this part of the world was so expansive, so immense. She'd never seen anything like California. It seemed to stretch on forever.

"It's a beautiful spot. How often do you camp here?"

Philippe continued unsaddling the horses. "Almost every time I come here. This beach used to be the campground for the Chinese fishermen until they were kicked out by the white men that run the city." He shook his head in disgust.

Philippe pulled a quilt from his saddlebag and spread it over a patch of cool sand. Together, they scoured the beach for branches of driftwood large enough to start a fire. As Philippe worked on kindling a campfire, Sara sat down on the beach. It was a relief to finally take off her hat and release her hair from its pins. She had no hairbrush, so she combed her fingers through her tresses and shook out the knots. The light, salty breeze was refreshing, and cooled her itchy scalp. She tied her hair back loosely with a leather cord she had stashed in her bag.

Sara dug into her bag for the leftovers from lunch—cold chicken, apples, bread and half a bottle of chardonnay—and transferred the food to tin plates from Philippe's saddlebag. They sat down to a satisfying meal, to revel in their accomplishment and plot their next triumph.

"A tavern? Really?" Philippe seemed cautiously interested.

"It wouldn't have to be a tavern. We could start small—a wine wagon, perhaps," Sara ventured.

"Hmm." Philippe popped another piece of bread into his mouth and chewed thoughtfully.

Sara brandished a chicken leg in her right hand as she expanded on her idea. "Hundreds of tourists travel by rail from

Napa Junction to Calistoga every year to take the waters at Aetna Springs. We could set up a wagon or a permanent stand at the station. It might be a nice cool place to stop in the summer heat for some refreshment. A glass of wine, some cake, a few bottles of chardonnay for the journey . . ." Sara beamed. The possibilities excited her. She took another bite of her chicken. "Mmm. It could be a gold mine."

Philippe shook his head and grinned. "That brain of yours never stops scheming, does it? Your ideas are very creative and— well, unexpected."

Sara wasn't very comfortable with flattery, so she persisted with the plan. "So you'll consider it?"

"I'll consider it. After the harvest. Hammer out some more details for me. Location. Cost of construction. Cost of upkeep. We'll talk about it at the end of September."

"Will do, boss." Sara mock-saluted him with her tin cup.

Philippe flashed a grin, then restlessly jumped up and stoked the fire with a branch. Sara watched the embers glow and sparks fly up, lighting the darkening sky like blue fireflies. When he sat down again he was closer to her side, closer than two people sharing a stretch of deserted beach would usually sit.

For the first time all day, Sara was self-conscious. She was here without a chaperone; in fact there was not another soul anywhere on the beach. She stared down at the colorful black, red and white geometric pattern of the quilt. As she ran her fingers along its stitches, she told herself she was being silly. If she were going worry about anything, it should be about Philippe discovering her crime, not being alone with him. A sick feeling washed over her, but she steeled herself. She had made her decision.

"Are you warm enough?" He was shoulder-to-shoulder with Sara now, resting his elbows casually on his parted knees. The fire's blue-orange flames were reflected in his eyes, muting their sharp blue-green, but painting them with an unimaginable brilliance.

"Um, yes?" It came out as a mumbled question, but Sara was so distracted by his nearness, she wasn't sure she had actually said anything. She would have felt utterly ridiculous had his eyes not rested on her.

"Yes?" he repeated, his face moving slightly toward hers. Now she could catch his scent—like honey and cloves. His face was close to hers now, yet she did not feel threatened by him. She did not shrink from his touch as he ran the back of his hand from her cheekbone to her jaw. She closed her eyes and felt a wave of desire like none she had ever experienced ripple through her. She pressed her lips together to keep from sighing. His nose grazed the length of her throat, and his lips brushed against the hollow at the base of her neck. She loved the feel of his warm, soft breath on her skin.

Then he lifted his head, searching her eyes again. The intensity was almost too much to bear. Her eyes flitted away from his, and she could feel herself flush. She hoped it was too dark for him to see her crimson cheeks. She was so inexperienced; she didn't know what to do. But at that moment, she desperately wanted to learn. She needn't have worried. Sara felt Philippe's fingers graze her chin, and he swept his thumb gently across her lower lip. Every inch of her body went soft. His eyes never left her lips as his fingers continued their caress. When he finally spoke, his voice was a whisper. "May I?"

Sara tried to answer, but the words caught in her throat. Her body took the lead over her addled brain and she nodded, just barely. He smiled gently, amused, she imagined, by her inability to form a coherent phrase. Then, ever so cautiously, he brought his lips to hers.

As they kissed, Sara felt an electrical current surge through her chest and begin to burn deep within her. She instinctively placed her hands on his warm, hard torso, and then, worried he would think she was pushing him away, moved them up shyly to stroke his stubbled cheeks. Her heart was beating so violently she thought it would explode out of her chest. Sara was shocked. How could she have been so oblivious to her desires? She had craved this since the day she had first seen him again in the vineyard. Philippe parted her lips with his tongue and pressed his hand to the small of her back to pull her closer to him. A low moan escaped from his throat. Yet, Sara thought, he was controlled, never violent, so *different* from . . . And the warm *taste* of him—she never wanted him to stop.

When he pulled away, Philippe's breathing was jagged. He stroked her cheek with his thumb and exhaled deeply. "I should apologize. I promised myself I'd be on my best behavior tonight. Honestly, this wasn't part of the plan." He smiled.

Sara shook her head and looked down at the sand, running her fingers through the cold granules in an effort to recover her senses. "No." Her mind took the lead again, and she started to say what a respectable woman would say upon finding herself alone on a beach at night with a man: *Take me home.* But somehow she couldn't.

284

"Are you very upset with me?" He brought his face down to hers, seeking her eyes, but she could only look down at her fingers, drawing lines in the sand.

"You're blushing?" He sounded surprised. How did he know that heat burned in her cheeks? He would wonder why—he would think she had practice at this, her having been married.

Sara touched her face. "I suppose so, yes."

"You needn't be embarrassed." He wound a loose strand of her hair around his finger and tucked it back behind her ear.

She pulled away and looked up at him. His face was luminous next to the dying fire. "It's not that. It's just that I didn't expect—I know I should leave, that we shouldn't be . . . together like this." She didn't know if she was making any sense. She inhaled sharply and gazed up at him again. "But I don't want to leave."

Philippe laughed lightly. "Neither do I." Before she could say another word, his hand was in her hair, and he pulled her gently toward him. He kissed her again eagerly. All Sara's reservations floated away like balloons snipped from their strings. She surrendered to the sensation and let the moment have her.

After a few minutes, Philippe pulled away again, this time abruptly, as if something had just occurred to him. "You don't know much about me."

"No, I suppose not." What did he mean?

"I asked you so much about yourself before I offered you a job. It's only fair that you have a chance to ask me a few questions. To know what you're getting yourself into." His expression suggested he was enjoying all of this a bit too much.

"I do know a little about your background, from what Aurora's told me."

"Oh, so you two have been talking about me behind my back?"

"A little," Sara said unapologetically. "I know you are from Vouvray, that your father is an important wine negotiant in the valley and that you are the younger of two sons."

"And that my brother was killed last year."

Sara could not bear to look at him. She shifted her gaze to the expanse of ocean. The crests of the waves were barely visible now in the encroaching darkness.

"I'm sorry," she murmured, managing to sound like any other sympathetic friend, but feeling a flood of regret.

Philippe's eyes followed hers out to the water. "It was sad and untimely, but you understand that all too well, I would suspect, having lost your husband."

Sara did not reply to this, nor did she glance in his direction. She kept her eyes fixed on the rolling waves. Philippe must have sensed she did not want to talk. When he spoke again, his voice was lighter, although Sara detected a hint of melancholy remaining. "*C'est la vie, n'est-ce pas?*"

Sara couldn't think about the past. She was separated into halves now—one part had despised Bastien enough to end his life and the other loved Philippe too much to leave him, though she knew she should. Tonight, she would listen to the latter.

"Aurora did tell me one other thing."

"That sounds ominous." He chuckled darkly. "What is it?"

"That you have a woman in town." Sara's eyes drifted toward the shadowy outline of the jagged rock cliffs beside them and then back to his face.

Philippe exhaled loudly before he formed his response. "*Had.*"

Sara was suddenly ashamed for having asked him about something so scandalous. Yet she burned with curiosity and wanted to know more. She glanced down at the sand.

His finger gently coaxed her chin upwards. "Look at me, Sara." His voice was almost pleading, and his eyes smoldered with an emotion that Sara couldn't decipher. "*Had.* I broke it off with her the day after Aurora's party."

"But why? You didn't even know me." Sara was unconvinced.

"I know it sounds like nonsense, but it's true. The day I first met you, in the vineyard, I was drawn to you, though I wouldn't admit it to myself. That night at Aurora's, when you spoke so fearlessly, with such conviction and intelligence, I knew how I felt."

Sara didn't know what to make of that. In truth, she knew she had experienced the same thing when she'd first seen him in California.

"Did you and she have . . . an understanding?" Sara wanted to be sure. She wanted to believe him.

Philippe shook his head and, for the first time since she'd met him, shifted uncomfortably under her scrutiny. "Not so much an understanding as an *arrangement.*"

Sara blinked, wide-eyed with surprise.

"Are you shocked?"

She instantly felt young and naive. She was nine years his junior and not at all familiar with the intimacies between a man and woman. He knew so much more than she did.

"A bit." She looked down to hide her expression. In truth, she was stunned.

Philippe was silent for a few moments, and Sara didn't dare speak. When he finally did explain, his candor was genuine and appealing.

"It's not something I'm proud of, nor is it something I sought out. It just evolved, and I did nothing to stop it. But I assure you," he said, taking her cold hand in his, "my intentions toward you are entirely honorable."

Sara shook her head—she had heard enough. Who was she, of all people, to judge his actions? "You needn't explain further."

"Ah—but I do. You need to know," he said as he kissed the back of her hand, "that after I saw you out in the vineyard, I didn't want anyone but you."

She could see the sincerity in his eyes, yet she didn't know if she could trust her feeling of elation. She thrilled to know that he desired her. But had he chosen her to be foreman only because of his attraction to her? What about her experience and ideas? She would always want to be valued for her mind. A flash of what she was feeling must have registered on her face.

"Does that upset you?" Philippe asked.

"Yes. I mean, yes and no." She shook her head, trying to think of the right words. In the end, she clumsily blurted out, "Is that the only reason you hired me?"

He tipped his head to the side, as if he thought her question absurd. "No! I hired you because you were the best man for the job. It wasn't until tonight that I really allowed myself to act on my—what would you call it?—my ulterior motive, I suppose."

Sara couldn't help but laugh. "I guess I can't blame this entirely on you. I was an all-too-willing accomplice."

"Hmm, yes. So it would seem." He pulled her tightly to him, and they sat in silence, listening to the gentle crash of the waves against the shore. Sara leaned against Philippe's chest, enjoying the comforting, steady rhythm of his breath. She could not remember the last time she'd been embraced. Maybe before Papa left her for the last time, or before Lydia died. She exhaled deeply, feeling content and secure for the first time in a long while. She felt him tighten his arms around her. Before long, she drifted into a deep, tranquil sleep.

Sara awoke alone inside the tent, to the screeching of seagulls diving for their breakfast along the shoreline. She surmised that Philippe had carried her inside and slept outside by the fire, to tend to the horses. She rubbed her eyes, raked her fingers through her hair and retied the loose strands. She wished she had some mint leaves this morning to freshen her breath, but perhaps a swig of leftover wine or a sip of water would do the trick.

She stepped outside, sheepish and flushed from the memory of the night before. She could not see Philippe near the freshly lit fire, though the horses were still securely tied up and feasting on apples and hay. She scanned the beach for him, then inhaled sharply. He was stunning in the morning light as he washed his face and torso in the frigid ocean water. The musculature of his back, even from a distance, was smooth and flawless, marked only by two faint scars that ran from his waist up to his right shoulder blade. Her heart sank when she thought of someone hurting him. Had it been his father, Jean Lemieux? When she regained her breath, she was terrified that Philippe might see her studying him so brazenly. She ducked back inside the tent before he turned around, hoping he wouldn't catch sight of her, and sat cross-legged inside her shelter, churning with confusion.

Until Philippe had kissed her last night, Sara could not fathom how a woman could truly want a man to do what husbands did to their wives. But embracing him had ignited something inside her. It was beyond desire—it was need. Sara now understood why Lydia had given herself to Bastien. Impossible as it seemed, Lydia must have felt for Bastien what she felt for Philippe. But really, what was she *thinking*? How could she get herself into something—a courtship—with the brother of the man she'd killed? What kind of person would willfully deceive another like this? Was she not setting herself up for discovery and disappointment?

Sara couldn't begin to count the number of mistakes she'd made so far and, in all honesty, she didn't care to. All she cared about was kissing Philippe again. She had become besotted overnight.

CHAPTER 16

Tremors

S ara scribbled down the date, 10 August 1897, and made a few notes in her field journal. The vines at Eagle's Run were healthy and free of insects; the fruit had almost ripened. Another two weeks, she estimated, until they'd begin harvesting the grapes. That left two weeks to finish cutting back the excess leaves so that the additional sunlight could accelerate the fruit's ripening process. She would inform Philippe at once.

She knew she would find him in the stables with Luc, for he had decided to start teaching the boy how to feed and care for the horses. Sara thought this was ridiculous—Luc was just a year old this month—but Philippe insisted that he loved being around Red and Lady. Sara had just rolled her eyes, knowing she was not going to talk Philippe out of it. When she entered the stables, she was greeted with a belly laugh from Luc as Lady ate right out of his hand, brushing his palm with her rough tongue. Philippe held Luc easily in one hand and, in the other, carried a bucket of feed. He turned to greet Sara with a broad smile.

"Wait until you see what your son can do." His eyes lit with excitement as he set Luc down on his feet. The child stood no higher than Philippe's knee. Taking Luc's pudgy hand in his, Philippe gently pulled him forward, step by half-step. Luc tottered, unsteady at first, and then gained enough speed and assurance to let go of Philippe's hand.

"Go see Maman. Walk to Maman," he encouraged the boy.

Luc crossed the five feet to Sara in no time and fell into her outstretched arms.

"Oh, Maman is so proud of you!" Sara kissed his plump cheeks. She did not expect the wave of sadness that washed over her when she drew Luc tightly to her chest. Lydia should be the one laughing with excitement and pulling him into her arms, not her. Sara hastened to wipe her damp eyes, but not quickly enough, for a single tear escaped down her cheek.

"Silly Maman," she chastised herself for allowing Philippe to see her so overcome with emotion. "You are such a good boy," she muttered into Luc's hair. He smelled of hay and sunshine.

Philippe was somber, silent for a moment. "What were you thinking just now?"

Sara shook her head in an effort to frame a believable response. "I'm just so proud of him. His first steps . . ."

Philippe was standing in front of her now, resting a warm hand comfortingly on her arm. "Were you thinking of your husband?"

"No, not at all." Sara dismissed the idea.

He stood silently, watching her eyes, waiting for her to continue. Clearly, she would have to come up with something more persuasive.

"It's just that we've been alone for so long. It's nice to have someone to share these . . . milestones with."

"Which is a polite way of saying it's none of my business."

Sara smiled. "No, it's a polite way of saying thank you."

Philippe bowed slightly. "You're most welcome." His words were genuine, but his eyes held their skepticism.

"You'll be happy to learn that we're right on track," Sara said, happy to change the subject. "The grapes, I estimate, will be ripe within the next two weeks. So far, no insects have been discovered."

Philippe was all business as they walked out of the stables. "How many vines have been inspected?"

"All of them, including the young ones."

"Excellent." He rubbed his palms together, lost in thought. "Any estimate on yield?"

Sara deliberated. "It's hard to say at this point. A solid hundred acres, but I'm not sure of the tonnage. Next week I'll have a better estimate."

"Very well, next week. Where are you headed now?" Philippe asked, taking Luc from Sara's arms and setting him free to walk on his own.

"To the barn for the pruning tools, then off to show the workers where they need to cut back. The grapes need more sun."

"Well done. Meet you back at the house for supper?" Rather

than waiting for her reply, Philippe simply tilted her chin up and touched his lips to hers. It took all Sara's willpower to pull away, to return to her work—to sleep without him every night.

The sun was hot on Sara's neck and shoulders as she loped from the stable toward the barn. Luc toddled along just a few yards ahead of her. Her mood was buoyant. Being close to Philippe every day—his easy smile, his energetic presence, but most of all the way he looked so intently into her eyes—always lifted her spirits. Seven hours was far too long to wait to see him again.

The quake hit at midday.

The absence of sound was what first made Sara uneasy. The chirping of the birds, the throaty anthem of the bullfrogs, the rustle of the swaying leaves on the trees—the buzzing din that usually hung in the air this time of day—had ceased. Everything was still. Besides the echo of Luc's laughter as he ran, all was quiet.

And then the earth began to shake.

It started as a trembling beneath Sara's feet and in moments felt like the fierce vibrations of a thundering steam train. Sara was thrown to her hands and knees instantly. Luc was oblivious to the danger and tottered right inside the barn. She watched in horror as the ground before her cracked, rupturing like a seam being split, right up to the barn door. The barn began to rattle, and its timbers peeled loose from their frame, crashing to the ground. Panic clutched her. Luc was nowhere in sight when Sara reached the doorway, clawing the earth with her fingernails to steady herself. She frantically called his name, but could hear nothing over the shriek of scraping metal and the dull thud of wood hitting earth.

Where could he be? She could hardly see now, but searched for Luc in the slits of sunlight that pushed through the broken and obstructed barn windows. The violent shaking made it nearly impossible for Sara to maintain her balance, and she stumbled again and again. Sara shouted his name repeatedly. Finally, she heard Luc's high-pitched squeal followed by a hysterical sob.

"I'm coming! Maman's coming!" He would not understand; he would not know to stay still. Sara ducked under the beams breaking around her and slid over shards of glass and metal, searching the debris-filled barn. *Oh God, Lydia, protect him!* Her thoughts nearly choked her. What if he'd been knocked down, his delicate bones crushed? Sara heard a deafening creak and then watched the northern wall break from its support beams and crash inward. When the dust began to clear, Sara trained her eyes on the area beneath the fallen wall. Her eyes followed a single ray of light shining upon what she thought might be Luc's dark hair.

"Luc!" Sara was almost at his side when a heavy weight slammed onto her shoulder and forced her to the ground. After the shock had passed, she realized that she was pinned down by one of the immense oak ceiling supports. Sara was consumed by the searing burn that radiated from her shoulder down to the tips of her fingers. Her vision blurred but she forced herself to look over to where Luc lay; she wasn't sure he was moving. She heard a scream so fierce and raw its agony resonated to her core and her own grief threatened to swallow her whole. Then the darkness overtook her.

Sara wasn't sure where she was. It was dark, but she could hear something. It sounded as though someone were calling her name through a long, metal pipe. The voice was getting closer, but it was not the one Sara wanted to hear. She listened instead for Luc—where was he? She struggled to fight her way back to consciousness.

"Sara. Open your eyes." This voice was loud, commanding. Sara tried to lift her eyelids, but felt as if someone were pressing iron weights down upon them. She squeezed her eyes repeatedly, and when she finally opened them, she saw nothing but a blinding blur of sunlight overhead. She drew an arm over her eyes to shield them. Pain charged through her left shoulder and down her arm, and she could not help but cry out. It was so intense, she thought she might vomit. She labored to catch her breath.

"Breathe, Sara, in and out. Slowly, that's it." The voice was very close to her now. She did as she was told and concentrated on taking long, deep breaths until she felt her heartbeat returning to a normal pace. Without opening her eyes, she uttered his name.

"Luc?" Her throat was bone-dry.

The voice was low and silky. "He's fine. Absolutely fine, just a few scrapes. Aurora's feeding him right now."

Sara's chest heaved with relief and a single, powerful sob escaped her lungs. "Try to open your eyes," the voice commanded.

Sara sniffed and coughed—the air was almost too thick to breathe. She shook her head. "Too bright." Then she finally recognized the voice. "Philippe?" Sara extended her right hand, and he caught it in his own and held it reassuringly against his warm cheek.

"Yes, yes, it's me. I've got you." His words were stilted, his voice hoarse with emotion.

"My arm." She let out a low groan.

"Yes. Does your head hurt? Your back? Where else do you feel pain?"

"My shoulder, my chest, my arm. Headache."

"Your left arm is broken and your shoulder is dislocated. You may have a concussion. I've just about stopped the bleeding, and I've sent for the doctor, but I don't know when he'll arrive. I'm going to give you some laudanum for the pain."

She struggled to open her eyes while Philippe cradled her head in his arm and slowly lifted her to a sitting position. Her shoes came into focus first. They were covered with a thick layer of dust, and she imagined that it was the same with her clothes and face. She coughed again, trying to clear the choking dust from her throat.

"Water?"

"After the laudanum." His voice was certain, controlled now. He lifted a small brown bottle to her lips. "Just one small sip—a teaspoonful."

Sara cringed at the bitter taste and forced herself to swallow. "Water?"

"It's coming," Philippe whispered. He held her in his strong grip, with his face now buried in her hair. She could feel him shudder beside her. She wondered if it was from fear or relief. Or something else.

"Sara?"

"Mmm?" Brutal pain—again.

"In order to stop the pain, I need to relocate your shoulder."

She was too shocked to respond, but he must have seen the fear in her eyes when she looked up at him, for he met her concern with a comforting expression of reassurance and determination.

"Trust me."

Sara nodded. She would do anything he asked.

"Try to relax your muscles. Keep breathing, deeply, even when it hurts. Breathe right through it. I'm going to lay you down now."

His words were soothing. Philippe seemed to know what he was doing. She closed her eyes again, not wanting him to sense her fear. She wanted to be brave. She wanted to retreat back into the dark place where she had felt no pain. She was only vaguely aware of his gentle touch as he lay her back down on the dirt floor and drew her elbow to her chest. He took her shoulder in one large hand and held her wrist with the other. As soon as he began to move her shoulder, she was gripped by pain. She gritted her teeth and fought the overwhelming urge to scream. It seemed to go on forever. Each movement sent a shock through her body, but finally, she felt a pop in her shoulder and her torment eased.

Philippe exhaled as if he'd been holding his breath the entire time. "There. Better?"

She opened her eyes to meet his. "Mm-hmm. Much." She tried to manage a quick smile, but the muscles in her face had gone slack. The laudanum, she guessed.

He helped her sit upright again. Sara's eyes searched the space in front of her, but all she could see was a pile of wooden beams and torn metal. She looked toward the sky and realized that the barn was now fully exposed to the sun overhead. The roof had collapsed. Sara could feel panic rising up within her. How had any of them survived this? Philippe must have sensed her escalating anxiety and tucked her face protectively into his chest. Then she spied the cloth smudged with blood in Philippe's hand.

Sara pulled away to examine him. Was he injured? What she saw shook her to the core. His face was covered in dust and dirt, and his shirt was ripped and matted with blood. One hand was bandaged. He looked as though he had been through battle.

His voice was steady when he answered her unspoken questions. "Luc is fine. It was an earthquake. The blood is yours, not mine. I'm unharmed. When the beam fell on you, it scraped an old wound." Philippe's eyes moved to her upper chest. "A fresh scar?" There was an undercurrent to his question. He was asking what, or who, had done this to her.

Sara recalled the injuries she had sustained from Bastien's attack, in particular, the burn of his teeth cutting her skin. She winced and her breathing accelerated. Sharp pain still throbbed in her left arm. "Yes . . . last . . . year." She answered his question, but did not tell him what he wanted to know. It didn't matter. Nothing mattered now except for finding a way to stop the pain.

He pulled her closer, taking care not to move her elbow, which was cradled again in his hand. "A few more minutes and the laudanum will take effect."

"Can I see Luc?" she asked desperately.

"Not now," he said. "I'll need to clean the scrape and bandage it."

She looked down. Her blouse had been torn open, revealing a small amount of blood where the wood had chafed her skin, and the old scar burned red again. She couldn't stop the humiliation from brimming over in her eyes. The last thing she wanted was to cry in front of him, to appear weak. She hated feeling defenseless. She turned her head away and tried not to whimper, but the tears streamed down.

Philippe did not try to console her with trite words. Instead, he held her, allowing the silence to envelop them. After a few minutes, Sara regained some composure. Philippe rested a warm hand on her uninjured shoulder.

He was right, of course. Infection would set in if it wasn't cleaned properly. Sara knew that she shouldn't be embarrassed about Philippe tending to her so intimately, especially at a time like this, but still she felt bashful, or perhaps she did not want him to examine the scar too closely. She wiped her face with her right hand and moved to face him. Without meeting his eyes, she whispered, "I'll do it . . . or Aurora."

Philippe sighed and shook his head. "With your broken arm? Aurora has Luc to look after and her own injuries to deal with." Her face creased with concern. "Don't worry, just a few scratches. She'll live," he said quickly. His expression softened, but now his voice was serious again. "I'm afraid I have to insist." He took her hand in his.

Sara hadn't the energy to argue. She nodded weakly. The laudanum was working. Her pain began to ebb, and a curtain of exhaustion began to close around her. Her eyes fluttered shut, and Philippe lifted her up and carried her out of the wreckage. She was vaguely aware of him placing her on a bed and mumbling something about water.

Sara managed to murmur one last request. "Luc?"

"Yes, Sara, soon, but for now, sleep." She felt his lips press against her forehead, then Sara drifted off.

Sara was in the long metal pipe again, back in the darkness. This time, she carried a lamp to light her way. Panic pushed down on her chest, and her breathing hitched as she searched, unsuccessfully, for her child. She called to him again and again until, miraculously, she heard his sweet voice light up the darkness. "Maman!"

Sara pushed toward him, feeling as though she were mired in mud. Finally, she burst out of the darkness into a muted light. She saw a golden field, an amber sky. She called to Luc again, whirling in every direction and straining to hear his voice. His laughter played on the breeze that whipped through her hair. His features were delicate and glowing, his hair dark, his brown eyes warm. But he was slung over the shoulder of a tall, raven-haired man who was walking, in broad strides, away from her. She shuddered. Where was he taking him? She reached her arms out and started to run toward the boy. He belonged with her; she was his maman. Luc ducked down, burying his tiny face in the man's neck. When he looked up to smile at Sara, his face was smeared with bright, fresh, dripping blood.

"No!" Sara's shriek stopped the man in his tracks. He turned and sneered at her. A river of blood flowed out of the gaping hole in his neck. Her body seized, and she clamored for air. Someone was squealing. She realized it was her.

She awoke to feel Philippe's cool hands on her face. "Sara!"

She could not speak; her terror was real. She had seen Bastien, seen the boy. Her eyes were open now, but she was not breathing. She felt her fingers and upper lip begin to numb.

Philippe's lips were at her ear, his voice urgent. "You're all right—it was just a dream! Breathe, Sara. You must breathe!"

She gulped for air, then squeezed her eyes tight and shook her head, trying to shake away the truth. The magnitude of what she had done bore down upon her. She had killed Luc's father, Philippe's brother. She did not deserve Philippe's faith; she had done nothing to earn his trust. She deserved to be in constant pain. Sorrow filled her chest and she exhaled deeply. Then her mind darted in another direction. What had Philippe heard? Did he hear her screaming Bastien's name? Oh God, please, *no*.

When she opened her eyes again, Philippe was stroking her cheek and staring at her, the alarm still clear on his face. His eyes were rimmed with red, his dark irises a vivid blue. The beauty of his expression—one of aching concern—sent a jolt of electricity through her veins. If he only knew that the pain she felt inside was ten times worse than her physical injuries.

"I'm so sorry," she said before thinking. She wanted to reassure him that she was fine, but her heart hurt too much.

He shook his head. "There's nothing to be sorry for, love." He wiped her face with a white towel, and she realized that her hair was matted wet with perspiration. Her skin felt clammy, her stomach nauseated.

She looked around and discovered she was lying in a large wrought-iron bed, a pale blue quilt thrown across her and two fluffy pillows beneath her. She was in Philippe's house, the room where she had slept when she had stayed there with Aurora. She was wearing her white nightgown, and there was a makeshift sling on her left arm. She flushed a thousand shades of red and instinctively pulled the quilt to her chin with her good hand.

Philippe stifled a laugh and tried to take her mind off what he must have realized was her profound embarrassment.

"Luc wants to see his maman." He smiled broadly. "Aurora?"

Aurora appeared at the door with Luc. His little face lit up when he saw Sara. He threw his hands up in the air and strained toward her.

"Is that your maman? It's good to see you awake and alert." Aurora's voice was cheerful, albeit laced with concern. She put Luc down so he could toddle to Sara's bedside.

Sara reached her good arm out toward him, and Philippe, who sat on the edge of the bed, picked him up effortlessly and placed him in the crook of Sara's arm, where she knew he would not want to stay for long. He babbled and giggled while he pulled Sara's hair and gave her kisses. She beamed in spite of the pain. She buried her nose in his shiny, fresh-smelling hair and kissed the little dimple at the back of his neck.

"How long have I been asleep?"

"Asleep? Try nearly unconscious—for sixteen hours." Philippe chuckled with relief. "If you hadn't had a nightmare and awakened with such a start, I would have taken you for dead."

Sara felt the shadow cross over her face again. Philippe began to fill in some of the missing details. "Dr. Pratt came around seven, and you barely stirred. He examined your injuries, bandaged your arm and placed it in the sling. You have a slight concussion. He wants you to remain in bed for the next few days."

"*Days?*"

"Don't give me any trouble, Sara. Doctor's orders, and it's my job to make sure you follow them." The sharpness of his voice was tempered with a radiant smile that made Sara forget her fears altogether. "You can't escape me," he teased. Sara knew she couldn't win that argument with her pitifully slung arm, concussion and scrapes.

Luc wriggled out of her arms and slid off the side of the bed. He bounded out the bedroom door toward the kitchen, Aurora trailing him the whole way.

"And Aurora?" Sara's voice fell to a whisper. "She will be all right?"

"Like I said, she was scraped up a bit from the spill she took, but luckily she was outside the house when it happened."

"Was anyone else hurt? How's Rose?" Sara searched his face.

"She's fine, but in town, several people died. The damage is extensive, but we'll rebuild." He gazed out the window toward the barn, looking as though he were holding something back. His voice lightened. "How's the arm feeling?"

"I've had worse," she said quietly. Was he protecting her from something?

"Yes, I know." His expression was grave again.

Sara looked away. She would never tell him how she had sustained the injury to her chest. She could tell he had been the one to dress it. Surely he had been able to tell it was a bite mark. She turned back toward him, but this time, he was the one to look down at the quilt between them.

"I can't—I don't understand how—" Philippe was shaking his head now. Sara silenced him by placing her hand over his.

"It doesn't matter, and I don't want to talk about it. What does matter is that you found Luc and me, and we're safe."

"The thought of someone hurting you . . ." Philippe's voice trailed off, and Sara saw anger flash across his eyes. The tug she felt on her heart was quickly overruled by her throbbing head.

"Let it go," she said, more sharply than she had intended. He sat back in surprise.

"You're so stubborn."

Her tone was gentle, repentant now. "Yes. And so are you."

He lifted his head and flashed her the crooked smile she so loved. "That could be my best trait."

Sara gazed at the blue sky, its far reaches wrapped in a haze of translucent cloud on this unseasonably warm September evening. It looked as though God had taken a bale of cotton and stretched it as wide as the eye could see. The harvest was finally complete.

Eagle's Run had fared much better than some of the surrounding wineries in the earthquake. Miraculously, the winery's structure had remained intact, with the exception of shattered windows on the second and third floors. The old storage barn had been destroyed, but every last piece of equipment had been salvaged from its wreckage. Fortunately, only two windows and a lantern had shattered in the barn where Sara and Luc slept.

While Sara had spent a week reluctantly resting in bed, Philippe had finished cleaning up the glass and debris and counting the remaining inventory. Of the almost twenty-seven thousand bottles that were stored when the earthquake hit, just over nineteen thousand had survived. Over the next four weeks, Philippe and an assembly line of workers had bottled the surviving sixty-two barrels of 1896 cabernet sauvignon. The new bottling machine helped to expedite the process, but they still had to manually foil, label and box the wine after sterilizing, filling and corking the bottles. Meanwhile, Sara had supervised a crew of more than fifty laborers picking the ripe fruit. By the end of the harvest, they had picked 550 tons of grapes.

Sara had spent today in the winery, overseeing the de-stemming and partial crushing of the cabernet grapes, which left some of the berries intact. With Philippe's approval, she had added a large helping of stems back to the grapes to add spice to the wine's flavor. The mixture would now soak for another two or three days before the wine would be drawn off the skins and moved to the fermenting barrels. Sara didn't take the responsibility lightly. Constant vigilance was required to create wine of quality and character. Also, Sara had to make sure the Roman Catholic Church's strict directive was followed: sacramental wine must be naturally made from the grapes of the vine only, not corrupted with sugars or other flavor-enhancing additives.

Sara could feel fatigue press upon her shoulders, and her healing arm began to ache. Although this was the time of day she most looked forward to, when she and Philippe would settle Luc down to sleep and enjoy dinner together, Sara thought she'd rather retire early this evening. Lost in her thoughts as she ambled toward the barn, Sara nearly jumped out of her skin when Philippe caught her good arm, tucked it in his and started leading her back toward the winery. He was holding something in his right hand, deftly concealing it from her. She caught the delicious scent of his soap and shaving cream on the evening breeze.

"You're wearing a new shirt," she observed suspiciously as she tried to keep up with him, "and you've shaved."

His eyes were bright and fixed on the winery.

"I have something to show you," he said excitedly.

He led her down the winery stairs to the cellar. Sara smelled the cool, musty air and her eyes strained to adjust to the darkness of the vast stone room. The evening light slipped through the narrow windows near the cellar ceiling and shimmered off the rows of gleaming bottles before them. Philippe put down the glass goblets he'd been carrying, pulled a bottle off the rack and, cradling it in his hand, held it out for Sara's inspection.

The bottle's label bore a beautiful sketch of the Eagle's Run winery and the winding road leading up to it. A delicate rendering of grape vines wound its way around the design, and Sara's heart filled as she read *Eagle's Run, Carneros, Zinfandel, 1896*. Sara ran her hand over the smooth ivory paper, as if to make sure it were real. It was a work of art. She was choked with emotion.

She stretched up on her tiptoes and threw her arms around his neck. "I'm so pleased for you! You've worked so hard for this."

His face was exuberant, filled with a joy that echoed Sara's own. "Pleased for both of us."

He reached in his pocket, pulled out a bottle opener, and opened and poured the wine. Sara swirled the wine in her glass and inhaled deeply. The smell reminded Sara of spiced cherries.

The taste was even more delightful—smooth, with just a hint of raspberry. It was by far the best zinfandel she'd ever tasted. She laughed with relief. "It's superb, Philippe."

His voice was unexpectedly serious. "I couldn't have done this without you, Sara."

"I have no doubt that you would have done it all without me, but I've certainly enjoyed helping out."

His eyes glanced at the stacks of bottles, then back at her. "I found another occupation for you—something to pass the time until your arm has healed."

"And what is that?" She was almost afraid to ask.

He took her glass and placed it with his on a nearby barrel. Then he guided her down the long cellar row.

"The best man in the county can complete eleven thousand bottle turns in twelve hours. How do you think you'll fare with the riddling?"

Sara wasn't amused. Nothing was more boring than turning bottles. Not to mention that with only one good arm she'd only be able to turn half as many. She swatted Philippe playfully on the chest.

He took her hand and guided her back up the stairs and over to the workbench on the other side of the winery. "Come here."

Philippe gently lifted her up onto the bench, seating Sara so he could look into her eyes. His lips sought hers tenderly, and she felt a familiar, deep longing. Her head began to spin. His fingers caressed her spine, and he moved his lips down to her neck, where they hovered just below her earlobe. "When are you going to agree to marry me?"

"Um . . . I"—Sara struggled to regain her faculties—"I hadn't thought . . ." Her voice trailed off. Of course she dreamed about marrying Philippe, but she couldn't imagine how it would be possible.

He continued his contemplation of her décolletage. "Nonsense. All you *do* is think and plan and scheme." She could hear a smile in his voice as his nose traced its way down, and back up, the length of her neck. "The only way I know of to remove that little crease of contemplation between your eyebrows is to kiss you—and often." He traced her lower lip with his tongue and then took it between his own two lips, sucking gently. Sara shuddered. "I fear it may have to become a full-time occupation for me," he murmured. "So, back to my question. A simple 'yes' would suffice." He pulled away and gazed at her expectantly, with a trace of humor in his eyes, his hands resting on her waist. "Will you marry me, Sara Landry?"

Her alias rolled off his tongue in perfect French, but the sound of it snapped her right back to reality. Sara knew she had teetered on the knife's edge for too long—there was a delicate balance between loving him and leaving him before she ruined everything. And now, here it was: the moment she would have to reject him, against every instinct she possessed.

"I can't marry you," she whispered. In the silence that followed, she almost convinced herself that she hadn't said anything at all, that she could begin anew, that somehow she could answer "yes" without reservation. She looked down at her skirt, but saw nothing.

When he spoke, the roughness in his voice splintered her daydream. "Can't or won't?"

"Both."

"You sound confused," he said.

"You don't want to marry me." She struggled with each word.

He tipped her chin up with his fingers and drew her eyes back to his. It was unbearable. The only sound was the softness of his breath. His eyes blazed as they searched her own—for what, she didn't know.

"Yes, I do. I want you . . . always."

"You have me," she said lightly, trying to sound relaxed. But Philippe would not be deterred.

"No." He brought his lips to the corner of her mouth and whispered, "I want *all* of you." He intertwined his fingers with hers. She hoped that he didn't feel the shudder that rippled through her body. "And you want me, too." He said the words so simply, so earnestly, that she couldn't hold back her smile, but behind it was a sinking sensation that the end of her time with him was near. She was so eager to be close to him. Her body folded into the contour of his chest as she wrapped her hand around his neck and pulled him toward her. Her lips sought his urgently, almost violently. Somewhere deep inside her, she knew there wasn't much time.

When she finally got hold of her senses and broke away, he laughed softly, keeping one arm securely around her waist while he touched his forehead to hers. "See?" he teased.

Sara was breathless. She shook her head and looked down again. "I can't marry you."

"Ever? Or just now? Is it time you need?"

"Not just time. You don't . . . *know* me. There are things that I've done. Things I need to tell you. I just can't—"

He kissed her once again to silence her. When he pulled away, he looked thoughtfully at her.

"You're young, I know, but you are already widowed and a mother to a boy whom I adore." Philippe took her hand and pressed her palm to his cheek. "I would venture to say you've already lived a lifetime." His eyes were solemn as he continued, "But you have to understand, I'm older, and I know what I want—what I *need*. You could have been killed in the quake." His voice broke at this. He shook his head and sought her eyes again. "The thought of it was too much for me to bear. I can't—I won't live without you. And I know you love me, too, so you needn't try to convince me otherwise. But whatever the problem is, whatever impediment you see to our marrying, tell me now." Sara detected a hint of frustration in his voice. "Let's figure it out, because it can't be worse than spending a lifetime apart, can it?"

The smile that appeared on his beautiful face was so warm and generous that tears blurred her vision. As long as she lived, she knew she would never love anyone this intensely ever again. How could she let him go? She would have to find a way to tell him the truth and then allow him to decide what he wanted.

"I would never hurt you like he did." The words stung her. He had completely misinterpreted her reticence. He thought her late husband had abused her, since he could never know that her old wounds had been inflicted by his own brother. His sympathy made her feel all the more sorrowful for what was to come. She was a selfish creature. She should have left Napa before their friendship evolved into something deeper. She should have left Napa as soon as she heard his name.

Her agony must have registered on her face, for he quickly added, "If time is what you need, you have it." He stopped abruptly and his head snapped up.

Sara and Philippe both tensed at the sound of thundering hooves outside. When the rumbling stopped, a single gunshot rang out and a man shouted Philippe's name. Philippe pulled Sara down to the floor, and they crouched below the open window. He held her head down while he stole a glance outside.

Ducking down again, Philippe spoke in hushed tones, "Stay here, flat on the ground. Don't move, no matter what you hear, no matter what happens, do you understand?"

Sara nodded. He climbed on a nearby cask. Balancing precariously, he felt along the joist overhead until he found the rifle and shells concealed there. He loaded and cocked the gun and stepped out the winery door, calling out to the men.

The reply was hostile: "Philippe Lemieux?" After a few moments, Sara heard murmurs of their conversation, but was unable to interpret the words.

Anxious to see, Sara poked her head up for an instant and tried to comprehend the scene outside. Four men, unshaven and unkempt, all carrying guns, fanned out in a semicircle around Philippe. No one looked injured; it must have been a warning shot. Philippe pointed his rifle downward and raised his hand in a gesture of compliance. Sara was alarmed to recognize Jip Montagne atop his horse with a smug look on his face.

After what seemed like an eternity, Sara stole another glance. This time, she spied Philippe returning from the house. He handed the group's ringleader a stack of bills, then dismissed the gang with a flick of his head. The man tipped his hat and signaled to his men to mount up. Philippe watched as the horsemen reached the main road and broke into a full gallop. He stood motionless for minutes, staring down the road at the cloud of dust billowing in their wake.

Then Philippe dropped his head, rested the rifle on his shoulder and walked away from the winery where she was hiding, back toward the barn. Philippe did not cast even a fleeting look in her direction. What was happening? Sara felt her heartbeat stutter, then intensify until it was pounding so loudly she thought it would beat out of her chest. She looked at the spot where Philippe had just asked her to marry him, and leaned back against the door for support. Her legs gave way and she sank to the floor. Sara tightened her arms around her knees, dropped her forehead down upon them and stared into the darkness of her lap.

The truth of what had just transpired crushed down upon her. Those men had been sent. Montagne had led them here. They were bounty hunters, and they had come for *her*.

CHAPTER 17

Truth

H e knew. Sara was certain.

Had Marie divulged her identity? Even if she had, Sara had told her she was headed for upstate New York, not California. Had Bastien's family found her name written in the ship's manifest, and hunted her all the way across the country? Jip Montagne, she'd bet, had been eager to point them toward Eagle's Run.

After dining alone with Luc that evening, Sara retreated to her apartment. Now, as she stared at the books on her bedside table, she realized the answer to all her questions was right in front of her. She ran her fingers along the cracked binding of her mother's Bible. Between its curled pages was Bastien's deed to Saint Martin.

She'd always kept her books and documents neatly stacked in a crate under her bed, never out in the open. Yet here they were tonight, in plain view on her table. Philippe must have searched her little apartment for evidence of her identity, of her crime. He had found it in the Bible, which her father had signed when he had given it to her mother. There, on the inside cover, Philippe must have read Sara's record of Luc's birth date. By leaving the Bible in a conspicuous place, he confirmed that he knew, beyond any doubt, that she was Sara Landry Thibault.

But rather than turning her over to those ruffians, he had bought her freedom, possibly even her life. Surely that must count for something?

Sara barely slept that night. Even when Luc wasn't awake fussing, her thoughts were dark, and she was inconsolable. In the pale light of a new morning, her stomach twisted with anxiety.

She was disgraced, but she would not retreat without a fight. Philippe was going to stand there and listen to every word of what she had to say before she let him cut her loose. He was the first man she had ever needed—like air, or water. And while she had tried to resist, she knew she loved him. All she could hope for at this point was that she could make him understand that she'd never intended to kill his brother.

Sara hitched Luc to her hip and crossed the wide yard to the kitchen door. "Rose?" she called. The housekeeper appeared instantly, apron on, skillet in hand.

"Ma'am?"

"Good morning, Rose. Where is he?"

Rose contemplated her shoes. When she finally looked up,

Sara could see a flash of fear in her eyes. Rose gestured toward the stables. "Saddlin' up, ma'am."

"Take Luc and feed him some cereal, would you, Rose? I'll be back soon." Sara tried to rein in the desperation she felt. She set Luc down in a chair and marched toward the stables. It took every ounce of self-respect she had not to break into a run.

When Sara walked in, Philippe was saddling Lady, with his back toward the door.

"Philippe." He stiffened at the sound of her voice. *He may not want to hear what you have to say, but you must make him listen,* she reminded herself. "I need to explain."

"California is a long way from Saint Martin," he retorted, turning to glare at her. Sara was shocked by the loathing in his eyes. He continued, his tone cutting, "They never found you or your sister that night. Only my brother's burned body." Philippe choked out the last words. "I see that surprises you. That's right. They pulled his body out before the fire destroyed the entire house, and do you know what they found?" He moved to face her, tall and threatening. His eyes bored into hers. "A puncture wound to his neck. The fatal blow, it seems. How many months has it been? And *now* you're ready to explain? Now that you've been discovered."

Sara was numb with fear, unable to answer.

"So—where is she?"

Sara was startled by his question. Did he mean Lydia? Maybe Marie wasn't behind this after all. Maybe it was someone else . . .

"Are you hiding her? Did she even kill my brother, or was it Chevreau? I want the answers you promised."

Sara backed away slightly and bowed her head to think. What

317

did he suppose had happened? Her voice shook with uncertainty. "I don't know what—"

"Don't play with me, Sara." He cornered her, forcing her back up against one of the oak beams in the wall. "Who killed my brother?" he asked hoarsely.

Sara inhaled deeply and uttered the two words that would ruin everything. "I did."

Philippe stood silent, frozen.

"Let me tell you—" Sara's voice was soft, repentant.

Philippe would not hear her. "What? Why?" He looked bewildered, and then his face twisted with revulsion. "Oh, I see. Bastien was not the best of men. He must have made life . . . uncomfortable for you and your family. So you took his life? Why not just *leave*?"

How dare he presume to know what they had endured at his brother's hands? Sara could feel the blood begin to boil beneath her skin. "You don't know anything," she snapped.

"I know he stole your land." Philippe's voice was laced with fury. "Killing him must have been quite convenient for you and your sister. You didn't get your land back, but you secured your freedom." He brought his face close to hers and grasped her chin tightly in his palm, making it impossible for her to look away. "And your revenge. I assume that includes me."

Sara drew back and abruptly slapped him across the face. Philippe was stunned, but she wasn't finished. All those months of desperation, of hiding, of fear, of shame—all because of one man who had destroyed everything she had in the world. Without thinking, she raised her left arm from its sling to slap him again, but he was ready for her and caught her hand in his. She winced in pain and struggled to break free, but he'd soon captured both her wrists, pinning them together.

Her anger flowed forth, and she spat the words at him. "Your brother beat my sister every night for months, and that night— that night he hit me, forced himself on me, and almost . . ." She squeezed her eyes shut at the memory. "My sister is dead—*dead!*" Sara almost broke as she screamed the words, but her anger won out, and she opened her eyes to face him. "Don't you *dare* stand here and accuse me. I killed him to save myself and Lydia and her child, and I'd do it again!"

Philippe still held her wrists tightly, and Sara continued to watch his face. He shook his head slightly as if he were trying to make sense of what she'd said. Slowly, he eased his grip on her wrists, but he did not release them. For the first time since she'd known him, she could see raw grief in his eyes. She had caused him this pain. She'd never wanted that. Philippe stared at her for a long time. His eyes eventually softened with sadness.

Then he did the unimaginable. Without a word, he let go of her wrists, raised her chin gently with the tips of his fingers and pressed his lips to hers. They were soft, searching. Sara was not prepared for this. She kissed him back, tentatively at first. His mouth tasted sweet and warm. His hand moved down the length of her spine and rested at the small of her back, sending a charge all the way down to the tips of her toes. His lips brushed her eyes, her cheeks, the hollow of her throat, before they found their way back to her lips, parting them greedily.

She wanted so much more of him. She knotted his hair between her fingers, and he tightened his hold on her, pressing her to his chest. She felt his body stiffen, and then, without warning, he broke from their embrace. He turned away from her. She could feel her cheeks redden with confusion. What had she done now?

He shook his head and whispered, "I can't. I won't—do this." Before she could protest, he turned, took Lady by the bridle and walked out of the barn.

Sara's stomach tightened. She stumbled back against the wall, stricken with shame.

Philippe was gone for ten days. Sara didn't know which was worse: his physical absence, or not knowing what he was thinking. Both were exquisite forms of torture. Yet she also dreaded his return and the recriminations that would ensue, the pain that would inevitably flash again across his face. She would have curled up into a ball and wallowed in her despair, if it hadn't been for Luc. Changing, feeding and comforting him were her distractions, along with her work in the vineyard. Until Philippe told her to stop, she would keep on racking the wine and riddling thousands of bottles every day.

When he finally returned, he came to Sara in the damp darkness of the winery cellar, where she was turning bottles. The light spilling down the stairwell was bright, but the tall outline of his figure blocked the entryway.

"Sara." His rough, familiar voice melted something deep inside her, even before her eyes could see him clearly. She stood silently, waiting.

He leaned against the stone wall next to the stairs, across the room from her, and her eyes took him in. His arms were crossed, his eyes tired. He was still wearing his traveling clothes and muddy riding boots.

This time, his voice was pleading. "Tell me more. I need to hear all of it."

Sara tried to remain calm, although her heart thudded and adrenaline rushed through her. She had never told anyone the full story of what had truly happened with Bastien. Philippe deserved to know. In a strange way, she was glad he wanted to know—that he would allow her to tell him. She sighed and began, trying to keep her emotions in check. To cry or stammer would be selfish, an indulgence. It was his brother who had died.

"We struggled. I was trying to push him off me and get away, but he was too strong. I grabbed—" *Dear God,* she thought, *how am I going to say this?* She took a deep breath and stared down at her shoes. "I had to stop him, and there was a fork that had been knocked to the floor. I didn't think—I just grabbed it." She felt his eyes upon her, but she couldn't look up.

When she finally summoned the courage to raise her eyes, she wished she hadn't. The agony on Philippe's face was unendurable. He did not say anything, but just squeezed the bridge of his nose between his fingers, struggling to keep his composure.

Sara could offer no words of comfort. She continued on. "I lost consciousness. What happened after that is unclear to me. When I awoke, Bastien was on the floor beside me. He wasn't moving." Saying his name sounded strange to her. She had avoided it for so long.

"Did you tell anyone?"

"Jacques found me. You mustn't blame him—he was trying to protect us. He and Lydia feared that I would be sent to the guillotine. I was seventeen and knew nothing of the world beyond Saint Martin. I trusted Jacques and did as he said. We set sail two days later for America."

"So that makes you—what?—eighteen now?" He was surprised.

She'd forgotten he might assume she was older. She had told him she'd been married. "Just nineteen."

"So you were never . . . married."

"No."

He paused, staring at the floor, trying to piece together the whole truth from her words. "And Luc?"

"He is your nephew, Lydia and Bastien's son."

Philippe exhaled and smiled slightly. "My kin, my blood."

"Yes." Sara watched his features soften.

"So why did you come here? If you feared capture and the guillotine, why did you seek out the very person who'd want your head?" His voice was both curious and confused.

Sara met his eyes. She could lie and tell him that she had come to seek his forgiveness, just like the priest had instructed her. Maybe, somewhere in her mind, she had almost convinced herself that her motive was that honorable. But Philippe knew her too well, understood her ambition too acutely, to be deceived.

"I didn't seek you out. I was picking grapes with the Chinese workers, traveling from vineyard to vineyard. When Aurora found me working at Eagle's Run, I had no idea that all this was *yours*.

But once I found out, I decided to stay. I stayed because I wanted *my* vineyard back—Saint Martin." She spoke the name with reverence. "I didn't expect—"

"What? What didn't you expect?" The look in his eyes filled her with regret.

She smiled wistfully. "To admire you, to respect you. I began to question myself, to wonder whether the course I'd set for myself was right, whether it was just. Philippe, I am so sorry for hurting you."

Philippe grimaced. "But you're not sorry that you killed my brother?"

"I'm sorry it had to come to that. That I couldn't convince my sister and mother to leave before . . ."

"Before . . ." Philippe crossed the room and stood before her. His fingers followed his eyes to her chest, and rested on the delicate fabric concealing the scar that was her reminder of Bastien's violence.

"Before he did this to you? Before he almost *raped* you?" His voice was edged with pain.

"Yes."

Philippe drew Sara tightly to him. She sank into him, relieved. She drank in his heady scent—musk and horse. The heat of his chest warmed her cool skin. He understood. He believed her. For the first time in over a year, Sara felt as if she could exhale. She didn't know how long he held her, his chin resting on her head, occasionally brushing his lips across her hair. Time stood still for Sara. When he pulled away, his face was less serious, and his eyes lit up as they found hers.

He held her by the shoulders. "Enough confessions. We can't change what happened. Besides, I have something for you. It's the reason I was away." He pulled some pieces of paper from inside his coat. They were loosely tied together with string, which he slid off with one finger before handing Sara the papers.

She did not need to unfold the documents to know what they contained. She stared down, clutching the rough paper tensely, but could not bring herself to move into the light of the stairwell to read them. She knew it was the deed to Saint Martin. Philippe had just handed her everything she wanted. She should feel excitement, vindication. What was wrong with her? Instead, she felt only despair.

Sara could feel Philippe's eyes upon her, yet she could not find any words. He broke the silence first. "It's yours—all of it, less the debts. I've paid them all." Philippe smiled, probably waiting for her to awaken from her stupor.

"Thank you." Sara's response was hollow. There was so much more to say, but the words caught in her throat. She wanted return to their embrace, to press her body against his muscular chest, and inhale the intoxicating scent of his skin. Instead, she could only lean against the wall, dazed and still.

Philippe pulled another envelope from his pocket and, looking down at it, continued thoughtfully. "I assumed you'd want to leave at once, so I've booked passage for you and Luc back to New York by rail, and then on to Calais by ship," he glanced at Sara. "Second class—it's very comfortable. You leave next Saturday."

Sara stared at him, her eyes wide with disbelief. Philippe's voice then took on a formality that chilled her. "Oh, and here are the sixty dollars you put toward the purchase of those ten acres. I'm buying them back so you'll have some cash for your journey home. Take it," he encouraged.

Sara accepted the money, but struggled to understand what was happening. Her mind froze. When she looked up at him again, she was near tears.

"You want us to *go*?"

His answer broke her heart. "I thought you'd be eager to get home to your mother, *your* vineyard, as soon as possible, now that all the charges have been dropped." His smile was warm, but his eyes were impenetrable.

"Oh . . ." He was handing her freedom and a livelihood, and gratitude suddenly washed over her.

"I . . . my family . . . won't trouble you anymore," he said sadly. "I would like to ask you one favor, if it's not too much?"

"Of course." Sara was still in shock. She wasn't ready to leave yet, to leave her life in California, to leave *him*.

"I would like to stay acquainted with my nephew, perhaps visit when I'm in France." His words were tentative, as though he thought she might object. "I've grown attached to him."

Did he not know her at all after these months together? He'd like to *visit*? What happened to their life together? Why was he sending her away? Then the truth hit her with staggering force. Despite what they had shared and how urgently she loved him, *he* could not continue to love *her*, to share a life with the woman who had killed his brother. He did not seem vengeful toward her—but his feelings had changed, that was clear. Dejection washed through her, threatening to destroy what was left of her composure.

"Visit. Yes, certainly." She tried to mimic his even tone. "You will always be welcome." Sara turned away and wiped her tears.

She could hear him move toward her. His eyes found hers, and his fingertips skimmed the line of her jaw, from ear to chin. Her knees weakened at his touch.

"It's what you wanted," he reminded her without bitterness, without reproach. "Now you can give Luc the life you wanted and the legacy he deserves."

"Yes. Of course you're right. And we're thankful for all that you've done." Sara managed a strangled smile.

"It is no more than what I owe you. No more than what my family has taken from yours. Now I'm in a position to restore Saint Martin to its rightful owner, and into very capable hands." He took her palms in his and rubbed his thumbs in circles along the back of her hands. It was what she'd always wanted to hear: that she was more than a vintner's daughter. To Philippe, she was a vintner.

She examined the rough, suntanned hands holding hers so protectively, and something inside her began to ache.

She looked up at him imploringly. "But what do *you* want?" She searched his eyes now for a sign that he needed her as much as she did him, but she saw only a fierce determination to set things right.

"I want you and Luc to be safe and happy, back in your rightful home."

Home. But what if she'd been wrong? What if she had been struggling and fighting for the wrong thing? The chasm between what she'd always wanted and what she knew she needed now was too much to endure. Should she return to Saint Martin to reclaim the land that had been stolen from her family, or stay in California to stake her claim for the heart of the man she loved? She knew Philippe was her home now. It broke her inside to know that he didn't want her here.

"May I ask you for one other thing?" she said slowly.

"Of course."

She placed her palm on his cheek. "Forgive me."

His eyes reddened, and he shook his head. "There is nothing to forgive."

"For what I did to your family."

"I'm afraid we—well, Bastien and my father—brought this upon themselves."

"Please," Sara entreated him. "I need to hear you say it."

Philippe held her shoulders. He placed his forehead to hers and whispered, "I forgive you, Sara."

"But you don't . . . love me?" she whispered.

He closed his eyes and sighed. "I can't love you."

When Philippe pulled away, Sara could see his distress. But when he spoke, his voice was distant, his heart retreating already. "Go home to Vouvray," he said. "You need to pick up where you left off with your mother, with Saint Martin. You're going to work wonders with that place, I can feel it."

Hearing Philippe say what Sara knew to be true, she snapped. She remembered the promise she'd made to herself: to never allow herself to feel powerless in the shadow of a man. She clenched her teeth and stared Philippe straight in the eye.

"I *will* work wonders with Saint Martin." She raised her voice. "My father resurrected that vineyard, and I'll not only make it profitable again, but when I do, I'll buy up the surrounding land and establish an international winery to rival Eagle's Run!" Sara was trembling so fiercely she clenched her fists to steady herself.

Philippe was silent. They suddenly stood a world apart, even though they'd shared a life for the past three months. Sara would leave and make her own way, as she'd always planned. The Lemieux family had brought her nothing but pain—why would Philippe be any different?

He shifted uncomfortably under her glare. "Aurora and Tan will take you to the station next Saturday," he said evenly. "I have to head back to the city for a week. I'm sorry I won't be here to see you and Luc off."

Sara nodded and blinked back her tears. Her grief, and her fury at losing him, swallowed her whole.

He leaned over and kissed her forehead. "Safe journey."

Then Philippe was gone.

They rode in silence to the station. The only sounds from their carriage were Luc's excited outbursts as he pointed to the wagons and bicycles that swarmed around them as they approached Napa Junction.

Aurora brought the rig to an abrupt stop in front of the station and set the brake forcefully, as if to emphasize the point she was about to make.

"He can't force you to leave, Sara. You're my friend, too, and you and Luc can stay with me indefinitely. You know I love your company, and there's plenty of work."

"I'm not sure what Philippe told you, but I've decided to return to France. My mother is alone there, and she must see Luc grow up. At last I am taking over my father's vineyard, and I have big plans for its expansion." She tried to sound cheerful. "Besides . . ." Sara felt the tears pooling in her eyes and looked away, ashamed. She was overwhelmed with sorrow. Sorrow that she had to leave her friend, sorrow that she had to leave *him*. Sara's shoulders shook uncontrollably, betraying her pent-up anguish. Aurora draped her arm around Sara and offered her a hanky. Sara wiped her eyes. "I can't live near to him and not be with him. It's better this way. I will miss you more than you know, Aurora."

The two women huddled together until Luc broke their embrace by squirming his way back into Sara's arms.

Aurora laughed. "And you, little man, how could we forget you? Always vying to be the center of attention." She placed her palms gently upon his cheeks and sniffed. "I will miss you, Luc. Be a good traveler for your maman, all right?"

Sara pulled Luc into the crook of her arm and rummaged through her satchel. She couldn't believe she'd almost forgotten it.

"Will you do one more thing for me, Aurora?" She handed the note to her. "I didn't have the opportunity to tell Philippe everything I needed to before he left. Will you give him this?"

Aurora took the note and tucked it in her jacket pocket. "Of course, my sweet girl. He's insane to let you go. You are the smartest, most hard-working, handsome young girl I've ever met. A fool he is—and I'm going to tell him so."

"No, Aurora, don't do that. Trust me, I'm the bigger fool." A fool to think he could love her. A fool to have come here in the first place.

"You'll write me? At least once a month, now, I insist."

"Of course. You've been so kind and generous. I could never repay you."

"Nonsense," Aurora said, shaking her head vehemently. "You have given me more happiness than anything since my husband died. A family—that's what you'll always be to me. And you'll always be welcome here." She ruffled Luc's hair and kissed his forehead.

"You'll come visit us? In France?"

"Yes, certainly. Now you two better get along or you'll miss the train."

"And you'll remember my note?"

"Of course. I'll give it to Philippe when he returns Monday."

Sara slowly pulled Luc down from the wagon. "Thank you, Aurora, for everything."

Aurora smiled ruefully and blew them a kiss.

Sara turned to face the station and took the first step back toward her old life in Saint Martin.

CHAPTER 18

Regret

T he following Monday morning at Eagle's Run, Philippe picked at the eggs and potatoes on his plate, and then glanced at the pages of the *Wine and Spirit Review*, eager for distraction from his thoughts. He'd been wrong not to see Sara and Luc off at the station. His visit to town was a fiction he'd invented to avoid saying goodbye. He had feared that when the time came he would beg her to stay, when he knew deep inside she had to leave. He wasn't sure whether he had done it for her sake or for his, but alone at the table, in this empty kitchen, he wanted nothing more than to touch her again.

Before he had even read the first line of the paper, he heard the creak and slam of the screen door. He didn't need to look up to know who it was. He felt her eyes burning a hole through the pages between them.

"Aurora." He folded the paper, placed it down neatly and waited.

Without a word, she marched over to him, stood across from where he sat and slid a small envelope across the table. It bore his name. Aurora was uncharacteristically silent; it was the calm before the storm, he presumed.

"Did they get to the train safely?" he asked as nonchalantly as he could manage.

Aurora turned toward the door.

"Aurora, you and I have been friends for a long time, and I know you disagree with what I did, but you have to trust me. I had a good reason."

That did it. She whirled around, teary-eyed and ready to explode.

"Pride is not a good reason, Philippe. In fact, last time I checked, it was still one of the seven deadly sins." Her hands went to her hips and she stood ready for the challenge.

"You don't know all the facts."

"No, I suppose I don't. Even when I called you a fool to her face, she defended you and told me I was wrong. That *she* was the one who had been foolish." Aurora shook her head and held up a hand to rebuff any objection. "I don't need all the facts. She loves you. You love her. You love her son. And you just cast her off, like she means nothing to you?"

Philippe took a deep breath to steady his emotions. "She lied to me, Aurora, and covered it up. She lied about who she was and what she'd done."

Aurora eased herself into the chair opposite Philippe. "It can't be all that bad, Philippe! She's just a girl. What did she *do*?"

"I can't tell you right now. But what she did makes it impossible for us to be together."

"Another man?" Aurora looked confused. "That can't be. I've seen the way she looks at you."

Philippe waved this away. "Nothing like that. Worse, if you can imagine."

"You're not going to tell me? I suppose you think it's none of my business. But I found Sara in the vineyard that night and invited her into our lives, and she is my friend, just as you are. It's not happenstance that you two were brought together, that you share a love of winemaking and, from what I have seen, of each other. You were intended for her, and she for you. Yet you push her away—you spit in God's face." Aurora shook her head disapprovingly.

"What do you expect me to do?" Philippe retorted angrily. "Marry the woman who killed my brother?" He paused as Aurora's face registered shock. "Yes, it's true."

"Oh." Aurora's voice quivered. She reached across the table and placed her hand over Philippe's. "Why? What happened? Sara is not violent by nature."

"Of course not." As he explained, Aurora listened wide-eyed. Philippe's final words were the hardest. "My brother attacked her, and tried to rape her. She fought back."

Aurora examined her hands. When she looked up again, there was a new light of understanding in her eyes. She asked softly, "If you had walked in on your brother trying to rape Sara, would you have stood by and let it happen?"

"Of course not." Philippe clenched his fists. "I would have killed him myself."

"Yes. Yes, I believe you would have." Aurora inhaled deeply, wiped her eyes and stood to leave. "I'm sorry, my friend. You've had a lot to contemplate these last few days. You were right. I didn't know the facts, but here's what I do know. Sara's affection for you and her passion for the work you shared were all very real. She's only nineteen years old, Philippe. She's lost her father, her sister and now you. For God's sake, go after her."

Philippe rubbed his tired eyes and looked up at Aurora. "I can't, Aurora. I had to let her go. I *have* to."

"I'm disappointed, Philippe. I never took you for a coward."

As Aurora left the house, Philippe stared down at the sealed envelope. A coward? He loved Sara and he had let her go. Hadn't that required infinite strength and selflessness? He had sent Sara home for good reasons, he thought. She was young. She needed to return to her family and to Saint Martin, the vineyard she had always wanted. And how could he live with the woman who had killed his brother?

But then he understood. How could he live *without* her? He couldn't sleep or eat. He couldn't finish a thought without feeling a desperate need for her. He hadn't realized how deeply he'd miss the elegant line of her neck, the curve of her hip, the defiant lift of her chin when she disagreed with him. Her green eyes pierced his soul, and in their depths he had recognized her desire for him too. Aurora was right. If he was going to give Sara up to appease his pride, he was indeed a coward.

Philippe's heart hammered in his chest; he ran his hand over the delicate lettering on the envelope Aurora had given him, feeling both hope and fear. He tore it open carefully.

October 2, 1897

Dear Philippe,

I cannot repair the damage I have inflicted upon you and your family, in deed and word. However, allow me to set one thing right. Although I am grateful to you for restoring Saint Martin to me, I have decided to transfer the ownership of Saint Martin to Luc Thibault, our mutual nephew, and will serve only as its steward until he is of age.

Thank you for your friendship and your faith in me. May God bless you and keep you safe.

Yours,

Sara Landry Thibault

He folded the paper and tucked it absently into his jacket pocket. Her message was clear. Her words shattered his resolve. In all his life, he'd never felt like such a fool.

CHAPTER 19

Home

A s Sara, Luc and Jacques turned down the road to Saint Martin, Sara expected to see Maman running to welcome them home. But her mother was nowhere in sight. Instead, Sara spied two gendarmerie wagons parked outside the watchman's shed. Her heart sank. She had thought the ordeal of Bastien's murder was over. How could she have been so naive?

Jacques squeezed her hand and advised, "You stay in the carriage with Luc. I'll speak with them." Sara nodded, too nervous to reply.

Four tall uniformed men armed with rifles and bayonets appeared from behind the shed accompanied by a gentleman dressed in a derby and frock coat. He looked like a town official. The shed door opened and Maman stepped out, her face creased with worry. She approached the carriage where Sara sat, afraid to move.

Jacques greeted Maman. Then he marched over to the men and extended his hand. After a brief conversation, the official called to Sara.

"Sara Landry Thibault?"

"Yes," Sara replied. As she stood, her knees buckled, and she felt as though she might collapse. The concern in Maman's eyes as she helped Sara down from the carriage was only slightly overshadowed by the radiance in her face as she embraced her grandson for the first time. Holding Luc tightly, she kissed her daughter, whispering, "My dear, brave Sara." Maman's wistful smile broke Sara's heart.

"I am Monsieur Morel, the magistrate in charge of investigating the murder of Bastien Lemieux. We've been anticipating your return."

"Why?" Sara knew why, she just wasn't ready to face it.

"A murder has been committed, and I am responsible for interviewing all parties involved, most importantly you."

Sara was confused. "But the Lemieux family has dropped all the charges against me."

"Yes, but until my investigation is complete, I cannot decide whether to close the case or send it to the state prosecutor." The short, brusque magistrate turned toward the shed. "This way, mademoiselle."

"I will come with you," Maman declared. She handed Luc to Jacques, linked her arm through Sara's and escorted her inside. Mother and daughter sat at the table near the fire, while Morel paced back and forth.

He barraged Sara with questions about her identity, about how she had killed Bastien, and why. He did not react to any of her testimony; he simply recorded everything in his leather-bound notebook.

"Mademoiselle, do you have any proof that Monsieur Lemieux attacked you?"

"Other than the testimony of Jacques Chevreau, who found me unconscious and bleeding on the scullery floor?" Sara retorted.

Morel cleared his throat. "Yes, other than that."

Sara stood up, removed her gloves and coat, and began to unbutton her shirtwaist.

"Sara." Maman shook her head.

"Maman, he must see." *And so must you.*

Sara pulled her blouse down to reveal the crescent scar that marred the skin of her chest. Her eyes blazed. "This will have to be sufficient, monsieur. I cannot, in all decency, show you the more intimate injuries I suffered from Bastien Lemieux's attack." Tears streamed down Maman's face; she gripped Sara's hand. Morel closed his journal and his eyes shifted to the floor.

When he looked up, his voice softened. "Mademoiselle, if Bastien beat your sister and threatened you, why didn't she seek a divorce, or leave?"

Maman stood up. "That is my fault, monsieur. Sara urged me to help Lydia escape, knowing that Bastien would never consent to a divorce. But I refused. I should have protected my daughters. I am the one responsible for Bastien's death."

Sara was stunned.

Morel exhaled, made a few notations in his journal, and then clapped it shut. As he moved toward the door, he turned and offered Sara an understanding nod. "Thank you for your time, mademoiselle. We won't be troubling you again."

After Mass, Sara knelt before the statue of the Blessed Mother in the nave of the Église de Tous les Saints, her hands clasped in prayer. She studied the serene features of the statue's white marble face. The figure's robes cascaded smoothly down to her delicate feet; she stood upon a serpent's head to symbolize the defeat of Satan. Sara had finally made her confession and received absolution for her sin. Yet her heart was still heavy. She would not face prosecution for Bastien's death, but was enduring something that felt worse: the absence of Philippe. On this late November day, she thanked the Lord for Luc's health, and for the peace and contentment Maman seemed to have found. She prayed that Papa and Lydia would be brought into the light of eternal salvation. Lastly, she asked the Lord to heal the gaping hole in her heart.

Sara had found that nothing was the same at Saint Martin. She'd been shocked when she arrived to see how much damage the manor house had sustained from the fire. It was now no more than a burnt-out shell of crumbling, blackened clay and rock. Only the two chimneys still stood intact. The roof had collapsed, pulling the dormer windows and the second floor exterior walls down with it. She barely recognized her childhood home.

When Sara told Maman about Lydia's last moments, how hard she had fought to give birth to Luc and how happy she was to hold him, their mother grew tearful, but never reproached Sara. Sara had expected Maman to blame her, to resent her for having taken Lydia away. Yet Maman never uttered a word in anger. Instead, she seemed to blame herself. "If only I had listened—if only I had been strong enough to help Lydia," she had whispered during Sara's sorrowful account.

Sara had withheld from Maman the nature of her relationship with Philippe Lemieux. It pained Sara greatly to even utter his name. Instead, she explained that they'd come to a mutual agreement about the vineyard and that he'd been generous and kind. Maman might have suspected more, but did not pry.

Maman was a changed woman. Somehow, despite everything, she'd emerged from the dark tunnel of depression that followed Papa's death. Her cheeks were rosy now, and her eyes danced with emotion. Once the magistrate closed his investigation, Maman was positively radiant. She hadn't stopped embracing Sara and Luc in the five weeks since their arrival. Even more surprising was Maman's interest in the vineyard. Sara thought she'd returned to the wrong farm when she caught sight of her very own maman on bended knee, picking grapes. It was obvious that the reason for Maman's metamorphosis was none other than Jacques Chevreau.

Apparently he hadn't wasted any time. After receiving the news of Lydia's death last winter, Jacques had feared for Maman's sanity. The two of them were alone at Saint Martin during the winter months, with only a skeleton crew of hired hands to help in the vineyard. By March, Jacques had realized he was in love with Maman; they had been married this past June. When he recounted the story to Sara, it was all she could do not to burst out laughing. It seemed absurd, but they both seemed entirely enamored of one another.

Jacques had eagerly shown Sara what he'd done with Saint Martin in her absence. It was a sight to behold. Jacques had followed Philippe's instructions and sold the estate's remaining barrels of wine to pay off some of Bastien's debts. He'd worked the undamaged seven hectares of vines expertly the previous year and extracted two hundred barrels of premium chenin blanc. They'd fetched a decent price and Jacques was able to turn a small profit. This year's harvest had just been completed, and the total yield was a hundred tons of fruit. Sara couldn't help but notice how small Saint Martin was in comparison to Eagle's Run, where the harvest was five times that.

Sara would save two-thirds of their profits to cover the coming year's expenses and use the rest to start constructing a small family house to replace the manor house she'd grown up in. Jacques had moved into the gatehouse with Maman, and now Sara and Luc were living in one of the cave dwellings. She'd promised herself that she'd never borrow money if she could avoid it, and that meant making sacrifices. Sara's sole focus was keeping the vineyard afloat.

She had journeyed through two continents and many cities to find her way back home. She was no longer merely a vintner's daughter. After creating the Eagle's Run 1897 vintage, Sara Thibault had become what she'd always known she was destined to be: a vintner in her own right. She looked forward to expanding Saint Martin in the years to come, although there was little joy in this life without Philippe.

Jacques had found a buyer from New York who was interested in tasting and possibly purchasing their wines. Sara was excited at this new prospect and had agreed to meet the man today, directly after church. When Sara was finished with her prayers, she made the sign of the cross and began the walk home. She thought about what would be happening there: Luc was probably stuffing Maman's hot currant buns into his mouth, smearing frosting all over his cheeks. Maman was thoroughly enjoying her new grandson.

As Sara walked down the lane, her thoughts drifted back to Philippe, as they so often did. When she passed the spot where he'd pulled Saul Mittier off her, when they both were so young, she thought of how kind he'd been, never patronizing her like someone nine years her senior might have. Then Sara's mind flashed, for the millionth time, to their last conversation, their final embrace. He'd seemed so sure that she should leave. Perhaps she should have refused. Maybe she should have stayed and fought for him. In the end, it didn't matter. He could no longer love her because of what she'd done. It was, she thought ruefully, her long-overdue penance for her crime.

As she neared Saint Martin, she noticed the figure of a man standing near the front gate—the wine buyer. The sight immediately cheered her, for she had always dreamed of shipping Saint Martin's wine to the New World. After having lived there, Sara knew that their sweet Chenin Blanc would sell, especially in the eastern markets. She allowed herself the momentary pleasure of imagining Philippe dining at a San Francisco restaurant, surprised to find Saint Martin's Chenin Blanc listed at the top of the wine list, right next to the Eagle's Run Chardonnay. She smiled with satisfaction. Sara pulled her mind back to the present as she drew closer to the end of the lane. As the waiting man came into view, she thought she was imagining things again. Philippe? How could it be?

Then he smiled, and he was beautiful. Her memories did not do him justice. He was real, standing in front of her in a tailored suit, something he rarely wore. Sara hesitated, searching his eyes for anger or doubt. She found none. Then Philippe stretched out his arms, beckoning her to him. She closed the space between them in a heartbeat and clung to him for fear he might vanish again. Philippe lifted her up and pressed his lips to hers. She drank in his delicious taste—and felt faint. When Philippe finally broke their embrace, he kept one arm locked firmly around her waist. She gazed up at him and blushed, overwhelmed by his rugged beauty.

"So it's a good thing I came?" He flashed a brilliant smile. She had missed him so much.

She took a moment to catch her breath. "What took you so long?"

His brow creased and she took his hands in her own. They stood silently, studying their clasped hands. Sara was the first to speak.

"So you're the buyer from New York Jacques spoke of?"

"In the flesh."

Sara felt a renewed surge of resentment. "Why did you send me away?" she asked boldly.

"Why did you leave?" he countered.

She examined his long, elegant fingers, and the words tumbled out: "I killed him, and you said you couldn't love me!" Her eyes flashed to his.

He pulled her close, the warmth of his chest comforting her.

Philippe's voice was steady and sure. "I was wrong to say that. All you did was defend yourself. You didn't set out to kill him—you were trying to stop him. I would have killed him myself if I'd been there." He looked at Sara intently. "I was such a fool. I convinced myself that you'd be better off without me, or as far away from me as possible. I convinced myself that it would be selfish to ask you to marry me. That every time I touched you, you would remember how my brother—" Philippe rested his hand gently above her heart, upon the scar. "How he did this to you. I feared that you'd resent me, for asking you to give up what you always wanted. You'd already lost so much—how could I ask you to give up your land?" His eyes locked with hers. "I had to set you free."

"But you didn't set me free," Sara protested. "You sent me away, without asking me what I wanted."

"I didn't think you would suffer like I would—that you could feel for me a fraction of what I feel for you. How could you, with everything my family had put you through? But then Aurora gave me your note. That you would give up Saint Martin—the thing you desired most in this world—to try to make amends . . . well, it leveled me." He shook his head again, but she caught his chin in her hand. He smiled ruefully.

"No, you're wrong," she said. "I didn't sign Saint Martin over to Luc to make amends. I did it for my own reasons. You see, I realized"—Sara's eyes darted toward the vineyard, and then came to rest on Philippe—"that this isn't the thing I most desire in this world." The relief of finally expressing this truth aloud filled her with satisfaction.

Philippe swiftly countered her. "I don't want you to give up

Saint Martin." He waved his hand toward the vineyard. "Saint Martin is, by right, yours."

"Yes, and that's why I'm free to sign it over to Luc. It's going to be his someday anyway. It makes me proud that I can give it to him now."

Philippe tried to interrupt, but Sara continued, "I didn't want there to be any doubt in your mind. I couldn't live with your believing that I'd used you just to get Saint Martin back."

"I did think that when I first discovered what happened. I've since altered my view." He tucked a strand of chestnut hair back behind her ear and smiled. "I visited Marie Chevreau when I came through New York two weeks ago."

Sara smiled at the memory of her friend. "And how are they, she and Adeline?"

"They're well and send their regards." His voice became serious. "Sara, she told me what happened with Lydia, and how brave and unselfish you were."

"I only did what any sister would do," Sara insisted.

"Perhaps, but she was impressed enough to send those bounty hunters on a wild goose chase to Virginia, which is why it took them so long to find you. Not to mention that she deceived *me*—someone she trusts. She didn't tell me about her friendship with you until now."

Sara was overwhelmed. Marie had probably saved her life.

"She also told me about Bastien." Philippe continued. "About what he did to you."

Sara was stunned. Marie had obviously discovered her identity, but how had she unearthed the rest? "Marie knew? All this time?"

"All this time."

"But how?"

"Jacques Chevreau wrote her last July and, although he didn't tell her about Bastien's death, he did explain that Bastien had attacked you. He told Marie that you two had fled to New York, and asked her to be on the lookout for you. He thought you would probably stay in the city until the baby was born—that maybe you'd cross paths with Marie, because she was a midwife. Little did he know . . ."

"That we were at the convent the entire time." Sara shook her head in amazement.

Philippe seemed amused.

"What's so funny?"

"I'm just trying to picture it—you in a *convent*." Philippe pulled her into his arms. "I need you, Sara Landry Thibault."

"And I you."

Philippe brought Sara's fingers, chilled in the cool morning air, to his warm lips and murmured into them, "Come back with me to California."

"Stay here with me in France," she commanded playfully.

"My vineyard is larger," he trumped her.

"Mine requires more attention." Sara tilted her head for emphasis.

Philippe shook his head, laughing. "You're impossible."

"Hardly. I'm just intent on replanting our land and creating a legacy for Luc."

"I can't object to that." Philippe smiled and, looking across the road to Saint Martin's vines, announced, "I have a plan."

He held her by the shoulders, excitement blazing in his eyes.

"We'll replant with resistant rootstock from Eagle's Run. We'll merge the two vineyards and sell our wines to our combined contacts in Europe and America. Both vineyards will benefit, and it'll only be a matter of time before our wines are well-known on both continents, maybe even in Australia, Asia—who knows?"

Sara admired his enthusiasm, but still had reservations. "Where will we live? I have just returned to my mother."

He placed her hand in the crook of his arm and started walking around the perimeter of the vineyard. Sara recalled that Philippe always thought more clearly while in motion.

"Hasn't Jacques managed the vineyard well while you were gone?"

"Indeed, but Jacques and Maman are older now," Sara said skeptically. She didn't know how long they'd be able to maintain the vines on their own.

"So we'll hire more help, and we'll visit once a year."

Sara was warming to the idea, but she couldn't let him off too easily.

"The Saint Martin wines must keep the Thibault name," Sara insisted.

Philippe nodded, and his eyes filled with understanding. "Luc Thibault?"

"Of course," Sara replied, thinking of her father, who would have been so pleased.

Philippe circled his arm around Sara's waist. "Then I suppose there's nothing left to negotiate, is there?"

Sara stopped and looked up at him. "Yes, there is," she said firmly.

"What is it?" Philippe's brow bunched with concern. Sara suppressed a smile.

"If I return to California with you, I need one more assurance," she persisted.

"Anything," he whispered, his lips gliding over her hand again.

His touch stirred Sara so deeply that she struggled to remember what she'd intended to say. She closed her eyes, and her thought returned. "That you'll bring me home as your wife." She searched his face, waiting for his answer.

"Hmm." Philippe edged away and looked at her appraisingly. "That could be a problem."

"Why?" Sara was bewildered. Had she misinterpreted his intentions again?

"There will be talk, you know."

Sara decided to play along. "What kind of talk?"

"You are my father's enemy, my nephew's aunt, and the woman who wrangled Saint Martin right out from under me," he said, skimming her cheek with his fingers. "It's highly improper."

"Perhaps," she said, throwing her arms around his neck, anticipating the feel of his smooth lips on hers, "but I wouldn't have it any other way." He kissed her deeply, more desperately than ever before.

Sara knew that she could never repair the damage she'd done. She could never bring Bastien back to life. Nor could Philippe restore the father and sister she'd lost. Out of their hurts, they would work to create something new—a life defined by love of family and friends, and the joy of making exceptional wines. In Sara's mind, only one question remained: could they truly let go of the past and forge a future together?

Acknowledgments

T*he Vintner's Daughter* would not exist without the generosity of my friend, the accomplished writer Holly Payne, who introduced me to my agent, April Eberhardt. When Ms. Eberhardt offered me representation, I was overjoyed. Since then, she has championed my work with intelligence and verve. I am deeply indebted to you both.

My heartfelt thanks to my publisher, Iris Tupholme, and amazing editor, Lorissa Sengara, for their eagerness to tell Sara's story, and their diligent and gracious collaboration during the editorial process. I was fortunate to benefit from the expertise of Senior Managing Editor Noelle Zitzer, copyeditor Sarah Wight and proofreader Helen Guri. My gratitude also extends to Alan Jones, HarperCollins Canada's art director, who designed a cover more beautiful than I could have imagined.

I would like to express my appreciation to many who have offered their expertise and guidance: Joe Donelan of Donelan Family Wines, winemaker Tyler Thomas of Dierberg and Star Lane Vineyards, Max Roher of Max Napa Tours, Steve Stone and Paul Torre of Napa Valley Bike Tours, Andy Burr and Susanne Salvestrin of Salvestrin Winery, Rebecca Martin of Chase Family Cellars and Greg Gauthier of Bouchaine Vineyards. I'd also like to thank the Napa County Historical Society, of which I'm a proud member, and my historical guide there, research librarian Alexandria Brown, for reviewing the manuscript and for answering every esoteric question I posed with efficiency and enthusiasm.

Thank you to my first readers, who critiqued my work and encouraged me to keep writing: Mary Ellen Army, Maxine DeBard, Pat Donelan, Susan M. Harnisch, Uma Khemlani, Sharon Onorato, Mary Rys and Richard Rys. I'd especially like to acknowledge Dr. Robert DeBard, S. Taylor Harnisch, Autumn Howard, Elizabeth Murphy, Frank Lacroix and Maryellen Lacroix for their detailed reviews, which greatly enhanced the novel.

To my celestial brother, Commander Matt Lacroix, USNR, whose positivity propelled my writing forward and who continues to be a guiding light; to my sister, Katie Lacroix, for researching winemaking history; and to my cousin John Donelan, who helped create my website, *www.kristenharnisch.com*, I thank you.

The unrivaled staff at the Darien Library, in particular Tina Bothe, Sally Ijams and Blanche Parker, assisted me in researching French and Loire Valley culture, New York City and California history, and turn-of-the-century winemaking. Thank you for your patience!

I'd also like to acknowledge the excerpt on page 152 from Edward Roberts's "California Wine-Making," which appeared in *Harper's Weekly* on March 9, 1889. He was one of the first to write about the growing popularity of California wines in the late 1800s. Robert's article was also cited in William Heintz's *California Napa Valley*, Scottwall Accociates, 1999. The quote from suffrage activist Mrs. B. F. Taylor was cited in Lauren Coodley's *Napa: The Transformation of an American Town*, Arcadia Publishing, 2007. Both books provide wonderful insights into the history of Napa Valley winemaking. Lastly, the quote from suffrage leader Elizabeth Cady Stanton was found in her book *The Woman's Bible*, European Publishing Company, 1985.

Finally, I offer my sincerest appreciation to my parents, Frank and Maryellen Lacroix, for their unwavering love and faith in me, and to my husband, David, and children, Ellen, Ryan and Julia— you make every day worth living.

About the Author

KRISTEN HARNISCH's ancestors emigrated from Normandy to Canada in the 1600s. She is a descendant of Louis Hébert, who came to New France from Paris with Samuel de Champlain and is considered the first Canadian apothecary. She has a degree in economics from Villanova University and now lives in Connecticut. *The Vintner's Daughter*, her debut novel, is the first in a series about the changing world of vineyard life at the turn of the century.

A Note on the Type

THIS BOOK WAS SET IN BULMER. Designed in 1792, the typeface is named not after its designer, William Martin, but after the printer, William Bulmer, who used it extensively in his Shakspeare [*sic*] Press editions. Originally, Martin's type was the English answer to the sharp, fine letterforms of Italy's Bodoni and France's Didot type foundries. But Bulmer was more than an imitation of these stark, modern-style types. By condensing the letterforms, giving the strokes higher contrast, and bracketing the serifs slightly, Martin made his typefaces both beautiful and practical. As well as providing an elegant and versatile text face, Bulmer is often used as a display face because of its high contrast and distinctive letter shapes.